CHIVALROUS

CHIVALROUS

PEGGY HOFFMAN

www.peggyhoffmanauthor.com

This effort is dedicated with love
to the memory of my mother,
Marylin McAlonan Carlson,
who gave me the little red notebook.

I

ENGLAND, EAST SUSSEX,
YEAR OF OUR LORD 1066

Raymond de Graville was covered with blood, so much so that it dripped from him. Some of it was his own, but just as much of it was the blood of other men. Men that he had wounded, men that he had killed. His chain mail and the gambeson beneath it had been sliced through diagonally across the chest. Though the wound bled still, it had cut through the flesh only, and while the hairs on his chest were now matted and sticky with blood, the injury, though painful, was not mortal, and the English knight who had inflicted it now lay dead at Raymond's feet.

"Serves you right," he muttered at the dead Englishman. "I liked that horse."

The horse in question also lay dead on the field, slashed by the same sword that had cut Raymond's chest, wielded by the same now-dead English knight. The horse's wound had, unfortunately, been fatal.

Not only were Raymond's horse and adversary dead now, but around him lay much of the English army that Raymond and his Norman countrymen had engaged this day upon Senlac Hill. The English aristocracy, nobility and its usurper king Harold Godwinson all lay slaughtered and defeated, his banner trampled and ruined in the mud under the hooves of Norman destriers.

Raymond sensed the presence of someone standing behind him, and turned quickly, sword at the ready to engage whatever enemy still stood.

But it was not an English soldier there, and Raymond immediately dropped to his knees onto the muddy, bloody English earth beneath him, his sword held point down.

"Your Grace. Forgive me." He bowed his head to William, Duke of Normandy, sometimes called William the Bastard, for obvious reasons, though never to his face.

"I believe we are victorious," William noted, gazing over the field covered with dead enemies. "History has been made here this day, de Graville."

"Indeed, my lord," Raymond agreed, breathing in the cool October air. "May I be the first to offer fealty to the new King of England?"

"You may," Duke William said. "And may I be the first to offer congratulations to the Baron de Graville."

"But, my lord," Raymond replied. "Baron de Graville is my brother."

William, Duke of Normandy and now King of England, smiled.

"Yes. In Normandy. But now, here, in England, you are Baron de Graville. I proclaim it, as reward for your bravery here today."

Raymond bowed his head in gratitude.

"There will be lands for you, my new baron," William went on. "I charge you to build a fortress to help defend my new kingdom. We may have conquered Harold's army here today, but I surmise there will be some resistance to be quashed elsewhere. You have a son, don't you?" He looked at Raymond.

"Yes, my lord. He is an infant. He and his mother are with my brother in Rouen."

"I have three. And four daughters," William informed him. "Always fighting, they are. But their mother keeps them in line, despite her small size. You will have a heritage for your boy. Raise me more of those de Graville horses. We will need a source here in England."

"It will be my honor, my lord," Raymond assured his new King.

William looked across the field towards where Harold Godwinson, the usurper and oath-breaker who had dared to steal the throne that was William's by right, lay dead with a Norman arrow in his eye. "I shall build an abbey here, in thanks for my victory, and place the altar at the spot where Harold fell."

"What will you do with his body, my lord?" Raymond asked.

A grim smirk crossed Duke William's face. "I should have it thrown into the sea without ceremony, usurping traitor that the man was." He glanced toward the edge of the battlefield, where anxious new widows were already gathering, hoping to retrieve corpses. "I presume his mother, his wife, or his mistress, will want his corpse returned to them. But they won't have it, not even if they come to me on their knees and offer me its weight in gold. I will not allow his grave to become a shrine for rebels. We will bury it right here, where he fell, but in secret, and none but you and I will know its location. I request that you dig the grave and bury his corpse yourself, once darkness has fallen. I realize that it is a task beneath the dignity of a baron, but I must have the location kept secret. Place no marker on the spot, and reveal its existence to no one. You are sworn to secrecy, de Graville."

"Of course, my lord," Raymond replied sincerely. He was a loyal knight, and grateful for his new rank and the promise of lands. He would not demur at performing this menial task for his lord.

His new King nodded. "Let them think Harold rots at the bottom of the Narrow Sea. But I won't have that sin on my conscience. When your son becomes a man, you may bring him here, to the abbey that will be built on this spot, and tell him that Harold Godwinson lies here. But only to your firstborn son, and he may tell the secret to his firstborn in due time, so that there will always be someone who knows, and who can stand before God on the day of judgment and reveal that Godwinson's remains were at least treated with respect, though he didn't deserve it, after attempting to thieve away a crown that was mine by right."

Raymond bowed his head again. "It will be my honor, my lord, to keep the whereabouts of Harold's body in confidence. I shall bring my boy here when he is man-grown so that he may see the spot upon which the Conqueror prevailed."

William nodded in approval, then looked back at Raymond.

"Christ, de Graville, you are still bleeding. Have that seen to."

William waved Raymond away and moved on to speak to another of his commanders. Raymond bowed and offered thanks again as he went in search of a barber-surgeon to dress his wound, a wound which somehow no longer pained him quite so much, as he contemplated all that had passed here this day.

Around him, birds began to twitter, as if they realized the battle was concluded and it was now safe to sing again in the autumn twilight.

History has been made here today. Raymond considered his Duke's – his King's – words as he sat having the barber-surgeon apply honey to the slice across his chest to retard the bleeding. It was certainly true. The dead English nobles whose bodies were now gathering flies and crows would leave England without leadership, as well as kingless. The Norman conquerors would rule here now, with William as their king.

As soon as it was full dark, Raymond returned to the silent battlefield covered with dead combatants, and fulfilled his lord's request to secretly bury Harold Godwinson's body in an unmarked grave. It would be covered later with the altar of the abbey church that William had pledged to build on this spot. But nobody other than Raymond de Graville and his king would know whose remains were beneath that altar, until the day when Raymond would return here with his son, now an infant at his mother's breast, but hopefully the first of more progeny to come, when the boy was grown to a man, and reveal the truth to him along with his responsibility to pass the knowledge in secret to the next generation in due time.

Raymond would like to return immediately to Normandy to share his good news of the Norman victory, his new title and the promise of lands of his own with his brother, his wife and his baby son. But that would not be possible for some time. His commission to create secure fortifications took priority. When he took possession of his promised lands, when he completed the construction of the fortress and a home there, then he could return to Normandy to retrieve his wife and son and bring them to their new English home. He wondered how long that would take.

Build me a fortress, King William had commanded. *Raise me more de Graville horses.* The tasks sounded simple, coming from William's lips, but it would be anything but simple. The construction alone would take years, and the reaction of the English people to the death of their old king and the conquest made by their new king was still uncertain.

*****

ENGLAND, DEVON,
YEAR OF OUR LORD 1071

Geoffrey de Graville was five years old when he first saw the castle that was to be his home and his heritage. Seated in front of his father on Raymond de Graville's tall black stallion, the boy's eyes widened with excitement as they came to the crest of the hill. After following the river Lyd west from England's southern coast, and skirting the mysterious moorlands and heaths of Dartmoor, they arrived at a wide green valley with farms laid out in neat checkerboard patterns, secluded in the hills of western Devon. The river was shallow through the valley, and thus gave the name of Lydford to the village situated on its banks.

But it was the castle located just beyond the village that drew young Geoffrey's excited eyes. Five years in the building, it had just recently been completed. The boy bounced eagerly in front of his father, anxious to explore the imposing castle on the hill. Raymond put a restraining hand on his son's shoulder, and urged his horse forward. He too was eager to reach their new home.

"Is that our home?" the boy asked with wide-eyed wonder, then hesitantly added, "Father?"

The name was still unfamiliar on his lips. He had only just met his father a month ago.

Raymond nodded. "I have named it *Belvoir* – beautiful view. You will see why when we get inside." He gestured towards the uppermost level of the castle's walls.

As soon as they passed under the raised portcullis and entered the bailey, grooms hurried forward to take their horses as Raymond and his men dismounted and Geoffrey was set on his feet. The grooms murmured words the boy didn't understand, but which sounded respectful.

Another man, stocky and redhaired, approached and bowed to them. A miniature of the redhaired man stood next to him, staring, and offered his own bow after a subtle jab from his father's elbow. Raymond spoke to the redhaired man in the same incomprehensible language the grooms had used, and turned to Geoffrey.

"This is Dunstan," Raymond said. "He is our bailiff here, to assist in the managing of the estate. And his son."

The redhaired boy turned to his father with a question, but again Geoffrey did not comprehend the words. He looked up at Raymond with his own question.

"What are they saying?" Geoffrey asked. "I don't understand them." Did the people of this island not speak the civilized language of the Norman French?

"It is English," his father told him. "The native tongue of this land. You would do well to learn it also."

Geoffrey stepped towards the other boy. He looked to be the same age, though smaller in stature than Geoffrey, with hair the color of sunset, a wild smattering of freckles across his round face, and eyes the green of summer grass.

"I am Geoffrey," he told the boy in French, placing his hand on his chest to indicate an introduction.

"I am Edmund," the boy replied in English, with another bow under his father's eye. He raised one hand to hold it at the level of the top of Geoffrey's head. From his look, Geoffrey could guess that the redhaired boy was saying something akin to, "You're big."

Geoffrey repeated the English words, though he didn't understand them, and his new friend chuckled, shook his head and pointed back at Geoffrey.

"I am bigger than my cousins also," Geoffrey said, but having Edmund comprehend his words was apparently going to be another lesson for another day.

"Tell me how to speak in your English," Geoffrey requested, but Edmund did not understand the Norman French words and his face squinted with a lack of comprehension. Raymond spoke to the bailiff, and Dunstan replied, as Raymond put a hand on his son's shoulder.

"Dunstan says his son will be honored to assist you in learning English. Later, however." He gave a dismissive nod and the redhaired father and son turned away, though behind their father's backs the two boys looked back at each other with smiles, and a friendship was born.

"Father, when is Mother coming here?" the boy asked as they passed through the main gate of the inner wall. Like the first gate in the curtain wall, it faced east, but was offset so that those entering the curtain were forced to make a sharp right turn to gain access to the keep, to inhibit any attackers should the wall be breached. The portcullis under which they had passed was a heavy wooden grating, spiked along its lower edge and raised and lowered as the need occurred by men-at-arms stationed inside the wall.

"Geoffrey," Raymond said. "Do you not recall? Your mother has died." He glanced at his cousin, Father Mathieu, hoping that the priest whom he had persuaded to emigrate to England with them to tend to their spiritual needs and act as his scribe, could help in easing the boy's confusion.

"I told you when I returned to Rouen. She is never coming to England."

It was not surprising that Geoffrey had overlooked his father's explanation about his mother. He had been very seasick as they crossed the Narrow Sea between Normandy and England, in spite of the calm seas and favorable breezes that brought them from Dieppe to Exeter. They had spent several days in Exeter at the manor of one of Raymond's fellow commanders in the war of conquest, Lord Baldwin de Meules, while Geoffrey recovered and father and son attempted to acquaint themselves.

"Never?" the boy repeated, his lip trembling a bit.

Father Mathieu now attempted to explain the situation to the boy.

"Your mother's soul is with God now, Geoffrey."

"But I want her to be here with us," Geoffrey insisted, looking to Raymond. "Why did you make her go away?"

Raymond sighed. "I did not order it nor wish for it," he insisted. "She became ill and she died. You must understand, Geoffrey. It was the will of God." He looked harshly at his son's trembling lip and moist eyes, and as a tear threatened to escape, yanked at the boy's arm, pulling him through the doorway before his men-at-arms should see the brat crying like a girl.

"Sit," Raymond ordered as they entered the great hall, the principal room in the castle keep, the main building of the fortress. Here, meals were to be served, tenants and guests received, and major estate business conducted. Geoffrey's confusion over his mother was set aside for a moment as he took in the grand, rectangular room, boasting carved oak beams to support the soaring ceiling, and a raised wooden dais at one end where the family could sit away from drafts and intrusion. Above the dais was a window, arc-shaped, made with real glass, a true luxury. Raymond even went so far as to commission a mason to carve the stonework along the wall behind the dais into decorative patterns and images of saint's faces, which could appear either sinister or protective, depending upon which way the firelight flickered.

The remainder of the castle folk, retainers, guards, and the household knights would eat at tables set upon temporary trestles below the dais. These tables were dismantled between meals and their benches pushed against the wall until needed. On either side of the room, huge fireplaces were capable of holding several whole logs each.

Geoffrey climbed up onto a chair and his father immediately made a sharp shooing motion.

"Not there, you ignorant pup. That is the lord's chair. My chair. You sit there." He indicated a less ornate seat and with a pout Geoffrey moved to it.

"Your display of emotion out in the bailey was unseemly," Raymond said. "You must understand, Geoffrey, that you are a Norman man. In a few years, you will begin training for your knighthood, and in the full-ness of time, you will become lord of this estate after me. Norman men, knights, barons, do not weep. Do you comprehend this?"

Geoffrey nodded obediently and wiped his nose and eyes on a grimy sleeve, which prompted an aggrieved look from his father. But he still didn't quite understand about his mother. He might be a Norman man, but he was still only five years old.

"Now," Raymond said, with a serious look at his young son, "Do you understand why I was gone these past five years?"

Geoffrey nodded. "Mother said you were fighting with the Duke to help him claim England."

"Yes," his father said. "That is correct. I have always been a soldier, since the day my father presented me with my first sword. But I was the second son, so I never had hopes of inheriting the family estates in Nor-mandy when he died. Your uncle Alain is the lord there now, and he has his sons, your two cousins to follow him. My choices, therefore, were a life of soldiering or the church. I do not have the religious vocation of our cousin Father Mathieu, and therefore I have taken up my sword in the service of our Duke."

As one of Duke William's commanders, respected by the duke for both his skill and his loyalty, Raymond had been a part of the Norman invasion which had landed in England to claim the throne which had been promised to William by the oath of its late king, Edward. Edward had sworn to his cousin, William, Duke of Normandy, that William would inherit the English throne after him, as Edward had no son to succeed him. Edward had even sent his brother-in-law, Harold Godwin-son, the Earl of Wessex, to William's court to swear his oath of alle-giance to William as his personal lord. The Duke's inheritance seemed assured.

"Understand, Geoffrey," Raymond said, "A knight's honor is para-mount, and that honor is based upon the sanctity of a man's oath. That is the bedrock of chivalry, the code by which we live. Nothing is more reprehensible than a broken oath, and the knight who breaks it is with-out honor."

This was a lesson every Norman child had been taught from birth.

No sooner had King Edward died in January 1066, than Harold Godwinson forsook his oath, seized the throne, and in spite of having not one drop of royal blood in his veins, had himself crowned King of England before Edward's body was even cold.

This was the ultimate betrayal. With the blessing of the Pope, Duke William organized an invading army of his own knights, including Raymond de Graville, to claim his promised inheritance. It was a huge force of men, horses, and ships that embarked across the Narrow Sea, bent on conquest. Raymond was forced to leave his wife, Nicolette, and infant son Geoffrey in the care of his brother as he answered his duke's call to arms. He left with the hope that, if the Norman forces were successful in their invasion and conquest of England, he would be able to obtain an estate for himself and his family.

Landing unopposed at Pevensey, the Norman forces quickly erected a wooden fortress there and pressed inland. The decisive battle was fought on October 14 at Senlac Hill near Hastings, and lasted the entire day. Raymond de Graville fought at his Duke's side, and though both were wounded, and William had three horses killed underneath him, neither man's wounds were life-threatening. For a time during that long and bloody battle, it appeared that Harold's forces might after all succeed in fending off the Norman invaders. But the more experienced Norman forces eventually prevailed. They had gone into the fight fresh and rested, where the defending English forces, having recently repulsed a Viking invasion in the north, were battered and weakened. When the Norman army pretended to retreat, the English forces had taken the bait and pursued them, abandoning their dominant position at the top of the hill, after which the clever Normans turned, surrounded them, and cut them down. Harold, his two brothers, and most of the surviving English aristocracy, died under the onslaught of Norman ferocity, and Duke William was crowned King of England on Christmas Day.

The new king rewarded those who helped him secure his throne with the lands of those English nobles who had resisted him, most of whom had perished at Hastings or in one of the subsequent rebellions that William ruthlessly obliterated over the next five years. Raymond de Graville's rewarded lands were located in the southwest, in Devon.

These lands were not merely bestowed upon de Graville and the others outright, but in fief to their lord. In turn, each Norman lord granted lands was required to repay the king by maintaining a certain number of mounted, armed knights and soldiers, and to lead those soldiers in battle as the need arose.

Raymond immediately began construction on his castle, the definitive symbol of the new ruling society, to be erected on his new estate in western Devon. Both the castle's completion and the elimination of the English resistance to Norman rule were to be a lengthy process, and he could not risk bringing his wife and son to England until he felt it was safe and the new castle was completed, secure and fully staffed.

By the spring of 1071, the English resistance was virtually eliminated, and the de Graville castle was almost complete. Raymond returned in triumph to Normandy, to the wife and son he had not seen for five years. But when he arrived at his brother's estate east of Rouen, it was to the news that Nicolette had died of a fever only weeks earlier, and the only one there to welcome him home was a confused five-year-old boy with no memory of the father who now came to take him away.

"We are charged to provide protection and defense for this part of the country, and the people living here," Raymond said now. "Before Duke William became king, Devon was ruled by Harold Godwinson, Earl of Wessex. But he paid little heed to its needs during his time as the usurper King. Dunstan has said that some of the older people here can recall their parents telling of Viking raiders venturing even this far inland. Now that Belvoir castle has been built, and our garrison of knights and men-at-arms is in residence here, they need not fear any more such attacks. The people of Lydford will feel safe, and it is our continuing duty to ensure it.

"Come," he said, rising from his chair, "There is more to see."

Raymond had taken great care with the planning of his castle, building an impressive stone fortification rather than the simple timber motte and bailey style structure which could be constructed in a matter of weeks, but was insubstantial and vulnerable to fire. Raymond wanted a more lasting and permanent heritage for himself and his family. His lifelong desire had been lands of his own, an estate upon which to raise his family and the horses for which the de Gravilles were famous. After years of hardship and warfare, he had finally attained that goal. It was too bad that Nicolette would not be there to share it with him, but they had not been very close so he did not miss her very much, and there was the boy.

The small hill half a mile west of Lydford village was the perfect site for a castle. It commanded a strategic view of the valley, the river, the village and the woods beyond. At the top of the curtain wall surrounding the fortress, the battlements of alternating solid merlons and crenel spaces gave it a square-toothed appearance. A walkway on the inner side of the battlements enabled guards to observe anyone approaching.

Within the curtain wall, the keep had a tower supporting each corner. The towers were round rather than square, to more easily repel an attacker's missiles. The outer walls were whitewashed, giving the building the appearance of being constructed from a single immense block of stone. Outbuildings housing stables, workshops, a smithy and the dovecote ringed the inside of the curtain wall. The gatehouse, under whose portcullis Geoffrey and his father had passed, protected the entrance.

The keep was comprised of three stories, in addition to the donjon, a windowless basement used for storage. The main floor housed the great hall, with kitchens and other service rooms such as buttery and still-room adjacent. Outside the kitchen lay the garden, the fishpond and the well. A short corridor led to a chapel for the family's devotions, where Father Mathieu now went to give thanks for their safe arrival.

The second story contained the family bedchambers and the solar, a private chamber for the lord's use, and extra chambers to accommodate guests. The third story housed servants and men-at-arms. Spiral staircases connected each story, built so that they turned to the right when ascending, and to the left when descending. If an attacker should somehow breach the defenses and enter the keep, they would find their sword arms hampered by having the stone wall on their right, while the defender coming down the stairs would have a free swing.

Most of the workmen employed to build the castle and service buildings had finished their work and departed for other employment. The few still working on finishing touches bowed respectfully as the father and son passed by. The new lord and his boy made a handsome but contrasting pair. Where Raymond, a typical Norman, was dark of hair and eye, Geoffrey had inherited his mother's blond hair and deep blue eyes. Raymond had a reserved, almost arrogant nature, as befitted a Norman lord, but Geoffrey, now that he had recovered from the disastrous sea voyage, was a merry, high spirited, reckless child who tried his father's patience sorely as he dashed through the castle, asking seemingly endless questions and insisting on exploring every inch. He was a big, sturdy boy and his energy seemed limitless.

As they walked the battlement at the top of the outer wall, Geoffrey's earlier illness was forgotten as a wondrous sense of home, of belonging took hold of his young heart. He even managed to set aside, for a little while, his grief and confusion over his mother's death. However, Raymond's patience with his son soon began to wear thin. He had answered a thousand, no, a million, questions and still the boy was not tired. They looked out through the crenels and Geoffrey was so entranced by the commanding view of the countryside that for once he was silent. It was because of this vista that Raymond had named his new estate *Belvoir*, meaning beautiful view.

Raymond was just beginning to breathe a sigh of relief, when Geoffrey leaned so far out over the edge that he came perilously close to falling over the side. Only his father's quick lunge, grabbing him about the waist and hauling him back, saved the boy from certain death. In the process, Geoffrey sustained a nasty gash on the forehead which bled profusely, turning his hair an interesting strawberry color. As Raymond tore off the bottom of his tunic to staunch the flow of blood, he resisted the urge to stuff the cloth into his son's howling mouth, and told himself, tomorrow, no, today, a nursemaid must be found.

*****

The nursemaid's name was Maud and she was a motherly peasant woman, a widow with no children of her own, whose kind heart immediately went out to the motherless boy, in spite of the scrapes he frequently got himself into. Even her diligent care could not always keep him out of trouble, which, as they settled into life in their new home, often led him to find himself on the business end of his father's belt. Raymond did not believe in tolerating disobedience in his son. Each time Geoffrey returned from one of these usually well-deserved whippings, with his pride as badly bruised as his young arse, Maud had to restrain the urge to smother him with too much motherly pity.

Geoffrey chose for his bedchamber a room at the top of one of the keep's towers. Fortunately, Maud was a sturdy woman who did not mind climbing the extra steps. Because the tower peaks were too high for an arrow to reach from below, the windows here were larger than the small, slitted windows in the lower rooms. Wooden shutters could be secured by an iron bar when the weather was foul, but on fine days, the shutters were opened wide and Geoffrey could gaze out over the fields and woods. After his near disaster on the battlements, however, he was careful not to lean out too far.

But neither that memory nor his father's stern hand could curb the energy, merriment and mischief that was his nature. He was curious, friendly and intelligent, and quickly made friends with all the castle inhabitants from lord to servant, indifferent to rank.

Raymond was glad to leave warfare behind and concentrate on his new estate. With the aid of stock sent by his brother from Normandy, he set about to establish a new breeding and training facility for the de Graville horses. Although Raymond hoped that his soldiering days were behind him, he knew that there was always a war being fought somewhere, and knights needed the best-trained horseflesh available under them in order to survive and prevail.

Training the expensive destriers used in battle was a skill that came naturally to all the de Gravilles. Each steed must be strong enough to carry the knight as well as his arms and armor, which weighed half again as much as the man. It was also vital that each horse continue to respond to its rider in spite of the confusion, noise, and smell of blood they would encounter in battle. A knight's horse was the most valuable asset he owned, and would be given food and water before the knight himself ate or drank.

It was the custom for young boys of the nobility to be fostered out at about eight years of age, to be sent to other noble estates to learn the skills of a knight. But this was one tradition Raymond chose to disregard. In spite of their disparate personalities, Geoffrey was his only child, and besides, who better to teach him the skills of knighthood than his own father?

So Geoffrey remained at Belvoir, and was glad of it. He would have been devastated to have to leave the peaceful valley in the Devon hills and his beloved horses. They were his pets, his children, his brothers and sisters. There was little doubt he would carry on the de Graville tradition of raising the finest horseflesh in the land, and in order to hone that skill, he was spared the fate of most other boys of his rank, that of leaving home at a tender age.

If he had been fostered out, he would have served as a page in another nobleman's household, running errands, learning proper behavior, courtesy, riding, and other valuable lessons, such as not to sit until bidden, not to speak until spoken to, not to fidget in the presence of his betters. Raymond attempted to teach his son these lessons himself, and although Geoffrey did excel in riding and hunting, the lessons in courtesy and behavior were an ordeal for both father and son, especially with no lady of the manor to instill the gentler aspects of chivalry.

Raymond had immense respect for King William, called the Conqueror, and would ever be a Norman lord, ingrained in Norman ways. Like his King, Raymond found the English language to be harsh and guttural compared to his native Norman French. But unlike the King, he troubled to learn the language and use it when necessary, although he never lost a distinct accent. Geoffrey, however, who spent much of his time in the company of Edmund and the other village boys, was quick to learn the speech of his new homeland and within a very short time, spoke English as if born to it.

The villeins and peasants of Lydford were affected far less by the Norman conquest than had been the nobility. The common people simply carried on paying their rents to the new lords, and provided none succumbed to the temptation of poaching deer from the forests, there was little change in their lives under the Norman administration.

In addition to Maud the nursemaid, Raymond also found it necessary to bring other English men and women into his service. On Raymond's behalf, Belvoir's new bailiff, Dunstan, hired a marshal and stable hands to supervise the stables and care for the horses, a hayward to maintain the hedges, a clerk to assist Father Mathieu with the accounts, and a domestic staff to see to the feeding, clothing and cleaning up after the family, retainers and garrison knights. The garrison required an armorer who made and repaired weapons and armor, and a blacksmith who shod the horses. The employment provided to many of the inhabitants of Lydford eased the fears of those villagers who had watched with trepidation as the castle rose above them.

Raymond was fortunate to have found an excellent bailiff to assist him in the administration of his estate in the form of the redhaired Dunstan. Surnames being rarely used by the common people, Dunstan was simply known as Dunstan, or sometimes Dunstan Red due to his titian hair. Dunstan's son, stocky, freckled-faced Edmund, was the same age as Geoffrey, and the two boys quickly became partners in mischief, and inseparable friends. The villagers in Lydford soon became accustomed to the sight of the two heads, one red, one golden, together plotting misbehavior and devilment.

2

They had been in England three years, and Geoffrey had just passed his eighth birthday, when a servant approached him as he was helping to muck out the stables, informing him that his father wished to speak to him. Pausing to wash the smell of manure from his hands, Geoffrey somewhat warily entered the small chamber off the great hall where estate business was conducted.

He had just that morning endured a sound thrashing, in punishment for setting loose in the gardens a dozen chickens who had been awaiting, in several large sacks in the kitchen, their eventual fate as the evening meal. He could still feel the sting of his father's belt, for Raymond was a man who believed in carrying out this fatherly responsibility himself, and not delegating it to others as many other men did. Geoffrey was secretly glad when neither Raymond nor Father Mathieu, who stood next to Raymond's chair, bade him to be seated. But he also wondered what disgrace he was in now. He was fairly certain he had already been punished for most of today's transgressions.

"Geoffrey," Raymond said, "I have something of importance to speak to you about. It is news which I trust you will find pleasing."

Geoffrey was relieved. At least his father had not unearthed any new sins on his part. But Raymond's next words quickly erased the smile of relief from his face.

"You will recall our recent journey to Warwickshire to deliver the horses purchased by Lord Turkill?" Raymond asked. Geoffrey nodded.

Turkill of Arden was one of the few English nobles to retain his estates after the Norman conquest. His father continued, "My son, you will very soon have a stepmother. In one month's time, we will return to Warwickshire, and I will wed with Lord Turkill's daughter, the Lady Alyssa."

His father to marry! Geoffrey felt as if the floor had dropped from beneath him, as if he'd been punched in the stomach. Surely this could not be true - his father could not betray his mother's memory like this. Geoffrey had met Lady Alyssa when they had been at Warwickshire, and had actually thought her to be very nice, for a girl. She had given him a fresh simnel loaf, and had not told anyone that she had caught him splashing in the fishpond with a couple of pages, trying to catch fish in their hands. Though she was a sweet and friendly girl, she was a maid of but eighteen years of age. How could Raymond, at the seemingly ancient age of thirty-three, contemplate such a thing?

"No!" Geoffrey shouted. "You cannot marry her! She will not be my mother. It is wrong! You cannot," he repeated.

Raymond sighed. "Geoffrey," he said, "It has been three years since your mother's death. It is no sin for me to marry again. The estate needs a mistress, and Lady Alyssa will bring a handsome dowry as well. I am certain you will grow to be fond of her. She will be a good mother to you."

It was no exaggeration that Raymond's estate required a mistress. Their bachelor existence was wearing thin. Though there was no lack of servants to see to their needs, the need for a chatelaine to supervise the household was apparent. Geoffrey was outgrowing his tunics, again, and though Maud tried her hardest to keep him decent, she could not do everything.

But Geoffrey did not see the situation in the same light as his father. He did not realize, nor did he care, that his father was lonely, that the servants needed guidance, that Lord Turkill's daughter's sweet smile had captivated Raymond. Geoffrey only shook his head stubbornly. He could not accept another woman taking his mother's place. One thing he and his father had in common was that they were slow to anger, but when that anger was sufficiently roused, their tempers could be fearsome. He unleashed that anger now as he stamped his foot childishly.

"She will never be my mother, never! I will never love her! I hate you! How could you do this to Mother? I hate you!" His face was red with fury.

Father Mathieu stepped forward and laid a placating hand on Geoffrey's shoulder. The boy shook him off. "My son," the priest began, but Geoffrey rudely interrupted him.

"I am not your son. And I wish I was not his son either." He pointed at his father.

At this, Raymond's patience snapped. He stood up and stepped menacingly towards his son. "That is enough, you rude little pup. You will apologize to Father Mathieu, and you will…"

But he was talking to air. Geoffrey had already fled.

*****

The clearing in the woods was his special hiding place, a place known only to Geoffrey and Edmund. The two boys had discovered it together, but Geoffrey frequently came here alone. It was a grassy area next to a small lake just large enough to swim in. Perhaps the local people believed the clearing to be haunted, for he was never disturbed when he came here.

He threw himself to the ground beside the lake, pulling up fistfuls of grass and throwing them into the water in impotent anger.

Although to his dismay, he found his memory of his mother fading as he grew older, he had never lost the sense of missing her; her gentle hands that had soothed his babyish hurts and sung him a small child's songs in a sweet, clear voice. Somehow in his child's mind, she became confused with the Madonna whose calm loving face looked down at him from her niche in the chapel during Mass. Surely, if he wished hard enough, prayed hard enough, she could come back to him.

But he knew now that it would never be. The statue in the chapel was the Mother of Christ, not the mother of Geoffrey. After a long while, he stood and stared unseeingly into the water of the lake, wiping the tears from his cheeks with his sleeve, a sleeve that was dirty and torn at the elbow. This Lady Alyssa might become his father's wife, but she would never be his mother, he vowed to himself.

Looking up, he saw the sun was low in the sky. Reluctantly, he turned in the direction of home. There would be another whipping awaiting him there for his tantrum, he was certain. His arse still smarted from the first one.

"She will never be my mother," he said aloud. But only the trees were there to hear him, and they had nothing to say on the subject.

*****

It was done. They were married, and now sat at the high board in the bride's father's hall, celebrating the nuptials. Raymond was beckoning Geoffrey forward to greet the bride. The boy bowed politely, but his eyes were sullen as he offered perfunctory congratulations.

Alyssa, a pretty, auburn-haired girl, thanked him gravely, but easily saw the resentment that showed clearly on her new stepson's face. She would not let it bother her. She came from a large family, and she was perceptive. She knew a confused, disconcerted boy when she saw one, and she couldn't fault this motherless boy for resenting her. Give him time to get used to her, she thought, and perhaps she could win him over.

Geoffrey escaped gladly to his seat further down the long table, away from his father's scowl. He toyed with the food on his trencher and wished Edmund was with him. Together they could have concocted some diversion to help him forget his misery for a while.

He looked up at the sound of jesting voices from the head of the table. He didn't understand the bawdy jokes the other men now seemed to be regaling his father with, but it seemed to have something to do with the fact that Lady Alyssa had left the table and was ascending the steps at the far end of the hall with several of her women. She disappeared into the chamber above, and Geoffrey was amazed to see several of the male guests pulling Raymond to his feet and pushing him in the direction of the stairway, a few of them even daring to lay drunken hands on his father, pulling his tunic over his head and laughing with mysterious suggestions. Surely the dignified Lord Raymond de Graville would not suffer this familiarity! But the dignified lord merely grinned broadly and downed his cup of wine. Bowing swiftly to his new father-in-law, he headed for the same chamber Alyssa had entered, followed by more loud, incomprehensible jocularity.

Geoffrey stared open-mouthed after his father for a moment; then his eyes sought out Maud, sitting with the other servants at the far end of the hall. He made his way to her side and sat silently next to her. She looked lovingly down at his bright golden head. She would have liked to gather him in her arms and comfort him against her ample bosom as she had done when he was a child of five, but now that he was a young man of eight, and in the presence of all these people, she knew that a swift comforting pat on the knee would have to do.

*****

The frogs were the final straw, Raymond vowed. The last, final, ultimate straw. He was beginning to regret his decision not to foster Geoffrey out. It was no use considering it now, however, Raymond told himself. No one else would have the boy.

Geoffrey had recovered somewhat from the fog of sullenness that had consumed him at his father's wedding, and back in his familiar surroundings at Belvoir and Lydford village, had regained his merry, head-strong life with Edmund and his beloved horses. He was polite as was required to his father and stepmother, but not polite enough to resist the urge to make their lives miserable with his pranks. He seemed sincerely penitent when he made his confessions to Father Mathieu, and never shirked the penances the priest imposed, but once shriven, simply found more ways to plague his father's forbearance.

The sand in the wine had been almost funny - the first time. The fire in the garderobe was more serious, but at least no one was injured.

The teasing of the castle dogs until they growled menacingly had been stopped by one harsh look from Raymond. But he should have suspected something more serious was afoot the evening a month after his wedding when he observed Geoffrey and Edmund huddled together in a corner of the great hall, pop-eyed with poorly suppressed anticipation.

Raymond was about to demand explanations from the pair, when Alyssa opened the workbasket containing her embroidery threads, and out hopped half a dozen large, slimy frogs. Suddenly freed from their captivity, they bounced frantically into the laps of Alyssa and her maids, trailing bright-colored silk threads from their little green feet.

As the women screamed and Geoffrey and Edmund collapsed in hysterics, Raymond and Dunstan rose together and stalked towards their sons, who were now rolling helplessly on the floor with tears of laughter running down their faces. There was absolutely no doubt in the mind of either father as to who was responsible for the frogs. Briefly, the two men exchanged glances. One was a lord and the other a peasant, but at this moment the desire to commit infanticide made them equals.

The two boys found themselves dragged to their feet by their respective fathers, and the laughter quickly died from their lips as they saw the murderous looks in their fathers' eyes. They looked at the ladies, still shooing the panicking frogs from their skirts, and Edmund whispered quickly, "Was it worth it?"

Geoffrey ventured a glance at his father's face. "I'm not sure," he whispered back. Further conversation was impossible as they found themselves swiftly hauled out to the stables, their feet barely touching the ground the entire way.

Both boys considered it a point of honor not to cry with pain and humiliation as they found their young arses bared and receiving the most severe beating either had ever endured. It took all the willpower in their souls to satisfy that honor.

After that, the number of pranks abated somewhat. Geoffrey and Edmund decided that it was not always worth it. But what puzzled Geoffrey was that while his father had punished him severely for all his escapades, or at least the ones he knew about, the lady Alyssa had never once raised her hand or voice to him. Other than her startled screams during the frog incident, she had virtually ignored his best efforts to plague her. She merely treated him with a calm, steady courtesy, never forced her presence on him, and never tried to mother him. The only demand she made on him was that he stand still for a few minutes while she measured him for new clothes.

He bore the ordeal with petulance, responding only with grunts to his stepmother's attempts at conversation, and escaped from her presence at the first opportunity. He did not thank her when she presented him with several pairs of braies, tunics and smallclothes, but later, when she could not see him, he ran his hand over the sleeve of one of his new tunics, enjoying, despite himself, the way his new clothes fit him and the comfortable feel of fresh clean fabric against his skin. When Alyssa asked him if the garments were satisfactory, he merely said, "They will do," expecting her to become insulted at his rudeness, but she merely nodded and went away to work on clothes she was making for his father.

He didn't understand it, but a small kernel of respect began to grow reluctantly in his young heart. Perhaps, just perhaps, she was not so bad after all.

It was a few months later when he first met Emma, the midwife. Geoffrey and Edmund were on their way out as she bustled in, giving them a quick nod as she hurried past them. Geoffrey stared after her as she made her way quickly up the steps to the lord's chamber. "Who is that?" he asked Edmund.

Edmund followed his friend's look, saying, "She brought me into the world, my mum said."

Geoffrey pushed his friend playfully. "Poor woman, to have to be the first one to see your ugly freckle-face," and he ducked as Edmund swung a mock punch in his direction. Laughing and shoving, the two boys left the castle.

Geoffrey never did find out exactly why Emma had visited them, though he did overhear some of the maidservants talking about a miscarriage. He didn't understand what that was, but somehow, he felt it was something he could not ask about. All he knew was that it made his stepmother cry. Somehow that did not give him the satisfaction he had thought it would.

A year later, Emma came to the castle again, and this time the result was a happier one. For several months, Geoffrey had been trying to ignore Alyssa's growing belly. His father had informed him that, God willing, he would soon have a brother or sister, and he did not know if he liked that idea.

Edmund was scornful. He had several brothers and sisters, and informed Geoffrey from his experience in the matter, "Babies are useless creatures. All they do is cry and stink."

So Geoffrey was determined not to be impressed when his father brought him into the lord's bedchamber to meet the crying, stinking, useless little creature. His stepmother was sitting up in the big curtained bed, looking tired but very happy. She held a swaddled bundle in her arms. Geoffrey stopped at the foot of the bed, but his father prodded him forward.

"This is your brother," Raymond said. "His name is Stephen."

Geoffrey looked down at the tiny face held proudly in Alyssa's arms. He wasn't crying and he did not stink - yet. Could Edmund have been mistaken? He didn't quite know what to make of this small person looking up at him with the solemn brown eyes. He knew he was expected to say something, so he merely muttered, "Very nice," in a bored voice and looked away.

Raymond clenched his fists at his sides to restrain himself from boxing his son's ears then and there. He did not wish to upset Alyssa by punishing the boy for his rudeness in her presence, with her still weak from the strains of childbirth. But just wait until he got him out in the stables!

But Alyssa was not upset. She merely smiled at Geoffrey. The boy's emotions always showed plainly on his face, and she clearly saw the confusion there, the reluctant jealousy. "I was hoping, Geoffrey," she said, "that you will be able to help me with Stephen. When he is bigger, of course," she added quickly. "He will need the guidance and strength of an older brother." Geoffrey began to look at the baby with a little interest, as his stepmother continued, "And if we are very, very fortunate, I think he may even look like you. When he is bigger, of course."

As she spoke, Alyssa also told herself not to forget to include her lie in her next confession. Stephen was a beautiful baby, to be sure, but the soft down on his head was the exact same shade as her own auburn tresses and his solemn brown eyes would never be the sapphire blue of his brother. The two boys would most likely bear little physical resemblance to each other. But Geoffrey was unaware of her deception as he looked anew at his brother with a proud, almost preening expression.

Raymond relaxed his fists and now hid a smile under the pretext of stroking his beard thoughtfully. So the pup was vain, was he? Well perhaps this time, in honor of his new son's birth, he would forgive his older son's rudeness. Just this once.

*****

Geoffrey's twelfth birthday proved to be an auspicious occasion, for it was on that day that he began the training of a knight. Until then, he had merely played with a wooden sword. But today his father put a real sword into his hands and let him feel the weight of it.

Although it was heavy, Geoffrey hefted it easily, moved it back and forth slowly, accustoming himself to the feel of it. As the bright Devon sun flashed on the wickedly lethal blade, honed to a killing sharpness on both sides, Geoffrey tossed the hilt lightly into the air and caught it with his other hand. Back and forth, forty-four inches of gleaming death, it glittered obscenely in the innocent sunshine.

Raymond let his son show off for a few moments. He had to admit, the boy showed the promise of growing to be a fine specimen of a man. Tall and well-built, he had avoided the gangly, clumsy stage of most growing boys, moving instead with a graceful elegance. That grace would stand him in good stead in avoiding tangling his legs in the long straight scabbard that hung from the sword belt draped diagonally across his chest.

But it bothered Raymond that his son looked and acted so, there was no other word for it, so English. To look at him, it would be difficult to tell that Geoffrey was a Norman by blood. He wore his hair long in the English fashion, the thick blond waves brushing his shoulders. To the English, this was not merely vanity. Although there were no slaves in Lydford or at Belvoir, it was a well-known fact that male slaves had their heads shaved as a symbol of their slavery. Therefore, free English-men wore their hair long as a symbol of that freedom.

Geoffrey also preferred the English way of dress, wearing the same loose-fitting braies and short tunic worn by the English peasant boys in the village. Raymond looked much more dignified in tight-fitting breeches that molded to his legs and a longer, almost knee-length tunic with embroidery at the neck and hem. But dignified was a word that could rarely be applied to Geoffrey.

Raymond stopped his son's playing with a look and began to teach him the real lessons of sword fighting. Parry and thrust, drawing the blade smoothly from the scabbard, Geoffrey took to it with a joy and skill that made his father think that perhaps the boy would become a Norman lord after all.

"Look here," Raymond said, holding his sword straight up. He hit the heel of his hand sharply against the flat of the blade just above the hilt. "See where the blade vibrates."

The blade's vibration shimmered at its percussion point – several inches down from the point.

"This is the part of the blade that will do the most damage to an opponent. Each sword will have its own personality, its unique area of maximum impact on your enemy. Try to strike with your blade at that point. However, you will need to adjust for position when fighting from horseback. Your opponent will not conveniently stand there and wait for you to strike. You must line up that sweet spot with your horse's shoulder to impact your opponent the most effectively, and with the least discomfort to you."

Raymond illustrated the lesson with a savage swing of the blade that made Geoffrey glad it was not aimed directly at him.

"Try it," he instructed his son, and Geoffrey lifted his own sword to strike the blade as his father had done.

"Notice also, the vibration of the grip when you strike it so. This is the best place for your hand to grasp the hilt. It will prevent the vibrations from coming back up your arm when you strike."

Geoffrey ran a finger down the shallow groove running the length of the blade, then looked at his father with a question in his eyes.

"That groove makes the blade lighter and easier to wield," Raymond told him, "but does not weaken it. It is not a blood channel." He reached out his own finger and flicked the end of Geoffrey's blond hair. "Despite this, we are not Vikings."

But there was more than handling a sword that Geoffrey had to learn as he grew from boyhood to manhood. He also had to accustom himself to the weight of the shield held on his left arm while he wielded the sword with his right. The leather-covered wooden shield was four feet tall from rounded top to pointed bottom, in order to protect the body and the legs, and Geoffrey could see from the gouges in his father's shield that it must have saved Raymond's life in many a battle.

Archers had been one of the deciding factors in the Norman victory at Hastings. Though bows and arrows were used by foot soldiers rather than mounted knights, still it was a skill worth cultivating. In addition to the bow, there was the mace, axe and lance in the knight's repertoire. Not only must the knight excel in handling the various weapons on foot, but he must also fight from horseback and in helmet and armor. It was a long, arduous and demanding training whose reward was knighthood, but before it was completed the knight-in-training was expected to serve as a squire to an experienced fighter, caring for the equipment and horses and assisting the knight with his arms and armor. Unless a young man distinguished himself in battle, he could not expect to be knighted until at least twenty-one years of age. Since Geoffrey showed such promise in the fighting skills, Raymond planned to use him as his own squire should the need arise. Although England was at peace now, war could erupt at any time, especially in Normandy.

*****

Geoffrey looked at the huge horse with distaste. Actually, it was not the horse he minded but the saddle. He much preferred riding bareback, with the wind in his hair and his long strong legs around the horse's flanks. But for battle a knight was mounted upon a destrier, a horse heavier and somewhat slower than animals used for other purposes. It was the destrier's strength and stability that made it invaluable in battle, where unstoppable power was its most important attribute. The rigid saddle, built high in the front and back, kept the knight steady in his seat during the clash and confusion of battle. Geoffrey hated the confinement of the military saddle, but it did help him stay steady on the horse's back when handling the various weapons.

When he was not training with his father or the other knights in Raymond's service, Geoffrey was in the stables or paddocks. He had a touch with horses that Walter, the marshal in charge of Raymond's stables, found invaluable. Soothing a skittish animal or restraining a fractious one came as naturally to him as breathing. He was as perfectly at home on the back of a horse as on his own feet.

Despite the rigorous training. Geoffrey still managed to find a little time for sport, usually with Edmund and the other boys in Lydford. Although as they reached their teens the boys felt they had outgrown most of the pranks of their childhood, that did not mean that fun could not be had.

Fun was exactly what Geoffrey had in mind as he brushed his favorite horse in the stable next to the training paddock. He had a special fondness for this particular horse because the young stallion's coat was a golden color almost the same as his own hair. He had named the stallion Storm, but he would not tell his father that for fear Raymond would ridicule him for being frivolous. Norman knights did not give names to their horses. His horse was a tool, not a pet.

As soon as he was finished, he planned to sneak off to meet Edmund to go swimming at the river. He hummed a little English tune as he gave Storm's glossy coat its finishing touches.

Suddenly his attention was captured by the high-pitched cry of a horse in pain. Dropping the brush, he dashed out into the paddock, and what he saw there brought a sudden stab of nausea to his stomach.

One of the mares, a fine roan he had been training himself, was laying on the ground with her front legs splayed out at an unnatural angle. Several men, including Raymond, were standing around her, and they all looked uneasy as Geoffrey approached.

"She tried to jump the fence, but she took it too low. Broke both her front legs," Walter was explaining. "The poor beast will have to be destroyed."

"Destroyed!" Geoffrey exclaimed, as he dropped to his knees beside the whimpering horse and gently stroked her ears. "Surely something can be done to save her..." his voice faltered as he looked hopefully at his father, but Raymond could only shake his head.

"Nothing can be done for the mare," Raymond said firmly. "She will only suffer, and then die eventually anyway. She must be released from her misery." He hesitated. "In fact, perhaps it is a task you should learn to do yourself. This is bound to happen in the future, and you should be aware of how to do it quickly, with the least pain caused to the beast."

Geoffrey stared disbelievingly up at his father, and for a moment, seeing his son's stricken look, Raymond almost wished he could rescind his words. After all, the boy was only fourteen; perhaps he was too young to take on this difficult task, especially since they were all aware of Geoffrey's devotion to their horses. Each of the men looked distinctly relieved at not being chosen to dispatch the beast in Geoffrey's presence.

Well, Raymond reasoned, the opportunity was here to teach his son a valuable lesson. It would only make it worse to put it off. It was time the boy started to grow up and learned some of the harsher lessons life had to offer. Slowly, he drew the knife from his belt and held the hilt out to Geoffrey.

Geoffrey looked at the knife, gleaming wickedly in the sunlight, and he wanted desperately to refuse to touch it, or to take it from his father's hand and fling it far away. Walter and the other men were all watching him, and he could see from the look in his father's eyes that Raymond would be shamed before them if Geoffrey did not summon the courage to euthanize the horse.

That horse was thrashing and whining now, her eyes rolling with pain. Geoffrey swallowed hard, and willing his hand not to tremble, reached up and took the knife from his father's hand.

For a moment, he could only stare stupidly at the blade. Then he looked up again at his father. From Geoffrey's kneeling position next to the horse's head, his father looked very tall and very forbidding. He gazed up at Raymond with a look that clearly said, *please do not make me do this.*

Raymond merely crossed his arms over his chest and nodded towards the roan mare.

Walter knelt down next to Geoffrey. "Here, lad," he said softly, but firmly enough that Geoffrey's attention was drawn away from his father's stern face. Walter pointed to the large throbbing vein in the mare's neck and continued, "Here's the spot, now make it swift and sure and you will soon both be freed from your pain."

Geoffrey swallowed again. He had gutted and skinned animals before, at the hunt, but this was different. This was not a mere animal; it was one of his horses. He looked at the horse's eyes and he could swear she looked sad. He fondled her ears one last time, leaned forward and whispered, "I am sorry."

Turning his face away, he felt for the spot Walter had indicated.

With his stomach rolling as wildly as the horse's pain-racked eyes, and praying for his nerve not to fail him, he plunged the blade in and slit the beast's throat.

The mare jerked hideously and then was still. Her warm blood flowed out from the wound and soon soaked Geoffrey's legs and the ground beneath them.

The knife dropped from Geoffrey's suddenly nerveless fingers. He felt himself growing dizzy. *I will not faint*, he told himself, *I will not*.

His face pale, he jumped up and ran, ignoring his father and the others, until he was behind the stable. His knees gave out from under him, and he was suddenly and violently sick in the grass.

He vomited until his stomach was empty, and then he retched some more. A hand gripped his shoulder, and he jumped in startlement.

Wordlessly Raymond handed him a wet rag. Geoffrey pressed it to his eyes for a moment, then wiped his face.

"Jesus," he groaned, as his father helped him to his feet. "Mother of God!"

"Such a task is always difficult the first time," Raymond said.

"The first time!" Geoffrey moaned, feeling sick and weak again. "Sweet weeping Jesus on the cross, I will never do that again. I cannot."

Raymond sighed. "Geoffrey," he said firmly, "You will most certainly be called upon to perform such a task again. Death is a part of life. It is something you will have to face. And I do not think Father Mathieu would appreciate your cursing."

Geoffrey shook his head weakly. "He would if he had to do that," he declared.

Raymond sat down on a nearby bale of hay and motioned for Geoffrey to sit next to him. "My son," he began in his this-is-a-lesson-for-you-to-learn voice. "You are a knight's son. You are training for knighthood yourself. What do you think this is all for? It is not a game. It is preparation for war, should it happen. And it could happen again, at any time. Oh, we are at peace now, but there is always something happening, somewhere. I fought for five years to bring us the peace we enjoy now. But I would be a fool to think that I may never have to go to war again, or that you may not have to fight someday. And in war, there is death. For men as well as beasts. You think it sickens you to have to destroy that horse. It is nothing, nothing, compared to the destruction of battle. But those battles are necessary in this world, and if you are going to run away every time you see blood, I may as well enter you into St. Nicholas Priory now."

At Geoffrey's blank look, he added, "In Exeter. Where boys are trained for the priesthood."

"No, no that will not be necessary," Geoffrey said quickly.

Raymond smiled. "Good. I did not think you would be suited for the religious life. I am certain the good fathers at St. Nicholas's would take an even dimmer view of frogs in workbaskets than I did."

Geoffrey managed to smile at that. "In that case, Father, I shall try very hard to be more courageous in the future. I would rather face any warrior than an angry father-be it you or a religious-with a switch in his hand. But," and here his voice became serious, "I will never enjoy it. I mean, having to put down a horse. I will not lie to you on that."

Raymond nodded, satisfied. "I know. You may try me sorely at times, but I have never known you to lie." He squeezed his son's knee in a rare show of affection. "Now go along and wash."

Geoffrey looked down at his legs, covered with the horse's blood, and felt his stomach rebelling again. Quickly he forced himself to contain the nausea as he stood and returned to the castle, where he threw the blood-soaked braies into the fire.

*****

Geoffrey picked himself up off the ground and walked over to capture his horse's reins. He glared at Edmund who sat on the fence laughing at him. "Let me see if you can do it any better," he said sulkily, holding the reins out to Edmund.

"No, thank you!" Edmund declared. "I have no desire to be a knight. I shall be quite content to be your bailiff after my father." He began to laugh again. "Maybe you should try it again."

Again! Geoffrey had been trying it for hours. His body felt like one large bruise, but he was determined to best the quintain.

The post sunk into the ground towered over his head even on horseback. Across its top was a cross beam that pivoted easily. At one end of the beam was suspended a shield-shaped target, at the other a bag of sand. The object was to approach the target at a gallop, lance couched under his right arm, and strike the shield in the center. This in itself was not difficult, for the target was fairly large. But as soon as the lance struck the shield, the beam swung around quickly. The hard part was avoiding being knocked off the horse by the bag of sand suspended from the other end of the beam. The wooden knight never missed his stroke. Geoffrey's father had instructed him that the quintain was designed to overcome a man's instinctive checking before an impact, and to teach the rider that the purpose of the charge was to not only attack one's opponent, but also to gallop through the enemy's ranks to make them panic and flee.

Geoffrey dusted himself off and mounted his horse again, walking the stallion away from the quintain and then turning to face it. It would be his last attempt today. Neither he nor the horse could take much more. He settled the long, heavy lance under his arm, took a deep breath, and kicked the horse into a gallop.

This time he made it. The lance struck the shield, but he had approached it fast enough that he was able to beat the swing of the sandbag, although he did feel it brush his back. He looked at Edmund in triumph. "You see, it can be done!" he panted, patting the horse's sweating neck.

"Yes, my lord Geoffrey," Edmund said, still laughing. "But will you be able to do it again tomorrow?"

Geoffrey rubbed his rear, which had taken the most punishment that day. "Perhaps I will wait a few days. But I will do it."

Just when he had mastered the quintain to a point where he was slugged by the bag of sand only once in a while, his father had him try it while wearing armor. The weight of the chain mail hauberk, knee length and split in front and back to allow the knight to ride, slowed him down enough to make the quintain a source of new pain, and it took more hours of practice to best it wearing the heavy uncomfortable hauberk and the quilted jerkin that went underneath.

He dismounted his horse and walked over to his father, who stood watching him with his helmet under his arm. Raymond held the helmet out to Geoffrey. "This is why a Norman knight cuts his hair short," he told his son.

Geoffrey took the helmet and put it on his head. It fit snugly and had a flat nasal guard on the front. He purposely shook his hair forward and when he pressed the helmet down, it held his hair in front of his face. Laughing, he staggered about with his hands outstretched like a blind man.

Raymond stepped forward and snatched the helmet roughly from his son's head. He smacked Geoffrey on the side of the head with a blow that made the boy's head ring, and reached for his knife. Geoffrey backed off, holding his sore ear.

"Wait, wait," he implored, not laughing anymore. He took the helmet back from Raymond and combed his hair back from his forehead with his fingers. Holding the hair tightly away from his face, he replaced the helmet on his head. This time his eyes were unobstructed. "See," he said to Raymond, "I can be an Englishman and a knight both, Father."

4

Raymond de Graville was a tall man, but by the age of fifteen, Geoffrey was as tall as his father, and still growing. He was outrageously handsome. His golden blond hair, still worn long in the English fashion, and dark blue eyes were a heritage from his mother, and from the Vikings who had raided and settled in Normandy a century and a half earlier. From his Viking ancestors he had also inherited the high cheekbones, firm square jaw and strong straight nose that might have given another man an arrogant demeanor. But Geoffrey's quick smile and friendly manner dispelled any hints of arrogance. His skin was bronzed from the years of outdoor work and horseback riding, and the strenuous military training he had started at the age of twelve had made him strong, broad-shouldered and muscular.

His father still tended to treat him like a child occasionally, as on the day he bade Geoffrey return to the castle from a hunting trip, while Raymond and the others camped in the woods to continue their hunt in the morning.

Geoffrey was resentful and sullen when he arrived. His father could very well have sent a servant or one of the grooms to tell his stepmother he would not be home that night. But no, he had sent Geoffrey, and now he would miss the rest of the hunt.

He knew he would most likely find Alyssa in the solar, and he was right. She was there with several women, working on the sewing which was a never-ending task. "My lady," Geoffrey said as he entered the room, "my father bade me inform you,"

He stopped. There was a girl there, curtsying to his stepmother, turning apparently to leave. He had never seen her before, so she could not be one of his stepmother's maids or a servant. A seamstress, apparently, because as she turned towards the door, one of the maids handed her a bolt of cloth.

Geoffrey stood in the doorway staring at her, his message from his father forgotten. If a warhorse had charged him at that moment, he would not have been able to step out of the way, so entranced was he at the vision of the pretty brown-haired girl now standing in front of him. She was standing there because he was blocking the doorway. She looked up at his face, probably wondering why he refused to let her pass, and her eyes widened at the intensity with which he stared down at her. For several minutes, or perhaps only for a second, their eyes were locked, until the titters of the maids watching them penetrated the trance they seemed to find themselves in. Finally, he stepped aside, and the girl looked down and quickly slipped out the door. He continued to stare after her, and he had to force himself to turn around and pay attention when his stepmother spoke to him.

Alyssa had to put her hand to her mouth to cover a smile as she watched her stepson stare awestruck at the young seamstress. "Geoffrey?" she prodded gently, "you have a message from my lord?"

Geoffrey looked around and saw that his stepmother's maids were all giggling at him, at the fool he had made of himself gaping at a girl like a moonstruck calf. He felt his face flush hotly and knew he was turning as red as a ripe apple. But damn, the girl was beautiful! His stepmother's maids, the other maidservants he saw every day, had never affected him like that. But there was something about this girl that caused a new and previously unexperienced sensation to sweep through him like a rushing river, and to his embarrassment he found himself stuttering as he tried to remember his father's message.

"H-he bade me tell you that he and," he found he could not remember the names of the other men in the hunting party, although he had been with them only a few hours ago. "He and the others will not be returning until late tomorrow, my lady."

"Thank you, Geoffrey," Alyssa said, trying very hard not to embarrass him further, but she did find it difficult to suppress a smile at her stepson's perturbation. After he left the room, practically falling over himself in an effort to get away from the teasing glances still being directed at him from the maids, she did, however, allow herself a small smile at his expense, shaking her head in silent laughter. Her stepson was growing up, she thought maternally.

*****

Raymond and Father Mathieu were returning to the castle one afternoon just a few days later when they paused to water their horses at the river. Raymond had recently returned from Exeter and was anxious to have a private moment with his cousin.

"And how does my lord de Meules?" Father Mathieu asked.

"He does very well," Raymond replied. "And so does his daughter. In fact, I am considering offering for her as a bride for Geoffrey. They are of an age."

"Oh?" Mathieu raised an eyebrow. "And does Geoffrey know about this?"

"He will, when the time is right," Raymond replied.

"The boy is a bit young, do you not think, cousin, despite his size?" the priest said.

"Perhaps," Raymond admitted, "but he is my heir, not a second son as I was, and it will be his responsibility to produce an heir of his own someday. Best for him to wed young. It will settle him down."

"That should make for an interesting wedding night, if you are planning for him to wed so soon," Mathieu chuckled, "with both the bride and groom virginal."

"What!" Raymond was astonished. This was something he had not considered.

"I may be celibate, cousin," the priest continued, "but I am not blind.

Unless I am badly mistaken, and I do not think I am, Geoffrey has not yet discovered, uh, shall I say, the pleasures of the flesh."

Raymond frowned, but Mathieu merely laughed. "You keep him too busy, Raymond," he said. "If he is not in the bailey practicing some warlike skill or other, he is on a horse or caring for one."

"Perhaps you are right," Raymond said reflectively, recalling how Geoffrey had fallen asleep again at Mass that morning and only a sharp poke in the ribs from Stephen had sent him to the communion rail.

Father Mathieu was amused at the disconcerted look on his cousin's face. Despite his religious calling he was not without a sense of humor. "Perhaps," he joked, "you should find a woman of experience, a comely widow or some such, and have her teach the boy what he will need to know on his wedding night. He is intelligent and quick to learn. Now that would be a birthday gift to remember," he concluded, reminding Raymond that Geoffrey would turn sixteen in a week's time.

"That is an excellent idea!" Raymond exclaimed. "There must be some such woman in the village, virtuous but experienced, willing to teach a good-looking lad like Geoffrey. If my negotiations with Baron de Meules proceed favorably, the boy may find himself a bridegroom very soon."

"Hold, cousin, it was merely a jest," Father Mathieu cautioned. "Surely you would not seriously consider..."

"Why not?" Raymond countered. "If my father had done such for me when I was that age, it would have saved me some awkward moments."

Father Mathieu shook his head, sorry he had brought up the whole subject.

A moment later a shout brought their attention away, up the dirt road toward the village, where the object of their discussion, unaware of his father's and Father Mathieu's presence, was leaping from his horse to go to the aid of one of the local farmer's sons, whose ox-drawn cart had slipped into a deep, muddy rut.

A recent rainfall had turned parts of the track into a quagmire, and it was in one of those areas that the cart's wheel had lodged. The boy who jumped down and looked at his mired cart with dismay was named

Dewi. Raymond and Father Mathieu did not know that, but Geoffrey did. Dewi started to bow as his lord's son approached, but Geoffrey waved his hand at him and put his shoulder to the cart.

Raymond watched with a frown as his son and heir, standing ankle-deep in the muck, strained and pushed and sweated in concert with the peasant boy. The cart began to move infinitesimally, but then Dewi's feet slipped out from under him and he fell against Geoffrey's shoulder, knocking him off balance and causing both of them to land on their hands and knees in the mud.

Geoffrey laughed at Dewi's dismayed, mud-streaked face. Sitting up and pushing his hair away from his face with his own filthy hands, he attempted to get to his feet, but slipped in the oozing muck and found himself face down in the mire. Quickly pulling himself back up into a sitting position, he looked at Dewi, who was sitting there trying very hard not to laugh at him. It was a losing effort. In a moment both boys were laughing heartily at the sight of each other, covered with slimy mud and ox droppings. With a mischievous gleam in his eye, Geoffrey noticed a clean spot on Dewi's shoulder. He scooped up a handful of mud and flung it, obliterating that one clean spot.

Dewi's face filled momentarily with shock at being pelted with mud by the lord's son. But Geoffrey was laughing at him in such an unlordly manner that after merely a moment's hesitation, Dewi also scooped up some mud and threw it back at Geoffrey, splattering it against his ear. Suddenly the two of them were hurling handfuls of mud at each other, laughing hysterically as each attempted to avoid the mud thrown by the other, until an impatient snort from the ox still hitched to the mired cart brought them to their senses.

Reluctantly, they ended their small muddy battle in a tie. Geoffrey grabbed the wheel of the cart, pulled himself to his feet, and put out his hand to help Dewi up. Again the two young men worked at the mired cart until finally, as the sweat rolled down and dripped off the ends of their noses, they lifted the stubborn cart from its rut and got it up onto a drier part of the road. Geoffrey waved off Dewi's effusive thanks as, mud-covered from head to toe, he leaped back on his horse's back and continued up to the castle.

Raymond was too far away to hear what the two boys said to each other, but he did not like what he had seen; did not like it one bit. His son was too friendly and familiar by far with these English peasants. A Norman lord, Raymond reflected sourly, would never lower himself to give aid to a mere serf, and yet here was Geoffrey doing just that, literally getting down in the mud to do so.

Raymond's voice was hard as he turned to his horse. "The boy is going to have to learn who are the conquerors, and who are the conquered here."

Father Mathieu raised one eyebrow. "The military conquest may have been yours, cousin," he said as he and Raymond mounted their horses, "But when you look at your son, I think you must ask yourself, in the long run, who has conquered whom?"

*****

When Geoffrey returned to the castle after helping Dewi with the cart, his stepmother took one look at him, covered from head to foot with mud, and merely pointed in the direction of the kitchen. He grinned, his teeth looking very white in his face, because they were the only part of him not blackened with mud. He bowed quickly to Alyssa and headed for the kitchen.

Enid, the cook, shrieked when she saw him, not realizing at first that it was merely Geoffrey and not some large black monster. "I have been banished from my lady stepmother's presence," he told her with a rueful smile.

Enid looked him up and down. "It is a well-known fact that my lady is a very wise woman." She turned and called out to a scullery boy, "Go fetch some water from the well and fill the big cauldron in the hearth to heat for my lord's bath." She glanced back at Geoffrey. "And get Wat or one of the other boys to help you. We will need a great deal of water." Then she pointed to a secluded corner. "Sit there, master Geoffrey, and do not move so much as a muscle until we have the tub filled. I will be back when it is ready."

Obediently he went to the corner and plunked down on a stool there, to wait until the big wooden tub that sat in the garderobe just off the kitchen was filled.

After a few minutes, the mud on his face and arms started to dry, and it itched. He'd been sitting in the deepest part of the mire during his mud battle with Dewi, and now it was oozing and itching in places he couldn't scratch in public. He was tempted to at least brush off some of the dried mud from his arms, but he knew that Enid would box his ears if he scraped the dirt off of himself anywhere in her clean kitchen. She was a large, plump woman, but moved swiftly in spite of it, as he had found out on many occasions when as a child, he had attempted to filch some morsel or other from under her nose. Hence his banishment to this lonely corner until his bath was ready.

Suddenly he looked up at the sound of footsteps, and just as suddenly shrank back into the corner. The girl, the brown-haired seamstress from his stepmother's solar, had just entered the room, walked past him without seeing him, and was now talking to Enid at the other end of the large kitchen, her back to him.

He pressed himself back against the wall, trying not to make any sound. He didn't want her to see him like this, covered with mud and other assorted filth, and smelling of sweat and the less pleasant end of the ox. The mud fight which had seemed like so much fun at the time, seemed silly and childish now. If she turned around and saw him, what would he say? Nothing, he knew, because if she looked at him he would find himself just as speechless as he had been the first time he had seen her.

He watched silently as she chatted with Enid, apparently not having noticed him skulking in the corner. Long, honey-colored braids hung down her back and swayed slightly as she laughed at something the cook said. Geoffrey held his breath as he stared, at once afraid she might turn around and see him, but also wishing she would, so that he could glimpse her face again. But she did not notice him, and after a few moments she left through the garden door. Geoffrey began to breathe again.

A few minutes later, the scullery boy came to tell him the tub was full and Geoffrey scurried into the garderobe, a small room behind the kitchen which housed the large bathing tub, closing the door behind him and quickly shedding his clothes. He climbed into the wooden tub and felt the warm water enfold him as he sat on the seat built into the inside. It was large enough that even he could stretch out his legs, and it felt wonderfully relaxing after a day in the saddle. He could not linger long, however; the water was quickly turning dark with mud. He used his hands to scrub at his face and arms industriously.

The door opened and Maud walked in, clean clothes in one arm and carrying another bucket of water in the other. Panicked, he looked around for something to cover himself with, but even his dirty clothes were out of his reach.

"Jesus! Maud, go away!" he exclaimed, but she just laughed, set her burdens down, and put her hands on her ample hips.

"You need not be modest with me, master Geoffrey," she declared. "Have I not cared for you since you were five years old? Who was it, do you recall, who picked splinters from your arse, when you fell from the hayloft that time? And did not inform your father of where you had been?"

"I did not fall; Edmund pushed me," he grumbled. Then he said pleadingly, "But, Maud, I was seven years old then!"

"And you think you are man-grown now?" Maud asked disbelievingly. She smirked at him. "Lady Alyssa told me you had begrimed yourself, and I see she did not exaggerate. Just where did you think to go when you were clean, if you ever are clean again, did I not bring you these?" She indicated the clothes she had placed on a stool. "I do not believe you would wish to wear these again," and she picked up the mudcoated tunic and braies he had discarded, holding them away from her as if they were a dead animal. With her other hand, she reached into the bucket she had set on the floor, withdrew a cloth and handed it to him, admonishing him, "For your face."

At least, he thought frantically, the water in the tub was now dark with mud, covering him somewhat. And he could attribute the redness of his face to the strong scrubbing he applied with the rag Maud had given him. He was tempted to duck his head under the water as well. "Thank you, Maud," he croaked in embarrassment, hoping she would leave now.

But she merely continued to chuckle at him. "What, pray tell, have you been doing? Wrestling with the pigs?"

Obviously, she was not going to give him the luxury of privacy, Geoffrey thought. With a sigh of resignation, and trying to wipe mud from his hair, he began to explain. "There was a cart, stuck in the mud. I was trying to help Dewi right it, and we fell." He began to smile at the memory of what had happened next. "Then I threw some mud at him, and well..." He saw there was no need to finish the tale, as Maud was laughing again, and shaking her head. "Do not tell my father," he pleaded, unaware that his father had already seen him.

"Saints preserve us, Geoffrey, big you may be, but you shall ever be a child," she declared. Then she picked up the bucket of water she had brought in with her, and without warning poured it over his head. "There!" she declared. "Now you are clean!"

Sputtering and choking from the unexpected deluge, Geoffrey wiped his eyes and glared at Maud. "You could warn a man!" he declared.

"A man!" Maud laughed, again holding up Geoffrey's dirty clothes. "I think not, young sir!" Still laughing, she turned to leave with the muddy clothes. Geoffrey suddenly thought of something, and leaned over the edge of the tub with his arms folded on the edge.

"Maud, wait," he called. Maud stopped, turning to look at him from under raised eyebrows.

"You must learn to make up your mind, Geoffrey," she declared. "First it is, Maud, go away, now it is, Maud, stay here."

"I wish to ask you something," he said with his most charming smile, but trying nonetheless to appear nonchalant. "Do you know who that girl was, talking to Enid in the kitchen?"

"Girl? What girl? There are many girls here," Maud said.

Geoffrey felt suddenly disconcerted and embarrassed now as Maud looked at him appraisingly. She obviously still thought of him as a child though he was almost sixteen, and of herself still as his nursemaid though it was his brother Stephen who was her charge now. He looked down at the floor, staring at a small puddle of water next to the tub, and mumbled, "The girl who was here but a few minutes ago. Brown hair, the color of honey. Who is she?"

"I did not see her, Geoffrey," Maud said, "so I do not know what girl you are talking about."

"No matter," he muttered, wishing fervently he had refrained from asking Maud about the girl. Now she would tease him as well. In fact, she did step towards him and muss his wet hair.

"Ah, Geoffrey," she said with a sigh. "It seems only yesterday you were a naughty child playing in the hayloft, and in mud puddles. Now you look at girls and they have hair the color of honey. You make me feel old, my boy." Still shaking her head, she left the room, taking his dirty clothes with her.

Quickly Geoffrey climbed out of the now-cool water and dried himself with the towel Maud had brought with his clean clothes. Although he had been embarrassed when she had walked in on him, it was, after all, a good thing that she had. He had not given a thought to the fact that he had neglected to bring anything clean to don after he washed. His mind had been too full of the pretty brown-haired girl to think of practical matters. He wished he knew her name.

He also wished he had kept his mouth shut and not asked Maud if she knew the girl. He wondered when, or if, he would see her again. Just thinking about her made him feel hot inside, and he didn't even know her name.

Several times in recent weeks Geoffrey had awakened in the morning to find his as-yet-unused manhood as hard and upright as a sword shaft, and a sticky white substance in his bed, on the skin around his genitals. He did not know what it was, but he knew that somehow it had to come from him. He had furtively tried to wipe it away and hope that Maud did not notice or comment on it when she came to clean his bed coverings.

Despite his ignorance, he instinctively felt that this had something to do with his attraction to the brown-haired seamstress. These embarrassing nocturnal emissions had never occurred before he saw her.

*****

In spite of his irritation at Geoffrey's over-familiar attitude, or perhaps because of it, Raymond did not forget his plans for preparing his son for his soon-to-be arranged marriage. Being an honorable husband, he rarely paid much heed to the young women and girls coming and going about the castle, but now he made a few discreet inquiries. In only a few days Raymond was meeting with a young woman from the village.

When the castle on the hill had been completed, Raymond had also ordered the construction of a church in the village. Before Father Mathieu's arrival, there had been no priest in Lydford for many years and the tiny church there had fallen into disrepair. A new stone church dedicated to Saint Petroc now stood in its place and Father Mathieu divided his time between the chapel at the castle and serving the spiritual needs of the local people.

It was in the rectory of this village church that Raymond awaited the young woman who was conducted into his presence. She was shaking with nervousness, her face downcast as she stood before him. He could see that she was passably pretty, though no beauty.

"What is your name?" Raymond asked in his accented English, for of course this peasant girl did not speak Norman French.

"Milesenda, my lord," she replied.

"You are a widow?"

"Yes, my lord."

"Do you have children?"

"No, my lord." She was still trembling and he could see she was afraid of him.

"Do not be frightened," he said quickly. "I will not harm you in any way. I would ask you several things. I may request your assistance in a very important matter, if you are willing. How old are you?"

"Twenty, my lord." Perhaps a little young, Raymond thought, for what he had in mind. Still, she had been married and widowed already.

"And how long were you married?"

"Three years, my lord. My husband died a year ago."

"And was your husband a ... virile man?"

She looked up at him, startled and fearful again.

"No, no," he soothed. "I said you would not be harmed, and I meant it. You will not be forced to do anything you do not wish to do. But I ask these things of you for a reason. You know my son, Geoffrey?"

"He has never spoken to me, nor I to him, but I know who he is. He is very handsome."

"Yes, he is," Raymond said proudly, forcing himself not to grin at the girl's shy admiration. "What I wish to ask of you may shock you, and if you decline, I will understand." He drew in his breath. This was going to be the hard part. "My son will soon be sixteen years of age, and I wish to arrange a marriage for him. I do not believe he has lain with any woman yet, and I would not have him go to his marriage bed ignorant. But I would prefer that he not gain his experience from whores. There were many such following the army, and they are for the most part a sorry, diseased lot. A prudent man does well to avoid such.

"Therefore, I seek a woman who would be willing to teach the lad so that he may feel confident on his wedding night. A woman with experience, but not promiscuous. A widow, such as yourself, would be the best choice."

Milesenda reddened with embarrassment and did not answer.

"I realize this an unusual and difficult thing to ask. And if you do decide to help me, I will see that your reputation will not be besmirched. Should you marry again, there will be a dowry provided for you. Take some time to think on the matter," he finished, expecting her answer in a few days, if at all.

To his surprise, she hesitated only a moment. Then she looked up and said simply, "I will do it, my lord."

5

Most evenings the family, their retainers and servants gathered in the great hall after the day's work was completed. On the evening of Geoffrey's sixteenth birthday, his father called him aside.

"Geoffrey, I would like a word with you. Today you are sixteen years of age, and I am of a mind to find you a bride."

"A bride!" Geoffrey exclaimed. "You mean, marriage?"

"Yes, a bride is usually associated with marriage," Raymond said dryly. "You are my heir, and it will be your duty to produce an heir of your own. My friend Baron de Meules - you remember him from Exeter - has a daughter close to your age. I would like to bind our families together, however, before any arrangements are finalized, I must ask you something. Am I correct in assuming you have not yet lain with any woman?"

Geoffrey quickly blushed a bright red, and shook his head. Lain with a woman? He couldn't even talk to one!

"I thought not," Raymond continued. "When you do marry, your bride will be a virgin, and innocent. It would be better for both of you if you entered marriage with some experience. I have taken the liberty of arranging for you to gain that experience, for I will not have you seeking out any harlots."

"But, Father!" Geoffrey protested.

"I am not accusing you of considering it, boy," Raymond said. "I just wish to make sure you do not consider it in the future. Therefore, when you go to your bedchamber tonight, there will be a young woman there. She is no harlot, but a widow of good reputation. Her name is... oh, I'm sure she'll tell you, if you care to know. She has agreed to be your ... tutor in this delicate area."

Geoffrey was astounded. Never in his wildest adolescent dreams had he anticipated this! Speechless, he picked up the wine glass from the table and drained it in one swallow, not even realizing it was his father's cup. Finally finding his voice, he stuttered, "Thank you for taking such an interest in my education, Father." He looked nervously at the stairs leading to the tower chamber, and in his hand the wineglass shook slightly. Raymond took the cup from his son's hand.

"Go ahead, lad," Raymond urged, trying to suppress a smile. "I assure you, she will be gentle with you."

*****

Geoffrey mounted the stairs to his bedchamber slowly, his heart pounding. He wondered, in fact was dying to know, if his father had faced such a situation before his parent's marriage, but he knew it was a question he could never ask of him.

He was not entirely ignorant of the physical relationships between a man and a woman. He had, after all, grown up in the company of rough knights and stable hands, though he had to admit he did not always understand the jests they told. But he was not as oblivious to women as Father Mathieu believed him to be, although he had yet to summon the courage to speak to any female except for his stepmother, and being his stepmother, she did not count. But there was one girl he would like to speak to, were he brave enough, and that was the pretty brown-haired seamstress he had first seen in his stepmother's solar.

He opened his door, and in his bed, the fur coverlet drawn up to her chin, sat the girl he had just been thinking about, her eyes wide with apprehension. He drew in his breath, not at first believing his eyes. It was really her, the brown-haired girl he had been so attracted to. He remembered seeing her with his stepmother, and in the kitchen, and thinking she was the most beautiful creature he had ever seen.

For a moment, he could only stare at her. Her hair, shining and brown, flowed over her shoulders like soft honey, glowing with soft highlights in the light from the fireplace and the flickering candles. He had never seen a woman's hair unbound before. Both Norman and English women kept their hair plaited and veiled by day, and never left it unbound outside the bedchamber. Her eyes were blue, not the bright sea-blue of his own, but a softer, grayer shade. She had a pert nose with a smattering of freckles, and beneath the coverlet he could see the outline of a lush bosom. She was undoubtedly the loveliest creature he had ever beheld.

Nervously, he closed the door, his mind and his blood racing. It was a lesson, he told himself. Merely another lesson. He had always been quick to learn whatever he had been taught. When his father had taught him to ride and train horses, he had proved exceptionally skilled at it. When the knights had instructed him in the handling of sword, dagger and lance, he had learned these skills well also. He had learned to snare, skin and dress rabbits, birds and other small game; even to cook them himself if necessary. This should be no different-a lesson to be learned as part of his future responsibilities. Why, then, was his heart pounding, his hands sweating, and his mouth as dry as dust?

"Hello," he finally managed to say, and immediately he realized how stupid that sounded. Here he was, in his bedchamber with the most beautiful woman he had ever seen sitting naked in his bed, and all he could say was hello? He felt himself blushing. She inclined her head, murmuring, "My lord."

He might have stood there staring all night, but when she looked down and bit her lip he realized that she was probably almost as nervous as he was. He took a tentative step towards her, almost surprised when she did not scream or try to run away. For a moment, she looked frightened, but then apparently remembering what she had promised Lord Raymond, she lifted her chin and smiled at him.

Her smile was to him like the sun coming out from behind a cloud, and he found himself smiling back at her. "I am Geoffrey," he said, thinking that in view of what they were here for, they might as well get to know each other. "And you are?"

"Milesenda, my lord."

"Milesenda," he repeated. "That is a very pretty name."

"Thank you, my lord."

She had been fearful and nervous when he had first entered the room, wondering just what she was doing here. He was so big, so tall, so strong looking, but when he blushed and smiled nervously she realized that despite his great size, he was still a boy. A boy about to become a man. A boy who despite his nervousness was looking at her as if she were the most beautiful woman on the face of the earth. She felt her apprehension disappearing as she looked into those deep blue eyes and thought she had never seen a man, old or young, as handsome and well-built as Geoffrey de Graville. She patted the bed beside her and he sat down, kicking off his boots at the same time.

He looked down at her and there were so many things he wanted to say to her, that she was beautiful, that he had thought of nothing but her since the day he had first seen her, that he would be willing to kill or to die to be able to touch her. But though she smiled at him encouragingly, he still found himself speechlessly shy, and the hammering of his heart made it even more difficult for him to speak.

"My father," he finally managed to say. "My father sent me ... he said..."

"Yes," the girl said. "He spoke to me ..."

Their sentences went unfinished. They were sitting so close Geoffrey could feel the heat of her skin and the softness of her hair against his arm. Having her sitting there, looking up at him was wondrously exciting.

"I saw you," he began.

"In the solar," she finished for him, and they both smiled at that memory, the first time they had seen each other. Now they had actually met, and he knew her name.

"Milesenda." Her name flowed from his tongue like a poem. "I have wondered what your name was."

"You have thought of me?" She was genuinely surprised. He was after all, a Norman lord, even if he did speak English like a native rather than with the strong French accent his father had. She was only a peasant woman, far beneath the notice of any of the de Gravilles.

"Of course, I have thought of you," Geoffrey affirmed. "I have thought of nothing but you since the day I first saw you. And now you are here."

"I am here." She seemed a bit surprised at that fact as well.

Geoffrey completely forgot the fact that his father had sent this woman to him to prepare him for a future marriage. All he could consider was the fact that this dream woman, Milesenda, was here with him, in his bed. He wondered, with a brief frisson of panic, if he would be able to do this exciting, mysterious thing.

She placed one of her hands on his, and instantly he felt himself hardening just from the mere touch of it. He looked into her eyes, and his other hand moved towards her cheek. At her continued smile of encouragement, he touched her face with his fingertips. She closed her eyes for a second. He moved his hand around into her hair and felt its thick softness around his fingers. It was finer than the softest silk, and his heart raced.

Her one hand was still holding his, but the other touched his arm, then moved to his shoulder. He could hear her breathing quicken even as his was, and as they turned, shifting their positions to face each other, he could see the pulse beating rapidly in her throat. He could also see that the coverlet she had been holding when he had entered the room, had now dropped to her lap, and the sight of her round pale breasts filled him with a sensation like drowning.

Her hands now moved to his waist and tugged at the fabric of his tunic. Quickly he pulled the garment over his head and it dropped to the floor, but when her hands went to the top of his braies he froze in embarrassment. A small giggle escaped her and she looked away as he stood and divested himself of the rest of his clothes, which had been feeling much too tight in any case. Quickly he returned to the bed and slipped his legs under the bedcovers, sitting next to her.

She put her hands on his chest. They were small and gentle, but he was just as captured by them as if they had been leather straps or iron bands. He held his breath as she moved those soft hands slowly up to his neck. She looked up at him and slid closer in the bed, so that her thigh touched his and he could feel one of her breasts against his arm. He exhaled then and the breath came out of him as a small groan. One of her hands was in his hair now and he leaned down towards her, his own hands touching her shoulders and moving along her back to draw her closer. Her skin was satiny smooth and he wondered, briefly, if she would mind that his hands were rough and callused. She did not appear to notice. Sensations he had never felt before were igniting like small fires inside him.

Her lips were pink and moist looking. "I do not know-" he began to say, breathlessly.

She smiled. "I will teach you what you do not know," she murmured, and her hand in his hair, drew his lips to meet hers.

Her soft lips parted beneath his, and a small tongue touched his, clung to him, fenced restlessly and warmly with his. Her arms were about his neck now and he could feel her smooth round breasts against his chest. He wanted desperately to touch one of those breasts and as their kiss ended she seemed to sense his wanting. She took his hand in hers and slowly, their eyes locked on each other's, drew his hand around over her shoulder to fit snugly over her breast.

His breath hissed between his teeth as he felt the soft flesh beneath his hand, and he instinctively let his thumb tease her nipple. She moaned slightly and together they slid down in the bed until he was laying over her. He kissed her again, hesitantly, hoping she would not think his inexperience foolish.

But apparently, she thought him not at all foolish, for her legs parted, and, her lips against his neck, she reached down one hand to guide him.

He was more than ready, but at her touch he glanced down. "Holy Jesus God," he gasped, "Surely not-" but she silenced him with a kiss.

"Surely yes," she insisted, her other hand against the small of his back to press him into her.

He gasped with pleasure and newly awakened desire as her warmth enfolded him with an almost unbearable sensation. She moved beneath him, holding him tightly and guiding him until he found his rhythm.

At first, he felt clumsy and awkward, but it was not long before he responded to the instinct as old as mankind. Is this real, he wondered dazedly; this velvet mouth and soft tongue caressing, inviting him, these small hands guiding him, enthralling him, this warm supple female body entwined with him? It had to be real, for no one could possibly merely imagine the rapturous passion he was feeling. When she cried out, her face pressed against his shoulder, he stopped, thinking he had hurt her, but she merely urged him on, her hands slipping down to cup his buttocks. His hands were pressed into the bed on either side of her head, the fingers unconsciously opening and closing with each thrust.

And when his cry of ecstasy mingled with hers, he felt as if he had died, and not minding it at all, and yet at the same time, as if he would live forever.

*****

Milesenda awoke to find Geoffrey's head cradled on her shoulder, and somehow it felt right and natural for it to be there. The candles in the room still glowed, guttering softly in the breeze from the open window. In sleep, his blond hair tousled, Geoffrey looked even younger, like a little boy. No, she thought, a boy no longer. Daringly, she brushed the hair from his forehead.

At her touch, Geoffrey's eyes flew open. For a moment, he stared at her unknowingly. Then, as remembrance returned, he could feel himself blushing again.

Impulsively, Milesenda leaned forward and kissed his ear. "When you blush, my lord," she whispered, "even your ears turn red."

His blood began to race at her touch, but he managed to mutter, "Tis the curse of fair coloring."

Then he looked up at her with a question in his eyes, which she seemed instinctively to understand. "Yes," she said gravely, "you were very good."

"Did I... please you?"

She nodded. "Yes," she said again, "very much so."

He relaxed then, and smiled. Sitting up against the wall, he pushed the hair away from his face. "I was afraid I had hurt you," he said hesitantly.

She shook her head. "No, my lord, you did not hurt me."

"Good," he said with relief. Then, shyly, "You are so very beautiful."

"Thank you, my lord," she replied, looking away shyly at his compliments.

He picked up a strand of her hair, inhaling the soft scent of it. It smelled faintly of wildflowers. He buried both his hands in the thick brown tresses, then leaned down and pressed his face against her neck, murmuring huskily, "Teach me more."

*****

Milesenda spent three nights in Geoffrey's bed, three nights of the most incredible ecstasy he could have imagined. Boyhood was left behind without regret, or even a backwards glance.

But there was something more than merely the physical pleasure that bloomed for Geoffrey in those three nights. Looking into Milesenda's eyes was like looking into the other half of his own soul, like being found after having been lost all his life. Sometime in the third night of their idyll, before he slept he drew her close, pressing a kiss against her neck, and whispered, "I love you."

The next night she did not come to him. Perhaps she was tired, he said to himself as he yawned mightily. Lord only knew they had slept little these past three nights. But three more nights passed without her return, and then he was upset.

Her cottage was at the edge of the village, and he hesitated at the door. Should he knock, or merely walk in? He took a deep breath and pushed open the door.

She was tending the fire as he strode into the cottage and closed the door behind him. She turned quickly, startled at the intrusion. It was early, and she had not yet braided her hair. The long tawny tresses swirled about her face and framed her alarm-filled eyes.

"Where were you?" he demanded, stepping towards her.

She stepped back, unable to take her gaze away from his angry blue eyes. The truth was, she was afraid of the suddenness and intensity of her feelings for this young Norman lord, this boy-man who now seemed to fill the cottage with his presence.

She had agreed to go to his bed almost on a lark, because she was lonely and he was the most gorgeous man she had ever seen. She had tried to tell herself it was merely lust that she could confess, do penance for, and forget, but she was lying to herself. In spite of the short time they had spent together, he had touched something in her that told her she would never be happy without him. But she knew in her heart that there was no real future for her in his life. He was the lord's son, and in spite of his easy, friendly manner, she was after all merely a peasant woman. A woman who had been sent to him to prepare him for a soon-to-be-arranged marriage.

She tried to sound casual. "I have taught you all I can. You know that your father..."

"Yes, I know my father sent you to me. But can you say that that is all it was to you? A lesson taught, and learned? Is that all?" He smashed his fist down on the table, making the crockery there dance dangerously. Frightened now, she stepped back again, and found her back to the wall. He moved closer, his gaze never leaving hers.

She was pressed against the wall now, and he put his hands against the wall on either side of her. He was tall enough that she could have easily ducked beneath his arms to escape, but she found herself incapable of doing so. She felt as if she were drowning in the sea of those blue, blue eyes. When she began to tremble, the anger suddenly drained away. Taking her chin in his hand, he said softly, "Do not fear me. You need never fear me. Do you not know that when I look in your eyes, I look into my own soul? I love you, Milesenda, I need you, and I cannot bear the thought of you not being near me. Can you truthfully say that you do not feel the same?"

She swallowed. How closely his words had echoed her own thoughts! *I need you*, he had said. When her mother had died, her father and brother had needed her, but only to cook and clean and tend the chickens. That was definitely not the same need she now saw shining from the eyes of this handsome, golden young Norman "No, my lord, I could not in truth say that. But, my lord..."

"You need not call me my lord. My name is Geoffrey," he said, running one finger along her jawline and over her lips. She shivered at his touch. He put his hand in her hair, gathering up the long brown tresses which hung to her waist and wrapping them around his own neck as she held her breath.

"You see, I am bound to you now, and I will never let you go," and he bent his head and kissed her. That kiss was Milesenda's undoing. No longer the hesitant boy's kiss of their first encounter, but the confident kiss of a man, strong and lusty and possessive; he molded her mouth to hers with a concupiscence that left her breathless. "Do you love me?" he demanded, his lips against hers. His irresistible, hungry mouth convinced her that love was not bound by wealth or rank. She wanted him, and it was obvious that he wanted her as well.

"Yes, my lord, God help me, but I do love you," she whispered. "But, my lord-"

"Geoffrey," he insisted. "I want to hear you say my name."

She reached up and put her arms around his neck. "Geoffrey," she murmured, as he held her close and kissed her again.

Then he looked down at her, the desire showing plainly in his eyes, and pleaded, "Please, Milesenda, my love, never leave me again. I love you so very much."

"I love you too, my - Geoffrey."

He grinned. "My Geoffrey," he repeated. "I like that. I am yours, my Milesenda, yours always."

Her hesitation disappeared as he drew her to the bed, loosening the laces at the neck of her gown. As the garment fell to the floor, with his own clothing soon following, he proved to her just what an apt student he had been in the lessons of love. Indeed, she realized, as his body claimed hers, the student had now become the teacher.

6

To Geoffrey it did not seem at all strange that he should fall in love with this girl whom he had met in such bizarre circumstances, nor did he question the strength of that love in light of the short time they had known each other. It was part of his nature to know what he wanted without taking very long to think about it, and he knew he wanted Milesenda. The potential obstacles to their relationship were of no consequence to him. He knew she was a peasant woman, and one who had been sent to him in the role of a tutor, but he dismissed the disparity in their social standings. It was unimportant in his eyes. He knew she was older than him, but the difference in their ages was only four years and equally unimportant to him. He knew also in the back of his mind that his father probably had not intended their relationship to continue after their initial encounter, and he forced himself not to think about what his father had said about arranging a marriage for him. None of these things mattered to him at all, because he loved Milesenda and she returned that love.

Raymond was fully aware that Geoffrey was spending many of his nights at the cottage in the village, and that on other nights he smuggled Milesenda in through the postern gate and up to the tower room, but he made no mention of it. Let the boy have his fun. Raymond was certain that Geoffrey would soon tire of the liaison, and decided it would not be worth the effort to put a stop to the affair, at least not until Geoffrey's betrothal was finalized. If he was still involved with the peasant girl when he married, then of course Milesenda would have to be sent away. Raymond had no idea of the intensity of the feelings which had blazed like flames to consume Geoffrey and Milesenda.

The clearing by the lake that had been where he went to be alone, now became the place he brought Milesenda to be alone with her. They would lay on the grass and, now that he had conquered his speech-numbing shyness of her, talk for hours, for he found he could tell her anything he felt without fear of ridicule. He told her of his love for his adopted homeland, his dreams of becoming a great knight like his father, and the ambiguity of his feelings for his father and stepmother.

She, in turn, told him of her life before she had met him. Like Geoffrey, Milesenda had lost her mother at a young age. But her father had not remarried, and when he died, her older brother had already married and moved away from Lydford, and had no room in his home for an orphaned sister. So, at the age of sixteen, she had found herself married, at her brother's arrangement, to a man twice her age, only to find herself widowed three years later. Fortunately, she had by then developed a skill as a seamstress and was able to use that skill to support herself in the small one-room cottage after her husband's death, and was able to avoid becoming a burden in the home of her brother and sister-in-law. She had been chaste as a widow, until meeting Baron de Graville's son had awakened a surprising desire in her.

"Did you love him?" Geoffrey asked her, referring to her husband and trying not to sound jealous. The man was, after all, dead, and had Milesenda not been married before she met him, they would not be together now.

She shook her head. "He was a good man," she said, "and kind to me, but no, I did not love him. There was something, I did not know what at the time, but something missing that prevented me from loving him. I know now that something was you, my Geoffrey."

He smiled at her use of the endearment. He was laying with his head in her lap, shielding his eyes with his hand while the warm Devon sun shone down on them. In this temperate corner of southwest England, summer sunshine was plentiful. Both Geoffrey and Milesenda knew there were other places they were supposed to be, other things they were supposed to be doing, but neither cared when they were together.

He had pulled off the light jerkin he usually wore in warm weather in place of the heavier tunic, and he shivered as Milesenda ran her fingers over the bare, sun-warmed muscles of his shoulders and chest. She smiled at the way his skin went all over with goosebumps at her touch. There were so many things about him that made her smile, such as the endearing habit he had of pushing back his hair with his hand as he was about to speak, and how, despite his great size and new-found manliness, he would still blush at times.

As they lay there, drowsy and peaceful, Milesenda noticed the small white scar near the hairline over Geoffrey's right eye.

"How did you get that scar?" she asked him.

Geoffrey rubbed his chin as he remembered. As soon as his beard had begun to sprout, he had started to shave it smooth, another English custom his father deplored. "I was five years old when my father brought me here from Normandy," he told her. "The castle was almost completed. Father took me to the top of the battlements. From there we could look out and see, oh, I thought the whole world. I was so enthralled by that view that I leaned out so far, I almost fell over the edge. If my father had not quickly grabbed me and pulled me back, I would not be alive now to tell of it. Fortunately, my only injury was to gash my head on the edge of the wall-which according to my father, was small punishment for my recklessness."

"That must have been quite painful," Milesenda said.

"I thought so at the time," he answered. "But when this happened," and holding up his left hand, she could see the little finger was slightly bent, "I decided that was the most painful thing I had ever experienced. A horse stepped on it."

Milesenda giggled-not at Geoffrey's childhood hurts but at the wry face he made when contemplating his injured finger. She took his hand and tenderly kissed the crooked little finger.

Curling her fingers in his, she said softly, "You seem so different from your father, though I have only spoken to him once."

"Thank you," he said with a grin. "I take that as a compliment."

She smiled. "He seems so stern, so grim, so..."

"Norman?" he supplied.

She nodded. "You do not seem like a Norman at all, my Geoffrey. When I first met you, and heard you speak, I could not believe you were not an Englishman. You have no accent when you speak English, as your father does."

"That is because I am an Englishman," he said. "Oh, I know I was born in Normandy, but I lived there only as a child. Now I am an Englishman."

She put her hand on his head and ran her fingers through the bright hair, saying, "You do not look like your father either."

"I know," he replied. "I take after my mother's folk, so I am told." He looked thoughtful for a moment. "I barely remember her, I was only five when she died, before we left Normandy." His father rarely spoke of his mother, and had never done so after he'd married Lady Alyssa, so that Geoffrey's memory of her was tinged with a hazy vagueness, like remembering an angel.

"I was eight," Milesenda said sadly.

They were both silent for a minute, thinking about their mothers, and then Geoffrey chuckled. "Maud once called me a bloody Viking, but I am not sure if she was referring to my looks or to the fact that I was brutally attacking a defenseless tree, pretending it was a mighty fortress, with a stick that I was pretending was a sword."

He looked up at her, and she no longer looked sad, but was smiling down at him, and he said, "But I am not a Norman, nor a Viking, but an Englishman. Your Englishman." He captured her hands in his, and sitting up, drew her to her knees and nuzzled her neck. She shivered when he licked her ear. Then he leaned back slightly, and looking at her face intently, asked, "Do you know that you are the most beautiful woman ever born?"

She blushed and looked away, embarrassed because she knew that it was not true, despite Geoffrey's effusive compliments. "No, I am not," she said. Her nose was a bit too snub, her mouth a bit too wide for beauty, but Geoffrey, looking at her with the eyes of love, would hear no argument on the subject.

"Do not dispute me, woman," he said with mock severity. "I have a fearsome temper when I am crossed."

Milesenda laughed. Except for his brief anger on that first morning he had come to her cottage, she had never seen Geoffrey in any disposition other than tender and loving, and she could not imagine her gentle lover in a fearsome temper.

He smiled also, saying, "Come swim with me," and before she could answer, he stood and ran to the lake's edge, discarding his braies and diving into the water.

When he surfaced, shaking his wet hair so that droplets of water flew off and glistened in the sunlight, she was still standing at the lake's edge. He waved for her to come and join him, and she hesitantly put one foot in the water, wetting the hem of her gown.

He waded in until the water was waist deep, then stood with his hands on his hips. "You cannot swim in your clothes, silly goose. Do you want to drown?"

She looked at the water, then at Geoffrey. "I will most likely drown with or without my clothes, my Geoffrey. I cannot swim."

"Then I will teach you," he said, striding towards her out of the lake, all wet and nude and golden. She put her hands over her eyes but he could see her peeking through her fingers. "Come," he told her, "after all you have taught me, it would only be fair of you to allow me to teach you something. Not that the two can compare. Trust me, I will not let you drown. But this will only weigh you down when it gets wet," and he helped her remove her gown and shift and led her into the water as bare as a fawn.

They waded out waist deep and he floated on his back and spit water up at her. "See? It is easy."

"I am afraid," she said.

He stood up and laughed. "Afraid? Do you know how afraid I was the first night we were together? Lord, my stomach felt like this," and he splashed the water with his hand, letting it drip from his fingers. "But it was foolish of me to be afraid, and now you need not fear either. I swear to you, I would never let anything harm you, in the water or out of it. Do you trust me?"

She nodded.

"Good. Now let me teach you to swim."

He was a patient teacher, and soon had her paddling about the lake, although she would never be the strong swimmer that he was. He dove under the water and when he did not surface, she panicked. Fortunately, she was not in deep water and she was able to stand, the water just below her breasts as she looked about frantically, calling Geoffrey's name.

He came up behind her with a great splashing noise and she whirled about in fright, throwing her arms around his neck in a panic. "I was afraid you had drowned," she cried, clinging to him.

"I would risk it for this," he said, feeling her breasts pressing against his chest. "I am quite safe, and I am sorry if I frightened you."

She looked up at him and said simply, "I do not wish to swim anymore."

With a groan, he took her hand and led her to the shore, barely making it out of the water before they fell to their knees in a passionate embrace. She arched her head back, her face towards the sky and her eyes closed, and her wet, heavy braids brushed the ground behind her as Geoffrey trailed hot kisses down her throat. Her hands grasped his arms for support as he pressed his lips to her breasts, murmuring, "Soft... Oh, God..."

The feeling of the soft flesh, wet from their swim, beneath his cheek and the ecstatic trembling of her body in his strong hands made Geoffrey's heart and blood pound faster than the hooves of a galloping horse. She put one hand in his hair, urging him, offering herself, and his mouth found her breast, the flesh soft, the nipple erect under his tongue's attention. She whimpered, and he transferred his affections to the other breast. Consumed with the heat of desire, he moaned, "My love, I want you so!"

Still on their knees, Milesenda returned every kiss Geoffrey had given her, tasting him, clinging to him tightly with both hands and lips, murmuring against his skin as she did so. The blood sang in Geoffrey's ears and he could not understand what she said, but the words mattered not, only the feelings. They fell to the ground and there were flowers around their faces though their feet still splashed in the water at the lake's edge. Geoffrey felt grass tickling his nose and Milesenda's wet hair tickling his chest, and then he could bear it no longer and pressed her to the ground beneath him, crushing the fragrant flowers.

He cradled her in his arms and it was as if nothing in the world existed now except the two of them and their single purpose, their urgent desire to be one. She entwined her arms around his neck, and as they joined made a moaning sound that almost drove him wild with desire. They clung to each other tightly, almost fiercely in their passion, and she wrapped her legs around his to draw him even closer, deeper, their skin slick with lake water and perspiration. The rhythmic thrust and arch consumed Geoffrey's senses; he was lost, dizzy, throbbing in erotic waves of sensation, and she was his anchor, compelling. His world was the center of her.

He emptied himself into her with a convulsed groan that sounded-and felt-as if his heart was about to burst, and felt her quiver and tremble beneath and around him. A million stars shot through his body, and he quivered as well, feeling hot inside and moaning her name as the climax overtook him; overtook them both in a rushing, erotic wave of exquisite sensation.

The intensity of their lovemaking drained him and he had to lay on the grass until his heart slowed. Milesenda was warm and breathless beside him; he held her close as they breathed and panted back to sanity. "I love you," he said as soon as he could speak again, pushing his hair and some strands of wet grass away from his face. "I love you, love you…"

Milesenda stroked his chest with weak fingers that moved gently over smooth skin and hard muscles, until a cool breeze sprang up to chill them and remind them of reality and the lateness of the day. With great reluctance they rose and dressed, coaxing Geoffrey's horse from its contented grazing across the clearing to take them back to Lydford. Geoffrey knew he was expected to put in an appearance at home at some point, so he reluctantly parted from Milesenda at the edge of the woods to trudge up the hill to Belvoir as she returned to her cottage in the village, but not before exchanging a kiss replete with promises for tomorrow.

*****

Geoffrey skidded to a stop outside the doorway to the great hall and peered around the corner into the room. If his father was already at the table for the evening meal, Geoffrey would rather go without and be hungry, than to endure Raymond's questions about where he had been and why he had been neglecting his other duties.

Fortunately, neither his father nor stepmother were in the room, and he breathed a sigh of relief.

"Geoffrey, wait." He jumped as he heard Alyssa's voice behind him, and turned to face his stepmother warily. She stepped close to him and reached up, standing on tiptoe though she was tall for a woman, and began to pick pieces of grass and leaves from his still-wet hair. Slipping the debris into her pocket, she said, "Your father has been looking for you."

"Jesus," he grumbled, looking about for an avenue of escape.

"Perhaps you should tell him that you merely went swimming," Alyssa advised, as Geoffrey stared at her. Did she know? But, "Turn around and bend down," was all she said.

He presented his back and bent his knees, and she picked a few more scraps of greenery from his head. "There," she said, patting his back.

He turned and grinned at her, combing his fingers through his hair. "Thank you, my lady," he said, and went in to dinner.

*****

"He is the most impossible, pig-headed, arrogant..." Geoffrey sputtered in anger as he ran out of ways to describe his father.

Milesenda giggled. "Yesterday you said he was the greatest knight in Christendom, and you could only hope to become half as skillful as him."

He looked at her sideways. "I did say that, did I not?" She nodded. He flopped on her bed on his stomach, propping himself on his elbows and resting his chin on his hands. "He is a great knight, a skilled soldier," he admitted grudgingly, "but do you know what he told me to do to-day?" Without waiting for her reply, he went on, "He said I was not to take a step until every horse in the stable had been curried, merely because one was missed yesterday."

"You must be a very fast worker," Milesenda said, sitting next to him.

"Oh, I did not do it at all," he replied. "I left as soon as his back was turned."

"He will be very angry with you, my Geoffrey."

He shrugged. "He will not know. Fortunately, horses cannot talk. Stephen, on the other hand..." his eyes glittered merrily.

"What have you done to Stephen?" she asked suspiciously.

He covered his face with his hands, but she could see his shoulders shaking with laughter. "Tied him up in an empty stall," he admitted.

"Geoffrey, how cruel!" she admonished.

"Oh, I did not hurt him," he said defensively. "And I left the ropes loose - he could wriggle out after a while. But I did have to gag him."

"But why?" she asked.

He sat up and shrugged. "He wanted to know where I was going and could he come with me. What a nuisance the lad is! You should hear him." He pitched his voice higher in imitation of Stephen's childish tones. "You should not curse, Geoffrey. You should show our father more respect, Geoffrey. You should stay awake in the chapel, Geoffrey. Weeping Jesus, what a plague!" He rolled his eyes melodramatically as Milesenda laughed.

"I cannot believe Stephen is as bad as all that. He seems like a sweet young lad," she insisted.

"Perhaps. Occasionally," he was forced to admit. "I just hope he is sweet enough to not tell our father what I did to him. Not that it would matter if he did or not - the old man will find something to be displeased about in any case."

Milesenda moved closer to him and slipped her arm through his. "I have seen Stephen many times when I have been at the castle. I think he admires you very much."

"And well he ought," Geoffrey boasted. Milesenda laughed softly. "Are you laughing at me?" he asked in mock severity.

She nodded, her hand over her mouth. "And why, pray tell?" He tried to look fierce and stern, but she continued to giggle.

"Because you look so funny when you boast, my Geoffrey."

He put his hands on Milesenda's waist and pulled her down as he lay back on the bed, so that she was leaning over him. They looked deep into each other's eyes, and then she stopped laughing. "You say that Stephen admires me. And what of you? Do you admire me?" he asked in a low, husky voice. He reached up and removed the small veil she wore over her braided hair, and she trembled in anticipation.

"Oh, yes, my Geoffrey, I admire you very much. But not in the same manner as Stephen." Now he unbound the heavy braids, spreading her brown hair about her shoulders. It fell like a curtain around their faces.

"And in what manner do you admire me?"

"In this manner." She kissed him, and his arms went around her to hold her tight as he deftly rolled them over so that he was now leaning on his elbows over her. One of the first things Milesenda had taught him, out of necessity, was to carry his weight on his elbows so that she could breathe.

"I admire you also," he murmured, kissing her forehead, then the tip of her nose, feeling as he did so the burning rush of desire that swept through his body whenever he touched her. She put her arms around his neck; ran her hands through his hair, ruffling it so that it fell over his forehead. Then she pulled him down to her and he laid his head on her breasts. When he spoke again, his voice was so low it was almost a whisper. "No, admire is not the right word. I love you. I need you near me. Every time I am with you, I want you more. Sweet Jesus, Milesenda, you intoxicate me." He raised his head to look at her and cupped her round face in his large, strong hands. No further words were possible as his lips touched hers, and she made a small moan, low in the back of her throat. He moved over her, strong and sure, and wondered how he had ever existed before she had come into his life.

*****

Later they lay cuddled together, half asleep with her head on his chest and his arm about her shoulder. She could hear the thump of his heart and feel the rise and fall of his breathing, and he felt the heavy warmth of her hair laying tousled across his chest. His arm tightened around her, and he murmured softly against the top of her head, "You will always be my love." Then sleep overtook him.

*****

As the gray light of dawn began to fill the cottage, Milesenda sat up and reached for her shift. "Where are you going?" Geoffrey mumbled sleepily, reaching for her.

"To feed the chickens," she said. She kept a few in a coop behind the cottage, and she could hear them scratching and cackling hungrily.

He didn't open his eyes, but mumbled something that sounded like, "Help you."

She pressed him back down in the bed. "There is no need," she said with a smile and a kiss, picturing the ludicrousness of the heir of Belvoir feeding a peasant's chickens, especially as he was now, as naked as the day he was born. "I will be back very soon," she assured him. He turned over and went back to sleep as she slipped from the bed, dressed and went to the door.

As she opened the door, she stepped back, startled, when she saw her friend Carys standing there with her hand raised to knock. "My mother sent me to ask if you had any eggs to spare," Carys said, and then her mouth rounded in amazement as she looked past Milesenda's shoulder to see Geoffrey in her bed, peacefully asleep with one arm flung out over the edge. The bright golden hair was unmistakable, and there was no doubt as to the identity of Milesenda's lover.

Quickly Milesenda pushed Carys out the door and shut it gently but firmly behind them. "What is he doing here?" Carys hissed.

Milesenda glanced briefly back at the door. "Sleeping," she said simply.

"That is Lord de Graville's son!" Carys exclaimed, as if Milesenda was unaware of it. "What...how? Milesenda, why?"

"He is very tired." But Milesenda could tell from the look on her friend's face that that was not what Carys had meant. Milesenda sat down in front of the door, and after a moment Carys sat next to her. Briefly, she explained to her friend the circumstances of how Geoffrey de Graville came to be sleeping comfortably in her bed on this bright summer morning. Carys looked shocked when Milesenda told her of the arrangement with Geoffrey's father.

"And what will you do," Carys asked, "when he marries?"

Milesenda wrapped her arms around her knees. "I do not know. He has not spoken of any marriage arrangements. But if-when-he does marry, if he still wants me, I will be here."

"But why?" Carys asked.

Milesenda's eyes were bright with unshed tears as she looked at her friend. "I love him," she said simply.

*****

The next time they were able to escape from their respective responsibilities to their hidden rendezvous by the lake, she asked him about his life in Normandy. Milesenda had never been more than a mile away from Lydford, and to her eyes Geoffrey seemed very well traveled.

"I remember very little of Normandy," he told her.

"But you have family there?" she asked.

He nodded, wrinkling his brow as he tried to remember. "An uncle, my father's brother. Some cousins, one my age, one a year or two older, I believe. We fought frequently."

"Have you never been back?"

He shook his head. "My father has gone several times, but I have not gone with him. England is my home, and I have no desire to visit a group of haughty Normans. Besides, to go back to Normandy would mean traveling by ship." He shuddered at the memory.

Milesenda had never seen the sea, and could not imagine what it would be like to sail upon it. "What is wrong with sea travel?" she asked him.

He patted his stomach. "*Mal de mer*. Seasickness," he explained. "Though I remember little of Normandy, I do remember the voyage here. Being aboard a ship does not affect everyone in that way, but I spent the entire time with my head in a bucket. I was only a child then," he said in his defense, "and my mother had just died. Perhaps that is what made me so sick. Father Mathieu even gave me last rites at one point, although he said he had never heard of anyone actually dying of it. At that time, I almost wished for death." He laughed at the memory, now that it was safely behind him. "I will be very glad never to set foot on a ship again. I wish only to spend the rest of my life here in England, at Belvoir. With you," he said softly, putting his hands on Milesenda's shoulders and pressing her down among the grass and flowers, kissing her so passionately that all talk of ships and seasickness was forgotten, and only the words 'with you' echoed in their minds.

7

❧

It was impossible for Geoffrey to avoid all of his duties on the estate merely because he was in love. So he found himself one fall day kicking his heels at the blacksmith's forge while Brand shod two of Raymond's horses. Geoffrey had been instructed to wait until the work was done and then to return the beasts to the stable within the castle walls. Bored, he wandered around Brand's small shop waiting for him to finish, until he saw two small lady's brooches laying on a workbench. They were simple yet elegant, lover's knots that appeared to have no beginning or end.

"What are these?" he asked.

Brand looked up from the horse's hoof for a moment. He was a huge and muscular man, as was required for his trade, with arms like trees and hands like hams. He was the only man in Lydford who made Geoffrey feel small.

Brand grinned when he saw what Geoffrey was looking at.

"Morning gift," he said. Geoffrey looked at him questioningly.

"I am going to be married in a week's time, my lord," Brand explained. "It is an English custom for a man to give his bride a gift such as that," he indicated the brooches, "in the morning, after the wedding, you see, to show that he is pleased with her."

"They are very attractive," Geoffrey said, fingering the delicate brooches thoughtfully. "Who made them?"

"I made them myself, my lord," the blacksmith replied.

Geoffrey was a bit surprised that those large, meaty hands could have fashioned something as delicate as these small ornaments. He looked up at Brand, his eyes bright. "And would you have time, before your wedding, to make another pair?" he asked.

"For you, my lord?" Brand asked in surprise.

Geoffrey nodded. "I will be marrying soon also."

"Congratulations," Brand grinned. He liked Geoffrey. Everyone in Lydford liked Geoffrey. He was friendly and open and not at all lordly like his father, who would never had deigned to engage in conversation with a blacksmith. But Brand was surprised to hear Geoffrey mention marrying. Surely something as important as the wedding of Lord Raymond's son, and the arrival of another noble bride such as Lady Alyssa, would have been rumored of in the village.

"I would be honored to make a morning gift for you, my lord," he said.

Geoffrey set the brooches carefully back on the bench. "Just like these?" he asked.

Brand nodded. "But they are very simple," he said.

"They are perfect," Geoffrey replied.

*****

Within a few days the weather turned chilly, with tingly promises of frost in the morning air, when Geoffrey awoke one such morning to find himself alone in Milesenda's bed. He sat up and looked around but she was not in the cottage.

After a moment, he heard a coughing sound, coming from outside. Scrabbling on the floor for his trews, he pulled them on hastily and hurried outside.

He found her behind the cottage, on her knees vomiting quietly into the grass.

"Milesenda!" he cried, kneeling down beside her and putting his arms around her. "What is the matter? Are you ill?"

She shook her head, and Geoffrey could feel her shivering in the cool morning air. She put her hands against the cottage wall, and breathed deeply, then with Geoffrey's help, stood up. Still she said nothing, so Geoffrey picked her up, resting her head comfortably against his shoulder, and carried her back into the cottage.

He deposited her gently on the bed, found the pitcher of water, and poured some into a cup for her to sip. Wetting a cloth with the remainder, he gently wiped her face.

"Better?" he asked, and she nodded.

He climbed into the bed next to her and put his arm around her, drawing her head to his shoulder. He loved the feel of her in his arms like this, as she lay her head trustingly against him. The thought of her being ill upset him.

"Did your dinner not agree with you?" he asked, trying to sound casual.

She looked up at him, her eyes searching his. Taking his hand in hers, she laid it on her stomach.

"My Geoffrey," she whispered at last. "I am with child. Your child."

He stared at his hand laying on her stomach, then looked at her face.

"Oh, Milesenda," he whispered. "A child!" He grinned and hugged her. "A child!" he repeated. "A child of ours! Then we must do it immediately. I will speak to my father today." And he swung his legs off the bed and stood up.

"Do what, Geoffrey?" she asked, surprised but gladdened by his happy reaction.

"Why, we must be wed, of course," he replied. He looked down shyly. "I should have spoken sooner, sweetheart. Do not think that it is only because of the child. I have known since we first met that I wished to be with you always."

To his surprise, her eyes filled with tears. "We cannot marry," she whispered. "Your father would not allow it."

He sat down next to her and took her hands in his. "Of course, we can marry, my darling," he declared. "My father has said it is my responsibility to produce the next de Graville heir, and it looks as if we have done just that." His large hand slid again over her stomach, and it did seem just slightly fuller to him.

The tears in her eyes spilled over. "My Geoffrey, he intends for you to marry a noblewoman, not someone like me. He told me so, when-when..."

"He told me, too," he said, trying to wipe away her tears with his thumbs. "But none of that matters now. It never did, not to me. I have no intention of marrying anyone but you. Whatever negotiations he may have made, his noble heiress will have to find someone else, because you are going to be my wife. I am sure that once I explain to my father how much I love you, he will agree. He may be difficult to get along with, but I am certain I can convince him," he declared with all the confidence of youth. He cupped her face with his hands. "You do love me?" he asked.

"Of course, my Geoffrey," she said through her tears.

"And would you not like to be my wife? To live with me openly, at the castle? I know my father is not always pleasant to be near, but my stepmother is kind, and Stephen is agreeable, when he is not being a pest. And then, of course, there is me. Am I so awful to be with?" He grinned comically.

"Oh, Geoffrey," she sighed, putting her arms around his waist and laying her head against his chest. "You are not awful. You are wonderful, and I would want to be with you no matter where we were. But..."

He hushed her with a finger on her lips. "Then it is settled. Do not worry, my love, I will convince my father that you are the perfect, the only, wife for me. He should be proud to have such a beautiful daughter-in-law." He dropped a kiss on her forehead, then stepped back and took her hands in his. "I swear to you, on my honor, that I will marry no one but you, and I will always care for you, and for our child. Our child!" he repeated, hugging her close. "I will be back soon," he promised, leaving her to shake her head disbelievingly behind him as he pulled on the rest of his clothes and hurried to seek out his father.

*****

Raymond was in a foul mood. This morning someone had left a gate open in the paddock and two valuable horses had wandered out. One was still missing. He suspected his son had been the one to leave the gate unlatched. But that was minor compared to the news he had received only an hour ago. The daughter of his friend Baldwin de Meules, to whom he had just been finalizing a betrothal for Geoffrey, had died in a clumsy fall down a flight of stairs. There was a younger sister not spoken for, but the child would not be old enough for marriage for several years.

When Geoffrey entered the room, it only added to Raymond's irritation to realize that his son was now taller than he was. Christ, would the boy never stop growing! At least Raymond had been spared the effort of trying to find Geoffrey to speak to him. Geoffrey's attention had been decidedly difficult to come by for the past several months.

Geoffrey hesitated before speaking to his father. Why was it, he wondered, that even now, when his father gave him one of his stern, dark looks, that he was still able to make Geoffrey feel like a naughty child? *Courage, Geoffrey*, he told himself, *you are no longer a child. You are sixteen years of age, a man now and about to become a father yourself.* He took a deep breath, pushed back his hair with his hand, and looked his father in the eye.

"Father, I wish to marry."

Raymond almost groaned aloud. Now the boy took an interest! He began to explain about the death of the de Meules girl, but Geoffrey forestalled him.

"Father, I intend to marry Milesenda."

Raymond looked confused. "Who..." he began.

"Milesenda," Geoffrey repeated, amazed that his father had forgotten her name. "Surely you must remember." He felt his face reddening. "My birthday."

"The peasant girl? Absolutely not," Raymond replied dismissively. "Baldwin's other daughter is still a child, but there are other girls of your own rank to be considered. Perhaps my brother Alain knows of some suitable possibilities. A Norman bride might be a steadying influence for you…"

"Father!" Geoffrey interrupted Raymond's ramblings. "I do not wish to marry anyone else, and especially not a Norman woman. I love Milesenda, and I am going to wed her, and only her. I am not asking your permission, merely your blessing."

Raymond sighed. "Geoffrey," he began, and Geoffrey cringed at the condescending tone to his father's voice. "First of all, sit down. I cannot talk to you with you towering there like a tree."

Geoffrey flung himself onto a bench. "Now," Raymond continued. "You must understand something. You are my son; you are a Norman lord. You cannot marry some common peasant girl. It is simply not suitable. She may be a pleasant dalliance, and I will not deny you that. But when it comes to a bride, you must bind yourself to a woman worthy of you, and who brings an appropriate dowry with her."

Geoffrey could feel his face flushing with anger, and he struggled to keep his voice calm. "If you do not think Milesenda is worthy of me, then why did you send her to my bed?"

"To teach you a lesson you needed to learn," his father replied. "And did you learn it?"

Geoffrey's red face was his only answer.

"You may be grateful to her, and that is fine," Raymond continued. "But you do not have to marry her. I will not allow it."

Geoffrey's jaw was beginning to ache from clenching his teeth. "Father, I love Milesenda. I do not want some haughty Norman girl, no matter her fat dowry or great name. Milesenda is worthy of me, especially since…"

"Since what?" Raymond asked, his dark eyes glaring at his son.

Geoffrey forced himself not to quail under his father's scowl. "She is carrying my child. Your grandchild, Father."

Raymond did not sound very angry, but Geoffrey could see the tightness in his father's face. "In that case, she will have to be sent away, when a new bride is found for you. I do not have personal experience in the matter," he said hastily, "but I have been told by those who do that wives can become most fractious when a husband's leman and bastard are nearby."

Geoffrey jumped to his feet as his father spoke, angry beyond reason at the insulting words. He had to clench his fists tightly at his sides to keep himself from striking his father.

"I will not allow you to insult Milesenda, and I will marry her. Can you not understand, Father, I love her, and she loves me. Our child will not be bastard born, and she will not be my..." he could barely force himself to say the word, "she will not be my leman. She is going to be my wife."

"That girl is a tenant on my demesne, and you are not going to marry her, no matter if she bears you a litter of bastards," Raymond declared. "You will marry a woman of my choosing, as is suitable. You forget, as the overlord here, no marriages can be performed without my approval. Not yours, nor your mistress's, nor anyone else's. Remember that!"

Geoffrey turned his back on his father for a minute. He wanted this, needed this marriage with Milesenda, more than anything he could imagine, but his pride refused to allow him to beg. Turning back to face his father, he willed his voice to stay calm. "Father, have you not taught me that a knight's honor, his word, is sacred? That a knight who breaks his oath is less than a man?"

Raymond nodded, surprised at Geoffrey's changing of the subject.

"I may not have earned my knighthood yet," Geoffrey said, "but I feel myself just as bound to its precepts. And I have sworn an oath to Milesenda to care for her and our child, to protect her, and to prove my love to her by marrying her no matter what opposition we must face. And I will marry her, with your approval or without it." Before Raymond could reply, Geoffrey swiftly strode from the room, leaving Raymond cursing silently behind him.

*****

Raymond wondered if his son would have desired this unsuitable, unallowable marriage if he had been fostered out and spent more time in the company of Norman boys of his own rank, rather than roistering like a savage with Edmund and the other local boys. Perhaps he had spoiled the boy by keeping him at Belvoir. Perhaps he should have found an older, less attractive woman to initiate Geoffrey into the mysteries of the bedchamber. Perhaps he should not have concerned himself at all with the level of his son's sexual experience, and let the boy figure things out for himself. Or perhaps, he reflected, Geoffrey was merely a reckless, headstrong fool who jumped into situations feet first and with his eyes closed. In any case, Raymond told himself, he could do nothing to change the past, but by Christ, he was not going to allow his son to marry a peasant woman. With a determined step, he set off in search of Father Mathieu.

When Geoffrey returned to Milesenda's cottage, he could only hold her close and did not trust himself to speak for several minutes. He felt as if he had failed her by not being able to secure his father's permission for their marriage.

Milesenda was not surprised. She had not really believed that Lord de Graville would allow his son and heir to marry her.

"We will be married, Milesenda," he declared, his lips against her hair. "We do not need my father's permission." He put his hands on her shoulders and looked in her eyes, which were filled again with tears. "I am going to fetch Edmund to be our witness, and then we will seek out Father Mathieu. We will be married by nightfall, and my lord father," and he put an ugly sneer on the word, "will have to accept us, like it or not." He patted her stomach protectively. "Do not fear, little one, your mother and I will soon be wed, I swear it!"

He left her only long enough to find Edmund and to explain his plans to his friend. Edmund had suspected that Geoffrey was involved in some sort of liaison, because he had seen little of him these past months. But he was very surprised when he heard of Geoffrey's plans to marry.

The three young people walked quickly to the small church of Saint Petroc located in the center of the village. Father Mathieu divided his time between the chapel at the castle and this church. They found him in the rectory.

"Father Mathieu, I wish you to marry us," Geoffrey told the priest, holding Milesenda's hand.

But Father Mathieu shook his head. "I cannot marry you to this girl," he said.

"Why not?" Geoffrey challenged. "Neither of us is contracted to another."

"Your father has forbidden it," Mathieu replied. "He left here but minutes ago. He has forbidden me to perform any marriage for you that he has not approved. He is my cousin and the lord of this demesne, Geoffrey," he said, as he saw the anger rising in Geoffrey's face. "I cannot disregard his orders. You know it is his right to forbid this marriage."

"God's wounds!" Geoffrey cursed. "Are you a man of God, or my father's toady? I demand that you join us in wedlock, today."

But Mathieu would not be persuaded. "I am sorry, Geoffrey, but I cannot do it. I have promised your father that I would abide by his orders."

Geoffrey was furious, and he fought back a desire to hit something, smash something. He glanced back at Milesenda, weeping silently, and Edmund, his face pale and fearful under his red hair. Turning away from the priest, he took a deep breath.

"If we cannot be married by a priest," he said to Milesenda, "then we will pledge ourselves in handfast. An English custom," he said over his shoulder to Father Mathieu, "and quite legal."

"I am not ignorant of the existence of handfast marriages," Mathieu said. "But you are wrong, Geoffrey. Handfasting is not truly legal. You must understand that, both of you."

Geoffrey turned and looked at the priest briefly. "We don't need you," he said harshly. He took Milesenda's hand and led her from the chapel, with Edmund following quickly behind them.

* * * * *

Geoffrey and Milesenda went to the clearing in the woods, leaving Edmund behind in Lydford to ward off any who might try to follow the lovers. Leaves of yellow and orange were drifting from the trees and crackling under their feet.

Geoffrey took Milesenda's hands in his and gazed lovingly at her. "I am sorry, my love, so sorry that my father has done this to us. I wish I could take you somewhere else, someplace where they don't know us, to be married. But I doubt there is another priest between here and Bickleigh and I do not want to force you to travel so far in your condition. I know a handfast marriage is not truly valid, but in our hearts, we shall be man and wife and I swear to you I will do everything in my power to make you my wife in truth." He looked at her with such love and tenderness that she was forced to smile as he released one of her hands just long enough to wipe away the last remnants of her tears.

"Milesenda, you are my heart," he said. "I will always love you, always care for you, and I want nothing more in this life than to be your husband, and the father of our children," and he squeezed her hands tightly.

Milesenda looked up at Geoffrey, into his blue eyes filled with love. "My Geoffrey," she said, her voice soft but steady, "I love you more than life itself, and I will always be by your side. I would be proud to be your wife, in any circumstances."

He leaned forward to kiss her, and whispered in her ear, "I am certain, my darling, that once the child is born and my father sees the beautiful grandchild you have given him, he will relent and allow us to be married legally, by a priest." He folded her into his embrace and kissed her passionately, then murmured, "Let us go home, my wife."

They returned to Milesenda's cottage and as soon as they went in, Geoffrey drew forth a small package wrapped in a bit of cloth and bade her open it. He was too eager to give her his gift to wait until the morning. She gasped when she saw the twin brooches that he had commissioned from Brand.

"Morning brooches!" she breathed.

"Do you like them?" he asked.

She nodded, smoothing a finger over the delicate filigree. "They are beautiful. My mother was buried with hers." He looked shocked, but she told him, "Most English women are, because her morning brooches are the most precious gift she can ever receive." She stood up on tiptoe to kiss his cheek. "But I have no dowry to bring to you." She remembered that Geoffrey's father had promised her a dowry if she married again, but she realized that Raymond had most certainly not intended for her to marry Geoffrey.

But Geoffrey only laughed and held her close. "I need no dowry, I only need you," he said. "I would take you in your chemise, or out of it." And in his eagerness to prove his devotion to her, he tore that garment beyond repair. He looked so ashamed of himself at the ruin of her chemise that she could only laugh and kiss him, and as they tumbled to the bed, the chemise, and everything else, his father's disapproval, the dubious legality of their marriage, was forgotten in the simple joy of each other.

*****

"Are you asleep?"

"No." Her voice floated softly up to him, disembodied in the dark.

He turned on his side toward her, gathering her protectively against his chest. They fit so well together, he reflected, as if they had been made for each other. In Geoffrey's opinion, that was exactly the case. He smoothed her hair away from his nose and laid his chin gently against the top of her head, as she sighed in contentment.

"You are truly mine now," he murmured, "mine forever."

"I have always been yours, my Geoffrey," she replied. "From that very first day - do you remember-in your stepmother's solar. I saw you standing in that doorway, looking like a..." she paused a moment as if searching for a phrase, and he could hear the smile in her tone of voice when she found it, "looking like a bloody Viking, and I was yours from that moment." She cuddled closer to him, the smooth line of her back warm against his chest, and went on, "I was surprised when your father told me you were not yet sixteen. I had thought you to be older."

"Do you mind, my love," he asked anxiously, "that I am younger than you?"

"Did I mind," she returned, "would I be here now, with you?"

She ran smooth fingers along the muscle of his forearm, and then asked an anxious question of her own. "Do you mind, my Geoffrey, the manner in which I first came to you, at your father's arrangement?"

He laughed softly, hugged her, and repeated the answer she had given him.

"Did I mind, would I be here now, with you? I am glad of it. It is the one kind thing my father has ever done for me. Left to myself, I doubt I would have ever summoned the courage to even speak to you."

"I thought knights were trained to be brave and courageous," she teased.

"Bravery in battle is one thing," he replied. "Courage when facing a beautiful woman is quite another thing altogether."

"Oh, my Geoffrey," she said with a sigh, "I do love you."

"I love you too, my darling," he said softly. "You have made me the happiest man in England; no, the happiest man alive anywhere. And this," he laid his hand possessively on her stomach, "this is a miracle."

"I thought I was barren," she said, her voice almost a whisper.

"What!" he exclaimed in surprise.

"When I was married - the first time -" she added hastily, "I never conceived. I thought then that I was barren, that I would never bear children."

He turned her in his arms to face him, though he could barely make out her features in the dark, holding her face in his hands and smoothing his thumbs along her eyebrows. "We know now that you are not barren, and I am happy beyond words that I am the one to father your children. I hope that this baby is but the first of many for us, sweet Milesenda."

"That is my hope as well," she answered, putting her arms around his neck. "Can you imagine us, old and gray, with a brood of children about our feet?"

He considered for a moment. Despite impending fatherhood, at the age of sixteen, 'old' was twenty. His father, at twice that age, seemed ancient. "I can imagine the brood of children," he replied. "We should have, oh, six at least. Beautiful daughters, as gorgeous as their mother, and strong sons to protect them."

When they slept, it was locked in each other's arms, but the next morning, and almost every morning for the next several months, Geoffrey awoke alone as Milesenda retched miserably with her morning sickness.

A few days after their clandestine and invalid marriage, he brought her a length of cloth, filched no doubt from Alyssa's storerooms, with which she made herself a new chemise to replace the one Geoffrey had torn. She used what was left of the material to sew several garments for the baby whose existence became every day more real for them as her belly began to swell.

Geoffrey said nothing to his father about the vows they had exchanged, in fact did not speak of her at all to him. He had little if anything to say to Raymond, and avoided his father whenever possible.

As for Raymond, he could only hope that Geoffrey had given up the foolish notion of marriage with the peasant girl. He was still sending out feelers for a possible bride for Geoffrey, in the hopes that a nubile, wealthy young girl of his own rank would take his mind away from Milesenda.

But Geoffrey would not listen to anything his father said about marriage. "You may make what arrangements you will, Father, but I will not be participating in them," he said, and something in the firm set of his jaw made Raymond decide to put off betrothal arrangements for the time being. Raymond could, if he wished, contract a betrothal, could even, with enough assistance, physically force Geoffrey to the altar. But he could not force his son to say the marriage vows if he was unwilling. Perhaps a little time to cool off would make the boy more reasonable. So, he did not ask if Geoffrey was still seeing Milesenda, feeling that if he made an issue of it, it would only have the effect of pushing his son closer to the girl, if for no other reason than to antagonize his father. For this reason also, he did not send her away from Lydford, although it would have been within his power to do so, and there was nothing he would have liked more than to separate Geoffrey from her. However, Raymond feared that if his son's pregnant lover were to disappear from Lydford, Geoffrey would never forgive him. Even more vexing was the humiliation Raymond would feel among his peers if his son and heir were to abandon his home in search of a peasant woman, which he had no doubt Geoffrey would do if Raymond were to separate him from Milesenda.

Geoffrey no longer tried to smuggle Milesenda into the castle at night, but spent most of his free time at her cottage in the village. She still did embroidery and sewing for his stepmother, so he did sometimes see her at the castle when she came to deliver her handiwork, and he treasured those brief glimpses, even as he burned with the unfairness of her not being able to live there with him.

Through the winter as the child grew and moved within her, she found it more and more difficult to move about. Geoffrey was fascinated by the growing mound of her belly, petting her stomach and trying to cheer her up when she felt ill, which was frequent. Once, he teased her about waddling like an obese duck as the increased bulk in her front unbalanced her, but Milesenda did not find this amusing, so he did not tease her thusly a second time, although the comparison was valid.

He could not remember what his life had been like before her, and he did not want to. Geoffrey did however feel slightly guilty at his neglect of his friendship with Edmund. He could only hope that his friend would find someone to love as much as Geoffrey loved Milesenda, and then Edmund would understand.

Geoffrey had always attempted to preserve Milesenda's reputation by being as discreet as possible with his comings and goings at her home, but they realized that it was impossible to keep such a secret in a small village like Lydford, as they had discovered the morning Carys had seen him in Milesenda's bed. Their affair had become open knowledge in the village, especially as Milesenda's pregnancy became obvious. There were of course some who were scandalized by Milesenda's lack of shame, but neither Carys nor Edmund would allow anyone to insult their friends, and those who might be inclined to were usually silenced by Geoffrey's and Milesenda's obvious devotion to each other.

However, at the castle, the attitude was slightly different. Although everyone, the family, retainers and servants, were well aware of who the father of Milesenda's child was, it was tacitly understood that the subject was not mentioned in the presence of Lord Raymond. And no one, not Geoffrey, Milesenda, nor Father Mathieu, who suspected, spoke of the simple vows Geoffrey and Milesenda had exchanged in the woodland clearing. That particular piece of information was hidden, even from Raymond's usually perceptive vision.

8

Spring in Devon could be a beautiful time filled with flowers and newborn lambs and warm, sweet breezes. But that part of the season was yet to reveal itself. The very beginning of spring offered cold, wet winds that could cut through a man's flesh to chill his bones. Such a storm was developing, and blowing dark threatening clouds through the valley, when Geoffrey entered the cottage and rubbed his arms to warm them. Milesenda was sitting on a stool by the fire and did not look up when he came in.

He walked up behind her, sliding his hand over her shoulders and leaning down to caress the large mound of her belly, feeling the kick of the child soon to be born. He kissed the back of her neck and she pushed him away.

He backed up, startled. "Are you not feeling well, sweetheart?" he asked.

She rounded on him. "No, I do not feel well! I cannot sit, I cannot stand, I cannot lay down! My feet are swollen, my back hurts, and I feel as if I am carrying six babies!"

Geoffrey stared at her in horror. She had always been the sweetest, most even-tempered of women. He could not believe that his gentle Milesenda was being so shrewish. Before he could think of something to say, she burst into tears.

Instantly he knelt beside her, putting his arms around her and holding her close as she wept. "I am sorry, my Geoffrey," she gulped. "I did not mean to be so unpleasant. Please forgive me."

"There is nothing to forgive." Gently he helped her to her feet. She was awkward with the bulk of the child. "Bearing a child must be very difficult. I am sorry to put you through this. If I had known how uncomfortable it would be for you, I would never have…"

She put her finger to his lips. "Do not be sorry. I do not mind, truly I do not. It is just that this one," and she put her hand over her rounded stomach, "sometimes makes me do things I would otherwise not do. You are so kind to put up with me, my Geoffrey. I love you so much," and she leaned against him, slipping her arm around his waist.

This was the gentle, loving Milesenda he was accustomed to. He picked her up - it was fortunate that he was strong because she was heavy with the child - and set her gently in the bed. They had not made love since she had become so big and uncomfortable, but he was content for now just to sit next to her, his arm about her shoulder and her head resting against his chest.

After a few minutes she tried to pull herself up and get out of the bed. "I must go to the castle," she said. "I have some embroidered pieces for your stepmother that I must bring to her today. I promised her they would be ready." In sympathy for the young lovers, Alyssa had commissioned more sewing from Milesenda, although Raymond was not apprised of the fact. The managing of the household was not his concern in any case.

"No, you need to rest," Geoffrey insisted. "I will take your work to my lady later." He drew her head to his shoulder petting her much as he would a skittish horse. "Just sleep."

"You do not mind going back to the castle?" she asked sleepily. "Perhaps even encountering your father?"

"I suppose I can endure one evening in my lord's presence. You rest, and I will come back in the morning to see how you are."

She closed her eyes. "I love you, my Geoffrey," she murmured. He held her until she finally fell asleep, then picked up the embroidery from the table and left after placing a gentle kiss on her forehead.

He arrived at the castle just as the first raindrops began to fall, and found his stepmother in the solar. "These are the workpieces Milesenda has done for you, my lady," he told her, handing her the packages and turning to leave.

"Geoffrey, stay," Alyssa entreated. "My maids have all deserted me and I am quite alone."

He glanced around and saw that she was indeed alone, the ladies who usually attended her having apparently all found other errands to attend to. Not being able to think of any good reason not to, he found a stool and set it next to her chair, folding his long legs under him with a sigh as he sat down, resting his elbows on his knees and his chin in his hand.

"How is Milesenda feeling?" Alyssa asked.

"Poorly," Geoffrey replied. He would only talk about her now because he knew his father was not nearby. "She is uncomfortable and - not herself. It must be very difficult to bear a child."

"Yes, it is," Alyssa agreed. "But the results make it worth the difficulty." She paused. "You love her very much, don't you, Geoffrey?"

He looked up at her sharply, but saw only caring and compassion in his stepmother's face. "Yes," he admitted. "She is my life. Without her, I am nothing. With her, I can be anything. I just wish I could make my father understand that."

He looked away again, and Alyssa tentatively put her hand on her stepson's head, afraid he might pull away from her. She had loved this boy as if he were her own son since the day of her wedding when she had accepted his unenthusiastic congratulations. But she loved her husband too, and it broke her heart to see father and son so estranged.

He did not move away from her touch, just sat there in silence for a moment, then said in an anguished voice, "Is it so wrong to love her, my lady? Is it wrong because she is not a nobleman's daughter? My father would have me believe it is some sort of sin to want her. Why can he not accept us? Is it wrong?" he asked again.

"No, Geoffrey, it is not wrong," she said. "It is unconventional, but it is not wrong."

He relaxed, and then he rested his head against her knee. It was the first sign of affection he had ever shown towards her, and she treasured it.

Geoffrey was coming to realize that he felt differently now towards his stepmother than he had when his father had married her. It was a gradual transformation that had taken place so slowly over the years that he had been unaware of it until now. She had been nothing but kindness itself towards him from the first, in spite of all the horrible, childish things he had done. Had he been wrong, he wondered, to have been so resentful of her?

He was tempted to tell her of his plan, after their child was born, to again petition his father to marry Milesenda in a ceremony performed by a priest. But he held his tongue. Alyssa was, after all, his father's wife and he would not risk having his father hear of his plans prematurely.

"I am sorry, my lady," he said.

She was surprised. "Sorry for what?"

He closed his eyes. "The frogs. I am very sorry about the frogs."

*****

Geoffrey reluctantly agreed to join the family for the evening meal but had little to say to his father. Instead he sat with Stephen and talked and joked with his younger brother, who basked in the attention from his adored older brother.

A commotion at the doorway caught their attention. Geoffrey looked up and saw Milesenda's friend Carys, the daughter of the midwife Emma, pulling away from the guardsman who was denying her admittance to the hall.

"My lord!" she cried out when she saw she had their attention. Raymond looked up and frowned, signaling to the guard to remove her.

"Geoffrey!" Carys screamed. "I must speak with my lord Geoffrey!"

Raymond's scowl intensified. Had Geoffrey become involved with yet another peasant girl, this time one who boldly dared to accost him in the castle's great hall?

Geoffrey, looking up, had seen something in Carys's face as she called his name and tried to pull away from the guard that made him rise and leap over the table, striding towards her and ordering the guard to unhand her. The man did so reluctantly. Carys clutched Geoffrey's arm in a panic.

"Please, my lord," she said desperately. "It is Milesenda. It is her time." She cast a fearful glance at Raymond's rage-filled face. "My mother is with her, but she is in a bad way." That was all Geoffrey needed to hear. He took Carys's arm and they turned to leave.

"Geoffrey!" Raymond's voice thundered. "Where are you going?"

Geoffrey turned to face his father. "To be with my wife," he replied coldly, "while she gives birth to your grandchild."

"Your wife!" Raymond exclaimed, turning to glare at Father Mathieu.

"Oh, Father Mathieu refused to marry us as you instructed, Father," Geoffrey said. "But we pledged ourselves in handfast, and as far as I am concerned, we are just as bound as you are to my lady stepmother."

Raymond glared again at Father Mathieu, who could only nod miserably. "But such a pledge is not a valid marriage, Geoffrey. Surely you must realize that," the priest called out.

"Geoffrey, I order you to stay here," Raymond demanded, rising to his feet with his hands pressed flat on the table. "There is no need for you to go tearing out on a stormy night merely because some peasant girl is bearing your bastard."

The silence in the hall became absolute as Geoffrey and his father stared each other down, rage filling both their faces. Alyssa and Stephen, as well as everyone else in the room, stared in horror at the two of them. Geoffrey, with his hand still on Carys's arm, could feel her shivering as much with fear as with the cold and wet of the stormy night. She had come here to fetch him despite the certainty of Lord Raymond's anger, despite fears of the devil and gruesome creatures who walked abroad in the dark, and here was Raymond, trying to prevent him from going to the woman he loved in her crisis. Geoffrey's eyes were blue ice as he looked at his father.

"Go to hell, my lord," he said coldly, and escorted Carys out of the hall.

In the gatehouse, he took two cloaks from the guard's supply and put one over Carys's shoulders before swinging the other over his own. As they stepped out into the dark, wet, rainy night, Geoffrey saw one of the knights riding into the gate. No sooner had the man dismounted than Geoffrey took the reins from the startled knight's hands and swung up onto the horse's back. "Help her up," he ordered curtly, and the knight put his hands on Carys's waist and lifted her up behind Geoffrey.

"Hold on," he said to her, and she put her arms tightly around his waist as he turned the horse and they clattered through the gate and down the hill towards the village.

Although it was only a short distance to Milesenda's cottage they were soaked through by the time they arrived at her door. Geoffrey swung off of the tired horse and helped Carys down. He froze as he thought he heard a scream of pain that penetrated even the howling wind of the storm. For a moment he could not move, then without even bothering to tether the horse, he burst through the cottage door.

When he entered the small cottage, he was assaulted by the sharp, sickening smell of blood that permeated the air. Two women were doing something by the fireplace, and Emma the midwife was by the bed, but he had eyes only for Milesenda, laying still and ghostly pale under the covers.

He strode swiftly to the bed, trying to ignore Emma who was shaking her head at him, and slipped one arm about Milesenda's shoulders.

Her eyes were closed, but she opened them with apparently great difficulty at his touch.

"My Geoffrey," she said weakly, her voice so soft he had to lean close to hear her. "You are here."

He was shocked by her pallor, her weak voice. Only this morning she had been fine and healthy. But no, he remembered, that was not true. She had been sick and irritable. He tried to keep the dismay from his voice as he brushed damp tendrils of hair from her forehead, noticing that her skin was cold and clammy under his fingers, despite the fact that the room was warm and her hair was damp with perspiration. "Yes, sweetheart, I am here, and all will be well, I promise," he said.

"No," she whispered, "I..." She was having difficulty speaking, and fear wrapped icy fingers around Geoffrey's heart.

"My Geoffrey, please, I beg of you..." But that was all she could say. She gasped once, then her eyes closed and she was still.

A perilous horror began to fill Geoffrey's soul as he shook her gently. "Milesenda," he whispered.

But she was beyond hearing him. "Nooooh," he whispered, standing up, the blood draining from his face. "No! Oh, God, no!" His whisper became a moan, then a shriek. He backed away from the bed, staring blindly, his eyes wild with pain, and Emma put her hand on his arm. He shook her off.

"Geoffrey," she began, but he would not listen to her. He backed toward the door, pushing aside Carys who stood there with large frightened eyes, and stumbled out into the rain, his cry of pain and grief floating back on the moaning wind.

9

For three days and nights no one knew where Geoffrey was, though Raymond sent men out to search the village, castle and surrounding countryside for his missing son. Edmund quested to all the places where he and Geoffrey had played as boys, with no success. Only the cloak he had been wearing was found, a few paces away from the door of Milesenda's cottage. Fraught with worry, Alyssa could only pray for her stepson's safety. On the third morning, her prayers were answered as the family left the chapel following Mass. Alyssa discovered him slumped on a bench in the corridor, his face in his hands. He was wet, dirty, and there were leaves in his hair and stuck to his clothing.

Alyssa sat down next to him. "Geoffrey?" Her voice was full of concern. "Geoffrey, where have you been?"

At first, he did not appear to hear her, but after a minute he looked up. He did not tell her where he had been, because he could not remember.

The look in Geoffrey's eyes frightened his stepmother. Gone were the merriment and mischief, the twinkle that usually showed even in anger. Those blue eyes were now filled with a despair and grief that broke Alyssa's heart.

"She is dead," he said, and his voice sounded dead as well. "Holy God, she died in my arms, and I could do nothing to help her."

"I know. Geoffrey, I am so sorry," Alyssa replied.

Then Geoffrey did what Alyssa had never seen any man do, especially not her tall, strong stepson. He began to weep, hot tears flowing unchecked down his face. A lump formed in Alyssa's throat, and she put her arms around Geoffrey's shoulders. He laid his head on her shoulder, and shook like a child.

"Dead," he sobbed. "She is dead, and I could do nothing, nothing! She was so good. I loved her so much, Mother. Why did she have to die?"

*****

Raymond and Alyssa sat in the great hall, both looking at Geoffrey with concern. Raymond was exasperated, Alyssa was sad, and Geoffrey was drunk. Again.

It broke Alyssa's kind heart to see Geoffrey like this. Though he had fallen in love and fathered a child, he was still only sixteen years old, and in some ways he was still a boy, struggling now with a situation for which he had been completely unprepared.

It had been over a month since Milesenda's death, and during that time Geoffrey had barely spoken to anyone, seeming very embarrassed about his display of grief outside the chapel. He spent his days riding his horse over the countryside, pushing the animal as if the devil himself was chasing him, uncaring of the possibility of breaking his neck. On returning to the castle, he tossed the horse's reins to whoever was close by, he who had always cared for his own mount.

He spent his evenings sitting in the great hall with a sullen face, speaking to no one and depleting the castle's stock of ale and wine at an alarming rate. Most nights he was too drunk to climb the steps to his bedchamber and slept wherever he fell in an alcoholic stupor.

There were among Belvoir's garrison, several knights who had recently returned from a posting in the far north, along the wall built centuries ago by the Roman commander Hadrian. The men had brought back with them wild, half-believed tales of warriors from the north of Hadrian's wall, savages who went into battle naked and with their faces painted blue. In addition to their wild stories, the men had also brought to Belvoir a fiery, potent liquor called usquebaugh, brewed by the blue-faced northern folk.

In the past Geoffrey had listened rapt to these yarns, half uncertain of their truthfulness. Now he cared only for the usquebaugh the knights might share with him, and the stories went unheard. The taste was fair nasty, and burned like fire in his empty stomach, but it brought him the oblivion he sought much faster than wine ever could, and that was his purpose now. Never mind the pounding head and rolling stomach he suffered the next day. More wine and more usquebaugh cured those ills, if only temporarily.

The garrison knights, never ones to shirk from hard drinking, now hid their jugs when Geoffrey approached. The lord's son he might be, but he refused to share, drinking all he could lay his hands upon, and he was a sullen drunk. Most men became ebullient with drink, but Geoffrey descended into saturnine melancholy until he sank into unconsciousness. The whole pathetic scenario was repeated, day after day.

He refused to eat, because a full stomach inhibited the effects of the drink. He refused to bother with niceties such as bathing or clean clothing, because there seemed to be no reason for them. The one person he had cared to be close to was gone. It was a matter of supreme indifference to him if those around him were offended by his appearance or odor.

He was angry that the sun continued to shine and birds sang in the morning. How dare the grass turn green and lambs and colts frolic when all that Geoffrey loved and cherished had been snatched away from him. He reached for the wineskin that was never far from his hand now, tipped it to his mouth, and the world went on without him.

Raymond attempted to speak to his son, reminding him of his duties, his responsibilities, his neglected training. Geoffrey ignored him, even when his father in frustration threatened to beat him bloody. He merely looked right through Raymond as if the older man wasn't even there, mounted his horse, and rode away.

Edmund tried to talk to him. Geoffrey merely said, "Leave me alone," and turned away. To Alyssa he was at least civil, but all he would say was, "Please, Mother, I do not wish to speak of it."

Raymond was beginning to think that Geoffrey was not after all too big to have his insolent arse whipped. When Geoffrey slapped one of the servants, who had tried to pry the goblet from his fingers, his father had risen from his chair with just that intent, but Alyssa stopped him with a gentle hand on his arm.

Geoffrey had always treated their servants with kindness and consideration, and had in fact only a few weeks ago asked after the health of this girl's ailing mother. Thinking him asleep, since he was slumped in a chair with his head on the table and his eyes closed, she had attempted to remove the glass from his hand. The formerly considerate Geoffrey had risen up and dealt her a blow with the back of his hand that nearly knocked her over. The girl had fled, sobbing, from the hall, one hand held to her bruised cheek.

Alyssa had not failed to notice that Geoffrey now called her Mother, rather than the formal my lady he had used in the past. She had never before interfered with her husband's disciplining of his son, but now for the first time, she put her foot down and insisted upon her own solution to the problem. Raymond was so surprised at his usually obedient wife's defiance that before he knew what he was doing, he found himself acquiescing to her proposal.

The next morning, she sent a man-at-arms down to the village with explicit instructions.

*****

Geoffrey came straight from the stables to the great hall, striding across the room towards the jug of ale on the table. He had neglected to bring a wineskin with him when he had left that morning, and as a result he now found himself to be sober. He did not like the feeling. Sobriety made him remember, and remembering was driving him insane. He didn't intend to remain sober for long. He still bore a splitting headache from the excesses of the previous day, and the day before, and the day before that. He needed more strong wine to ease the pain.

He did not see his stepmother standing by the doorway. She called his name, and something in her voice made him stop and turn around, but he refused to look anywhere but at his feet. He knew he smelled of horse and sweat, and that he must look like a complete ruffian. He had not bothered with such niceties as bathing or shaving or donning clean clothing since Milesenda's death, but right now he just couldn't bring himself to care.

"Geoffrey," Alyssa said sternly. He did not look up. "Geoffrey, it is time for you to start living again. I know Milesenda's death is a shock and a grief to you, and I truly am sorry for your pain. But killing yourself like this will not bring her back. There are people here who love you, and we cannot bear to see you doing this to yourself."

He continued to stare at his boots. He felt ashamed of his behavior, but more than that, he was frightened. He could not bring himself to tell anyone, not his stepmother nor even Edmund to whom he usually confided everything, about the nightmares he had been experiencing since Milesenda's death, as he lay in his bed in the tower room where their love had begun, where they had conceived the child whose birth had killed her.

He had dreamt he was at the clearing in the woods, standing on the shore of the lake. Thick fog surrounded him, so dense it seemed as if there was nothing left of the world other than the few feet of earth on which he stood. He was afraid to move, for fear he would fall into the abyss he was certain loomed all around him.

Suddenly a portion of the fog receded, and there stood Milesenda. She looked so beautiful, her long tawny hair swaying gently in the breeze, but her eyes were sad and she looked at him beseechingly.

He tried to go to her, but his feet were rooted to the ground and try as hard as he might, he could not move. He tried to call her name, but no sound would come from his throat.

Although she did not seem to take a step, she moved away from him, her face becoming more sorrowful and woebegone as she moved further from him. She held her arms out to him, her look begging him to come to her, but although he used all his strength, every ounce of energy he possessed, still he was paralyzed. The mist began to close around her, blurring her image. Now he could see tears running down her face, but she appeared to be as unable to speak as he was.

The fog was getting thicker, closing menacingly around Milesenda as Geoffrey struggled to move, to speak, to save her. Then she was gone, and all he could see was a willow tree, the symbol of grief and lost love.

He awoke with a start, screaming her name. Sweat was running down his chest and his breath came in ragged gasps. He could not rid himself of the image of her imploring tears as he helplessly struggled to reach her. That night he began to drink, to forget his pain in the oblivion of intoxication.

Now here was his stepmother, admonishing him for his waywardness, and he could not bring himself to tell her why.

"Geoffrey!" Alyssa's voice became sterner. "Your daughter needs you."

Daughter! This at last drew his gaze upward. He had assumed that the child had died with Milesenda, but now he saw the swaddled bundle Alyssa held in her arms.

"She was born just before you arrived at the cottage. Emma and Carys have been caring for her, but she is your child, your responsibility." Alyssa drew back the blanket so that Geoffrey could see the baby's face.

Geoffrey stared at the baby's tiny face as she slept in his stepmother's arms. Milesenda's last word to him had been, "Please". Had she been trying to say, please care for our child? He remembered Emma grasping his arm, trying to speak to him after Milesenda's death, but he had run out and not listened to what she had tried to tell him. The two women by the fireplace-they must have been caring for the baby, and he hadn't even noticed. His only thought at that moment had been for Milesenda.

"Here," Alyssa said. "Take her."

Geoffrey backed up, his eyes wide, but his stepmother insisted on placing the bundle in his arms, cradling the baby's head on his elbow.

He gazed down at his daughter wonderingly. As if she sensed his gaze, she opened her eyes and looked up at him.

Milesenda's eyes. The exact same round, gray-blue eyes in smaller form. His heart filled with pain again, but also with love and awe. So he had something left of Milesenda after all.

He would have stood there forever, just staring, if Alyssa had not spoken. "She must be baptized, Geoffrey."

He looked up at her and swallowed, still astonished and amazed at the child's existence. For a moment, his voice failed him. Finally, he nodded. "Mother, would you, would you be her godmother?"

"Of course, Geoffrey."

He looked around. "Do you know where Edmund is?" he asked.

Alyssa signaled a servant with her eyes. "He will be found."

Geoffrey's eyes returned to his daughter's face. "Ask him to meet us at the chapel."

*****

It was an unusual little group that gathered in the chapel for the baptism of Geoffrey's daughter; an odd combination of Norman and English that made Raymond feel uneasy as he stood back and observed.

There was Geoffrey, his older son, who though a Norman by blood, was nonetheless an Englishman by inclination, even by appearance. The emotions of pride and grief were mingled in Geoffrey's handsome face as he held his tiny daughter in his arms.

Raymond realized grimly that he was now a grandfather, although not in the circumstances he would have preferred. But despite the ir- regularity of Geoffrey's relationship with her mother, and her dubious legitimacy, this child undoubtedly was his granddaughter.

Raymond glanced briefly at the others - Stephen, his half English younger son, assisting Father Mathieu as his acolyte; Alyssa, his English wife, standing as the baby's godmother; and Edmund, the English peas- ant's son, his granddaughter's godfather. Edmund was nervous in the presence of Lord Raymond and stumbled slightly over his responses.

When Father Mathieu asked what name was to be given to the child, they all looked at Geoffrey expectantly. He hesitated for a moment, and then said, "Tamsin." With a brief glance at his stepmother, he added softly, "It was," he faltered, unable to say Milesenda's name without risking falling apart, "it was her mother's name."

Then he turned to look at his father. "Mary Tamsin de Graville," he said distinctly, his eyes daring Raymond to deny her the de Graville name.

But Raymond did not protest, although by his expression he clearly disapproved, and Tamsin was duly baptized. As the family left the chapel, Raymond began to wonder, and not for the first time, what had happened to the Normans in England. A generation ago they had arrived as conquerors, but the Normans and the English had now settled down under the equal protection of King William. The two nationalities were drawn together; the process was transpiring which was rapidly making it nearly impossible to distinguish Norman from Englishman. Raymond and his son had contributed to the intermingling process by fathering children with English women, and there were many others as well. They all spoke English now. It seemed as if the Normans and their influence were slowly but surely disappearing, being absorbed and assimilated into the culture of the English.

*****

Geoffrey walked out of the chapel with his daughter in his arms, still a bit stunned and amazed at her existence. The very fact of her being opened a small aperture in the dark cloud of grief that had shrouded him since Milesenda's death. He touched the baby's rounded cheek, the perfect little nose. Her lips were like a tiny rosebud, delicate and sweet.

"Geoffrey, a word with you please," came his father's voice. Raymond stood at the door of his small office. Obediently Geoffrey followed his father into the room, his daughter still in his arms. Tamsin was a part of him, a physical extension of his existence.

Raymond also looked at the baby, with a small frown creasing his dark brow. He saw the child more as a nuisance than as the miracle she was in Geoffrey's eyes. Lord, that his son should have fathered a bastard at such a young age! And then the mother had to go and die, leaving the brat abandoned at their doorstep. At least if the girl-whose name escaped Raymond-had lived, he could have paid her to leave Lydford and to take her child away as well.

Geoffrey sat on the little bench against the wall, being careful not to joggle the baby. Protocol demanded that he not seat himself until and unless invited to do so by his father, but at the moment Geoffrey was more concerned with his baby's comfort than anything else. He adjusted the tiny blanket which covered Tamsin. The blanket looked familiar. He recognized it as one which had been used on his brother Stephen as an infant.

"What do you plan to do with it?" Raymond asked. Geoffrey looked up. His father was standing at the edge of his desk, leaning one hip against it as he looked upon his son and granddaughter with unfriendly eyes.

For a moment, Geoffrey was speechless. He had no thought beyond this moment. But it angered him that his father referred to his child as 'it.'

"I am sure we can find a good home for it," Raymond went on. "Someone in the village who has lost a child perhaps, can take it off your hands. You need not be burdened."

"My daughter has a name," Geoffrey declared with cold anger in his voice. "Her name is not it. Her name is Tamsin de Graville. De Graville, Father, the same as you and me. I most certainly do not intend to give her away to strangers. She stays with me, and I will do my best to raise her without ... without ..." He faltered and looked away. He could not say the words, without Milesenda.

Raymond was not swayed. "It is customary," he said stiffly, "for illegitimate children fathered by the nobility to be adopted out." He took a step towards Geoffrey, who hunched himself over the baby as if to protect her from his father.

"She is my child. I am not going to give her away."

"It is only bound to cause you problems in the future, Geoffrey. When you marry, your wife will not wish to have your bastard living under the same roof as your legitimate children."

Geoffrey flared in anger. "I will not allow you to call her a bastard, and I will not marry again," he declared, putting a slight emphasis on the word *again*, because he knew his father did not consider him to have been truly married to Milesenda.

"No matter what you choose to call her, the truth is she is a bastard." Raymond's voice was firm. "You were not married to that peasant."

"We were handfasted!"

"Who were your witnesses?"

Silence.

"I thought so. An illegal union, not a marriage at all. That child is a bastard, plain and simple, and should be sent to live elsewhere. I allowed Lady Alyssa to have it brought here for you to see, and against my better judgment allowed you to have her baptized here, because she is after all only a girl child and as a bastard will not be your heir. But now, the child goes. She is not a legitimate member of this family."

"Is that how you have dealt with your bastards, Father? Given them away to strangers, like a pair of cast-off boots?" Geoffrey asked with cold steel in his voice.

"I have no bastards, that I know of," Raymond replied, just as coldly. "You are the first de Graville to bring this particular disgrace upon our family."

Geoffrey stood up, clutching Tamsin to his chest. "I do not care for your opinion, my lord. I consider myself to have been married to Milesenda, and this is our child, my child, not some nameless bastard. If she is not welcome here, then we will leave Belvoir and go elsewhere to live."

"Go?" Raymond asked with suspicion.

"Yes, go. I will not stay where my daughter is not welcome. If that means we must leave Belvoir, we will leave." Geoffrey thought quickly. "We will go to the village. We can live in M—, in the cottage where Tamsin was born. When Tamsin is a little bigger and can travel, we will leave Lydford altogether."

Raymond's eyes bulged with a combination of shock and anger. "You? You, my son and heir, will leave your home for the sake of a bastard brat?"

Geoffrey's anger matched his father's. "No, for the sake of my daughter."

"And just how, my fine young pup, do you plan to live if you leave Lydford? Do you actually desire to leave your home?"

"I do not want to leave, but I will do it if necessary to keep her with me. I can sell my services to some lord or chieftain who needs a soldier. You yourself have said I have skill with a sword. Or, I can plow a field, muck out stables, clean other men's boots. I do not care what I do to earn our keep, but I will ...not ... be separated from my child!"

Awakened and frightened by the loud voices of the two arguing men, the baby in Geoffrey's arms twitched and began to cry. Stricken by her screeching, Geoffrey turned accusing eyes at his father. "Now see what you have done!" He joggled the wailing bundle a bit, but the movement only increased Tamsin's bawling. A suspicious warmth was spreading over Geoffrey's arm underneath her.

"I did nothing to the child!" Raymond declared in his defense. "Do not blame me if she cries."

Geoffrey moved towards the door in search of assistance. "You will not see us again," he threatened his father. "We shall leave here until you are gone and I may live as I please." He turned to go.

Raymond looked at his son's back, walking away from him, and said heavily, "Geoffrey, wait. Don't go. The child can stay. Neither of you need leave Belvoir."

Geoffrey stopped for a moment, almost turned around. Then Raymond said, "but I warn you, when a marriage is arranged for you ...."

The broad shoulders beneath long blond hair stiffened. Without bothering to turn and face his father, Geoffrey stated, "As I said before, my lord, you waste your time if you contrive any marital contract on my behalf," and Raymond knew that any such arrangements would be futile at this time. He would, however, not give up the idea altogether.

Geoffrey had one last statement to say to his father, in a slightly softer voice, though he still wouldn't look at Raymond. "Remember, it was you who brought us together at the first."

"An action I now regret," Raymond replied sharply. "From now on, you may find your own women."

Without deigning to reply, Geoffrey departed the room in search of Maud, desperate for instruction on what one was to do with a wet, crying baby.

And so Geoffrey's daughter Tamsin was installed in the nursery under Maud's diligent care, if not exactly with Raymond's blessing, at least with his permission. Maud for her part was only too glad to have another de Graville child to care for, now that Geoffrey had long since outgrown her care and even Stephen was growing up. Alyssa had hired a wetnurse to feed Tamsin, a plump, fresh-cheeked farmer's wife whose child had been stillborn, and had arranged for her to come to the castle with the baby. It was one more kindness for which Geoffrey had to be grateful to his stepmother.

The night after Tamsin's baptism, Geoffrey tossed restlessly in his bed, unable to sleep. It was the first night he had gone to bed sober since Milesenda's death, and though he was tempted to go down to the hall and again get himself forgetfully intoxicated, he knew he could no longer afford to succumb to that immature form of oblivion. He had responsibilities now; a child to care for.

Finally, he gave up trying to sleep, got up and groped for a candle, which he lit from the embers of the fireplace. Pulling on his tunic and braies, he padded barefoot down the dark stairwell, shielding the candle's flame with his cupped hand, and turning at the landing to follow the corridor past his father's bedchamber to the nursery.

As he pushed open the door, he saw another candle already glowing in a holder on the table, and heard the plaintive crying of a small baby. His daughter. He moved quickly across the floor to the cradle, but someone else was there before him, kneeling on the floor and reaching into the cradle with soothing words and gentle hands.

The girl looked up, startled, as Geoffrey loomed over her, and as the candle he held lit her face, he saw it was Olwyn, the wetnurse his stepmother had engaged. Maud had introduced her to him briefly outside the chapel after Tamsin's christening.

Olwyn relaxed when she saw that her visitor was her charge's young father, and returned to her task of changing the baby's wet wrappings as Geoffrey peered over her shoulder, drinking in the sight of the tiny, delicate creature who was his own child.

"She is quite loud for one so small," he observed in a whisper which the baby's crying almost drowned out. But Olwyn could hear him, and she smiled as she picked up the now dry baby and carried her to the chair.

"She is hungry, my lord," Olwyn explained, sitting down in a chair and reaching to open the front of her gown. She looked a bit self-conscious, but as Geoffrey made no move to leave, she shrugged and undid the laces, easing out a full, swollen breast and guiding the baby's mouth to the nipple.

Tamsin's crying ceased in an instant, to be replaced by a contented gurgling as she nursed, her tiny fingers gently kneading the soft flesh above her mouth. Geoffrey watched for a minute, and then turned his back, not out of modesty, but because it hurt too much to see another woman nursing Milesenda's child.

It was unfair, so damn unfair! That should have been Milesenda sitting there with their child at her breast, not some stranger hired to do the task. Geoffrey gripped the edge of the table and bit his tongue to keep from screaming out at the pain in his heart. He had been so certain that when their child was born, he would have been able to convince his father to allow him and Milesenda to marry legally. Now the point was moot, for Milesenda, his gentle, sweet love, was gone, and another woman was sitting in the chair behind him, nursing their daughter.

He waited until he heard Olwyn stand up, then he set the candle he had in his hand into another holder on the table. Olwyn's gown was demurely fastened now that Tamsin was fed and satisfied. "May I hold her?" Geoffrey asked shyly.

Olwyn appeared a bit surprised that Geoffrey should appear in the nursery to see his daughter in the middle of the night, but she replied, "Of course, my lord," and placed the baby in his arms.

"I will stay with her," Geoffrey said to Olwyn, "You may go back to your rest."

Olwyn was very dubious at the prospect of leaving a month-old baby in the care of a sixteen-year-old boy, but, she reasoned, he was Lord Raymond's son and the child was his own daughter. "Very well, my lord," she replied. She nodded toward an alcove across the room where a pallet was laid for her to sleep on. "If she wakes again..."

"I will call you," Geoffrey said, aware of the one thing he could not do for his daughter, and Olwyn returned to her rest.

He held his daughter gently against his chest, her tiny soft head cradled in his hand. She was asleep, now that she was dry and fed, and she sighed contentedly in his arms, her little rosebud mouth pursing and then relaxing. Geoffrey's heart constricted painfully at the thought that Milesenda would never hold the dainty, perfect little person who was their daughter, nor would Tamsin ever know the gentle, loving woman who was her mother.

Tenderly he placed his daughter back in the cradle. She stirred, her tiny limbs twitching once before calming, but remained asleep. Geoffrey knelt on the floor next to the cradle and laid his hand on the baby's back, gently so as not to wake her. She was so small, and his hand so large, that she almost disappeared under it. He heard Olwyn lie down on the pallet in the alcove in the corner, and he was glad to be left alone with his daughter as he watched her sleep in the dim light of the two candles. She was so tiny, so fragile, so innocent and beautiful. He rested his arms on the edge of the cradle and his cheek on his arms. "I love you, my little girl," he whispered at Tamsin's peacefully sleeping form. "I am so sorry I neglected you. I hope you can forgive me. I did not even know you were alive until today... Oh, God, I wish your mother could see you. You are so perfect, so beautiful. Just like her. Nothing shall ever harm you, I promise, and you will never be neglected again. I will always be here to protect you and care for you, my precious little one."

He continued to watch Tamsin sleep until the candles had burned down to waxy puddles. Tamsin did not wake again until after sunrise, at which time Olwyn and Maud discovered Geoffrey, sound asleep himself, still kneeling next to the cradle with his arms folded on the edge and his head resting on his arms.

Tamsin's hungry crying woke him, and he touched her cheek briefly with one finger before climbing stiffly to his feet. Olwyn had hung back a little when she had seen him there, not being as familiar with Geoffrey and the de Graville family as Maud was, so she did not see what Maud saw as Geoffrey stood up and turned away, the faint tracks of dried tears on his cheeks.

IO

To all who knew Geoffrey, it was obvious that Milesenda's death had changed him in ways that would never be put right. His smile, his laughter, his youth had all been buried with her. His seventeenth birthday came and went unremarked, for he felt no cause to celebrate. Although since Alyssa had brought his daughter to him, he no longer drank himself into a stupor every day, had apologized profusely to the serving girl he had struck, and gradually resumed his work with the horses and his military training, the joy he had previously found in those pursuits had disappeared. It was as if a bright fire had been all but extinguished, leaving only a small coal behind to show any life.

Even the villagers in Lydford saw the change in him. In the past, he had often stopped to have a word or share a jest with many of them. He had not been above stopping to lend assistance to anyone he thought might need it, in spite of the fact that his father had on more than one occasion insisted it was not appropriate for the future Baron de Graville to carry firewood for a peasant woman, even if she was elderly and the bundle was heavy. Raymond had been even more disapproving the day he had observed his son climbing a tree and ripping his clothes in the process, to rescue a kitten belonging to one of the local children.

That had all changed now. Now when Geoffrey rode through the village, his face was hard and he kept his gaze straight ahead. If anyone spoke to him, he merely responded as required by courtesy and went about his business, leaving them to shake their heads in pity behind his

109

back. He appeared to be alive - he walked, though he still ate little and spoke less; he rode his horse; he did a few other things that might give the appearance of being alive, but inside he was dead, and it showed in his eyes.

Once, he returned to the small cottage at the edge of the village. He half expected to encounter the sickening smell of blood that had preceded Milesenda's death, but this time it was only in his imagination. The cottage had been thoroughly cleaned and freshened, and somehow, he knew that this too was his stepmother's doing. For a moment, he sat on the bed where he and Milesenda had spent so many happy hours, then, remembering how she had died in that same bed, he quickly stood up, still struggling disbelievingly with the fact that she was gone.

Her presence seemed to fill every part of the room. When he looked at the table he could see her sitting there, remembered eating meals she had cooked for him, remembered watching her sew as she sat by the window to catch the sunlight. By the fireplace there was still a stack of firewood he had chopped and carried in for her. Hanging over the chair was a tunic of his. She had mended a tear in it just days before her death. He gathered it up, smoothing his hand over the tiny, even stitches she had sewn with love. When he pressed the fabric to his face he could swear he smelled the scent of her hair in it, that faint scent of wildflowers.

He recalled the threat he had made to his father, to live in this cottage with Tamsin if Raymond refused to allow her to be raised in the castle with the family. Geoffrey was glad now that he had not been forced to make good on that threat. Living here, with Milesenda's ghost all around him, he would not have survived a week. The nightmares would have consumed him and driven him over the brink of insanity, he was certain.

An urge to get as far away from the cottage as possible overtook him, as strong as the urge to come here had been. He quickly gathered up the few items he had there, and the infant garments Milesenda had sewn. He did not see the brooches he had given her on their wedding day. He would have liked to have kept them for Tamsin, something she could have from the mother she would never know, but with a sick sensation he remembered Milesenda telling him that her mother had been buried with hers.

In his heart, he knew also that the day they had pledged themselves to each other had been a real marriage only to him and to Milesenda, and that no one else was going to acknowledge that they had been married. He suspected that perhaps even Milesenda had not believed it to be a valid marriage, but had gone along with it out of love for him.

He was about to leave the cottage when the door opened and Edmund walked in, followed by Emma and Carys. Faithful, forgiving Edmund, he had waved away as unnecessary Geoffrey's attempts to apologize for his rude behavior during the time just after Milesenda's death.

"We saw your horse outside," Edmund said.

Geoffrey sat down on the bed again and looked at Emma. "Why?" he asked. "Why did she die?"

Emma looked upset, and behind her, Carys had begun to cry. Geoffrey remembered that Milesenda and Carys had been close friends. Edmund put a comforting arm around Carys's shoulders.

"When I got here, it was already too late," Emma explained. "She simply bled too much; there was nothing I could do to stop it. I am sorry, Geoffrey. I tried, but there was nothing I could do. It is a miracle the child survived."

Geoffrey looked at his feet. "It is my fault," he said morosely. "I should never have left her alone; I should have come back and stayed with her, should have been here to fetch you sooner. I knew she did not feel well. But it was raining, so I stayed..." he flapped his hand in the general direction of the castle. "I should have been here with her."

Emma and Edmund exchanged glances over his head. "No, Geoffrey," she insisted. "It would not have mattered. There would have been nothing you could have done had you been here sooner. I believe that only the fact that she knew Carys had gone to fetch you kept her alive a little longer, so that she could see you one last time. But you could not have saved her. It was the will of God."

Geoffrey nodded, trying to accept her words but still filled with self-recriminating guilt. But he did not want Emma to think that he blamed her in any way. He looked up at the midwife. Though Emma had in her career seen more than one husband grieving a wife's death in childbed, she had never seen one look as ravaged as this young man. Perhaps it had something to do with his size. Standing inches taller than his companions, he had always seemed to laugh the loudest, ride the fastest, proved to be the strongest in any wrestling match. Now, he mourned the most absolutely.

"Thank you," Geoffrey said. "Thank you for all you tried to do. And thank you for my daughter."

He retrieved the small bundle that represented what he still considered to be his brief marriage, and with a glance at Edmund, still trying to comfort the weeping Carys, walked out of the cottage for the last time.

Geoffrey did not go to see Milesenda's grave. He knew now that his stepmother had arranged for her burial while he had been wallowing in drunken self-pity, and he was ashamed of himself for the way he had been unable to cope maturely with her death. He had run away, not even realizing or waiting to hear that the child had been born and was alive. He had fled, not even said good-bye, nor attended to Milesenda's burial as a proper husband should.

He knew also that if he did visit Milesenda's grave, he would begin to weep again and never be able to stop this time. He had humiliated himself with his lack of control in front of his family and their servants, weeping like a child in his stepmother's arms, and he vowed to never, never, allow himself to show such vulnerability again. Even if it meant encasing his heart in a layer of ice as hard and as strong as the toughest sword, so be it. He would not be vulnerable again. He protected his heart with a bastion stronger than Belvoir's walls, more impregnable than its towers or barbican. Only Tamsin's smile could breach his defenses.

The baby girl was the one person who could reach his heart through that layer of ice. Neither Raymond nor Alyssa, nor even Maud, had ever seen a man more devoted to his child.

Geoffrey had wanted to have Tamsin's cradle moved into his bedchamber so that he could have her near him at night, but he was forced to give up the idea as impractical. Until she was weaned, where Tamsin slept, so must Olwyn sleep, and Geoffrey knew he could not ask Olwyn to sleep in his bedchamber with him, even if it was on a pallet across the room and only for the purpose of nursing the baby. Olwyn was a married woman, and Geoffrey did not wish to embarrass her or shame her husband. He was extremely grateful that Olwyn was willing to live at the castle while Tamsin needed her, even more so when he realized that the wetnurse could go home only occasionally for a few hours while the baby slept. Geoffrey did not wish to risk losing her services.

He did, however, spend much more time in the nursery than was considered normal for a father, hovering nervously whenever Tamsin was fretful with any childish ailment, whether real or imagined. Raymond did not approve of his son's behavior, but as usual Geoffrey cared little for the opinions of others, especially those of his father.

When Tamsin put her soft baby hand on her father's cheek and said her first word, "Da," he smiled, the first smile anyone had seen on his face since before Milesenda's death.

When at eleven months she took her first toddling steps and fell into his arms, he picked her up in his arms and hugged her, telling her what a wonderful, intelligent and amazing child she was. Then he took her down to the stables. He had one of the grooms saddle his horse for him, because he would not trust anyone else to hold Tamsin if he did it himself, and trotted out into the paddock with her held firmly in front of him as she squealed in delight. Raymond saw them, and he frowned in disapproval, but Geoffrey ignored his father, as he had been doing for the most part since the day Raymond had thwarted his plans to marry Tamsin's mother.

As Tamsin grew from adorable baby to charming toddler, her hair grew in as blond as her father's, although in Geoffrey's eyes she was the image of her mother, the mother she would never know.

Geoffrey's heart broke anew every time he looked at her. It would have been easy to resent his daughter, to think that she had caused her mother's death. But although Geoffrey would have given his life to have Milesenda back just for an instant, he still could not find it in him to resent little Tamsin, who depended on him and trusted him so completely. Yes, it broke his heart to look at her, but the fact that she existed also gave him the only reason he could think of for waking up in the morning, for bothering to draw breath and continue to put one foot before the other along the path of life.

Geoffrey now measured his life in terms of Tamsin's, and it was three months after she had turned three years old when he took his horse-the stallion he had childishly named Storm, in that other lifetime of his youth, out for a run. During the time just after Milesenda's death, he had ridden wildly at breakneck speed, mindless and drunk, almost hoping for a hole or a fence to kill himself on, but now he had something to live for. He still rode fast, but having a care for his safety and the horse's, knowing that when he returned home, Tamsin would be there waiting for him.

He heard, or rather sensed, hoofbeats behind him, and he pulled on the reins to slow Storm's gate and glanced behind him. It was his father, galloping behind him on his tall black stallion.

Geoffrey was tempted to spur his horse back into a gallop, but he knew Raymond would catch him eventually. Reluctantly he pulled his horse to a stop and waited for his father to reach him. Storm protested the end of their run by rearing up on his hind legs, and Geoffrey pulled the beast's head down sharply, patting the horse's twitching neck in apology as his father approached.

"My lord," he nodded politely, though coldly as his father's horse trotted up next to him.

"Good day, Geoffrey," Raymond said just as formally, nudging his horse into a walk and motioning for his son to accompany him. They walked their mounts in silence for a few minutes, listening to the hum of insects and the swish of grass in the warm summer breeze.

When they reached a small stream, they dismounted to allow the horses to drink. Geoffrey hunkered down in the cool shade at the stream's edge, splashing some water on his face and feeling the cool liquid trickle down under his tunic. Looking into the gently flowing creek, he knew that if he were to follow it upstream and into the nearby woods, he would after a few miles arrive at the little lake in the clearing. Briefly he allowed himself to remember the hours he had spent at that lake with Milesenda, teaching her to swim, making love among the wildflowers, dreaming about their future together. He had not been back to the lake since his dreams had died.

He sensed that his father wished to speak to him, but waited for Raymond to make the first overture. His father sat down on the bank of the stream next to him.

"I have had a message from the king," Raymond said after a minute.

Geoffrey was not surprised. The king frequently purchased horses from them, and Raymond had been to court several times. Geoffrey had not accompanied his father on these excursions, and actually had little or no desire to visit London, which he had heard was a noisome and foul-smelling place.

But the message Raymond had received had not come from London. "His Grace is in Normandy," Raymond said. "The king of France has invaded the Vexin again and has taken Mantes."

The Vexin, a temptingly rich province on Normandy's northeast border, was not far from Geoffrey's birthplace at the estate of his uncle Alain de Graville. France had long cast covetous glances at this plum situated so near Paris, and its possession had frequently been a bone of contention between the Duchy of Normandy and the Kingdom of France. Border wars such as this were frequent.

Geoffrey waited for his father to continue, and Raymond said, "We cannot allow the French to retain a foothold in Normandy. Having tasted such a triumph, they will only strive for more, and that could cost the king his dukedom.

"His Grace has called for reinforcements to repulse the forces France has sent into Normandy, and he also needs more horses. We have been ordered to join the king's army."

Geoffrey listened with only half an ear, caring little for what happened in Normandy, despite the fact that he had been born there. Normandy seemed very far away to him. Now, were the French threatening to invade Devon, he would feel differently.

"We will be leaving for Exeter in one week's time to take ship for Normandy," Raymond continued. "With as many knights, squires and horses as we can equip in that time."

Geoffrey looked up sharply at his father's face at the sound of the word 'we'. Raymond nodded. "You are coming with me," he told Geoffrey. "I will need a squire, and it is time you gained your first practical experience in battle. I am also putting you in charge of the destriers and the other horses we will be bringing."

Geoffrey's mind reeled at his father's words. Normandy! He could not go to Normandy! Not now, when he had Tamsin to care for. Besides, Normandy was nothing to him but a faded childhood memory. His life was here, in England. He sat back on his heels, pushing back his hair which had fallen over his eyes when he bent down over the stream.

"Normandy can defend itself," he said. "They do not need us."

"Geoffrey, you are a fool," Raymond declared, looking at his son with a disgusted glance. "It is not a matter for us to decide. The king has ordered us to assist him. We have been fortunate here these years, and I for one have not disliked being at peace, but that does not mean we are allowed to pick and choose when it comes to war. We are vassals of the king, and when he calls for us to join him, we must answer that call."

Geoffrey stood up and shrugged his shoulders. "It is still a foreign war," he said, "and concerns me not. I am not going."

The next instant he found himself flat on his back, his head ringing from his father's blow. He had not even seen Raymond stand up. His head felt as if a tree had fallen on it, and he stared up at his father's rage-filled face above him.

"You stupid, insolent young pup!" Raymond shouted. "Have you learned nothing of what I have tried to teach you? Look around you," he commanded, and Geoffrey sat up, moving away from his father as much as he dared, and followed Raymond's sweeping hand with his eyes as he indicated the lands around them. His father continued, his voice still filled with anger.

"Think you that these fine lands were given to me by a whim on the part of the king? Do you believe that we hold them on the basis of our good looks? No, you shaggy-haired fool, we hold them in fief. The price we pay for our estate is service when it is required. I do not maintain that troop of knights for the pleasure of their company, but because our overlord, the king, requires it in return for his granting us this manor. If, and when, His Grace calls for us to fight at his side, we go. We do not sit back and decide we do not like this war, or do not approve of that one. We obey our lord's command. Do you understand me, Geoffrey?"

Geoffrey had never seen his father look quite as angry as he did now, and he had seen Raymond's anger almost daily since he had been five years old. In truth, he did understand what his father had impressed upon him about a vassal's service to his overlord. If he did not have his motherless daughter to be concerned with, he would have looked forward to testing the skills he had been practicing for seven years. He loved England, and would have gladly given his life without fear to defend it. But he had to admit that what his father had just told him was true, that a knight, or even a knight-in-training, was bound to the service of his lord, with no questions asked. He stood up and brushed the dirt from his clothing, then nodded at his father.

"Yes, my lord, I understand. How many horses shall I prepare?"

Raymond was visibly relieved that his son had finally decided to accept his responsibilities. "We have only a week to prepare. We should be able to outfit a troop of twelve, plus you and I. Two destriers for each knight, plus a palfrey for us each to ride and pack horses to carry arms and armor. Select the strongest of the grooms to accompany us to assist with the destriers. We cannot allow those stallions to fight and possibly injure each other before we reach Normandy. I will have Dunstan instruct the armorer to have your suit of mail finished before we leave."

*****

The next week was a busy one as they prepared for battle. The best, strongest and fiercest of the destriers were selected. Each soldier needed at least two, in case one was killed from under him. The destriers were never ridden for transportation, however, for it would be folly to tire them before the battle was joined. That meant that each knight must also have another horse to ride until they reached the battlefield, while the destriers were led by the squires. Only ungelded stallions were used by knights, whether for battle or in the ordinary course of events; geldings and mares being ridden only by priests, clerics and women. All those stallions in close quarters could be extremely troublesome, so it was advisable to have a groom for every two horses to keep them from fighting.

In addition to horses, there were arms and armor to prepare. Each knight needed a complete suit of mail including a hauberk on his body, chausses on his legs also made of chain mail, as well as mail gauntlets over his gloves. This, coupled with the conical iron helmet with its nose guard and camail, a piece of chain mail hanging from the back of the helmet to protect the neck and shoulders, made a formidably heavy accouterment weighing forty pounds or more. That did not include the weight of the knight's shield and arms.

The iron chain mail rusted and tarnished quickly, and this rust was the knight's enemy almost as much as the opposing forces. The presence of rust could turn an otherwise minor scratch on the knight's body into a life-threatening infection. To clean off any accumulated corrosion, the pieces of mail were placed in a leather sack with a mixture of sand and vinegar, sealed and tossed back and forth strenuously between two men. Geoffrey played this awkward game of catch until his arms ached, and then he went on to the many other tasks awaiting him.

It was two days before their planned departure, and Alyssa left the keep with a basket full of foodstuffs and medicines on her arm. She was planning on going down to Lydford as she did regularly to visit any of the villagers who were sick or ailing, and she was hoping to persuade Geoffrey to escort her so that he could carry the heavy basket for her.

As she emerged from the gate, she noticed Edmund across the court-yard with his back to her, and where Edmund was, Geoffrey was sure to be nearby. So, she turned and walked over to stand next to her stepson's friend.

Edmund bowed as she approached. "My lady," he said politely.

"Good afternoon, Edmund," Alyssa answered. "Where is Geoffrey?"

Edmund looked away from her and nodded with his chin. In the center of the bailey Geoffrey and Raymond were practicing sword fighting, both in full armor, and the sight chilled Alyssa with fear.

Covered as they were from head to foot in the heavy mail, it was difficult to tell them apart. The bright blond hair that usually made Geoffrey stand out in a crowd was covered by the helmet and camail. But as she watched them, Alyssa was able to distinguish her husband and stepson. Geoffrey, somewhat taller, slightly broader across the shoulders than his father, had the advantage of greater size, and wielded his sword and shield well, but Raymond had the greater experience. They were almost evenly matched, but Geoffrey was forced to retreat a bit beneath his father's onslaught. Both Alyssa and Edmund had to remind themselves that they were only practicing, that neither was actually trying to kill the other. It was a difficult premise to convince themselves of, with the fierce determination on both their faces.

Each clash of sword on sword, each thud of a blow deflected by a shield, caused Alyssa to jump with fear, and when she dropped the basket at their feet, Edmund looked at her with concern, noticing she had become quite pale. "Would you like me to escort you inside, my lady?" he asked solicitously, but she shook her head mutely, not taking her eyes from her husband and stepson.

Geoffrey's suit of mail creaked with newness, for he was too big to wear anything that had been made for his father. Each suit of mail was custom made to fit the wearer, and alterations were next to impossible. The cost of it had made Raymond groan aloud, and had also made him very glad he had but two sons, and Stephen still a child. A soldier who did not have a wealthy father and who earned his livelihood with his sword would spend a year's income on his arms and armor, and even more on his horse. With some ceremony, Raymond had also presented his son with a new sword and scabbard of his own.

As Raymond and Geoffrey ended their swordplay, sheathing their swords and removing their helmets to wipe the perspiration from their foreheads, Alyssa put on her bravest face as they turned towards her, both of them pulling off the cotton-lined leather caps they wore under the helmets. These caps lessened the pressure of the heavy iron helmet, and also absorbed some of the shock from a blow to the head.

Although the father and the son did not look alike, their mannerisms were similar in some respects, and as they wiped the sweat from their faces, their gestures, the way they moved, were so alike that Alyssa had to smile despite her fear.

"You did well, Geoffrey," Raymond said as he stuffed the leather cap inside his helmet. "Be sure to keep your shield close to your eyes. By the way, your nose is bleeding." Near the end of their practice fight, Geoffrey had used his shield to deflect his father's sword, but the impact had been strong enough to push the shield back and smash it against the nose guard of Geoffrey's helmet. He could feel the blood running into his mouth and he turned his head to spit it out.

"Yes, my lord," Geoffrey replied, pulling off his gauntlets and running a hand through his hair, which was matted down from the weight of his headgear and drenched with perspiration. It had the effect of making grimy strands of hair stick up in wild spikes around his face, and Edmund started to grin at the sight, but he quickly hid the grin and bowed as Lord Raymond approached. Raymond took his wife's hand for a moment, and then he and Geoffrey went to the gatehouse to remove their armor and polish their swords with the solution of vinegar and water which removed tarnish and dirt.

When they were out of sight, Alyssa's brave face crumpled and Edmund took her arm as she swayed slightly on her feet. "Are you ill, my lady?" he asked with concern. "Shall I fetch Lord de Graville? Or Geoffrey?"

"No, thank you, Edmund. I am fine," she replied. "But please do me one favor." She indicated the basket she had dropped and requested,

"Please take this back to the kitchen for me. I think I will wait and go to the village later."

Edmund picked up the basket, thinking that Lady Alyssa was most likely going to follow Geoffrey and tend to his injury as she hurried back inside the castle. But he was wrong. Possibilities much more frightening than a bloody nose were worrying Alyssa as she hurried down the short corridor which led to the castle's chapel, where she knelt and prayed long and fervently for the safe return of her husband and stepson from war in Normandy.

*****

The familiar, homely scents of straw, manure and horseflesh filled the air as Geoffrey slowly, methodically brushed his horse's smooth coat. Usually this undemanding task relaxed him, but today his brain swirled with thoughts and doubts. After a while, he realized he had been brushing the same spot on the beast's side over and over for several minutes. He stopped and leaned one forearm against the horse's warm back and rested his head against his arm. He closed his eyes, and he wondered.

He wondered how he would react when, for the first time, he raised his sword against men seeking not to instruct him, but to kill him. He wondered if he would be a credit to his father, his training and the de Graville name. He wondered about the outcome of the battle they must fight. He wondered if, when they sailed to Normandy, he would experience the same seasickness he had as a child. And most of all, he wondered where he was going to find the strength to mount this horse tomorrow and ride away, leaving Tamsin behind.

A sharp poke in the ribs interrupted his reverie, and he whirled around, his hand going to the dagger at his belt. But he found only Edmund, grinning impishly as he held the long stick with which he had jabbed Geoffrey. With a frown Geoffrey retrieved the brush he had dropped and turned again to the horse.

"There was a time," Edmund said, balancing one end of the stick on his hand and swaying back and forth in an effort to keep it upright, "when we were boys, when you would have tried to make me eat this stick."

"We are no longer boys," Geoffrey said curtly, smoothing the brush lightly over the horse's flank and realizing the currying job was done. He turned to face his friend, and Edmund was no longer grinning. His green eyes were serious and concerned.

"When do you leave?" Edmund asked.

"Tomorrow, after Mass," Geoffrey replied. He tossed the brush into a corner and stepped towards Edmund, gripping his friend's arm in a grasp so tight and strong that Edmund was certain he would bear bruises from it, but from the blazing look in Geoffrey's blue eyes, he knew he dared not complain.

"I do not know how long we will be gone, fighting this silly war in Normandy." Geoffrey's voice was tight and angry sounding. "But until I return, I charge you with Tamsin's care. You are her godfather, and it is your duty as such to see that no harm comes to her. And if anything should happen to me, if I do not return, it will be your obligation to care for her, protect her, and, God willing, see to her happiness." He gave Edmund a little shake, and Edmund felt his teeth rattle with the force of it. "I must have your word on this, Edmund. I must know that I leave my daughter well protected."

Edmund attempted to pry Geoffrey's fingers from his arm, but he was no match for Geoffrey's determination. "Of course, Geoffrey," he said. "You have my oath that I would protect Tamsin with my life were it necessary. I swear it by all that is holy. And do not forget your stepmother, and Maud. You know that they too would never let any harm come to the child."

Geoffrey released Edmund's arm, and Edmund rubbed it to induce his blood to start circulating again. Geoffrey pushed a hand through his hair. "I do not doubt the good intentions of my lady, and of Maud, but they are only women. If I should fall in this absurd fight, and my father returns here without me, I do not trust him in regard to Tamsin. I must know that you will raise her should that come to pass."

Edmund nodded, and then gave his friend a playful shove. "I swear it, Geoffrey, but you need not be concerned. The French soldiers will take one look at you and run screaming for their mothers, I am certain."

Geoffrey smiled at the absurdity of Edmund's words, and from the triumphant look on Edmund's face realized that was just what his friend had been trying to make him do. He reached out and yanked on Edmund's hair. "Carrot-top," he said, using the old nickname he had given his friend as a child. Edmund pulled on Geoffrey's hair also. It was a longer reach for him because Geoffrey was so much taller.

"Straw-head," Edmund said. Then, "Go with God, Geoffrey. We shall all pray for you."

Geoffrey nodded, and Edmund continued, "And will I be allowed to see my goddaughter today, or will you be selfish?" Geoffrey gave the horse a final pat on the nose, and the two of them left the stable.

"No, I will not be selfish. Let us go find Tamsin"

*****

The moment Geoffrey had been dreading came to pass in the morning as he and his father took their leave of the rest of the family in the courtyard.

Raymond bowed formally over his wife's hand, any more personal good-byes having been said in private. Even the horses seemed impatient to be off, especially Geoffrey's, who stamped its forelegs and rolled its head until he pulled sharply on the reins to quiet the beast.

When he saw Maud approaching carrying Tamsin, he turned the fractious horse over to a groom and strode forward to take his daughter from the nursemaid's arms.

Tamsin's small face, with her eyes so like her mother's, lit up when she saw her father, and she eagerly flung her little arms around his neck. He held her tiny body close against his shoulder and stroked the soft blond hair.

How can I leave her, he thought desperately. Since the day his stepmother had placed her in his arms for the first time, he had never been away from her for more than a few hours. Now he was about to leave for months, perhaps not to return at all. He closed his eyes against the thought of it and held her tighter, cradling her head in his hand and pressing his face against her hair. She seemed to sense something was amiss, and clung to him like a soft little leech.

"Geoffrey, we must be off," Raymond said, already mounted as were the dozen knights accompanying them. At the sound of her grandfather's voice, Tamsin raised her head and looked up at him for a moment. This dark, stern man frightened her and she quickly turned back to the safety of her father's shoulder.

Geoffrey knew that he should hand Tamsin back to Maud's care and mount his horse, but he could not force himself to let go of her. At a glance from Lady Alyssa, Maud came forward to take Tamsin.

"My lord," Maud said gently, trying to pry the child from Geoffrey's grasp. When neither of them responded, she presumed upon her years of service to the de Graville family to call him by his Christian name in the presence of his father.

"Geoffrey!" she said sternly, "Did I not have the care of you as a child, and your brother as well? Think you that any harm will come to this child while I draw breath? Go now, your lord father is waiting for you and," her voice lowered for Geoffrey's ear alone, "we both know he is not a patient man."

Praying silently to God to give him strength, Geoffrey unwound Tamsin's arms from about his neck. "Go to Maud now, sweeting," he said softly, "and I promise you I will be back as soon as I can." He placed her back into Maud's arms and quickly, before his strength failed him, put his foot to the stirrup and mounted his horse, noticing as he did so that Edmund was hovering discreetly in the background, apparently taking his godfatherly promises seriously.

Tamsin sensed somehow that this was no ordinary leave-taking. Though she was only three years old, she could discern from the way her father had held her tight and from the anguished look in his eyes when he handed her to Maud, that this was no mere one-day hunting trip taking him away. As Geoffrey turned his horse's head towards the gate, Tamsin squirmed and twisted in Maud's embrace. She started to cry, and the sound of it broke Geoffrey's heart, but he knew he could not turn back. As the troop moved away, Tamsin's shrill cries of "Da! Da!" struck him like physical blows, and it took everything he had to keep his back straight and his head high as the horses clattered through the portal and down the road to Exeter.

*****

Ordinarily it would take a mounted man, traveling light, three or four days to journey from Lydford to the port of Exeter. Slowed by the strings of destriers and the pack horses loaded with arms and armor, the de Graville contingent took twice that long to make the journey. During that time Geoffrey had his hands full overseeing the horses and grooms, and was glad they would be spending a day in Exeter before embarking for Normandy.

Baldwin de Meules, Lord Sheriff of Exeter, was a longtime friend of Raymond de Graville. They had fought together in Normandy and in the conquest of England, and it was at his castle that the de Graville forces stopped to refresh themselves before boarding ship for Normandy.

And if, Geoffrey reminded himself, his father had had his way and if Baron de Meules's daughter had not died, the man would now have been Geoffrey's father-in-law. He had never met the girl to whom his father had attempted to betroth him, but Geoffrey hoped he would be forgiven for being glad she had died. He had nothing personal against Baron de Meules, and he knew his father's friend would have been insulted to know Geoffrey would have refused to marry his daughter. It would not have helped matters to explain that it was not the girl herself that Geoffrey would have rejected, but rather that he would consider no bride other than Milesenda.

The night before their departure, Lord de Meules hosted a feast for the de Gravilles and their retinue. Although there had been promises of entertainment in the form of jugglers and singers after the meal, Geoffrey was in no mood for frivolity. He excused himself as soon as he finished eating, wiping his dagger on the leg of his braies and slipping it back into his belt as he left the castle in search of quiet and solitude. His father caught his eye with a look that said, where are you going, but Geoffrey merely shrugged his shoulders and left the keep.

Exeter, like Barnstaple and Totnes, was a walled city, and Rougemont, the de Meules castle, had been built within its confines, so Geoffrey found that quiet and solitude were not to be found outside its gates. At home in Lydford, an open village, Geoffrey knew that a short walk would bring him to fragrant fields and quiet woods. But not so here in Exeter. The summer evening was still light, and the streets were full of the sounds and smells of a bustling port. Geoffrey walked through the streets for a short while, and he could smell the salt of the sea not far away. When he heard the creak of ships at dock, he quickly retreated back inside the castle walls, dreading the thought of boarding one of those ships in the morning.

He had been here several times before with his father, most recently when he had been about twelve years old. Raymond had frequently brought Geoffrey with him on his various journeys, in the hopes that exposure to other noble Norman families might have what Raymond considered to be a favorable effect on Geoffrey. It had for the most part been a wasted effort.

What Geoffrey remembered most about his last visit to Exeter was the journey home afterward. As soon as they were out of sight of the town, Raymond had stopped their retinue and ordered Geoffrey from his horse. Then his father had dragged him into the nearby woods, bent him over a fallen tree, and blistered Geoffrey's arse with his sword belt, in punishment for sneaking into the gatehouse of the de Meules castle and filling the boots of several off-duty guards who were sleeping there with stones. Or perhaps it had been for climbing into an apple tree just outside the castle walls, along with several local boys he had recruited, and pelting hapless passers-by with half-ripe apples. It was difficult to remember now which punishments had been for which crimes. They all seemed to blur together in his memory.

What he did remember was that it had been hellishly painful to sit his horse for the next two days, which was probably exactly why his father had chosen to punish him then and there, rather than when they returned to Lydford. Not only had his arse felt as if it were on fire, but also his lower lip, which he had bitten completely through until he swallowed blood, in his efforts to keep himself quiet during the whole ordeal of the beating. It was an attempt to retain his dignity in the presence of his father's men-at-arms waiting in the roadway only a few yards away, but he might have spared himself the effort, for they had known perfectly well that their lord had not suddenly decided to take his son on a fishing expedition. It was obvious from the sympathetic glances the men had given him that they had heard every smack of the leather strap, punctuated by Raymond's grunted exclamation, "Damn it, Geoffrey, you are getting too big for this!"

The guard on duty at the castle gate, who had seen Geoffrey leaving less than an hour earlier, stepped forward when he saw him returning.

"If ye be looking for the whorehouse, young sir," the man said with a conspiratorial wink, "I can direct ye."

For a fee, no doubt, Geoffrey thought, and replied curtly, "No, thank you," although he had to admit to himself that he was tempted. It might, for a while at least, take his mind off of what lay ahead of him. But he resisted the temptation. One piece of his father's advice that he had heeded was the avoidance of whorehouses.

Instead he went down to his host's stables to check on their horses. Most of the warhorses were tethered out in a field under the watchful eyes of the grooms, but a few of the other horses were here in Baron de Meules's spacious stables.

As Geoffrey patted a nose here, checked a leg there, he felt the hairs on the back of his neck rise as he experienced the eerie feeling that he was being watched. Under the pretext of bending over to check his horse's foot, he glanced behind him, one hand reaching quickly for the dagger at his belt.

There was a girl standing at the stable door, a child really, with long black braids hanging to her hips. She wore no veil, and her blue gown was of a cut and material fine enough that Geoffrey knew she must be a member of the de Meules family. He did not recall seeing her at dinner, but with a hall full of knights and squires, children would have been kept to the nursery. He wondered how long she had been watching him.

Leaving his dagger in his belt, he straightened up and turned, bowing formally at the girl as if she were an adult. "Good evening, my lady," he said, and was rewarded by her look of surprise at his courtesies. He spoke in English, whether she understood him or not. He was tired of the babble of Norman French he had had to listen to all evening.

The girl's black eyes snapped. "Who are you?" she demanded imperiously, and also in flawless English, which surprised him, for she was clearly a Norman girl. "And what are you doing in my father's stables?"

So she was Baron de Meules's daughter. He was taken aback by her directness. It bordered on rudeness.

"I am tending to my horse," he said sharply. He did not give her his name. He could be rude as well, if he chose. "And who are you?"

She lifted a small chin. "Solange," she said proudly. "Solange de Meules."

"Your servant, my lady." He bowed again, a little mockingly, and turned back to his horse.

"Are you in Baron de Graville's service?" she asked.

He turned back and looked at her in surprise. "In his service? He is my -"

He stopped and looked down at himself. He was wearing the exact same worn, grubby clothes as the grooms, and none too clean at that. He had been too busy to shave since they had left Belvoir, and the weeks' worth of itchy stubble on his face must have made him look disreputable indeed. If he told this child that Baron de Graville was his father, she would never believe him. So he merely said, "Yes, I am in his service." It was true, after all.

"Is that your horse?" she asked, looking up at Storm, who, sensing attention, was stretching his neck towards her in search of a treat. Geoffrey nodded. "He is a beautiful horse," the girl said in an awed voice.

She could not be all that bad, Geoffrey thought, if she appreciated fine horseflesh. He decided to be gracious despite her rudeness. "Would you like to give him a treat?" he asked.

The black eyes brightened and she nodded eagerly. Looking around, he spied a barrel of early apples in the corner. Plucking one from the top, he broke it in half and handed her the broken piece.

She reached up to give the apple half to Storm. She was such a tiny thing, she stood on tiptoe to come close to the horse. Suddenly Geoffrey lunged forward with an oath and grabbed her wrist, dragging her away from the horse's eager teeth.

She flashed angry eyes at him. "Why did you do that!" she cried, the slice of apple falling to the floor. "You said I could give him the apple!" Then, as Geoffrey was not letting go of her wrist, she exclaimed petulantly, "You're hurting me."

He let go of her hand and shook a finger at her. "You silly child!" he scolded. "Do you know nothing?"

"Silly child!" she shrieked. "How dare you speak to me like that, you rude boy!" She stamped her foot childishly, and he almost laughed, though he was still angry at the girl's stupidity.

He picked up her hand again, gently this time. "Let me see. I did not mean to hurt you." Her tiny hand almost disappeared inside his large one. "You have pretty little fingers," he said. "It would be a pity to see them bitten off."

The girl looked up at Storm with fear. "It would not be the horse's fault," he explained. "Look where his eyes are. He cannot see your hand when it is below his mouth, and his mouth is much larger than your hand. You must place the food flat on your palm, like this." He put the other half of the apple on his own palm and held it out to Storm with his hand stretched flat. The velvety lips grasped the morsel eagerly and sniffed for more.

"Oh," she said, appearing somewhat mollified. She picked up the slice he had shaken from her hand, put it on her palm, and, as Geoffrey watched paternally, let the horse take it from her. As soon as the bit of apple disappeared, she wiped her hand on her skirt and put it behind her back.

Geoffrey glanced surreptitiously at the girl for a moment. She was a pretty little thing, with black hair and eyes, fair skin, red lips. She would be a beauty when she grew up.

He did not think that a stable was the appropriate place for a pretty, unescorted young girl to be wandering about in. He himself was not in the habit of molesting children, but there were many other unknown men; knights, squires, entertainers, around the de Meules castle today, and they might not all be so courteous as Geoffrey. But this girl was probably too young and naive to realize that.

"How old are you?" he demanded abruptly.

"Seventeen," she said, too quickly.

Geoffrey did not believe she was a day over thirteen, and he put his hands on his hips and glared down at her.

"The truth, girl."

She imitated his posture with her hands on her own hips, and declared, "Very well, sixteen."

He continued to glare down at her and finally she faltered under his gaze. Looking down at her feet, she admitted, "I will be sixteen...next spring."

"Then you are fifteen," Geoffrey said, and she nodded.

If she was truly fifteen, she was small even for that age, Geoffrey thought. Suddenly his nineteen years seemed to sit very heavily on him.

The girl - what had she said her name was? Ah, yes, Solange, glanced up at him through thick black lashes, appraising him with a look that attempted to be womanly. She tipped her head back to look up at his face.

"And how old are you?" she demanded.

What a rude little chit, Geoffrey thought. He was tempted to ignore her imperious questions, but instead he decided to play along with her game.

"Twenty-three," he lied baldly.

She saw right through him, and demanded, "The truth, boy!"

He tried not to smile. "Twenty," he amended. She tapped her foot impatiently.

"I will be twenty...next spring."

"Then you are nineteen."

"Ah," he teased, "a female who can do sums. A truly dangerous combination." Then, somewhat gruffly, he asked, "What are you doing here? Stables are not a place for children."

She grew angry again. "I am not a child!" she declared, stamping her foot once more. "I came here to get away from..."

"From your nursemaid?" he supplied when she hesitated.

"From my servant," she insisted pettishly.

"And why do you wish to escape from a servant?" Geoffrey asked with amusement.

The girl's lower lip trembled briefly. "She hit me."

"Hit you!" Geoffrey exclaimed in surprise. A servant would never dare to strike her employer's child. Nursemaids, on the other hand, had more leeway with their charges. On more than one occasion in his own childhood, Geoffrey had had his ears boxed or his hand smacked by Maud. Obviously, this girl felt she had outgrown the need for a nursemaid. Should he tell her, he wondered, that nursemaids had a most difficult time accepting the maturity of their charges, that his own former nursemaid still attempted to fuss over him, even though he had a child of his own? No, he decided, it might only upset her more.

"And why did your - servant - strike you?" he asked patiently.

"Because -" the black eyes began to glisten. Geoffrey sincerely hoped she wasn't going to cry. "Because I made a mistake on some silly old embroidery. She smacked my hand with a stick, and she said...she said..."

"What did she say?" Geoffrey tried to sound sympathetic.

"She said I had the hands of a horse handler!"

Geoffrey just could not help himself. He laughed out loud, something he had not done in a long time. The girl looked very offended.

"Let me see your hands," he insisted. After a moment's hesitation, she held out her hands, palms up.

He looked for damage but saw none. Obviously, her pride had been hurt more than her flesh. "You most definitely do not have the hands of a horse handler," he assured her. "Look," he held out his own hands for her to see, "these are the hands of a horse handler."

He almost never wore gloves, and as a result his hands were rough and covered with calluses from the years of holding reins and weapons. They were a far cry from the tiny, smooth white hands she had shown him. On Geoffrey's right hand there was a scar at the base of the thumb, a small gift from the teeth of a half-wild horse who had objected strenuously to the bit, and of course there was the crooked little finger on his left hand that another horse had trod upon.

"You may tell your nurse-your servant-that poor as your embroidery may be, you most assuredly do not have the hands of a horse handler."

He had meant only to tease her, but apparently it was the wrong thing to say, for her lower lip began to quiver and her eyes filled with tears.

Please do not cry, he said to himself. The tears of children had always unnerved him. Tamsin did not cry often, other than when he was forced to leave her, but when she did, he felt as helpless as a child himself.

But his silent request was ignored, as the tears spilled out from the large dark eyes. "She had no right," she started to say with a gulp, and then she began to cry in earnest.

Jesus, Geoffrey thought, *now what do I do?* The only thing he could think of was what he did with Tamsin. He sat down on the nearest bale of hay, pulled the girl onto his lap, wrapped his arms around her, and let her cry out her childish frustration on his shoulder.

For a minute she wept noisily, then began to sniffle, and wiped her face unashamedly on his sleeve. She felt so soft and sweet in his arms, the hair he found himself petting feeling so silky under his hand, that for a moment he almost forgot she was only a child. Before he forgot himself further, he tipped her up onto her feet, putting her away from him almost roughly.

As she struggled to regain her composure, he said, "You should go, before your nurse-, I mean, your servant or your mother misses you. I do not think they would approve of you lingering in stables and consorting with soldiers."

Her tears had ended as abruptly as they had begun, and she tossed her head so saucily that one black braid brushed his arm. Was she embarrassed, he wondered, at crying so childishly while at the same time claiming not to be a child?

"If I see any soldiers," she declared, giving him a withering glance, "I shall decide then whether or not to consort with them!"

She flounced away from him and out the door. Discreetly he followed her and watched as she crossed the courtyard towards the main gate of the castle keep. There was still enough light in the sky that he could see her approach the gate, and when the guard there bowed respectfully he knew she was safe, and returned inside the stable, telling himself he was never going to allow Tamsin to wander unescorted in any stables, not even at their own home.

When he was assured that the de Graville horses were well tended and comfortable, he also returned to the castle keep. His father, as a long-time friend of Baldwin de Meules, had been given the use of a comfortable guest chamber in which to sleep. But Geoffrey, along with the other squires, was expected to bed down on the floor of the hall, once the entertainment was finished. He did not mind; he had slept rough before. But as he rolled himself in his cloak and pillowed his head on his arms, he found himself missing Tamsin dreadfully. To try to take his mind off of his daughter for a while, he thought about the capricious de Meules girl he had met in the stable. What a little minx she was! One minute she was childishly naive and trusting enough to sit in the lap of a complete stranger, and the next minute she was mature enough to see right through Geoffrey's prematurely referring to himself as a soldier. Was it the age she was at, he wondered, poised on that fine line between childhood and adulthood? Was it just her nature to be petulant and changeable, or were all girls like that at fifteen?

Thinking about women in general brought his mind, painfully, to Milesenda. Even now, over three years later, the pain of losing her still clawed at his heart. *Oh, sweetheart,* he thought, *if you could only see our beautiful daughter. She is so like you. If you could only be waiting in Lydford for me to return...*

He tried to push all of these painful thoughts away, along with other uncomfortable thoughts of warfare, sea travel, and even of children wandering in stables as he wrapped his cloak tighter about him, tried to make himself comfortable on the stone floor, and tried very hard to sleep.

*****

As soon as he set foot on the ship in the morning, Geoffrey felt his stomach begin to rebel, and he realized his propensity for seasickness was not a childhood ailment he could outgrow. He did however manage to contain the nausea as he and the grooms secured the horses below decks.

Storm especially protested boarding the rolling ship, and only Geoffrey's patient encouragement induced the stallion up the gangplank.

"I do not blame you one bit," he murmured into his horse's ear. "Were it my place to decide, we would both be far away from here. But if I must travel on this cursed wallowing tub, then so must you."

By the time all of the horses and equipment were secured and they cast off from the shore, Geoffrey could positively feel his skin turning green. He was looking around for an obscure corner in which to quietly sit and die, when he encountered his father. Raymond took one look at his son's face, and with a noise of disgust, roughly shoved a bucket into Geoffrey's hands.

"Just remember," Raymond hissed, "there is no priest on board this ship. If you die, you go unshriven!"

12

The tent was small, just barely large enough for the two cots that Geoffrey and Raymond lay upon as they both stared at the cloth above their heads and studiously ignored each other.

In the tent next to them were Geoffrey's two cousins, Hugh and Robert, the sons of his father's older brother Alain. The three young men had had little to say to each other when they had met earlier, despite the fact that they had played and fought together as children. The same thought had run through all three of their minds as they had exchanged perfunctory greetings.

Foreigner. He is not like me. This despite the fact that they had all been born in the same house, had in fact been delivered by the same midwife. Geoffrey and his cousin Hugh had even been born within a week of each other. But the years of separation had made them strangers. Geoffrey's cousins seemed very haughty, very Norman to him, with their beards and their short, cropped hair, dark like most of the de Gravilles. Except for me, Geoffrey thought, and he knew that his cousins looked down on him, figuratively if not literally, for his English ways, his long hair and for the rough accent he now had when he spoke to them in Norman French. Despite the fact that it had been his mother tongue, he spoke it now only when necessary.

Geoffrey was trying to ignore the hollow feeling in the pit of his stomach. He tried to tell himself that it was a remnant of his seasickness, but he knew it was nervousness and dread at the thought of the battle which would be joined at dawn. He had been training for this since he was twelve years old, and yet still it was a chilling prospect to think of facing, for the first time, men trying to kill him, and ironically, trying to kill him because he was a Norman. Would it make a difference, he wondered, if on the morrow he stood up in his stirrups and shouted out something like, I am not a Norman, I am an Englishman? Yes, he thought, it would make a difference - instead of risking death in a battle against the French forces, he would experience certain and immediate death at the hands of his father.

"Geoffrey -"

"Father -"

They spoke almost in unison and Geoffrey hesitated, allowing his father to speak first.

"Geoffrey," Raymond said, still looking up at the tent's roof. "I would have your word on something. If anything should happen to me tomorrow, or at any other time, I want your solemn vow that you will always care for your stepmother and Stephen."

"Of course, Father," Geoffrey replied. "You need not even ask."

"She is with child."

Geoffrey sat up and stared at his father in surprise. Since Stephen's birth, there had been no other children for his father and Alyssa, and if there had been miscarriages Geoffrey was unaware of it. Raymond did not meet his son's eyes, perhaps feeling slightly embarrassed at the idea of becoming a father again, at his age and when he was already a grandfather. Geoffrey had grown accustomed to not speaking to his father, and did not know what to say to him now. Should he offer congratulations, or condolences? He began to see his father in a new light, and not only as a prospective father.

Because of the heat of the night, both of them had pulled off their tunics, and Geoffrey looked with some awe at Raymond's broad chest, covered with a pelt of dark curly hair, interrupted by one white scar which crossed from his left shoulder to the top of his belly. He had never seen his father's bare torso before. Raymond was a private man who preferred to do his bathing without witnesses. Geoffrey could not help but glance down at his own chest, just as broad as his father's but unadorned by any hair, except for what grew under his arms.

Raymond followed the path of his son's gaze and absently touched the scar on his chest. "This is from Hastings," he said. "As you can see, at a close enough range, a sword can cut through your chain mail. The armor can protect you, but only so much." Geoffrey nodded, acknowledging his father's instruction even this close to its practical application, but continuing to look, assessing the physical differences and similarities between himself and the man who had fathered him.

"It is your coloring," Raymond said after a minute. Geoffrey looked at his father with questioning in his mind and on his face. "The hair," Raymond explained, running one hand briefly over his own chest. "Fair-colored men such as yourself are rarely hirsute. I would not fret about it."

"I wasn't fretting," Geoffrey replied. "But I am curious-does it not itch?"

Raymond chuckled and scratched. "Occasionally, when it is hot as it is now. But your stepmother can soothe any itching I ever have."

Geoffrey's eyes popped in surprise, taken aback at this casual, intimate conversation with his father. It was unusual, unreal, brought on perhaps by the intense situation in which they found themselves, on the eve of battle and possible death.

After a moment he lay back down and put his hands behind his head. He had a request to make of his father also and, joking about body hair aside, perhaps they would both find it easier to speak of sensitive matters if they did not look at each other. It had, after all, been more than three years since they had had civil speech with each other, aside from what was necessary.

"Father, you have my word, my vow, that I would always care for and protect Mother - my lady - and Stephen and the new baby. But if something should happen to me, what of Tamsin? Will you promise to care for her as well?"

Raymond sighed. "Of course, Geoffrey. Despite, well, despite everything, she is my granddaughter. I give you my word that should anything befall you, I would keep her and care for her. Besides," and Raymond chuckled dryly, "did I not make that promise, your stepmother would kill me in my boots. She dotes on the child."

Geoffrey stared out of the open tent flap at the moon. The night was so hot and humid that they had tied the flap open in a futile attempt to admit any breeze. He realized the definite possibility that he or his father, or both of them, might die tomorrow, and he wanted very much to clear the air between them.

"Tamsin is all I have left of –" Even now and in the dark he could not bring himself to say Milesenda's name aloud, so he could only say, "She is all I have."

Raymond also was feeling the need to set things right with his son before they faced the French forces on the morrow. He had fought in many battles in his life and that prospect alone did not frighten him. But the prospect of having Geoffrey beside him, inexperienced in battle despite his skill, chilled him to the bone despite the warmth of the August night.

"Geoffrey," he began, also staring up as if searching for his words on the tent ceiling above his head, "I am not the uncaring monster you may think me to be. I believe that you loved that girl and I do not enjoy the pain you have suffered since she died. However," and here his voice became hard, "were I to do it over, I still could not have allowed you to marry her. You must marry a woman of noble birth, for the sake of the estate."

"What difference does the estate make, if there is no love with which to share it?" Geoffrey challenged stiffly.

Raymond sighed, knowing that no reply he could offer would convince his stubborn son. "Believe me, Geoffrey, I did not, do not, wish for you to be unhappy. I have always striven to do what I felt to be in the best interests of both you and our family. Please understand that." Raymond paused. "I have never seen anyone grieve as you have, and I am sorry for your pain."

To Geoffrey his father's words were both a comfort and a source of pain. It annoyed him that his father would not say, or could not remember, Milesenda's name. But his father's expression of sympathy encouraged him to ask things he had wondered about since his childhood but had never been able to ask his father about before. He sat up again and leaned forward with his arms on his knees.

"What of my mother, my real mother?" he asked. "Did you not love her? Did you not grieve when she died?"

Raymond turned his head to look at Geoffrey. "Geoffrey, you must understand how it was with your mother and me. I met her the day before we wed. It was arranged by our parents, as was proper. As I have been attempting to do for you. You were born less than a year after our marriage, and when you were but a baby I had to leave to go to war, and could not return for five years. And when I did, your mother had already died. I barely knew her, Geoffrey. Perhaps if we had been together longer, we would have come to love each other."

"I knew I loved Milesenda from the first day we were together," Geoffrey declared quickly, almost accusingly. "The time we had together was just as brief as the time you were with my mother. But we knew we loved each other from the start."

Raymond refrained from saying that he thought Geoffrey was too impulsive for his own good. He merely said, "That is the difference between you and me, Geoffrey."

"Were you faithful to her?" Geoffrey demanded.

Raymond's eyes widened in surprise at his son's temerity in asking such a personal question. He looked away.

"Geoffrey, we were apart for five years," he said almost pleadingly. "I am not a monk. Nor, I believe, are you."

Geoffrey was silent. It was true he had not been celibate since Milesenda's death, but he knew that had she lived, he would have been the most faithful of husbands. After a moment he asked, "And my stepmother, do you love her? Have you been faithful to her?"

This time Raymond met his son's eyes. "Yes," he said solemnly. "I love her, and I have not so much as looked at another woman since the day we were married. I hated having to leave her when she is with child."

Geoffrey was surprised. He had not thought his hard, cold father capable of loving anyone. Perhaps Raymond was not as cold as he had thought. As he put his hand to his forehead and pushed back his hair, he began to think of his father in a whole new light, as a human being with cares and feelings, a husband, a father.

"If you love her, Father, then can you understand how it would feel if someone had tried to prevent you from marrying her?" Geoffrey challenged.

"It was not an issue I needed to consider," Raymond replied honestly, "because the love bloomed after we were already married. That is what I had hoped for you when I attempted to arrange a marriage for you. You have a responsibility, Geoffrey, a responsibility to Belvoir. It is your obligation to marry and father a legitimate heir for the estate. Your child is illegitimate, and a girl. She cannot inherit the estate nor carry on the de Graville name."

Geoffrey had no reply to that, and turned his gaze to study his toes. "Tell me about my mother," he said. "That is, if you can remember her."

Raymond smiled slightly. "She was high spirited, and very beautiful. Your stepmother is beautiful too," he said quickly, "but in a different way, her own way. Your mother was blond, like you. You favor her, you know. Or rather, you favor her father." He chuckled. "Now there was a man to be terrified of. When I first saw him, I thought he was Rollo himself come to life."

"Who is Rollo?" Geoffrey asked.

"He led the Norsemen who invaded here many years ago and gave Normandy its name. I swear your grandfather must have been his descendant. The man was a giant, taller even than you if you can imagine such a thing. You almost weren't conceived at all, because every time I touched your mother, I imagined I saw her father standing there glowering at me, threatening me with fates worse than death if I hurt his girl."

The words popped out of Geoffrey's mouth before he thought. "I did not believe you were ever afraid of anything, Father," he exclaimed.

Raymond sat up on the cot, leaning forward as Geoffrey was doing. His face became serious. "Every man fears something in this world, Geoffrey. Even the most courageous knight, even the King himself, is afraid of something, though not every man may admit it. Your grandfather, that was nothing, a joke. There is something that I truly do fear more than anything." He glanced down at the floor for a moment, then up again at Geoffrey's face. He waved a hand towards the east, towards Mantes, where they knew the French forces awaited them. "The thing I fear more than anything, more than death, is the possibility of you being wounded or killed. That thought is what truly terrifies me."

Geoffrey found that he could not take his eyes from his father's. Raymond's candid words seemed to form the beginning of a bridge between the father and son that had not existed for a long time, if ever.

"The same thought frightens me, Father," Geoffrey admitted in a soft voice. "I mean, that anything might happen to you."

"Well then, stay close by my side and we shall protect each other's flanks," Raymond said with a grim smile. "And when this is all over, and we return to England, I will take you to Senlac Hill, where the battle was fought that made Duke William the Conqueror and King of England. There is something there, in the abbey which now stands on that spot, which I must tell you about in confidence, now that you are a man grown."

"What is it?" Geoffrey asked, but his father refrained from telling him the secret yet.

"I will tell you when we are there, at Battle Abbey's altar." He reached a hand out towards Geoffrey's head and for a moment Geoffrey almost flinched, thinking his father was going to strike him as he had done so often when Geoffrey was a child. But Raymond merely put his hand on his son's head and ruffled his hair. The action touched Geoffrey almost as if it had been a blow. He could not recall his father ever treating him with such affection. "Get some sleep," Raymond said. "We will need to be well rested in the morning."

Geoffrey nodded silently and both he and his father lay on their cots and closed their eyes, but sleep was a long time in coming.

*****

Under ordinary circumstances, a squire would not take part in the actual battle, but would stay in the background with his knight's spare horse. But Geoffrey was so big, strong and proficient that an exception had been made in his case. He would be fighting as a sergeant, an un-knighted soldier. So this morning found him fully armed and covered from head to foot in the heavy mail, mounted in the built-up saddle upon the back of a powerful destrier. The long stirrups kept his equally long legs straight, almost stiff. On his left side hung the heavy, deadly sword, on his right a smaller but equally as deadly dagger, honed to a sharpness capable of splitting a single hair. Geoffrey knew this because he had sharpened the knife himself and tested it on a hair he plucked from his own blond head. A mace was thrust through a loop attached to his saddle.

William, King of England and Duke of Normandy, had experienced an extraordinary stroke of luck in his bid to retake Mantes. His scouts had reported that the French garrison occupying the city had unex-pectedly left the city to push further into the Vexin. Attacking and besieging the town itself would be difficult, dangerous and uncertain. But out in the open, the French and Norman forces were almost evenly matched. The French army was a little larger, but William's Normans would have the advantage of surprise as they drew themselves up along the road out of Mantes to await the unsuspecting French. The air was eerily quiet with no hint of morning birdsong, as if even the birds knew there was about to be a battle.

Geoffrey pushed his hair away from his face as he placed the cotton-lined leather cap on his head. Up and down the line of mounted war-riors, other knights arranged knee to knee, including Geoffrey's two cousins, were doing the same, but the helmets themselves would not be donned until the last possible moment. Once on his head, the helmet would make it difficult to speak or hear, and it would be impossible to wipe the sweat from his face, sweat that was already beginning to form as his father gave him last-minute instructions.

"Remember," Raymond was saying, "your mail will protect you, but will not make you invincible. A blow from a sword may or may not pierce it, depending upon the strength of your opponent, but you will feel it nonetheless. An axe will definitely be able to cut through the mail-and you - quite easily. Keep the tail of your shield over your left thigh. And whatever you do, avoid at all costs being thrown or dragged from your horse. Dismount only if the beast is killed under you. If you fall, you may find it next to impossible to regain your feet, encumbered as we are. I once saw a man drown in a three-inch-deep puddle of water because he had been knocked from his horse and could not get up."

Although Geoffrey listened carefully to his father's words, he looked down the dirt road where the French forces were approaching. As soon as they came into sight over the rise, the signal to attack would be given. The Norman troops were drawn up in a continuous shallow line, four deep with mounted knights, and approximately the same number of foot soldiers arrayed behind them.

"Look you," Raymond continued, "there is the King."

Geoffrey followed his father's gaze to their left, where they saw the banner of William of Normandy fluttering in the early morning breeze. "I suppose I should refer to him as the Duke, since we are in Normandy," Raymond said. "At all costs, he and his standard must be protected. The King of France stays safely in Paris, but William of Normandy leads his own troops into battle. If William is killed or captured, we are lost."

"Yes, Father," Geoffrey replied, and he was surprised at how calm his voice sounded. He realized that, although he did fear death in a general way, as he set his helmet firmly on his head and hefted his lance, he was not afraid to move forward at the signal in concert with the rest of the cavalry, their lances held vertically, towards the opposing forces whose first knights had just topped the hill. This was the culmination, the confirmation, of seven years of training, of practice, bruises, and more practice. This was his destiny. He would not fear it.

The horses were at a canter now, lances were lowered and secured under the knights' right arms, and the two forces rapidly approaching each other. The Norman knights rode into the waves of battle as their

Viking forebears had sailed their longships into piracy. *I will make you proud of me, Father*, Geoffrey thought, *or I will die trying.*

As Geoffrey had been instructed to expect, his lance was shattered in the first charge, the end impaled in the chest of the French soldier who had had the misfortune to be in front of him, and he discarded the remainder of it and drew his sword. He barely realized it when the next man he killed went down under his blow with a blood-filled gurgle, as he used his legs to turn his horse to face the next opponent. All around him were the clash and clamor of sword on sword, the thud of blows parried by shields, the screams and groans of wounded and dying men and horses. Battles were not so much a fight between two armies as they were thousands of individual fights between a knight and his opponent, each one being a fight to the death and the victor being the man who survived. The victorious army was the one ending the day with the most men left alive. Though the smell of blood and death filled the air, neither Geoffrey nor his horse panicked. They had both been well trained.

Time seemed to lose its meaning as the two armies battled, first one side pressing forward, then the other. Geoffrey's sword sang a bloody song of death, much as it must have for his Viking ancestors who had once conquered this land. Though Geoffrey's heart belonged to England, he could sympathize with those who fought to preserve their homeland. As he crossed swords with another French knight, he imagined defending England thusly, and made short work of his opponent.

It could have been hours or only minutes later in this hell on earth when Geoffrey turned his horse quickly to dispatch a foot soldier coming at him from one side with a galive, a long, hooked knife used by the infantry to pull the knight out of his saddle. The galive fell unused to the ground as Geoffrey cut down its owner with a blow that nearly decapitated him.

In that swift, sideways movement he glanced around him, briefly, but it was enough to see his father, just a few feet away from him, and behind Raymond, King William, the two men fighting back to back, so close their horse's rumps were almost touching. Raymond was fending off a Frenchman on a huge black horse, and in that split-second glance,

Geoffrey could see the bright sheen of blood on the shoulder of his father's sword arm.

Your mail will protect you but not make you invincible. His father's words flashed through his brain. And also, *at all costs the king must not be killed or captured, or we are lost.* Raymond was all that stood between William and the French knight, and his sword arm was obviously weakened by his wound. Geoffrey spurred his horse toward his father with a loud, savage shout, drawing the attention of both Raymond and his opponent. Several arrows came flying toward him at the same time and he warded them off with his shield. Two of them embedded themselves in the shield and remained there.

Geoffrey engaged the Frenchman as his father fell back, toward the king. Several more arrows whizzed past Geoffrey's head, and at the same time, the Frenchman's sword impacted on his with a force that numbed his hand, and the other sword's blade slid down the length of Geoffrey's until it was stopped at the quillon which guarded the hilt and his hand, but the force of the blow knocked the sword from his grip and it fell to the ground as Geoffrey used his shield to ward off the next blow.

He was tempted to leap from the horse's back and retrieve his sword from the ground. *Do not dismount unless your horse is killed under you!* He heard the words in his head as if his father had spoken to him, though he had not. Geoffrey could no longer see Raymond, somewhere behind him now, but in the same instant the decision was made for him as two more arrows embedded themselves in his horse's throat and the animal fell to the ground.

Geoffrey narrowly missed being pinned under the dying horse as he leaped from the deep saddle. He was fortunate, he was able to stay on his feet in spite of the spurs on his heels which almost tripped him. The Frenchman who had torn his sword from his hand had now been engaged by another Norman knight. Geoffrey thought the Norman might be his cousin Robert, but it was hard to tell under the concealing helmet. The two of them moved away from Geoffrey, his father and the King.

At the moment Geoffrey's horse had been killed, he had been reaching for the mace hanging from its loop attached to the saddle, but that weapon was now pinned under the dead animal. He saw his sword on the ground to his left, but from his right approached a French foot soldier armed with a formidable axe, the curved blade looking absurdly like a smile. In that fleeting moment, before the Frenchman reached him, he slid his left arm from the straps on the inside of the shield and transferred it to his right arm, to protect himself while he reached across the ground with his left hand for his sword, just out of his reach. He knew he would have to drop the shield when he took the sword back into his right hand, for he could not effectively wield his sword with his left hand and there would not be time to shift the shield back to his left arm, but he also knew he would be better off with his sword and no shield than with the shield and no sword. He bent over and reached for the sword, not daring to kneel for fear he would not be able to get up again. The French soldier saw what Geoffrey was trying to do, and with a wicked snarl, changed the direction of the swing of his axe from Geoffrey's head, protected by his stout shield, to his left hand, which was inching along the ground towards the sword, just barely out of his reach.

Geoffrey glanced up, and in that moment time froze. He saw the blood lust in his opponent's eyes, which he knew was mirrored in his own, saw the man's teeth, which were rotten, could smell his breath, which was foul; but though he observed all of this, still the axe descended so quickly that there was no time to retract as the blade thudded to the ground, through the mail gauntlet and across and through the fingers of Geoffrey's left hand.

The blow knocked him to his knees, but curiously he felt no pain at first, only a shocked numbness. He looked at his hand for just a second but saw only blood. There was blood all over him, but how much of it was his own and how much was other men's, he couldn't tell. He pressed his hand against his side, pressed it hard to staunch the bleeding. The French soldier was raising the heavy axe again, its blade red with Geoffrey's blood, this time aiming for his throat. Geoffrey still had his dagger in his belt. He shook the shield from his arm, and in the same swift movement pulled the dagger from his belt with his right hand. He had only a fraction of a second to save himself. There wasn't time to try to struggle up from his knees, so with a strength and speed born of self-preserving desperation, he slashed upwards with the knife, between the two sections of his opponent's hauberk, and buried the dagger to its hilt in the man's groin, twisting it quickly before he pulled it out.

Blood spurted horribly, and the man screamed once before he died. He and his axe fell to the ground as his life's blood gushed from him and anointed Geoffrey's face, the heavy axe thudding to the earth only inches from Geoffrey's foot. "You should have gone for my throat when you had the chance," he said to the dead man.

Wounded, horseless and armed now only with his bloody dagger, swaying on his knees and kept conscious only by delayed shock, Geoffrey quickly looked around for the next threat but found none. The French forces were beginning to retreat and only a few were still engaged in combat. Two horsemen approached him-Normans, and he looked up into the faces of his cousins Robert and Hugh. They dismounted quickly, and Hugh, seeing his cousin's wound, pulled a cloth from under his saddle, tugged off what remained of Geoffrey's gauntlet, and quickly wrapped Geoffrey's mangled, bleeding hand before he had a chance to see it. The numbness was receding to be replaced by a fierce pain, which Hugh's rough ministrations only exacerbated.

"We are victorious!" Robert was saying exultantly as Hugh pulled his cousin to his feet. It was difficult for Geoffrey to understand what Robert said, what with the pain, the impediment of his helmet, and the almost unfamiliar Norman French Robert spoke.

Geoffrey felt as if he was suffocating under the suddenly intolerable weight of his helmet. He struggled with his unwounded hand to pull it off and threw it to the ground. "My father? Where is he?" he gasped. He had not seen Raymond since before he had lost his sword.

"Your father is dead," Robert said, looking behind Geoffrey, who turned and, to his horror, saw his father's body on the ground, one foot still caught in the stirrup, and a French arrow protruding obscenely from his throat, apparently one of the arrows which had whizzed by

Geoffrey's head earlier. Next to him, Duke William was being assisted from his horse by several of his retainers.

"I saw him fall, but I could not rid myself of that man on that damn black horse in time to aid them," Robert explained as Geoffrey stared in horror at Raymond's lifeless form. "The arrow was meant for Duke William and your father moved into its path. That left you, Geoffrey, the only man between the Duke and that one." Robert glanced at the blood-covered foot soldier now staring sightlessly at the sky. "Thank God you killed him, Geoffrey; if he had gotten to the Duke the French would have surely regrouped and cut us down."

Geoffrey paid little heed to his cousin's account, and started toward his father's body with a strangled cry. "Father!" His anguished lament attracted the attention of the Duke, but before Geoffrey reached Raymond, the pain, blood, shock, stress and grief overtook him. Hugh tried to catch him but Geoffrey was much taller and heavier than his cousin and they both crashed to the ground.

*****

When Geoffrey regained consciousness, he found himself on his back on the cot in the tent he and his father had shared the night before. His mail and gauntlets had been removed, as well as the gambeson, the padded leather tunic he had worn under the hauberk. Through the mist of pain and blood that blurred his vision, he discerned his two cousins, one kneeling on either side of him holding down his shoulders, and a third man, the barber-surgeon. He tried to see his hand, but Hugh's body blocked his view.

The barber-surgeon, seeing Geoffrey was awake, gestured at Hugh and Robert.

"I had hoped he would not awaken for a while yet, but as long as he has, you must pull him up to a sitting position. I will have to trim the wounds, and cauterize them to stop the bleeding, and if he vomits, he will choke on it if he is laying down."

The cousins stood, and as Hugh moved, Geoffrey saw that his left arm was stretched out on the chest which had been set next to the cot. But the hand was still wrapped in blood-soaked bandages, and he could not tell the extent of the damage.

His cousins grasped him under the arms to pull him up on the cot. As Hugh tugged on his left arm, Geoffrey screamed as the pain coursed from his hand, up his arm and through his entire body like a knife thrust into his very soul. He turned his head, and as the barber-surgeon had predicted, was very sick.

Robert, looking down at his ruined boots, said bitterly, "Perhaps we should let him choke."

Hugh was slightly more sensitive than his brother, and hissed, "Would you like to trade places with him? Thank the Blessed Virgin only your boots are ruined!"

The surgeon, busy unwrapping the gory bandages from Geoffrey's hand, snapped at them, "Give him wine! As much as he can hold, and more. And hold him still. This is going to hurt."

Going to hurt! Geoffrey thought desperately, as a flask was pressed to his lips. He swallowed weakly, tasting the blood of the soldier who had wounded him, and some of the wine ran down his chin, drooling onto his bare chest.

The surgeon drew a sharp short knife from his pack, instructed again, "Hold him still now," and applied it efficiently as Geoffrey screamed in pain again. Hugh's body still blocked Geoffrey's view, and he was afraid to ask to see his hand. The wine flask was pressed continually to his lips, tasting bitter and sour in his rebelling stomach, and he could not help but heap more ruin upon Robert's boots.

Then the surgeon looked out the tent's entrance, to where his assistant sat next to a merrily blazing campfire. The younger man held the cloth-wrapped handle of a large dagger, with the knife's blade in the flames. When the surgeon nodded, the young man withdrew the dagger from the fire, its blade now red-hot, and presented it quickly to his master. Geoffrey stared wide-eyed at the red, steaming blade, which looked positively huge to him.

Quickly, before the blade cooled, the surgeon once again instructed

Hugh, "Hold his arm *very* still." Hugh gripped Geoffrey's left arm in a vise-like hold and leaned his weight into Geoffrey's shoulder. With a glance at Geoffrey's face, the surgeon also said, to Robert, "Turn his head away." Robert grabbed Geoffrey's chin with a rough hand and with an effort turned his face away from the surgeon and the dagger, pressing Geoffrey's head down on the cot with one hand and his right shoulder with the other.

When the side of the blade touched Geoffrey's flesh, everything he thought he knew about pain was erased and replaced by that red-hot iron as it was pressed against the open wounds, cauterizing them by literally burning the flesh together. Only the combined weight of his two cousins kept Geoffrey's body still on the cot, and it took all of Hugh and Robert's strength to keep him down. But nothing could silence Geoffrey's agonized screams which they were all certain could be heard back in England. The sickening stench of burning flesh rose and filled the small tent. Geoffrey still could not determine the extent of the damage, because the pain seemed to be everywhere, but at least he did not vomit anymore, simply because there was nothing left to come up.

What seemed like years later, the barber-surgeon wrapped his hand tightly in clean bandages, too thick for Geoffrey to see the extent of the damage, and gently laid his hand next to him on the cot. "Leave them on for a month," he said briskly, and to the cousins, "You may clean him up now." And before Geoffrey could find the voice to ask the question whose answer he was afraid to hear, the surgeon was gone, to tend to the next wounded man.

Hugh found a pail of water, a clean cloth and sponged off Geoffrey's face, neck and chest while Robert rummaged in the chest for a clean tunic.

"Just leave me," Geoffrey said, his voice coming out in a little squeak. "Just let me die." He had spoken in English, and he had to struggle to repeat himself in Norman French so that his cousins could understand him.

Robert shook his head. "You will have to wait," he admonished. "The Duke has instructed us to bring you to his tent as soon as the surgeon was finished. He told me he wished to see de Graville's boy, the young man with the yellow hair."

"The Duke?" Geoffrey squeaked miserably, unable for a moment to think straight. "What Duke?"

"Duke William, you English mule," Robert retorted. "What other Duke is there?"

"Oh, you mean the King," Geoffrey replied as his cousins pulled the clean tunic over his head. Trying to jostle his damaged hand as little as possible, they managed to get him dressed and pulled him to his feet.

He swayed wildly and only Hugh and Robert's strong grip kept him on his feet.

It was not far to the King's - or the Duke's - tent, but for Geoffrey, assisted by his none-too-gentle cousins, each step was an exercise in agony. In his weakened state, even the minor cuts, bruises and scrapes he had suffered, which in ordinary circumstances would have been of little consequence, throbbed painfully.

He felt his knees weakening as they approached the tent flying the banners of the Duke of Normandy. Robert deftly grabbed another flask of wine from a passing servant and pressed it to Geoffrey's lips.

"Have a care!" Hugh warned. "I do not think the Duke will appreciate having his boots ruined either."

As Robert hastily jerked the flask away from him and returned it to the startled servant, Geoffrey joked feebly, "If you think I was bad back there, you should be on a ship with me."

"If you value your life, do not even dare to think of being sick in the presence of the Duke," Robert hissed.

"The King," Geoffrey insisted weakly. Even in his weakened, pain-wracked condition, he thought, *these Normans! They thought the world began and ended here.*

"Very well, you stubborn savage, the King," Robert allowed, giving his cousin a disgusted look. Then Geoffrey felt dizziness threatening to overcome him, and as his head lolled dangerously, Robert grabbed his hair and yanked cruelly. As Geoffrey yelped with this new pain, Robert declared, "At least that mane of yours is of some use. Now try to keep your head clear and your bile down."

The three of them entered the large tent and approached the Duke-the King to Geoffrey-who was standing at the far end conferring with his commanders. It took all of what little was left of Geoffrey's strength to make his bow without falling forward on his face.

Impressive was a word which came immediately to mind when observing William of Normandy. A large and dominating man, with a massive bulk just this side of corpulence, he had a full, fleshy face, russet hair, and a majestic demeanor that would have awed Geoffrey had he been in a more healthy condition. He was vaguely aware of one of the barons leaning towards the Duke and murmuring, "Young de Graville, Your Grace."

The Duke nodded and looked at Geoffrey. "I understand this was your first battle," he said. Without waiting for Geoffrey's confirmation, he continued, "You fought bravely, and had it not been for your quick action, and your father's sacrifice, we might not be here to speak of it. Such bravery must be rewarded. Kneel," and he indicated the ground before him.

Kneeling was another challenge that Geoffrey somehow managed to accomplish without disgracing himself. He saw the Duke remove his sword from its scabbard, and thought, *thank God, he is going to cut off my head and end this pain. I should be honored that the King himself...*

But the sword merely tapped his right shoulder, then swung slowly over his head to the left. It took him a moment to realize he was being knighted, not beheaded. Now William was saying, "Be thou a knight. You may rise, Chevalier de Graville."

Rise? Geoffrey found he could not. He looked up at his King, who summoned Hugh and Robert forward with a look to help Geoffrey to his feet. Was it his imagination, or was his cousin's assistance a little more gentle than before, their look a little more respectful?

"Your father was a courageous warrior," William was saying. "He shall be sorely missed, and I am sure he would be proud of his son. You are a credit to him."

Geoffrey nodded his thanks for the Duke's kind words.

William glanced towards Geoffrey's bandaged hand. "I shall pray you recover from your wounds." Then the Duke surprised Geoffrey by asking, "You are married?"

"No, my lord."

"The wedded state is a most propitious one." A shadow of sadness crossed the Duke's ruddy face, and Geoffrey remembered that his queen, the diminutive Mathilda, had died the year before. "I would suggest that you seek to acquire yourself a bride and an heir, now that your father is gone."

Geoffrey said nothing and the Duke continued, "We have scored a great victory today. My brother of France shall think twice in the future before invading here again."

Geoffrey's thoughts were bitter as he and his cousins bowed to their Duke and King. *Great victory for the Normans, perhaps*, he thought, *but at what cost?* His father was dead and his hand maimed. Even the fact that he had received his knighthood two years earlier than he had anticipated was of little consolation. The pain in his heart was almost as great as the pain of his body as he and his cousins were dismissed from the Duke's presence, and they returned to the battlefield to retrieve his father's body.

13

Hugh and Robert took Geoffrey home with them to his uncle's estate near Rouen, so that he could recuperate from his wounds and bury his father. As he stood at Raymond's grave, he could see the grave of his mother nearby. How ironic it was, he thought bitterly, that his parents, who had been together such a short time in life, should now lie near each other in death.

When Milesenda had died, he had wept in the noisy grief of a child. But the child in him had died also, and he would never allow himself to lose control like that again. Kneeling, he looked again at the graves of his parents, the mother he had never had a chance to know, and the father he had not appreciated. The boy had once wept loudly, but the man now grieved silently.

His uncle made him welcome in his home, and he found himself staying in the same bedchamber that had belonged to his parents during their brief marriage, when they had lived with Alain. It was the room, in fact the very bed, in which Geoffrey had been born.

His uncle and his cousins all came to visit him frequently, to see how he fared, extend their condolences on his father's death, and to congratulate him on attaining his knighthood. There were three female cousins. He could not seem to remember their names. They seemed inclined to forget the consanguineous nature of their relationship in the presence of this big, handsome Englishman, but he shooed them wearily away though all three were pretty. His only desire was to be left alone.

There came a night when the full moon shone so brightly that the night seemed almost as bright as daytime as Geoffrey lay sleepless on his bed. He stared up at the ceiling, trying to picture his parents living here, himself as a child, but the images eluded him.

The last night of his father's life had been lit by such a full moon and in his head he could hear the barber-surgeon's last words to him after bandaging his wounded hand.

"Leave them on for a month."

Now it had been a month, and as the morning sunlight slowly replaced the moonlight, there was no one to prepare him for what he might find under the bulky wrappings. The barber-surgeon had been too busy to discuss his wounds with him, and Geoffrey's mind had been far too clouded with pain and wine to understand much anyway. His cousins had been there, but had been too occupied with holding him still and trying to avoid his vomit to pay much attention to anything else.

So as the dawn light crept into the small window, he sat up on the bed, perspiring though the morning was cool, and was at once both eager and afraid to cut away the wrappings.

Finally, he stood and bolted the door into the room. Returning to the bed, he picked up his knife and sat looking at it for a long time. It was the knife he used to shave with and he kept it very sharp. He turned it back and forth, watching the morning sun glint off the blade, studying the knife as if memorizing its details for future reference, then set it down next to him and picked it up several times.

But no amount of delay was going to change what was under the heavy wrappings. He picked up the knife again, slipped it under the topmost layer of the bandages, and slit the cloth. Taking a deep breath, he quickly unwrapped them, letting them fall to the floor.

He almost wept with relief when his hand was uncovered, for the damage was less than he had feared, though it was still horrifying.

His little finger, the crooked little finger that Milesenda had kissed so tenderly, was gone, sheared off neatly at the base. The next finger had been cut off below the bottom knuckle, leaving a small scarred stump.

His middle finger had been severed through the bottom knuckle, and the tip of his first finger was cut off at the top knuckle. His thumb was intact. The Frenchman's axe must have struck his hand at an angle, but the partial fingers had been trimmed off evenly. That must have been what the barber-surgeon had done with that wicked little knife. His fingers - what was left of them - ached at the memory.

He sat and stared at his hand for a long while, turning it back and forth. Vaguely he became aware of a pounding at the door that finally became too persistent for him to ignore. He heard his uncle calling out his name.

Quickly he got up and unbolted the door to admit Alain, who looked both annoyed and relieved.

"I was beginning to think you had died in here," Alain complained. "I was about to have the door battered down."

Then Alain's gaze took in the discarded wrappings lying in a heap on the floor, the knife beside them, and Geoffrey, who had sat back on the bed with his left hand in his lap.

"How bad?" he asked simply, and Geoffrey lifted the hand for his uncle to see.

Alain surveyed the hand carefully, saying, "Not bad; I have seen much worse. You are fortunate it is your left hand only."

Geoffrey laughed bitterly. "Yes, Uncle, I am very fortunate. My father is dead and I am maimed. I am the most fortunate of men."

Alain looked at his nephew critically. "And Normandy is safe for now from French invasion. Such safety requires sacrifice."

Geoffrey shrugged and looked out the window. He knew it would only antagonize his uncle to say that he cared little for Normandy's safety.

Alain sat down in the room's one chair. "Have you sent word to England of your father's death?" he asked. Geoffrey shook his head.

"I feel it is news I should bring myself," he declared. "Mother, I mean, my lady stepmother, is with child and I would not want her to hear this from a stranger in her condition. It is bad enough that the child will have no father."

"As you wish, Geoffrey," Alain replied. "You are Baron de Graville now. The English Baron de Graville," he added, because Alain held the same title in Normandy. Alain looked around him, at the room Geoffrey had been born in. "I remember when you were a child here," he continued with a small smile. "Always into some sort of mischief, you were. Your aunt, may God rest her soul, felt that your mother was not strict enough with you. She often said your mother did not beat you enough to keep you tractable."

Geoffrey managed a small, grim smile as well. "My father made up for her lack when we came to England," he said, but without rancor. He knew that most, if not all, of his childhood beatings had been well-deserved. Looking at his uncle, he saw that Raymond had born a strong resemblance to his older brother.

"Are you betrothed, Geoffrey?" Alain asked him, and Geoffrey's smile disappeared. *Damnation*, he thought, what was this infernal interest everyone took in his marital state? First the King, and now his uncle.

"No, I am not," he said sharply. His uncle looked offended at Geoffrey's curt, almost rude, reply.

"Well, you should become so," Alain replied tartly. "Now that you have inherited your father's title and estate, you must father an heir of your own. I am surprised Raymond had not already negotiated a bride for you."

Geoffrey sighed in exasperation, and patiently explained to his uncle, "I have been married once already. She is - she died. I do not plan to wed again. And I have an heir in my brother Stephen."

His uncle looked surprised. "Your father never told me you had been wed," he said.

"My father did not approve of or acknowledge my marriage," Geoffrey told him, recalling the night of Milesenda's death when he had told his father to go to hell. There was no point now, he reasoned, in being angry at a dead man. And though Alain looked curious, Geoffrey said no more. He did not wish to discuss the circumstances of his relationship with Milesenda with his uncle.

Alain stood up and said, "If you wish my assistance, Geoffrey, I would be glad to help you find a suitable bride here in Normandy. Robert's wife, and Hugh's betrothed, both have comely sisters, one of whom might be induced to travel to that savage island of yours, with a good-looking young man such as yourself to warm her bed."

Geoffrey tried to remain patient as he shook his head at his uncle. "Thank you for the offer, but as I have said, I do not wish to wed again." Alain shook his head in exasperation.

"Very well, nephew, but I fear you are being foolish. You have become much too English, in my opinion. Raymond's mistake was not sending you back here to Normandy for fostering, where proper training could be had."

Geoffrey frowned, but did not bother to argue. There would be no convincing his Norman uncle.

"Should you change your mind, you need only say so," Alain continued. "You are welcome here for as long as you care to stay."

"Thank you again, uncle. But I would like to depart for home as soon as I can. My family will need me." He refrained from mentioning his daughter specifically, not wishing for his uncle to question her legitimacy as well.

Alain stepped towards the door with a nod. "Shall I send someone to bring you something to eat? A big fellow like you must need ample fuel."

Geoffrey shook his head, and his uncle left him alone. He could not eat just yet, so soon after revealing his damaged hand. He lay back down on the bed and held it up to the light, looking at the scars, the missing fingers. Even if he were inclined to take a bride, he thought, what woman would want to be held or touched by a hand like that? He set the left hand next to him, letting it slide under the fold of his tunic as he briefly pressed his right hand, his whole hand, over his eyes.

Then he sat up again, despising himself for his self-pity. He had a few things to attend to before leaving his uncle's estate to return to England, but before he left the room he found a pair of leather riding gloves and pulled them on.

*****

The last thing Geoffrey did before mounting his horse to depart for Dieppe, there to take ship for England, was to present his cousin Robert with a new pair of boots, which Geoffrey had commissioned from the local cobbler.

"With my apologies, cousin," he told the startled Robert. "These are to replace the ones I ruined."

Hugh laughed aloud at the look on his brother's face, and Geoffrey thought, *at least not all Normans are humorless.* He turned to mount his horse, feeling very grateful that his beloved, familiar Storm was not a warhorse like the one that had been killed from beneath him.

It felt awkward and difficult to hold the reins in his truncated hand, and he leaned forward to murmur in his horse's ear. In English, so that his Norman relatives did not understand him. They were already looking at him as if he were slightly touched, to be talking to his horse.

"You will need to be patient with me, friend. And be glad, for we are going home!"

He looked at his cousins. "You are both welcome to come visit me in England if you wish. It is a beautiful place, and Devon the most beautiful part of it. In fact, were you to travel there, you might wish never to leave it. No offense intended, uncle," he said to Alain. *God, I am glad to be going home*, he thought, and nudged Storm forward, using his legs to make up for his awkward hand. "Godspeed!" he called behind him as the troop of knights, smaller in number since they had arrived in Normandy by two, in addition to the loss of Raymond, left his uncle's home behind them and turned their horse's noses towards the coast.

The sea voyage back to England was just as disastrous as the previous one, and Geoffrey realized that his proclivity for seasickness was a permanent condition. They called it the Narrow Sea, and few men were bothered while crossing it. But despite his Norse looks, Geoffrey failed to do his Viking ancestors proud on the water. As soon as his feet left the stability of land, he leaned over the rail and gave up his breakfast to the sea, this time feeling not only sick, but embarrassed as well. What a fool he had been to bother eating anything. It would have been more practical to simply toss the bread and cider directly into the water and spare them the journey down his throat and back up again. The last time it had been somewhat of a joke among the other knights. *Lord de Graville's boy cannot keep his stomach on a ship.* But Geoffrey was Lord de Graville now, and expected to set an example of strength and maturity to the knights in his service. They all knew he was seasick, but he decided to spare them the sight of his retching and betook himself below decks for the duration of the voyage. Why, he wondered, could he not have been more like his Viking ancestors, who were great sea voyagers.

He prayed fervently that he might never be required to leave England again. As he curled himself up in agony in a corner of the small cabin aboard that accursed rolling ship, puking his guts out and feeling, and soon smelling, like something three days dead, that prayer alternated in his soul with another, more fervent prayer, a prayer for immediate death.

14

Geoffrey's first impulse when he disembarked in Exeter was to kneel and kiss the ground, so glad was he to be off the ship, but he refrained. It might have looked foolish in front of his father's men. In front of *his* men, he reminded himself.

Under ordinary circumstances he might also have felt obligated to pay a courtesy call on Raymond's old friend Baron de Meules, but he was too anxious to push on for Lydford, for home, to stop for courtesy. He hoped that he would be forgiven if he merely sent a messenger to his father's friend informing him of Raymond's death.

As soon as they topped the last hill before descending into the village, Geoffrey knew that he and his retinue would be visible from the battlements of the castle. He was bone-weary, dust-covered from the road, and his hand hurt like hell, but he still paused for a moment at the top of the hill and looked out over the valley, allowing his mind to wander back to the day when, as a wide-eyed child, he had first seen it from atop his father's horse.

The valley had not changed much since that long-ago spring day. There were the same neat fields sloping down from the forest's edge, teams of oxen working the long narrow strips, the same common pasture where sheep and cattle grazed. The river Lyd glistened in the sunlight as it meandered through the valley, past the village and on toward the sea. The village had grown a little in the last few years, but not much. And beyond, his home, the castle on the hill. He had been agog with wonder and anticipation the first time he had seen his new home, wriggling and bouncing so in the saddle that Raymond had had to restrain his son before the boy did his father some serious hurt. Geoffrey almost glanced around to see if his father recalled that day as well, but then he remembered that Raymond would never see this view again. This was Geoffrey's demesne now, Geoffrey's tenants harvesting now in the fields, working in the village and castle; Geoffrey's responsibilities.

He had traveled away from Lydford many times in his childhood and youth, journeying with his father to various parts of England. Although he had always been happy to come home from those expeditions, never before had he been quite so glad to descend that last hill and canter past the village towards the castle. *Home*, he thought exultantly, *we are home*! And yet at the same time, his heart was heavy with the news he was being forced to bring to his stepmother.

They were all waiting for him when he entered the great hall, having been apprised of his arrival by the guards on the battlements who had observed them as they approached and had sent down the word to raise the portcullis. Alyssa stood a little apart from the others; Maud, with an eager Tamsin in her arms, Steven, Father Mathieu, Edmund, and the servants and retainers all ranged behind her as they waited expectantly.

His stepmother's pregnancy was obvious to Geoffrey now, and he wondered how he had not noticed it before they had left for Normandy. But even as he wondered it, he knew exactly why he had not noticed. He had been too wrapped up in himself, in his own heartache over Milesenda's death, to pay attention to anything other than his own grief, and his daughter.

As he approached her, Alyssa looked behind him frantically, and not seeing her husband, her eyes begged Geoffrey to tell her that his father would be arriving home, that he had merely been delayed somewhere along the way and would be riding up to the gate shortly, but although it killed him inside to have to do it, Geoffrey could only shake his head sadly. Alyssa's eyes closed, and a small moan of pain escaped her as her body sagged. She would have fallen if Geoffrey had not stepped forward and caught her.

This time it was Geoffrey who comforted his stepmother as she wept, held her just as she had held him after Milesenda had died, murmured useless words of comfort against her hair. Behind her, he could see Stephen struggling manfully not to cry. The boy lost that struggle when Geoffrey held out one arm to his brother and enfolded him in his embrace as well.

Tamsin was squirming and straining in Maud's arms, interested only in the fact that her father was home. Finally, Maud was forced to put her down, and the little girl streaked across the floor, shrieking, "Da!" at the top of her lungs. Father Mathieu stepped forward to escort Alyssa to a chair, while Geoffrey turned to scoop his daughter into his arms and hold her tight.

In the joy of his homecoming, and the pain of the knowledge of Raymond's death, no one noticed that Geoffrey had come into the hall wearing gloves, a habit he had never had before, nor was it noticed that three of the fingers on his left glove flapped uselessly. But later, after Tamsin had been persuaded, with much difficulty and many promises on Geoffrey's part, to return to the nursery with Maud, and Stephen and Mathieu had gone to the chapel to pray for Raymond's soul, Geoffrey escorted Alyssa to the solar, dismissed the servants and closed the door. Only then did he remove his gloves and show his wound to his stepmother. Alyssa wept anew when she saw the maimed left hand, holding it in her own hands as her tears fell on it.

"Oh, Geoffrey," she sobbed, "Oh, my poor boy."

He patted her shoulder with his right hand and tried to make light of it all. "Do not weep so, please, Mother." It bewildered him to see his stepmother so disconsolate; he had always known her to be calm and strong. "It is only a few fingers and I can make do without them. And I would not wish for any harm to come to the baby by your grieving so." Actually, it terrified him to think of his stepmother's pregnancy, knowing as he did now that childbirth could be life-threatening.

She attempted to regain her composure and let go of his hand to wipe her eyes. Taking a few deep breaths, she was finally able to ask, without tears but still with a catch in her voice, "How...how did it happen?"

Briefly, and attempting to omit the gorier details, he told her the circumstances of the battle, his father's death in defense of his king and the manner in which he had been wounded. He hoped she would not ask him how many men he had killed, because to be truthful he could not remember. And he told her about being knighted at the hand of King William afterward, at which she smiled proudly in spite of her grief.

He sat back in his chair, stretching his legs out and looking around him, not really seeing the familiar room but gathering his thoughts. "Father and I," he said after a moment, "we spoke, before the battle, of, well, of many things. He told me about the child you are carrying, and I am sorry I did not realize it before we left." She shrugged slightly; such minor details were immaterial now. He went on, "I think, if he had not been killed," he saw tears welling up again in his stepmother's eyes, but she fought them back, "it is possible we might have resolved some of our differences. Who can say, now, but we did speak about...things, a little. He promised me that, if I were killed, he would have cared for Tamsin. I did not truly think that I would be the one to come home to honor my promise to him to care for you and Stephen and the new child in his place. But I will care for you, for all of you, as best I can," he said fiercely, taking his stepmother's hands in his. But then he remembered his wounds, and quickly pulled his hands back, embarrassed and self-conscious about his bad hand, and not wanting her to look at him with pity.

"Please forgive me, my lady," he said, and Alyssa looked at his face in surprise, then at his hands clenched in his lap. He realized she thought he was asking forgiveness for pulling away from her. "I meant, I would like to ask your forgiveness for making you wait here so long with no word. My uncle felt I should have sent a messenger to tell you about...about Father, but I did not want you to hear of it from a stranger. I felt it was my duty to tell you myself."

Alyssa nodded. "Thank you, Geoffrey. It was kind of you to think of me. I know this is all very difficult for you as well." She paused and looked at his face, set now in even more severe lines than it had been before he had left, all traces of boyishness and happiness as obliterated as if they had never existed. What had happened to the laughing boy who had put frogs in her workbasket? The tragedies he had experienced and the responsibilities he now carried had changed him, but Alyssa could remember when he had had the ability to smile, and she prayed that he would someday find that smile again, despite all that had happened to him in his short life. Though she certainly did not expect her stepson to go dancing around the Maypole as he had as a child, still she felt he deserved some happiness.

She reached out and put a hand on his arm. "Your father was always very proud of you, Geoffrey. He would be proud of you now as well."

He looked at her in disbelieving surprise. "It is kind of you to say so, Mother, but it is not so. I do not believe my father was proud of me at all. We were always at odds."

Alyssa recognized the wistful tone in her stepson's voice. Though he tried to conceal it, she knew him well enough to discern the desire of a young man for his father's approval. "I know you had your differences," she said, "but believe me, Geoffrey, he was proud of you. He told me so, before you and he left for Normandy. And it distressed him that you two could not seem to agree on anything. I know he appeared to you to be cold and unbending, and perhaps he was, but that was his way, and he could not change himself any more than you can. But you must believe that he cared for you." She began to falter at the realization that she was speaking about her husband in the past tense, that he would never speak for himself again. Taking a deep breath to keep herself calm, as much for Geoffrey's sake as for her own, she went on, "You and your father did have some things in common, dear boy, whether you will admit it or not, that being that you could both be as implacable and stubborn as a wall when you chose to be so, and also that neither of you was ever prone to lie. So you must believe me when I say that Raymond," another deep breath, "your father told me he was proud of your skill, your strength, your loyalty, and despite everything he was proud to have you as a son. Perhaps he could not tell you so himself, and that is a shame. And perhaps also it matters not to you, now that he is...he is gone, but I thought you should know the truth of the matter."

All the while she had been speaking Geoffrey had been looking at the floor, but he now raised his head. "I believe you, Mother. Perhaps we were both too stubborn for our own good. And yes, it does matter to me, even though it is too late now to do anything about it."

Alyssa stood up, placing her hand against her back as she walked to the window and looked out. The swell of her pregnancy was emphasized by her movement, and her face was pale with her grief. "When is the baby due?" Geoffrey asked.

"Emma believes soon after the new year begins, perhaps around Twelfth Night," she replied.

In three months then, it was now the beginning of October. He was suddenly haunted by memories, of Milesenda, suffering and dying in childbirth. The thought of the same thing happening to his stepmother as well petrified him, and though he struggled to keep his voice calm, Alyssa perceived his unease as he spoke.

"How - how do you feel, Mother?"

She turned and stepped toward him, laid a hand on his arm, and said earnestly, "I feel fine, Geoffrey, truly I do." She understood his concern, and sought to ease it. Patting his cheek maternally, she said, "You must be exhausted; go and rest now. Yes, I insist," she chided when he hesitated.

He yawned and decided to follow her advice, for he had barely slept or eaten since leaving Normandy, between the gut-wrenching nausea of the sea voyage and his hurry to reach home once they had landed. He bowed courteously to his stepmother, and seeing it, Alyssa realized that Geoffrey, as his father's heir, was no longer just her dear Geoffrey, but the Baron de Graville. She swept him a deep curtsy, graceful despite her pregnancy, and murmured, "My lord."

He took her hand and raised her up. "I would much rather be merely Geoffrey, Mother," he said softly.

Before he sought his bed, he sent his stepmother's maids to attend to their mistress, with strict instructions that she was to be carefully watched over. And after he had left the room, Alyssa sank into a chair, exhausted as well, and wept again for the loss of her husband and the wounding of her stepson.

Geoffrey did not realize just how tired he was until he started to climb the stairway to his bedchamber at the top of the tower. Tonight there seemed to be twice as many steps as he remembered. He was contemplating whether or not he had the strength to get undressed, or if he would rather merely fall into the bed fully clothed, when there was a timid knock at the door.

He yanked open the door with considerable irritation, annoyed at whoever was delaying his sleep, to see a trembling servant girl that he did not recognize with a tray in her hands, bearing bread, venison and a cup of ale.

"M-my lord," the girl stuttered. She was quite pretty, Geoffrey saw, or at least she would be if she did not look scared to death of him.

"What is it?" he demanded irritably, just wishing she would go away so that he could close his eyes and sink into unconsciousness.

She held up the tray, the dishes clattering with her trembling. "M-my lady sent you, s-sent..." Geoffrey took the tray from her hands before she dropped it. "She s-said you might be hungry."

Geoffrey's irritation disappeared. He realized that he was hungry as well as tired, and he was amazed at his stepmother's thoughtfulness. In the midst of her grief, on the day she had been told of her husband's death, her first thoughts had been that Geoffrey might be hungry! There was even a dish of frumenty on the tray. Alyssa knew that Geoffrey was partial to frumenty.

The girl curtsied and turned to go, but Geoffrey called out, "Wait. Please." She turned back, still trembling, and Geoffrey asked, "You are new here, are you not?" She nodded, shaking. "What is your name?"

"M-moll, my lord."

"Thank you, Moll, for bringing this. I am indeed very hungry. And please convey a message to my lady from me, thanking her for her kindness." He thought it would be polite to smile at her, but he was too weary to force his mouth upwards. Why was this girl trembling so? Was he so changed, in the few months he had been gone, that the servants were now afraid of him? What did this silly girl think he was going to do, drag her into his bedchamber and rip off her clothes? Even if he were inclined to do so, he was too tired right now.

The girl was still awaiting permission to leave, shaking with nervousness and twisting her fingers. "Shall I c-come back, my lord, to fetch the tray?" she asked tremulously.

"No," Geoffrey replied, having a distinct suspicion that she might faint if he were to say yes, "there is no need; it can wait until the morning. You may go."

The girl looked so relieved, that Geoffrey felt somewhat annoyed that she thought him such an ogre. She curtsied again, quickly, and turned to flee. Before he changed his mind? he thought uncharitably. She had gone down only a few of the stone steps when he stepped out the doorway behind her, the tray of food still in his hands, and called out, "Moll!"

She froze on the steps, her hand pressed against the wall as if for support, her fingers pale and quivering. She turned around very slowly, stammering even more. "Y-yes, my l-lord?"

"I do not bite, Moll," he declared, and then turned and stepped back into his chamber. He heard the girl scurrying down the stairs and hoped she did not fall and hurt herself in her haste to get away from him. Kicking the door shut behind him, he set the tray on the table, sat down and proceeded to demolish every crumb and down the cup of ale in one swallow, silently sending up prayers of gratitude to his stepmother as he ate. The meal gave him enough strength to remove his clothes before sinking, at long last, into the comfort of his own bed.

He was asleep only moments later, but in that brief minute before oblivion enveloped him, he realized that the trembling servant girl, though absolutely terrified of him, had not appeared to even notice his damaged hand.

He awoke late the next morning, and as soon as he was dressed hurried to the nursery to see Tamsin. He half feared that his daughter would be repulsed by his wounded hand, but she did not appear to notice anything different about him; she was just generally delighted that he was home. She sat on his lap, chattering in her half baby talk, kissed him, pulled his hair, and demanded a ride on his shoulders. It was while he was fulfilling this last request that Maud came in, her eyes crinkling with delight at seeing him.

"It is so good to see you home, my lord," she said.

"It is good to be home." He was surprised that she had called him my lord, something she usually only did in the presence of his father. But, he reminded himself, his father was dead and Geoffrey was the lord here now. He hoped that it did not mean that the people he cared about, people such as his stepmother, Maud, and Edmund, would now be formal and distant with him. At least Maud had not curtsied.

"I was so sorry to hear of your father's death," Maud was saying, "and your..." Her gaze rested on his wounded hand with a look of sympathy.

He set Tamsin down and she promptly sat on his foot, clinging to his leg. Flexing the scarred, stumped fingers, he said ruefully, "A bit more than splinters in the arse, is it not?"

"Oh, Geoffrey, if only I could mend that as I did the other," Maud said with a catch in her voice. At least it was back to Geoffrey now, no more my lord.

Her emotion embarrassed him. He turned away and picked up his daughter, tickling her neck with his nose and ruffling her hair. Tamsin giggled. "Were you a good girl while I was gone?" Geoffrey asked her.

Tamsin nodded vigorously, but Maud was shaking her head. "She was a terror," Maud said, but with a smile. "The entire time you were gone, all I heard was 'Where is my Da?' Every time she heard anything that remotely sounded like an approaching horse, she would fly to the hall like a little streak of lightning. And when it was not you that came in, there were storms, to be certain."

"Tantrums? From my darling little Tamsin?" Geoffrey asked disbelievingly, holding Tamsin away from him so that he could see her face. She looked guilty, then smiled pertly and hugged his neck. He could not be angry with her when she cuddled him like that, and he suspected that she was perfectly aware of it, even as young as she was. He was surprised though, that gentle Milesenda's daughter could ever be a terror. Looking so much like a smaller version of her dead mother, at least in Geoffrey's eyes, he had always assumed she would be like Milesenda in character as well; sweet, biddable, soft-spoken. A terror, Maud said? That sounded more like a heritage from Geoffrey than from Milesenda.

He held Tamsin tight and stroked her hair. He was so glad to be home, so glad that his wound, though hideous in his mind, did not prevent him from holding his daughter, that she did not object to him touching her or hugging her in spite of it, that he could not have been angry at her even if she had tried to set fire to the castle.

But it would not do to let his daughter realize how she ruled his world. He had to establish his fatherly authority. "Now that I am home," Geoffrey said to his daughter, "I shall expect you to behave as a proper young lady." Tamsin started at the stern tone to her father's voice, and looked at his face with trepidation. But when he smiled and hugged her again, she cuddled lovingly against his shoulder. Over Tamsin's head, Geoffrey and Maud exchanged looks.

"You spoil her, my lord," Maud said.

"I know," he admitted. His smile faded. "How can I not?" he asked, and Maud knew he was thinking of Tamsin's mother.

"Oh, Geoffrey, I almost forgot," Maud exclaimed, "Edmund is downstairs, wishing to speak with you if you have a minute."

Geoffrey nodded, and placing Tamsin in Maud's arms with admonishments to behave herself, walked slowly down the stairs to see his friend.

He had barely had the opportunity to nod a greeting to Edmund when he had returned yesterday, but now he found himself hesitating on the steps before seeking his friend out. How would Edmund react, he wondered, to the sight of Geoffrey's disfigured hand? Would he be horrified, disgusted, feel that Geoffrey was somehow now less than a man?

With that thought, Geoffrey stopped and sat down on the step halfway down to the hall, pondering what he would do if Edmund reacted with aversion to his wound. Geoffrey had, since Milesenda's death, expended considerable effort in hiding his feelings behind a mask of stone, in contrast to the frank openness his face had always exhibited before. But he had serious doubts as to whether he could keep that stone mask firmly in place if Edmund, his best friend and brother in mischief since they had been five years old, rejected his friendship now.

He was being silly, he finally told himself. There was no reason for him to think Edmund would rebuff him over the sight of a maimed hand, ugly though it was. As boys, Edmund had taught Geoffrey to speak English, and Geoffrey had taught Edmund to ride. They had played, fought, swum and hunted together for almost fifteen years, binding up each other's hurts and conspiring together, with varying degrees of success, to keep their fathers ignorant of their numerous misdeeds. That kind of camaraderie went deeper than physical deformities. At least Geoffrey hoped so.

Keeping that sentiment in mind, Geoffrey pushed himself off the stairs and clattered down to the hall.

No sign of Edmund there, so he strode over to the small office in which his father had conducted the business of the estate. Pushing open the door, he saw Edmund sitting on the bench against the wall, the same bench on which Geoffrey had withstood many a tirade from his father, in anticipation of more physical punishments to come.

Edmund jumped up when Geoffrey came in, and bowed. "My lord," he murmured respectfully.

"Oh, Christ, Edmund, not you, too," Geoffrey muttered. Then he saw the glitter in Edmund's green eyes, a mischievous gleam that belied his respectful posture. Edmund lunged, and in a moment the two young men were pounding each other's backs in greeting.

"God's feet, Geoffrey, but it is good to see you home safe and whole," Edmund exclaimed.

Geoffrey stepped away slightly from Edmund. "Safe, perhaps, but not quite whole," he replied, and he laid his left hand out flat on the table.

Edmund's breath whistled between his teeth at the sight. "Sweet Mother of God, how awful!"

Geoffrey's jaw stiffened, but he left the hand splayed out on the table, resisting the impulse to snatch it back and hide it from view. The flesh which had been sealed together by the hot blade was still pink and angry-looking, with ridged scars he would bear for the rest of his life. The two amputated fingers were merely useless stumps, although he could bend the middle finger a little, not that he could do much else with it. He refused to look at Edmund's face, not wanting to see his look of horrified pity.

Edmund peered over his shoulder, surveying the damage. "Well, Geoffrey, are you going to tell me what happened, or are you going to stand there like a fool all day?"

He glanced at his friend's face then, relieved at what he saw there. Horror, yes, at what had happened to Geoffrey, but not pity, nor loathing, just his usual frank curiosity and brotherly concern. Geoffrey hadn't been aware that his body had tensed, but he relaxed now, and sat on the table, swinging his legs under it.

"Not all of the French soldiery ran screaming for their mothers at the sight of me," he said to Edmund, "and one of those who remained behind had an axe."

Edmund winced. "Did it hurt?" he asked.

"Hurt? Of course it hurt, you red-haired oaf. My cousins filled me with enough wine to float an ox, but still, when the barber cauterized it," he hesitated, unable to find words to describe the pain he had felt. "Yes, Edmund, it hurt. It still does, sometimes, but I imagine I shall learn to endure it. My cousin Robert probably wishes he had never met me, for he bore the brunt of the effect of so much wine. God, it was awful stuff." He smiled grimly at the memory of Robert, trying hastily and in vain to clean Geoffrey's vomit from his boots with leaves he plucked from a tree just before their audience with King William. But there was more that had happened in Normandy than merely Geoffrey's wound, and Edmund knew it.

"Your father...," the redhead began, "My Lord de Graville..."

Geoffrey pointed to his throat, pressing his finger to the hollow where his life's blood pulsed strong and steady. "An arrow aimed at the king," he said briefly. "It was quick, I doubt he suffered." He let his gaze rest briefly on the chair behind the table that his father had always sat in. His voice lowered. "He did not have the opportunity to see me knighted."

"You have been knighted?" Edmund asked in surprise. "But I thought you said not until you were twenty-one years of age?"

"Exceptions are made on the battlefield," Geoffrey explained. "I wonder if Father would have been proud to know that the King did the job himself." He rubbed his left hand absently with the right, tracing the scars and the stubbed fingers, but looked up when he felt Edmund's hand on his shoulder.

"Of course he would have been proud," Edmund said, and Geoffrey tried to believe him. But there was more on Edmund's mind. "Geoffrey, while you were gone... My father..."

Geoffrey suddenly realized that he had not seen Dunstan yesterday in the hall. "Where is your father? I shall need his assistance with..." He waved his hand. "With everything."

"My father is dead, also."

Geoffrey was astounded, and he stared at his friend; saw the sadness that now filled Edmund's eyes. "What happened?" he exclaimed.

"It was a week after you left. We were walking along the paddock fence. Everything seemed normal, he was not ill at all. But I noticed that he was no longer beside me, so I stopped and turned to see what he was doing. He was standing as still as stone, and his face had gone white." Edmund turned pale himself as he remembered, the freckles standing out starkly against his fair skin. "He looked at me and opened his mouth as if to say something, but no sound came out. Then he put his hand to his head, and his eyes rolled up, and he fell in his tracks. By the time I reached him, he was dead. It happened so fast..." Edmund's voice trailed off, and this time it was Geoffrey who put a comforting hand on his friend's shoulder.

"Both of our fathers...? Geoffrey mused. "Dead at almost the same time. What shall we do, Edmund?"

Edmund drew a deep breath. "You have been trained to be a knight," Edmund replied, "and a baron, like your father before you. You know that my father had been training me as well, to follow him as bailiff. We shall now have to put that training to its test."

Geoffrey nodded. "But I do not feel like a baron," he admitted, "although the king has confirmed my inheritance. I fear that whenever I hear someone say, Baron de Graville, I look around, thinking he is behind me. Silly, is it not?"

He looked at the chair standing behind the table, the chair his father had used. While not as ornate as Raymond's other chair in the great hall, it was still undeniably the seat of authority. With a strength-gathering sigh, he walked slowly around the table and with only a slight hesitation, sat down, straightened his back, and looked at Edmund expectantly.

For the second time, Edmund bowed. "I await your pleasure, my lord," he said formally.

Geoffrey tried to assume a dignified demeanor. "My pleasure," he said, "is that you continue to call me Geoffrey. I do not care for this, yes, my lord, no, my lord. Perhaps for appearance's sake, it will be necessary in public, but otherwise, I command you to address me by my name. Is that understood?" He drew his brows together in what he hoped was a lordly scowl.

"Your wish is my command, Geoffrey," Edmund replied with a small grin.

Geoffrey rolled his eyes. "Weeping Jesus. Do you think the world is safe, with us two on our own now?"

"No," Edmund replied simply.

15

The view of the valley seen from Belvoir's battlements had always given Geoffrey a supreme satisfaction, a sense of belonging; eliciting a fierce attachment almost savage in its grip on his soul. And yet, as he stood and looked out over the fields, woods and village, it also had a calming effect that gave him peace, as long as he did not dwell on that edge of Lydford village where Milesenda's cottage was.

He had always loved coming up here, despite the fact that as a boy he had almost fallen to his death from this spot. The bloodstain from his head wound was still there, though worn to a faint brown spot by sun and wind. He put a finger there, not quite touching it.

The small spot was a part of him, a physical portion of his being that had become a physical portion of Belvoir Castle. As he looked at the bloodstain and then out over the fields, he touched the tiny scar the incident had left, and reflected how Belvoir was a part of him, not just his home but a real physical part of his body, and of his soul. His place in the world.

Today he stood there, watchful as a guard, looking out on a scene he had viewed many times; but now it was different. The scenery was the same; nothing had changed in the few months since he had been gone, but he was different.

Different physically, that was obvious. He was quite alone at the moment, so he removed his leather gloves, letting them fall to the floor, and flexed the remains of his left hand, stretching out the surviving fingers, then curling them into the partial fist which was all that he could manage now. Alyssa, who had considerable skill as a healer, had advised him to exercise the hand as much as possible, not to hide it away which might cause it to stiffen. Not that the maimed stump was good for much, he thought bitterly. Still, he tried to follow his stepmother's advice for the sake of his respect for her if nothing else.

Not only was he different physically, but emotionally as well. No longer could he afford to be the callow, indifferent youth, tempting though that might be.

He was a knight now, though not under exactly the circumstances he had envisioned during his childhood and youthful training. Had he been knighted in peacetime, the ceremony would have taken place on the first Pentecost after his twenty-first birthday. He would have spent the previous night fasting, in vigil in the chapel, with his very own shiny suit of armor and a brand-new sword crafted just for him laid out on the altar. At sunrise, he would make his confession, hear Mass and take communion. Father Mathieu would have blessed Geoffrey's new sword, that it might defend the church. Geoffrey would have then bathed thoroughly, after which an elaborate knighting ritual would have been performed in the presence of all at Belvoir. He would be dressed in a long white tunic, over which would be placed a red garment with long sleeves and a hood, to indicate his readiness to shed his blood in the service of God. His raiment would be completed with a black cloak, to remind him of the death all must meet. A lock of his hair would be cut off, to symbolize the sacrificing of oneself in devotion to God.

Then, with great solemnity, he would have knelt before his father, to give homage and swear fealty with his most solemn oath, while placing his hands between those of his lord. Raymond would charge him to be brave, ready and loyal; and would remind him of the precepts of a knight's honor, to never consent to treason or false judgment, to honor all women and help them in their need, to hear Mass every day if possible, to fast on Fridays in remembrance of the sufferings of Christ. The actual moment of his knighting would occur as Raymond, as Geoffrey's lord and father, presented him with a pair of golden spurs, the symbol of knighthood, followed by the accolade, with his sword tapping the new knight's shoulders. It would be the last blow he need suffer without retaliation.

The ceremony would have been followed by a celebratory feast in Geoffrey's honor, during which his horse would be brought to wait outside. Geoffrey would have been expected to leap into the saddle without touching the stirrups and show off his skill and prowess as a horseman and potential warrior with a charge at the quintain. It would have been a glorious day.

However, in the contrary way of life, his knighthood had not been conferred in the way he had planned. Instead, it had been awarded in a tent on a battlefield, with Geoffrey in shock from the death of his father and his own wounds, and the blood of battle still on him. But in spite of the haste and simplicity of the ceremony, Geoffrey still felt the pride and obligations of his knighthood, and would not neglect its ideals - to obey the commands of his lord and the gentle requests of his lady, to be brave and loyal, to be faithful to his king, defend the Christian faith and to protect widows and orphans, the old and the weak. He would be a man of honor.

Just as pressing was the physical changes warfare had wrought upon his body was the change in his status, now that his father was dead. Not only was he a knight; he was also a baron.

Baron de Graville. The title still conjured up images of Raymond in Geoffrey's eyes, dark, bearded, stern, hard, negative, unfair.

You are the one who is unfair, an inner voice chided, touching him from that newly mature part of his soul. *You judge your father too harshly.* Now that Raymond was no longer there for Geoffrey to butt heads against, he could look at his father in a more neutral light. Geoffrey had been too busy being stubborn to realize that it was their very similarities which had kept father and son at odds. Raymond had not always been stern and negative. There were times, Geoffrey realized with newfound clarity, when his father had been just as human and considerate as the next person. Until now, Geoffrey had ignored such instances, but now as he thought about it he recalled moments when his father had smiled and laughed, especially when Alyssa was present. In his selfish youth, Geoffrey had believed his father's sole purpose in life had been to make Geoffrey's life miserable. But of course that was not true. Stern and serious as Raymond had been, he had in truth only the best interests of his family and estate at heart. Geoffrey realized that now, now when it was too late.

A guard passed on the walkway, bowing briefly to Geoffrey as he continued on his rounds. Geoffrey responded with a nod, hiding his left hand behind his back, and looked out between the merlons of the parapet, as he considered his new responsibilities.

All that he saw was his now, the castle, village, fields and woods, as far as his eye beheld. It should not be a surprise to him; he had of course always known he was heir to Belvoir, but it was one thing to know it in his mind, and quite another to experience it.

The people here were his people now, depending on him for protection should war ever come to Devon, for solutions should the crops be bad or the livestock fall into decline, for justice when injustice threatened. It was an awesome responsibility, the care of not only his family, but the rest of Lydford as well. He had been training for this task for all of his life, but now that the time had come to shoulder the responsibility, he was still daunted by it.

But it was bearable, doable, because Geoffrey loved this place as if it were constructed out of pieces of his own heart. Every stone in Belvoir's walls, every field being harvested, every horse in the stable and sheep in the fold was a part of him. The fields here were the greenest in England in his estimations. He would never need to seek greener ones since they did not exist. He realized anew his love for the land, for the earthy smell of the soil, the simple satisfaction of seeing growing things.

And the sentient inhabitants of his domain, his people, were an even more important part of him. Of course he loved his little daughter with every fiber of his being, with more love than he could ever articulate, and his brother, stepmother and the new little brother or sister he would soon have were more precious to him than his own life. In addition, there were now all of the inhabitants of Lydford who were now his tenants. To Raymond perhaps they had been mere tenants, but Geoffrey had grown up among these people, had known them, as they had known him, most of his life. They were a part of him as well.

He might not be able to tell them just how important they were to him; the taciturn nature he had assumed after Milesenda's death was not easily shed. In fact, he found it even more difficult to communicate directly with people considering his newly maimed hand, which would surely revolt them. But he did care, and he would do everything in his power to assure the well-being of those in his demesne.

Shielding his eyes against the afternoon sun, he could see a group of village men harvesting in the barley fields, scythes glinting with every rhythmic rise and fall. He even thought he could see Edmund's red head in the group. Geoffrey could not stay up here cogitating all afternoon. His responsibilities as lord of Belvoir and father of Tamsin did not allow for excessive lingering merely to admire the view. Raymond de Graville had worked hard to establish Belvoir, creating a fine, efficient and lucrative estate where previously had existed a run-down fief virtually ignored by its previous lord. Before Raymond's time, the people of Lydford had been on the verge of starvation and neglect, now, under the de Gravilles, they prospered. Geoffrey de Graville would work just as hard as his father had, to maintain and improve Belvoir.

The estate beckoned, and Tamsin would be awake from her nap soon. He turned and stepped towards the doorway, but with every intention of returning, when time and duties permitted, to this treasured place.

16

It was a completely new life to which Geoffrey attempted to adjust himself that fall and winter, both as the lord of his estate, and with his disabled hand.

Edmund now took over his father's duties as bailiff, just as Geoffrey was now shouldering those of his own father. As boys the two of them had ridden out together looking for trouble, and usually finding it, but now they found themselves in more serious pursuits. There was the harvest to oversee, allotments of grain to decide upon for the tenant farmers and next spring's planting, rents to be collected, disputes to be settled. Michaelmas had passed a week before Geoffrey's return from Normandy, bringing in a new fiscal year. Father Mathieu had totaled up the estate accounts for Geoffrey's approval, as the villagers opened the hedges to allow the cattle to enter the harvested fields and graze on the stubble. It was a busy time for everyone at Belvoir.

It was customary for the lord to give a harvest supper to celebrate the completion of the harvest and Geoffrey took this as one of his first responsibilities as lord of Belvoir. In Raymond's time he had left the organizing to Dunstan and the celebrating to the peasants. But Geoffrey preferred to get involved with this event himself and attended with Tamsin in his arms. He wanted to get to know his tenants.

The villagers and servants were a bit in awe of Geoffrey, now that he had returned a blooded warrior. Although he tried not to show it, Geoffrey many times felt awkward in his role as their lord. He could no longer ignore the world as he had done after Milesenda's death. These people were his tenants and his responsibility, and he wondered what they thought of him. As a boy, he had been familiar and friendly with them all, and many of them had not hesitated to call him by his Christian name despite the fact that he was the lord's son. But now Geoffrey was the lord. He was Baron de Graville, and the people were reticent in his presence. For example, the young man who was now bowing respectfully as Geoffrey rode through the village. Years ago, when they were young, he had once knocked Geoffrey down and blacked his eye in some childish brawl, and Geoffrey had repaid him in kind. But that had been a long time ago, before the loss of Milesenda had destroyed his youth, and the loss of his father had thrust him into adult responsibilities.

He saw Edmund at the river's edge watering his horse, so Geoffrey walked his own mount over to where his friend was and swung down as well. They had been there only a minute when Geoffrey heard something.

"Do you hear that?" he asked Edmund, who shook his head. "It sounds like a child crying." His fatherly instinct aroused, Geoffrey handed Edmund his horse's reins and searched through the tall grass along the river's shore until he located the source of the sound, which was indeed a crying child. A little boy less than a year old sat on the ground in a grubby smock, sucking his fingers. Geoffrey picked the child up and carried him back to where Edmund waited, and the little boy's cries subsided to whimpers as Geoffrey bounced him on his hip.

"Look what I have found," he said, and then the child's mother, a peasant woman from the village, scurried towards them in search of her wayward infant. She stopped and stared, and then curtsied, when she saw who was holding her child.

"Does this young man belong to you?" Geoffrey asked.

"Yes, my lord," the woman said hastily. "My pardon, my lord. I am sorry the child bothered you. I but turned my back for a moment and he crawled away." She reached for the child but Geoffrey kept him in the crook of his arm and chucked him under the chin.

"You must watch them every minute," Geoffrey agreed, ignoring Edmund who was snickering on the other side of his horse. "A fine boy you have here, but he does not appear to be very happy at this moment." The child was still whimpering and sucking his fingers.

"His teeth are coming in, my lord," the mother explained.

"Ah," Geoffrey replied knowledgeably. "It is a most unpleasant experience for the child, and the parents as well."

From the other side of his horse, Edmund muttered, "Mother of God, do not let him get started. Show the man a child, and he turns into butter." The child's mother did not hear what Edmund said, but Geoffrey did. He ignored his friend, and leaned towards the woman, speaking confidentially, one parent to another.

"If you put a drop of wine on your finger and rub it on the child's gums, it will soothe him and give you some respite from his plainting. But not too much, or it will make him sick," he warned, recalling his own experience with Tamsin.

The peasant woman was staring at Geoffrey in astonishment, not quite believing her eyes or ears that Lord de Graville was standing in front of her casually holding her baby and exchanging advice concerning the raising of children. She stammered quickly, "Yes, my lord, I will do that." But Geoffrey glanced at her and realized from the look of her worn gown that her family most likely did not have the means to purchase wine. It was also obvious the young boy he now held would have a new brother or sister before long.

He handed the boy back to his mother and asked, "Do you have other children besides this one?"

"Yes, my lord. I have born eight, with five still living." He saw her hand rest briefly on the bulging front of her gown, and she did not need to add that number nine was soon to be born. He would wager that the whole family lived in one room.

"How old is your eldest boy?"

"Seven, my lord."

Geoffrey pondered for the briefest of moments, then said, "I am in need of another boy to help in my stables. Is your lad a good worker?"

The woman nodded, looking confused. "If you are willing then, and the boy does not mind hard work, another pair of hands would be of great help. He would have to sleep in the loft with the other boys, but it is not far from the village, and those stableboys who are diligent are allowed the use of a pony when their duties permit them to come home for a visit. Do you think your boy would agree to such an arrangement?" Geoffrey knew that removing one child from the family's crowded home would probably not make much of a difference, but the money the boy earned would hopefully help a great deal.

The woman curtsied again, and exclaimed, "Oh, yes, my lord, I am sure of it. Thank you, my lord, we are grateful."

"Very well, then, to seal the agreement, you must take this as an advance on the boy's first wages," and he took the wineskin that had been hanging on his saddle and handed it to her. "For the teething child, and for the parents as well."

"Oh, my lord, I could not possibly accept," she said breathlessly, but Geoffrey insisted on pressing the wineskin into her hands.

"You must, or I shall be insulted."

"Yes, my lord!" The woman looked suspiciously as if she were about to kiss his hand, and if she curtsied one more time he was afraid she might drop her baby, either the squirming toddler in her arms, or the unborn child squirming in her belly. He formed his face into what he hoped was a lordly expression, and said, "Your boy can come to the stable at the castle tomorrow to begin his duties. What is his name?"

"Ulric, my lord."

"Very well, tell Ulric he should report to Walter, the stable master."

"Yes, my lord. Thank you again." The woman hurried away with her child, and then Geoffrey remembered Edmund watching him with amusement.

"Remind me to tell Walter he needs another stable hand," he said, helping himself to a swig from Edmund's wineskin.

Edmund chuckled. "I believe you have made a friend for life, Geoffrey," he quipped, looking after the peasant woman hurrying home.

Geoffrey swung back into his saddle. "I do what I can," he said. "My father constantly impressed on me that it would be my responsibility to see to the welfare of these people," he waved his hand in a gesture to encompass the whole village, "and I am beginning to understand what he meant. These people, this estate, they depend on me; and I cannot allow any to suffer when it is within my power to improve their lot." It was uncharacteristic for Geoffrey, since Milesenda's death, to speak of things close to his heart, but it felt good to do so, to let what he felt inside come out into the light rather than being kept bottled up inside him until he felt sometimes as if he might burst from the fullness of it all.

Edmund mounted his horse and smiled at Geoffrey. "You had best be careful, my friend," he said.

"Careful of what?"

"I know how hard you strive to hide it, Geoffrey, but if you're not careful, everyone is going to know how much you care." He waved his hand in the same manner Geoffrey had done, indicating the village and the castle, and he wasn't offended when Geoffrey silently turned away and nudged his horse up the hill. Geoffrey did not turn away that quickly; Edmund had still seen the brief but real smile that had crossed Lord de Graville's face at his friend's observation.

*****

In addition to his demesne, there were the stables and horses to oversee. Although Walter was a skilled and competent marshal, it was ultimately Geoffrey's responsibility to decide which horses were to be bred, which to be trained as destriers and which unsuspecting yearling colts were to be gelded. Any horse which was to be trained to carry a knight into battle had to be of just the right quality. A stallion strong enough to carry a fully armed man, brave enough to bear wounds, fierce enough to take an aggressive part in the fight, loyal enough to stay with his rider should he be knocked from the saddle, was not easily found, and required meticulous training.

Geoffrey did not merely stand back and supervise when it came to working with the horses. As much as his maimed hand permitted, he worked alongside Walter and the grooms, even in the unpleasant task of cleaning stalls and the even more unpleasant task of the gelding process.

There were also his fighting skills to be tested, to determine what limits his missing fingers would place on his abilities as a knight.

Archery had to be forsaken completely. With only the thumb and first finger of his left hand whole, he could not hold the bow steady enough to aim the arrow. In addition, he felt self-conscious and vulnerable with his left hand held out in front of him for all to see. Though he had been an excellent hunter with the bow beforehand, he was now forced to hang up his bow and quiver of arrows forever, unless Stephen someday cared to make use of them. A knight did not carry a bow in battle; arrows being used primarily by foot soldiers while the mounted knights fought with sword and lance. But he did miss the hunting. Hanging on the wall of the great hall was a set of antlers from the first deer he had downed; it would be his last as well. He recalled with clarity the thrill that had coursed through him, when at age twelve his father had deemed him old enough to hunt with the men. The buck had been a regal animal with an impressive rack. It had been almost a shame to kill it. But he had dropped it with one well-aimed shot, and even his father had been impressed. Raymond and the other men in the hunting party had insisted that Geoffrey gut the animal himself, the responsibility of the man who makes the kill. But first they had instructed that he cup his hands under the flow of blood which appeared under his knife with the first thrust, and following the cheers and encouragement of the other hunters, Geoffrey brought his hands to his mouth and drank the still-warm blood of the deer he had just killed. Raymond had stood back a bit as his son swallowed the deer's blood and gagged at its pungent, coppery taste. As the lord of Belvoir and the cousin of a priest, Raymond had known he should not encourage this pagan ritual of the first kill, but despite his lack of participation, a small smile had played about his lips as he remembered his own first hunt back in Normandy.

But those were memories which Geoffrey was forced to push to the back of his mind. The deer's antlers hanging over the fireplace would remain a solitary decoration.

His sword arm was of course unaffected, for which he was grateful. And since his shield was held by straps attached to the inside that slipped over his left forearm, rather than held by the hand, his defense was not diminished. If he were called into battle again, he would still be able to fight effectively.

He had already discovered that it was more difficult to handle his horse's reins with his bad hand, so he made up for that deficiency by training the horses he rode to respond even more to the pressure of his legs. Any knight's horse should understand when to turn, canter and halt by the pressure of his rider's legs rather than the touch of the reins. However this was more difficult for Geoffrey when wearing the heavy mail chausses that had covered his legs in the battle in Normandy, so he decided that he would leave them off if he was called into battle in the future. It would be dangerous to leave his legs unprotected in that manner, but it would be just as dangerous not to have total control over his mount.

The possibility of having to put his skills to the test once again loomed like storm clouds, far away yet impossible to ignore, as messages arrived in Lydford from Lord de Meules in Exeter. Raymond's friend had always kept them apprised of news as he heard it, so that they would still be informed in their more remote home. He continued to do the same for Geoffrey, and it was in that manner that the new Baron de Graville heard of the death of King William.

Only a few weeks after Geoffrey had been wounded, William had re-captured Mantes, and had ordered the town burned in retaliation for its capitulation to the French. Apparently the French forces had taken the town not so much by military conquest as by persuasion. When he heard of the destruction of Mantes, Geoffrey was almost glad he had been wounded. It would have sickened him to have had to participate in such cruelty.

While riding through the smoldering ruins, William had been thrown against the high pommel of his horse when the animal had jumped in fright of a pile of flaming embers that had fallen at its feet. Geoffrey himself had received many a bruised abdomen against his own pommel, but William's injury was much more serious. He was ruptured internally, and his nobles had him carried to Rouen where he lay in agony for weeks until he died.

On his deathbed, William had ordered his dominions to be divided after he was gone, with the dukedom of Normandy to go to his elder son Robert, and the crown of England to his second and favorite son, also named William and called Rufus for his flaming red hair and ruddy complexion. It was a wise decision, for though good-natured, Robert was basically an incompetent ruler, while William Rufus, though a hard and severe man, was nonetheless of the stuff of which Kings were made. It was rumored that the feckless Robert felt himself to be cheated of what he considered his rightful inheritance.

Those nobles with lands on both sides of the Channel now found themselves with divided loyalties and conflicting interests, being obligated to pay homage to two masters. Many felt themselves more comfortable with charming, easy-going Robert than with his unpleasant younger brother. The Baron de Graville, whose only estate was in England, suffered from no such conflict. He was the King's man. He had been knighted at the hand of King William, and if it was that king's wish that William Rufus should rule England after him, there was no hesitation in Geoffrey's support for his new king.

Geoffrey also watched his stepmother, and he worried. As winter descended on Lydford and Alyssa's pregnancy advanced, Geoffrey could not help but remember Milesenda and her death in childbirth. As soon as he returned to the castle at the end of the day, he sought his stepmother out to inquire after her health, hovering over her in such a mother-hen manner that she would have found it funny if he had not been so deadly serious. Edmund and Alyssa both tried their best to ease Geoffrey's mind. Though he had become quite skilled in the last few years in keeping his expression closed and unrevealing, his friend and his stepmother, who knew him best, could perceive the anxiety he felt.

Alyssa tried to be patient with her stepson, but even her considerable patience had its limits.

One evening a sharp kick from the baby's foot caught her unawares at dinner, and she gasped slightly, putting her hand to her side.

Geoffrey jumped up, panic-stricken, knocking over his chair in the process. "Mother!" he exclaimed. "What is it? Is it the baby?" Ignoring the servant's startled stares, he strode to Alyssa's chair, his face pale and his eyes so dark with fear they looked almost purple.

"It is nothing," Alyssa insisted. "I am quite well." She looked up at Geoffrey and smiled. "It was only a kick that startled me, nothing out of the ordinary I assure you."

Geoffrey was completely unconvinced. "I am sending for Emma," he declared.

"There is no need yet for Emma's services," Alyssa stated. "It was only a kick."

"I'll carry you upstairs."

In exasperation, Alyssa looked around and caught Edmund's eye. "Get him out of here," she insisted. "I cannot even twitch without him having a fit."

His stepmother's rare display of annoyance only further convinced Geoffrey that she was not well, but he allowed Edmund to tow him out to the stable. A glance back at Alyssa as Edmund pulled him out the door showed Geoffrey that she was calmly finishing her meal, as salubrious as she had claimed to be.

Edmund had chosen the stable despite the cold wind that sliced through them as they crossed the bailey, because he knew if any place in the world could calm Geoffrey, it would be among the horses. Warm equine bodies and stout construction made the stable an oasis of warmth in the December cold. Geoffrey paced up and down the center of the building in impotent frustration, as Edmund leaned against the wall with his arms crossed over his chest, watching. After a few minutes of this, Geoffrey stopped suddenly and punched the wall with a force that made several horses jump and snort nervously.

He sank down to sit in the straw, rubbing his bruised knuckles, and leaned his elbows on his knees. Looking up at Edmund, he asked, "Am I being a fool?"

"Yes." Edmund had a gift for succinct observation.

"God," Geoffrey muttered, pushing his hand through his hair. "Weeping, bleeding Jesus on the cross." He glanced around to make sure neither Father Mathieu nor his brother Stephen was nearby to scold him for his language. "Edmund, what am I going to do? Mother of God, what if she dies? I could not bear it. She is my mother, for Christ's sake!"

"No, Geoffrey, she is not your mother," Edmund reminded him.

Geoffrey sent his friend an angry glare, annoyed that he quibbled over details. Edmund, as usual, refused to be intimidated.

"Do you want my opinion?" Edmund asked. Geoffrey nodded. "You are only making it worse. Yes, worse," Edmund repeated when Geoffrey glared at him. "You are afraid your stepmother may die in childbirth. You are worried for her. Do you not think that she, and I, and everyone else here, did not worry about you and your father when you left to go to war? We did, Lady Alyssa especially, but she was strong and did not show it. Her worst fears were realized when your father was killed, and still she is strong, though she is bearing a child who will never know its father."

"Just as Tamsin will never know her mother," Geoffrey murmured.

"I am sure that your stepmother is just as fearful and uncertain as you are, perhaps even more so," Edmund continued. "If you would make it easier for her, be her strength, even as she was your strength when Milesenda died." Edmund was silent for a moment, because he knew it still hurt Geoffrey to speak of Milesenda. Then he said, "There is no point in worrying over something you cannot predict. Carys says that your stepmother is healthy and strong, and we can only wait until her time comes."

Geoffrey managed a small smile. "Carys says? I thought it was her mother who was the midwife." He knew that Carys and Edmund had become quite close, and that their relationship went deeper than friendship.

Edmund blushed, his face going almost as red as his hair. But he smiled back. "Carys is learning the midwife's craft from her mother," he said with dignity.

Geoffrey stood up and brushed the straw from his legs. "And learning other things from you, no doubt," he teased. Edmund merely shrugged, as Geoffrey straightened his shoulders. "Very well," Geoffrey said, reaching into the nearest stall to give the horse there a friendly scratch on the nose, "I shall take your advice and do my best to be a strength and not a burden to my stepmother. Do you suppose, if I promise to be very good, she will allow me to return and finish my dinner?" Edmund shrugged his shoulders again, in a gesture that said he did not know. "I can be just as strong and as brave as my stepmother," Geoffrey said, as much to himself as to Edmund. "I am, after all, Baron de Graville."

Edmund grinned impishly and bowed. "Yes, my lord. No, my lord," he intoned, then scampered quickly out of the stable door before the blow Geoffrey aimed at his ear reached him.

Alyssa did indeed allow Geoffrey to return to his meal. She was annoyed with him, but she was not cruel by nature. Geoffrey kept to his word and did his best to keep his fears about his stepmother's pregnancy and coming childbirth to himself. He did continue to attempt to prevent her from doing anything strenuous, but he tried very hard not to hover over her or annoy her with his anxiety over the next several weeks. It was difficult, but he took his stepmother's calm strength as his example.

17

The twelve dreary days between Christmas and Epiphany were a fairly idle time at Belvoir. Geoffrey and Alyssa bestowed upon the servants their traditional Christmas perquisites of food, clothing, drink and firewood, but Geoffrey would not allow his extremely pregnant stepmother to stay on her feet for very long.

Snow was rare in Devon, but that January proved to be the exception. Large wet flakes clung to Geoffrey's hair and eyelashes as he entered the hall, and he stamped his feet, both to shake the snow from his boots and to try to force warmth back into them. He strode quickly to the fireplace, pulling off his gloves and holding his freezing hands towards the warmth. "I hate sheep," he said to no one in particular. "They are stupid, witless animals who have not the sense to stay in their folds where they may be fed and protected without needing to do a thing in return, but must go wandering about the countryside so that men with better things to do must go hunting them down in the cold and snow." His fingers (the ones he still had) were just beginning to thaw when he heard Edmund's voice behind him.

"Geoffrey." Geoffrey turned to look at his friend, who looked as if he had bad news to bear. Edmund cleared his throat. "Geoffrey, your step-mother..."

Geoffrey looked around and did not see Alyssa. Fear grabbed at his heart. "Where is she?" he whispered.

Edmund nodded towards the stairs. "She is in labor. But..." It was too late to finish his sentence; Geoffrey was already bounding toward the stairs, taking the steps three at a time.

"But you can't go up there!" Edmund called out, panting as he chased after Geoffrey, past the startled stares of the servants.

Heedless of Edmund's protests, Geoffrey made straight for the door to his stepmother's bedchamber, only to be stopped by Emma at the door.

"You cannot come in, my lord," she stated firmly, refusing to let him pass.

The door was stout and thick, but still Geoffrey could hear a moan even through the thick oak. It was not the pain-racked scream he had heard through Milesenda's door minutes before her death, but still, the sound filled him with an unreasonable fear. "Mother!" he called out desperately, trying again to dodge past Emma. But despite Geoffrey's considerable size, Emma matched him in determination.

"This is a woman's place," the midwife insisted. "You cannot come in." She planted herself even more firmly in front of the door, and even in his panic-stricken state, Geoffrey was too courteous to take advantage of his size and remove her by force.

He looked down at Emma, recalling the night she had sent Carys to fetch him to Milesenda's side, Carys practically dragging him from the hall despite her fear of his father's anger, because Milesenda had been dying. Were they trying to shield him from such an experience this time?

Emma caught the eye of Edmund, who had followed Geoffrey up the stairs. *Perhaps you can reason with him,* her look said. Edmund tugged at Geoffrey's arm. "Please go with Edmund, my lord," Emma pleaded. "I promise, we will send you word when there is something to tell." She put a comforting hand on his arm. "There is nothing to be concerned about at this point. Everything is fine."

Edmund pulled on Geoffrey's arm. "You heard her, Geoffrey," he coaxed. "Come downstairs and have some wine. Everything is fine."

With reluctance, Geoffrey allowed his friend to half drag him back down the stairs to the hall. Everything is fine, Emma had said, but the unspoken words hung in the air. So far.

He sprawled in a chair and Edmund thrust a cup of wine into his hand. Tossing down half the cup in one swallow, he sat clenching the cup so tightly that his fingers felt stiff when he finally let go.

He willed himself to stay calm, brave, strong. Lord, how he would have preferred to be fighting in a battle, using his sword against an enemy he could see, than to be sitting here in agonized suspense.

Finally he could stand it no longer, and stood up so suddenly that the cup he had set on the arm of his chair was knocked to the floor. The sound awoke Edmund, who had laid his head and arms on the table and fallen asleep. Edmund sat up now, blinking owlishly.

How long had he sat there, Geoffrey wondered, looking around him. The servants had all apparently gone to bed and the fire in the hearth was reduced to glowing embers. Still no word from upstairs to indicate how his stepmother was faring.

"I am going to the chapel," Geoffrey announced. Edmund rubbed his eyes and stood up as well, but Geoffrey shook his head. "Forgive me, Edmund, but I think I would rather be alone. Go to bed."

He didn't even bother to see if Edmund was going to take his advice or not as he strode across the hall and ducked through the doorway that led to the chapel. He groped automatically at the holy water font as he entered the small chapel, genuflected, then knelt on the cold flagstone floor, looking around desperately for inspiration and comfort.

Geoffrey had never been devout, much to the despair of Father Mathieu. He had probably spent more time sleeping in this chapel than attending to the state of his soul, and now he felt uncomfortable, unsure, out of his element. In what direction should he direct his prayers, and would they do any good? He had taken the name of the Lord in vain so many times that Father Mathieu was weary of repeatedly having to hear the same confession, and with little or no contrition on Geoffrey's part. Would the prayers of a sinner such as himself help his stepmother in her travail?

A prayer to St. Margaret, the patroness of women in childbirth, was half-formed on his lips, when his vision came to rest on the statue of the Blessed Virgin, gazing calmly, serenely from the niche in the semicircular apse at the end of the chapel. As a small boy he had thought it was a statue of his real mother, and although he had long since outgrown that notion, the maternal association still lingered in his heart. Now the woman who had replaced his long-dead mother needed the Virgin's intercedence more than Geoffrey ever had.

He clasped his hands in supplication, in his now habitual manner of the good right hand covering the maimed left, and gazed up at the Virgin Mother's serene face. Formal prayers escaped him, and he could only speak from the heart.

"Please, Mother," he begged, feeling himself beginning to tremble, "please... don't let her die. Please don't let her die!"

*****

A hand on his shoulder startled him, and he looked up into the face of Father Mathieu. The morning sun streamed through the window behind the priest's head, a cold light, but enough to make Geoffrey realize that he had knelt here, trance-like, all night.

"Mother!" he croaked in a panic, his throat dry.

"Lady Alyssa is fine," the priest said. "You have a sister. They are both alive and healthy."

"Thank God!" Geoffrey replied fervently. Then, "You are certain?" He was afraid to be relieved too soon.

"Yes, I am certain," Father Mathieu affirmed. "Go see for yourself. Lady Alyssa is asking for you." The priest's mouth curved in amusement. "She seemed to think you were concerned for her."

The stern mask behind which Geoffrey had attempted to hide his feelings was becoming difficult to maintain, and he forced himself not to blush at his cousin's teasing words. Then he felt even more embarrassed as he realized that his legs were so stiff from the cold of the chapel floor and the hours of kneeling in prayer, that they felt as if they had become one with the floor. He looked up at Father Mathieu.

"I believe I need your assistance, Father," he said ruefully.

Father Mathieu sighed. "I pray for your soul every day, Geoffrey," he said, but Geoffrey shook his head.

"I had something a bit more worldly in mind. Could you help me get up?"

*****

Geoffrey held his baby sister and looked down at her tiny face. He held her in his left arm with her head on his elbow, and touched her soft little face gently. At least this was one pleasure his maimed hand did not deny him.

Of his father's three children, it was ironic that this last, posthumous daughter was the one to resemble him the most. Her dark brown hair already showed the promise of turning curly like Raymond's, and Geoffrey could swear that he saw the same cool, haughty look in her dark eyes.

He looked at Alyssa, sitting in the bed watching him admire the baby. There were dark circles under her eyes and she looked weak and tired, but she was alive, and his heart sent up a silent prayer of thanks.

"Geoffrey," his stepmother said, "you are the only man I have ever known who felt so comfortable holding a baby. You are very adept at it. You should have more of your own."

Geoffrey ignored her hint. "Have you chosen a name for my sister?" he asked.

She nodded. "With your permission, my lord, I would like to name her Isabel."

He was surprised at the French name she had chosen, but it did seem vaguely familiar.

"Your father," her voice faltered briefly, "your father once told me it was his mother's name. Does it meet with your approval, my lord?"

He nodded, looking down again at baby Isabel, and Alyssa continued, "And would you consent to standing as her godfather?"

"Of course," he replied, "if that is your wish."

Alyssa looked down, studying her hands. Geoffrey turned towards the window, still holding the baby and making silly faces at her, which did not impress Isabel in the least. He was not prepared for his stepmother's next words.

"Geoffrey, have you given any thought to marrying again?"

He turned quickly and stared at her. She stared right back, refusing to be cowed by his scowl. It was on the tip of his tongue to refuse to discuss the subject, but he could not force out the rude words. She had done too much for him, meant too much to him, for him to be curt with her. Gently, he placed the baby in her cradle, the same cradle that Stephen and Tamsin had occupied, and pulled a stool up next to the bed. Sitting down, he took Alyssa's hand in his.

"Dearest mother," he said, and she smiled. "I know your intentions are well-meant, but I shall never marry again. Please try to understand. No one could ever be to me what Milesenda was," and he looked away for a moment, not wanting Alyssa to see his face as he faltered at the mention of Milesenda's name. "I can never forget how she died, giving birth to my child. I could not ask another woman to take that risk."

Alyssa reached out with her free hand and brushed a lock of hair away from her stepson's forehead. "Dearest Geoffrey," she said, forcing him to smile at the way she repeated the endearment he had used, "you are not to blame for Milesenda's death. You must not torture yourself by believing that it was in any way your fault. If a woman dies in childbed, it is by the will of God. It is a risk we take gladly. If we did not take that risk, mankind would cease to exist."

Geoffrey wondered if he should tell her how he had spent the night shivering in terror as she labored, how Father Mathieu practically had to pry his knees off of the chapel floor. He did not want to admit to her what a coward he had been while she had been bravely bringing her child into the world.

She was not his mother, not physically. But he had to admit that despite the childish resentment he had felt towards her when his father had married her, that he had eventually come to love her as he would have loved his real mother, had she lived. If a man could not admit his fears to his mother, then to whom?

"You may be willing to take those risks, Mother, but I am not brave enough."

She made a noise of disbelief. "Geoffrey, you and your father are the most courageous men I have ever known. Your father gave his life, and you risked yours as well, to protect our king. Do not tell me you are not brave."

He was unconvinced.

"Geoffrey, you need an heir."

"Stephen is my heir."

He was not prepared for the look of surprise he saw on her face. Why should his brother not inherit his estate after him?

"Then Stephen has not spoken to you?" she asked.

"I have not seen him today," he replied. "Why? What does he wish to speak to me about?"

She shook her head. "I think it would be best if he talked to you himself." The baby had begun to cry and Geoffrey released Alyssa's hand to pick Isabel up and place her in her mother's arms. He turned his back modestly as Alyssa opened her gown to nurse the baby. "Go find your brother," she said. "He has been waiting to speak with you."

✳ ✳ ✳ ✳ ✳

He found Stephen in the great hall with Father Mathieu. Mathieu was teaching the boy to read, and Stephen looked up with a smile at his brother's approach.

Reading was a skill that neither Geoffrey nor his father had ever bothered to cultivate, but Geoffrey was not ashamed of his illiteracy. King William himself did not read or write, and why should he? It was a skill used by priests and monks, and unnecessary for a knight. But Stephen had begged eloquently to learn, and Geoffrey could not deny his little brother his wish.

But the boy was not so little; he was eleven years old now, though not nearly as big as Geoffrey had been at that age. He had his mother's auburn hair and soft brown eyes, and the same look of quiet, calm strength that Alyssa had.

Stephen looked up at Father Mathieu who nodded and patted the boy on the shoulder. The priest bowed to Geoffrey and withdrew.

Geoffrey nodded back, still feeling uncomfortable in his new status as lord of the manor. He didn't like it when people bowed at him and called him my lord and he wished his father was alive to carry out the responsibilities that now rested on Geoffrey's shoulders. With a sigh of regret, he sat in the chair that had been Raymond's and accepted a cup of mead from the maidservant.

"Well, brother, have you met our sister yet?" he said to Stephen, who shook his head.

"I was waiting for you, Geoffrey, I mean, my lord."

"Your mother said you wished to speak to me of something important."

Stephen's face lit up with eagerness. "Oh, yes. Father Mathieu says I must have your permission. Please, Geoffrey," he begged, in his eagerness forgetting, to his brother's delight, to call Geoffrey my lord, "I wish to enter St. Nicholas Priory, to study for the priesthood. Please give me your permission, brother, for I want nothing more than to serve God."

Geoffrey's mind reeled. So this was the subject of importance his stepmother had sent him to discuss. How could Stephen wish to leave Belvoir, his inheritance?

Seeing the hesitation in Geoffrey's face, Stephen knelt down in front of him and clasped his hands in supplication. "I want this more than life," he said earnestly, and Geoffrey could see the conviction shining from his brother's face. He took a deep swallow from the cup in his hand before he spoke.

"But, Stephen, you are my heir…" he stopped as a single tear rolled down the boy's cheek. He felt like a cad for causing Stephen the pain of having his heart's desire denied. No, it would be cruel to be that selfish. "But if the priesthood is your desire, then of course you have my permission."

Stephen's face flooded with relief and joy, and the tears disappeared. He jumped to his feet and almost hugged his brother, but something in Geoffrey's face stopped him. "Thank you, my lord, thank you so much," he exclaimed joyfully.

"And when would you leave?" Geoffrey asked heavily, trying to keep the dismay from his voice.

"The next term begins just after Easter," Stephen replied. Obviously, the boy had thought this out, Geoffrey realized. It was no whim. He smiled to himself as he remembered all the times Stephen had indignantly elbowed him in the ribs when he had fallen asleep in the chapel. He should have realized then that his brother had the vocation for a religious life.

He reached out and put his hand on Stephen's shoulder. "You must promise me one thing," he said, trying to keep a light tone to his voice so that his brother would not notice how heavy his heart felt. Stephen nodded enthusiastically. "You must say some extra prayers for your reprobate brother, for I most certainly shall need all you can spare. Now go pay your respects to your mother and our new sister."

Stephen scampered off happily, throwing more words of thanks over his shoulder as he left. Geoffrey put his head in his hands. He was tired, tired to death. The past twenty-four hours had drained him. The sleepless, panic-stricken night spent in the chapel, the rush of relief at the safe delivery of his stepmother and sister, Stephen's revelations and the realization that his brother would not be his heir after all, combined to make him feel heavy and old.

He sensed someone near him and looked up at Father Mathieu. He narrowed his eyes at the priest. "Did you encourage him?" he asked accusingly.

Mathieu shook his head. "No, Geoffrey. Stephen has a true vocation. You will not be able to foist off your responsibilities on him." Geoffrey frowned but Mathieu continued, waving his hand to indicate their surroundings. "You are the lord here now. You have this castle, these lands to oversee, and a family of women and children to care for. Stephen will not give up his vocation, now that he has your blessing. If you should die, what will happen to them? Much as you would like to believe otherwise, your supposed marriage to that girl was not valid and your daughter is a bastard in the eyes of the church. Even if she were not, and were to inherit your estate, would you want her at the mercy of every unscrupulous, land-hungry knight in England and Normandy, who would abduct an heiress and force her to wed for her lands? Is that how you love your child? Or your sister? It is your duty to wed and father sons of your own, strong sons who will protect your heritage and your family when you cannot. You cannot ask your brother to do it for you."

Geoffrey had continued to frown at Father Mathieu while he spoke, not wanting to admit to the truth of his harsh words. Mathieu merely smiled and added, "I never saw any resemblance between you and your father until now. You have that same forbidding look Raymond had when he was displeased."

Geoffrey groaned. If he had developed the same mannerism as his father, then why did Stephen and Father Mathieu not cower like frightened children at the sight of his displeasure? He could think of no reply to what Mathieu had said to him about his responsibilities, because it was all true. He stood up, put down his cup, and walked away. "I have to piss," was all he said as he left the room.

*****

Geoffrey's last remark to Father Mathieu had been crude and rude, but it was also true. His bladder was full to bursting. Sleeping was not the only thing he had neglected last night. After leaving the privy, he went to the stable and saddled Storm. He was tired, but he also had much to think about and he knew he could not sleep just yet.

The stallion picked its way carefully over the frozen ground, the warm breath puffing from his nostrils like baby clouds seeking a mother. The snow had ceased. The air was calm but so cold it hurt to breathe, and the creak of his saddle, the leather stiff with cold, sounded loud as Geoffrey pulled his heavy cloak about himself, wrapped the reins around his left wrist and allowed himself to contemplate the future.

What would happen if he were to die, today or any time soon? It was always a distinct possibility. Geoffrey's father, though an experienced veteran, had fallen in battle and Geoffrey was not a foolish man. He knew that no one, including himself, was invincible and must enter any battle he fought in with the realization that it could be his last. What would befall the family he loved if he were not there to protect them?

The first person he thought of, of course, was his beloved daughter. His throat constricted at the thought of her being orphaned. He knew that in the event of his demise, Edmund would claim her, adopt her and raise her as his own. She was young enough that the transition from being the lord's daughter to the bailiff's daughter should not be difficult. Geoffrey desperately wished that he could make Tamsin his heiress, but he knew it was impossible. Although it was true that in England, unlike Normandy, females could inherit land in the absence of a male heir, Tamsin's illegitimacy precluded the possibility. Although Geoffrey considered himself to have been well and truly married to Milesenda, he was the only one who held that belief. As Father Mathieu had stated, Tamsin was a bastard in the eyes of the rest of the world. Though Geoffrey knew that Edmund would do all in his power to see Tamsin well cared for should the need arise, still, Belvoir was her rightful home until she married, even if it could not be her inheritance.

And Alyssa, his stepmother, what would happen to her if he died? She could of course return with her daughter to Warwickshire where her brother was now lord of Arden, since her father's death several years ago. There she and Isabel would live out their lives as poor relations, dependent on the charity of relatives. The chances of Isabel obtaining any type of significant dowry and therefore making a good marriage would be very slight. Not even a convent would take her penniless. *Is that how you love your sister?*

Stephen would soon be safe and happy at St. Nicholas Priory, but would be barred from inheriting Geoffrey's estate by the vows he would take when he entered the Priory in the spring. Geoffrey could not understand how any healthy male, even one as young as Stephen, could take a vow of celibacy. But the conviction and love he had seen shining in his brother's face had convinced Geoffrey that Stephen's devotion to the Church was just as strong, if less worldly, as Geoffrey's devotion to Milesenda had been. Though he did not agree with his brother's choice, Geoffrey had to accept it.

There was no doubt as to the legitimacy of his baby sister Isabel, but as Father Mathieu had reminded him, an unprotected young heiress was in constant danger. A girl's inheritance passed to her husband upon her marriage, and it was not unheard of for such girls to be abducted by those desiring their lands and being compelled to wed after having their virginity taken from them by force, and usually in the presence of witnesses so that there were no doubts. Even if Isabel were fortunate enough to escape such a fate, the king would most likely exercise his right to arrange for her to marry a man of his choosing, someone he wished to favor by granting him an heiress and her demesne, regardless of her wishes. No, it would be in Isabel's best interest not to be an heiress. When the time came, Geoffrey would hope that both his daughter and sister could wed with men they cared for, or not wed at all if that were their choice. He would not want either of them forced into anything. The responsibilities for the futures of the two little girls weighed heavily on him.

Briefly, he considered making his cousin Hugh his heir. Like Raymond had been, Hugh was a second son without hope of inheriting his father's lands. But he rejected the idea almost as soon as he thought of it. Such an arrangement would require the approval of the king, and with England and Normandy now under separate rule and in a state of wary tension, William Rufus would never consent to such a move. Besides, even if the king gave his consent, Geoffrey reflected, would he really want Hugh, a Norman even if he was his cousin, to take possession of his home, to take charge of the future of his small daughter, his sister and his stepmother? Though Geoffrey's brief acquaintance with his cousin had given him the impression that Hugh was a fair and honest man, the three females would represent merely a burden and expense to him, and a resentment for his wife. Hugh would not love and care for them as Geoffrey did.

The more Geoffrey thought about his cousin, the more unacceptable the idea of Hugh even being considered as his heir became to him. He put the thought from his mind, and would not consider it further.

That left only the inevitable solution, what everyone from the King to Father Mathieu, and even Alyssa, had urged him to do. To marry and father sons to preserve his legacy.

Everything in his heart and soul cried out against it. How could he call another woman wife, when Milesenda had been denied that title? Though he would like to have more children, how could he father them on someone else, when he and Milesenda had dreamed of having a large family? And most of all, how could he put another woman through what Milesenda had suffered? Although everyone had tried to convince him that her death was not his fault, still the fact remained that she had died giving birth to his child. As he had told his stepmother, he could not bring himself to force another woman to take that risk. It was no use whatsoever trying to convince him that she would have died even if someone other than Geoffrey had been the child's father.

His musings had brought him no answers, only a headache. Given his head, Storm had meandered about back towards the warmth of the stables, and when they arrived there, young Ulric, the newest and most diligent of the lads working in the stable, dashed up breathlessly to take the reins as Geoffrey swung down.

"Shall I rub him down for you, my lord?" the boy asked hopefully.

Geoffrey yawned and remembered that he had not slept at all last night. "Thank you, Ulric, I would appreciate that." The boy beamed proudly at the opportunity to care for his lord's own horse. He was such a cheerful, hardworking boy; so eager to please that Geoffrey could not help but smile at him, and for a moment, almost wish to trade places in life with him. Ulric's most pressing concerns were a full belly, a warm place to sleep and his master's approval, all of which he had. Geoffrey leaned down and ruffled Ulric's hair. "He likes to be scratched behind the ears," he added, and Storm, as if he understood what Geoffrey had said, moved his head up and down in a motion that did indeed look like a nod of affirmation.

"Yes, my lord!" Ulric exclaimed, and Geoffrey sought his bed confident in the knowledge that Storm would receive his fill of ear-scratching today.

18

It was a fine spring day when Geoffrey left Belvoir to escort his brother Stephen to Exeter for enrollment in St. Nicholas Priory. The sun shone, flowers bloomed, and birds sang. It was a time for beginnings, and Stephen was looking forward with happiness to the beginning of his clerical training.

Alyssa was now completely recovered from the birth of baby Isabel, although sometimes when she was not aware that Geoffrey was noticing, he saw her looking at the baby with such an expression of sadness that he knew she was remembering Raymond. It was a sadness Geoffrey could sympathize with. He felt it every time he looked at Tamsin. It was something of a revelation for Geoffrey to realize that his father and stepmother had truly loved each other, despite the difference in their ages and the fact that theirs had been an arranged marriage.

He suspected that Alyssa had been crying as she bade Stephen and Geoffrey farewell as they left for Exeter, but now, in the presence of the servants, she was outwardly her usual calm and dignified self. She kissed her son briefly in parting, but only her reddened eyes betrayed the more emotional good-byes they had exchanged in private. Geoffrey kissed his stepmother's cheek just before he mounted his horse, which startled her a little because he was usually much more reserved in the presence of others. He used the farewell as an opportunity to whisper in her ear, "I swear to you, Mother, I will make them promise to allow Stephen to come home to visit." He smiled at her and she could not help but smile back as her two sons rode away.

Tamsin had sniffled and pouted at the prospect of her father leaving again, but this parting was not nearly as traumatic as it had been the last time. This time, he did not mind leaving his daughter quite so much, because he could tell her with assurance that he would be back, and when.

Now, as he and Stephen journeyed toward Exeter with their men-at-arms, skirting around the treacherous bogs of Dartmoor, Geoffrey basked in the warmth of the spring sun on his shoulders as they rode along. It had been a long time since he had cared enough to notice if the weather was fair or foul, in fact, not since Before.

Before. That was how he had measured his life since Milesenda's death. Before, when he had been happy, young, in love. Alive. And After. Now, after losing his love, when he had nothing, except for Tamsin.

But despite his chronic unhappiness, it was a beautiful day. Even Geoffrey's horse seemed to be enjoying the fresh spring air, raising his head and twitching his nose as if sniffing the breeze. Geoffrey leaned forward to pat Storm's neck, and he thought about how many of the significant events of his life had occurred in springtime.

It had been spring when Geoffrey had first arrived in England, a wide-eyed five-year-old. His father had married Alyssa in springtime. It had been spring when Geoffrey had first met Milesenda, and the following spring when he had lost her. Tamsin had been born in the spring, and was now four years old. Geoffrey had been born in the spring as well. He had turned twenty years old just a week ago.

I will be twenty in the spring. He suddenly recalled himself saying that to someone, but he could not recall to whom he had said it. After he thought about it for a minute, he remembered. The black-haired little girl, Lord de Meules's daughter. She had told him she would turn sixteen this spring as well. Geoffrey was planning to visit his father's friend for a few days before returning to Lydford. He wondered briefly if he would see the girl again.

*****

There were no inns between Lydford and Exeter, so for the four nights they spent on the road, the de Graville brothers and their men-at-arms camped in the woods along the road, with a blazing fire to discourage wolves and sentries posted on the lookout for two-legged predators. Tensions still abounded throughout England, with rumors of a possible invasion by Duke Robert of Normandy to try to wrest England from his brother's rule, and Geoffrey would take no chances while traveling.

The last night before they arrived in Exeter, Stephen and Geoffrey sat at the campfire gazing into the flames. It was a clear night and through the trees above their heads, a canopy of stars winked at them. Geoffrey glanced at his brother's face and it looked so intense, almost rapturous, as he stared at the fire. For a moment Geoffrey wondered if the boy was praying. Picking up a branch from the ground next to him, Geoffrey began to break pieces off and toss them into the flames, watching the sparks fly up like a cloud of small insects on fire.

"It is not too late to change your mind, Stephen," he said.

Startled, Stephen stared at him. The fire's light lit amber flecks in his brown eyes and set the auburn highlights of his hair gleaming like copper.

"Change my mind? Geoffrey, do you think I would change my mind about the priesthood?" Stephen looked genuinely shocked.

"There would be no dishonor, if you did," Geoffrey muttered, pushing his hair back with his hand. "You have not taken any vows yet. I just wish you to know, that if you change your mind and wish to return home, I will not object."

"I won't change my mind," Stephen insisted. He tried to explain his conviction to his brother, who was still staring at the fire and aimlessly tossing in twigs.

"Geoffrey," Stephen said softly, "I remember when your Milesenda died. I was there at the chapel when Mother found you. Emma had come and told us what had happened, and Mother had been very worried about you, not knowing where you were all that time."

Geoffrey turned away from his brother's gaze. He didn't want to remember that time, but the memory overtook him regardless of his wishes. He was surprised that Stephen remembered it so well; he had only been seven years old, but, Geoffrey realized, his younger brother seemed to be very mature for his age. "I wandered for a long time in the woods, after...," he could not finish the sentence. Vague nightmarish remembrances flitted behind his eyes, images of running, falling, curling up in a ball on the ground and screaming. "I cannot remember how I actually got home." He wondered why Stephen had brought up this painful subject. What did Milesenda's death have to do with Stephen's desire to be a priest?

"You loved Milesenda very much, and you wanted her more than anything. Is that not so?" Stephen's voice was gentle, and Geoffrey nodded. "Please forgive me for bringing up something that I know is painful for you, brother," the boy continued, "but I love God just as strongly as you loved Tamsin's mother, and I want to become a priest just as much as you wanted her. Can you understand that?"

Was the boy only eleven years old, Geoffrey wondered. For just a moment it seemed to him as if it were Stephen who was the older of the two, with his calm and mature manner. He got that from his mother.

"Yes, I understand," Geoffrey said, "but that does not mean I have to enjoy it."

"But I will enjoy it," Stephen said with a smile.

"Your mother will miss you. So will I."

"I will miss Mother too," Stephen admitted. "And Isabel and that little imp Tamsin. And I shall miss you very much, Geoffrey, even if you did tie me up in the stable and gag me with a rag that tasted of horse dung." Even in the flickering light of the fire, Geoffrey's expression of guilt was evident. Stephen put his hand on his brother's arm and said, "But I forgive you," with such earnestness that Geoffrey's guilt eased.

He stood up and looked at the moon. "I am truly sorry about the gag," he admitted. "At the time it seemed like something I had to do.

I thank you for your forgiveness." He bowed to his brother, to emphasize his gratitude at Stephen's indulgence. If Stephen wanted the priesthood as much as Geoffrey had wanted Milesenda, then Geoffrey would no longer doubt his brother's conviction.

"It is my turn to stand guard," Geoffrey said. "You should go to sleep. Tomorrow we will arrive in Exeter. Don't stray too far from the fire," he admonished.

Stephen reached for his cloak to wrap himself in to prepare for sleep. "Goodnight, Geoffrey," he called out as his brother began to walk away to relieve the man on guard duty. Then Stephen added unexpectedly, "Perhaps you will find yourself a bride while you are in Exeter."

Geoffrey stopped in his tracks and his back stiffened. He did not turn to look at his brother. He didn't want to argue with the boy or be rude to him, so he merely muttered noncommittally, "Perhaps," and continued on to his sentry duty.

* * * * *

It was harder than he realized it would be to leave his little brother at St. Nicholas Priory. Ever since Stephen had started walking, Geoffrey had tended to think of him as a pest, a nuisance, an annoyance to be avoided. Now, as he was about to leave his brother in the care of the brothers at the Priory, he realized how much he was going to miss the boy. Who would elbow him awake at the appropriate point in the Mass now, he thought bleakly. Who would scold him when he cursed? Father Mathieu would certainly take over that function, but it wouldn't be the same.

The Priory was so quiet and still that Geoffrey felt very large and very loud as he bade his brother farewell in the visitor's room. *I would go insane here within a week*, Geoffrey reflected. Stephen was so young to be left here on his own, but the happiness and conviction shining in the boy's face made it obvious that he was not regretting his decision.

Geoffrey had planned on leaving his brother with a brief, dignified handshake, but to the surprise of both of them, he quite suddenly hugged the boy tight and said, "I will be at Rougemont Castle visiting Baron de Meules for a few days. My offer still stands, if you should change your mind, you need only send word and I will come to fetch you immediately."

Stephen smiled for a moment, then in that mature manner that seemed much older than his years, said, "Geoffrey, I will not change my mind, but thank you for the offer." Then he was again an eleven-year-old boy, leaving home for the first time. "You will come to visit me, won't you, Geoffrey?"

Geoffrey gripped Stephen's arms tightly. The dark blue eyes of the older brother locked into the soft brown eyes of the younger. "Of course, I will visit you. And I will bring your mother if I can. If you need anything, or if you ever wish to come home, you must send a message to Belvoir immediately. Also, I am going to leave one of our horses at Rougemont if Baron de Meules agrees to maintain it for us. It will be for your use should you need it."

Stephen nodded. "Go with God, brother," he said.

Geoffrey went, but he felt just a little empty inside as he did so.

* * * * *

It was somewhat of a surprise for Geoffrey to find that he actually enjoyed the company of Baldwin de Meules, Lord Sheriff of Exeter. He had expected this visit to be a tiresome courtesy call, but he discovered that he got on rather well with his father's friend, as the two of them shared a companionable jug of wine in Lord de Meules's great hall.

Geoffrey did not find it at all difficult to talk to de Meules about his battle experience in Normandy, because as a seasoned veteran himself, the older man had a common frame of reference. De Meules reminisced about some of the battles he and Raymond had fought in together, and then he sighed.

"I shall miss Raymond," he said. "He was a fine warrior, a good man to have at your back. We had some times together, Raymond and I, both on and off the battlefield." He looked into his cup with an amused glance of remembrance. Clearing his throat, he asked, "And how is Raymond's widow faring?"

"She fares well, all things considered," Geoffrey replied. "A week after Twelfth Night she was delivered of a baby girl whom she named for my father's mother."

"My felicitations on the birth of your sister, but it is a shame your father will not be here to raise her."

"Yes," Geoffrey replied. "A shame. But I will be there."

A movement at the doorway caught Baron de Meules's eye, and he stood up and beckoned. "Come in, girl," he called, "and pay your respects to Baron de Graville." Geoffrey followed his host's glance, and stood up as well at the sight of long black braids.

She had grown since he had seen her last summer in the stable, with new lissome curves that were beginning to replace the childish lines, though her head still did not reach his shoulder. Her new maturity could not, however, hide her surprise at the sight of him. Geoffrey knew he was considerably more presentable now than when they had first met; clean, fresh-shaven, and wearing clothes even his father would have approved of. It would not be appropriate for Baron de Graville to dress like a servant, no matter how comfortable it might be, and the longer, Norman-style tunic made it easier to conceal his left hand without being obvious about it.

The girl cast her eyes down as she approached her father, and curtsied prettily as Lord de Meules said, "My lord, may I present my daughter, Solange. This is Baron de Graville, child, from Lydford."

Geoffrey reached out his right hand and raised the girl from her curtsy, saying, "I am most pleased to meet you, my lady," thinking with amusement that it would be best if he did not inform his host that he had already made his daughter's acquaintance.

Solange snatched her hand away from his almost rudely, and the fine dark eyes flashed at him with a glance that seemed almost angry. Perhaps her nursemaid had spanked her again.

She managed to control her eyes before her father noticed, and de Meules, who had turned to refill his and Geoffrey's cups, said, "Find your mother, child, and tell her to prepare a chamber for our guest. Baron de Graville will be staying for a few days." No sleeping on the floor for him tonight, Geoffrey thought.

"Yes, Father," she replied demurely. She curtsied again, with a polite, "My lord," in Geoffrey's direction, but her expression was far from polite as she left them to their wine.

Later, when he went to seek the promised guest chamber, he had no sooner stepped from the doorway of the great hall when he was attacked by a kitten.

A hissing, scratching little kitten with flying black braids who pummeled his arm and kicked him in the shins. He was so surprised by the attack that it was a moment before he could react; then irritation surfaced and he pushed her away and pinned her arms down with his hands to keep her still.

"What the hell!" he exclaimed, as she struggled and kicked in his grasp. He was afraid to let her go; she might try to scratch his eyes out, if she could reach them.

"You lied to me!" she shrieked.

He was bewildered. "Lied to you? All I said was..."

"You told me you were a groom!"

"You are confusing me with someone else," he began to say, then understanding dawned. She was talking about last summer, in the stable.

"I did not lie to you. I never said I was a groom. Now behave yourself." He released her arms but remained on his guard.

"Yes, you did," she insisted, her eyes flashing daggers. She held out her hands in a mocking gesture. "These are the hands of a horse handler," she mimicked what he had said to her.

Oh, God, his hands. He had left his gloves back in the hall. Instinctively he thrust his left hand behind his back. Had she noticed it when he had grabbed her arms? It had been a protective reflex and he had forgotten all about his disfigurement at the time.

"I did, I do handle horses, every day. But I never said I was a groom."

"You told me you were in Baron de Graville's service. Now my father says you are Baron de Graville. You were trying to trick me!"

Geoffrey sighed. Weeping Jesus, she was annoying. "If you will stop shrieking like a fishwife, I will explain." Solange pouted, but listened.

"When we were here last summer, my father was still alive. He was Baron de Graville, and I was serving as his squire. So you see, I was in his service, as I said." He paused and looked down at her. "And why does it matter to you who I am?"

"It doesn't matter, not one bit," she declared. "I merely do not like to be lied to. My father said you are Baron de Graville."

"I am now," he replied, becoming irritated. "My father died in battle, and I am his heir. Would you like to know how he died?" Without giving her a chance to reply, he continued, his voice rising with suppressed emotion. "He took an arrow in the throat, and he was gone like that!" Geoffrey snapped his fingers. "He never had a chance to say good-bye to his wife, or to see his last-born child, his only daughter. He never had the opportunity to see his older son knighted, nor will he see his younger son take his priestly vows. And he is buried in Normandy, so his widow does not even have the comfort of tending his grave. So now I am the Baron de Graville, and must suffer being attacked by ill-mannered children who deserve to be spanked for their rudeness!" He took a threatening step towards her. "In fact, perhaps I shall do your nursemaid a favor and tend to the job myself!"

He had no idea what had provoked him to rant on about his father's death like that, but the girl had begun to stare open-mouthed at him, until he threatened to spank her. Then, with a shriek of fear, she turned, picked up her skirts and ran. He didn't bother to follow her. At the end of the corridor, she realized he was not chasing her and she stopped and turned around.

"I no longer have a nursemaid!" she informed him loftily. "I'm all grown up now." Then she stuck her tongue out at him and disappeared around the corner.

He was tempted to follow her and inform the little hellion that grown-up young women did not stick out their tongues at their family's guests, but thought better of it and went to bed instead.

*****

The next day he felt a little guilty for scaring her as he had. He was so accustomed to being bigger and taller than everyone around him, that it had not occurred to him at the time how frightening he might have appeared to a small girl like her. So when he encountered her the next afternoon in the great hall, alone except for a servant, he apologized, although he rather felt that it was she who should apologize first.

She was gracious, and much more mature than the day before. "I accept your apology, my lord. Perhaps I was a bit hasty in my assumptions. And please accept my condolences on the death of your father. I did not realize he had died."

He felt his lips twitch with amusement. Hasty was a bit of an understatement, but about all he could expect from a sixteen-year-old girl.

"Perhaps you would like to go for a ride outside the city walls?" he invited. "With a proper escort, of course," he added quickly.

Her eyes sparkled. "I would like that very much, my lord."

"And if you promise to be very good, I may even allow you to feed my horse an apple." She stuck out her tongue again.

After securing the necessary permission and arranging for an escort, they went down to the stable and Geoffrey saddled Solange's pony himself. Then he hesitated. She was waiting for him to help her up onto the pony's back; with her skirts, she could not climb up herself. Would she be frightened and revolted if he touched her with his maimed hand? He was wearing his gloves; perhaps she wouldn't notice it. Putting his hands on her slim waist, he hoisted her up onto the pony's back. He didn't realize he was holding his breath until she smiled at him and said, 'Thank you, my lord." Then he exhaled quite quickly and turned to his own horse.

He eschewed a saddle for Storm and leaped up onto the stallion's bare back. "I believe you have forgotten something, my lord," Solange observed as they left the city behind them, the men-at-arms following at a respectful distance.

He shrugged. "Nothing of importance."

Geoffrey was completely unaware of what an appealing image he presented to the young girl as they rode past the city gates with the half-dozen men-at-arms following behind them. The sun gleamed from his hair like molten gold, the shining blond strands lifting away from his face in the breeze, and his eyes, blue as sapphires, sparkled with pleasure at leaving the smells and confines of the city behind. Without the impediment of a saddle, the well-muscled bodies of horse and man seemed almost to be one, as Storm appeared to respond more to Geoffrey's thoughts than to any physical commands. The only discordant note was the leather gloves Geoffrey wore in spite of the fine weather, and the manner in which he wrapped his horse's reins around his left wrist.

He kept Storm's gait down to a sedate walk to keep pace with Solange's fat little pony. The girl seemed to know where she wanted to go, for she pointed her pony's nose to the south, saying, "Let's go this way," and following a natural rise until they found themselves at the top of a steep hill overlooking the sea. Below them were the colored rocks characteristic of Devon's coast, red, brown, yellow and green hues gleaming wetly as the sea's waves washed over them.

Geoffrey dismounted, leaving his gloves on as he helped Solange down, then hobbled his horse and her pony, as the girl walked to the crest of the hill and looked down.

"Don't go too close!" he warned. Lord de Meules would be most annoyed if his daughter were to fall to her death while in Geoffrey's care.

She made a face at him and said, "You sound just like my father," but she did move away from the dangerously sloping bluff.

He cocked an eyebrow in amusement. "And if you were to mistakenly think that your father had in some way deceived you, would you dare to kick him in the leg?"

"No," she admitted. "I am sorry I did it." He was about to accept her apology when she continued, "Because I am sure I did more hurt to my foot than to your leg, my lord."

"Ha!" he replied. "You should see the bruise you left. I thought I would be maimed for life." She knew he was lying through his teeth, and he knew she knew it, so he wasn't offended when she laughed at him.

She sat down on the grass, apparently indifferent to staining her skirt, and looked out over the sea. After a moment Geoffrey sat down next to her, leaning back on his elbows but keeping a wary eye in case Solange decided to venture too close to the steep side of the hill.

"It is so beautiful here, do you not agree, my lord?" Solange said, gazing out towards the sea, the foamy waves roaring and sighing below them.

Geoffrey agreed that it was a beautiful view. He was glad that the breeze was behind them so he could not smell the salty sea air. In fact the wind was now blowing hard enough that Solange's veil blew forward over her face, and Geoffrey felt a sudden urge to brush it back over her shoulder. He suppressed the urge. Let the child care for her own clothing.

"Do you miss your father?" she asked suddenly.

He was so surprised at what she had asked him that he couldn't answer right away.

She pushed her veil away from her face and looked at him with questioning eyes. She had the longest, thickest eyelashes he had ever seen, dark as midnight against her fair skin. "You said that your father had died," she said. "Do you miss him? My older sister Judith died. I miss her still, even though it was a long time ago. Do you miss your father?"

Geoffrey considered for a minute before he answered. The older sister she was speaking of must have been the one to whom his father had been attempting to betroth him. But Geoffrey had been in love with Milesenda then, and she had been expecting his child, his darling little daughter who was now all he had left to remind himself of his beautiful love...

Stop it, he told himself. You must try to stop thinking of her with every breath. To attempt to keep thoughts of Milesenda at bay, he considered what Solange had asked him.

"Yes," he answered. "I do miss my father. When he was alive, we never agreed on anything. Sometimes I even thought I hated him. But now that he is gone, I do miss him."

"Are you sorry you were not able to marry Judith?"

He stared at her. So she knew about the attempted betrothal. She confirmed her knowledge by adding, "My mother told me just today that my father and yours had been arranging to betroth Judith to you at the time she died."

Geoffrey would not, could not, insult this girl and her family by revealing to her that he had refused vehemently to marry this Judith, that he had been relieved when she had so conveniently died, and it would not have eased the insult to reveal that Geoffrey had not known, nor had he ever cared, if Solange's sister had been sweet-tempered or disagreeable, homely or pretty. Although if she had resembled her younger sister, she must have been beautiful. He took refuge in vagueness.

"I never met your sister. She died before anything was settled." The truth, if not the whole truth.

"But you have not married another since then. I thought perhaps you pined for her."

"No," he said quickly, then reminded himself, *be tactful now*. "I never had the opportunity to make the acquaintance of, ah, Judith. I am afraid I could not pine for someone I never knew. I have been, um, oh...too busy lately to consider another betrothal."

Too busy. That sounded like a plausible excuse. And it was true he had been very busy since his return from Normandy and the responsibilities of his family and Belvoir had encompassed him.

They fell into an uncomfortable silence then; the teasing mood of their earlier conversation having passed. In his youth, Geoffrey had been shy around females; though he no longer suffered from that affliction he suddenly had no idea of what to say or how to converse with this young girl. He was more accustomed to rough swordplay than gentle conversation with the tender daughters of noble households. Funny, but he hadn't felt tongue-tied in the presence of her father, but then Baron de Meules hadn't looked up at him with big dark eyes that gave him a sudden, unsettling glimpse of the woman Solange would someday be. After an uncomfortable moment, the woman receded and the child re-emerged, as she turned and crawled a few feet away to pluck a tiny white flower.

"Look," she said, holding up the blossom for him to see, "nothing was in bloom yet the last time I was here."

"You have been here before?" Geoffrey asked, heartened that he had thought of something intelligent to say.

Solange nodded. "Oh, yes. I love to come up here. It is my favorite place to go when I wish to be alone."

"You come up here alone?" Geoffrey exclaimed, shocked. He looked around at the lonely hilltop, suddenly feeling very paternal. "You are a very foolish girl, Lady Solange. Don't you know it is dangerous to be traipsing about the countryside alone, especially here, near a seaport? Does your father know that you come out here without an escort? I would wager not, for if he did, he would surely forbid it." Lord de Meules ought to keep a closer eye on his daughter, he thought indignantly.

Solange flushed angrily at his scolding, and her eyes narrowed at him. "Just because you are a friend of my father's," she hissed, "does not mean that you can order me about! I will go where I wish, and you cannot command me, my lord de Graville. Besides, I am quite capable of defending myself."

"Is that so?" he asked sarcastically. "And just how would you defend yourself against an attacker?"

"Like this!" With a flurry of fabric, she quickly withdrew a wicked dagger whose sheath was strapped around her ankle, and pointed it at Geoffrey's chest.

"Jesus! Give me that thing before you hurt yourself." Geoffrey reached for the hilt of her knife, torn between an impulse to spank her or to take her home and lock her in her chamber until she grew up. She twisted away from him.

"No, it's mine. Don't worry," she said, her voice more gentle now. "I won't hurt you." She returned the dagger to its sheath and quickly smoothed down her skirts over it so that Geoffrey had only the briefest glimpse of a shapely leg.

She wouldn't hurt him, was it? For the love of God, what a troublesome little runagate. He was glad she wasn't his daughter!

He was very tempted to pin her arms down and force her to relinquish the knife to him, for her own safety, but he dared not lay hands on her with Lord de Meules's guards who had accompanied them relaxing not far away, though fortunately out of earshot.

"Where," he asked in a low, deadly voice, "did you get that thing?"

"My brother gave it to me," she said, but wouldn't meet his eyes as she spoke.

Geoffrey could think of many things he would like to give to his sister, but none of them included a knife like that one. It made the dainty eating knife that all ladies carried at their belt look like a toy. He had not yet met Solange's brother, but he did know that he was overseeing some property their father held near the Welsh border.

"And does your brother know that he has given it to you?"

Solange blushed and looked away, confirming Geoffrey's suspicion that the brother was unaware that his sister had taken his dagger. "He would give it to me if I asked him for it," she insisted defensively.

"I doubt it," Geoffrey muttered.

"Do you call me a liar?" the girl asked indignantly.

Geoffrey reminded himself that despite those big dark eyes, she was only a child who most likely did not understand the consequences of her actions. "Lady Solange," he said patiently, "I do not intend to imply that you are a liar, nor am I attempting to command you. I am merely concerned for your safety, and I am certain that your father is as well. It is not safe for a pretty young girl to roam the countryside alone in times such as these." He wasn't going to waste his breath trying to explain the unsettled political climate to this young girl; she would have to trust that he knew what he was talking about. "You may believe that you can defend yourself, but that dagger is a man's weapon and I merely fear that you may injure yourself with it. I am certain that your parents would be grieved if any harm were to come to you, and as your father's friend, I would also be upset if anything were to happen to you." He had no idea what had prompted him to add that he would be concerned over her welfare, and he seriously doubted that his concern would influence her.

Her angry expression softened. "Very well, Lord de Graville, I appreciate your concern and I promise I will be careful. If you do not think I should come here alone, would you escort me here again tomorrow?"

"Tomorrow I leave to return to Belvoir..." Geoffrey began, but then she put her hand on his arm. His skin under her fingers suddenly felt warm, and he found himself saying, without knowing why, "but I believe I can delay my return for a day or two," and feeling inexplicably breathless at the sight of the brilliant smile she rewarded him with.

19

When he left Exeter a few days later to return to Lydford, he had a squire of his own, young Henry de Lessay, a beardless boy of fifteen who soon developed the disconcerting habit of looking at Geoffrey as if he were God.

The boy was a nephew of Baldwin de Meules, and like his young cousin Solange, Geoffrey had met Henry in Lord de Meules' stable.

Henry had been grooming his horse when Geoffrey walked in. Not only grooming the horse, but talking to him as well, as if the beast were his closest companion.

A man after my own heart, Geoffrey thought as, unobserved, he heard the boy pouring his heart out into his horse's patient ear, telling him how much he missed his family in Normandy, and how he hated being cooped up in the confines of a crowded, smelly town.

It had not required much of an effort to persuade Baron de Meules to release the boy into Geoffrey's service. At Rougemont he was but one of several fosterlings. Geoffrey had been contemplating procuring the services of a squire since his return from Normandy, and Henry soon proved to be dedicated and intelligent. In his turn, Henry seemed to regard the arrangement as a stroke of great fortune, and a release from a situation he had not enjoyed. He was awed and respectful as they prepared to journey back to Lydford, and Geoffrey spoke to him about the people he would meet at Geoffrey's home.

"There is my stepmother, the lady Alyssa," Geoffrey said. "You must show her the utmost respect, for she is a great and wonderful lady." His voice was serious and his eyes stern.

"Yes, my lord!" Henry replied, dark eyes fervent under his mop of curly brown hair.

"My brother Stephen is back in Exeter, studying for the priesthood at St. Nicholas Priory," Geoffrey continued, "and my sister Isabel is but a baby." He mentioned the others, Edmund, Maud, Father Mathieu, before looking at Henry solemnly. "And then there is the most important person in Devon, with whom you should be honored to associate."

"Yourself, my lord?" Henry asked with complete sincerity.

"No, my daughter, Tamsin. She is five years old, and the light of my life."

"I did not know you were married, my lord," Henry replied.

"I am not." Geoffrey's suddenly stern expression brooked no questions on the subject.

Chastened, Henry was silent until Geoffrey spoke again. "There are two things I will require of you while you are in my service, Henry. In addition, of course, to your diligence and hard work."

"Yes, my lord?"

"One, that you make an effort to improve your English. I prefer it to Norman French, which you will have little use for at Belvoir." In truth, now that Geoffrey's father was dead, Father Mathieu was the only one left at Belvoir who spoke French as his first language. "And the second is that I insist that we find you a more worthy mount from my stable." He cast a disparaging glance at Henry's placid roncey, and as the boy opened his mouth to protest, went on, "No doubt this one has been a good friend to you, but a knight, or even his squire, must have a horse with a bit more spirit and strength." As he spoke, Geoffrey leaned forward to give a small pat to the neck of Storm, who was spirited and strong as well as being a good friend.

Henry promised heartily to make every effort to improve his English, and declared he would be honored to ride any horse Geoffrey saw fit to provide him with.

Geoffrey's new squire was surprised when they did not travel directly north to Lydford. Despite the days it would add to their journey, his lord insisted upon turning east rather than north and in a few days, they found themselves at Senlac Hill near Hastings, where stood the magnificent abbey built by King William after his victory on this very site.

Ever since his father's death, Geoffrey had been pricked by curiosity regarding words Raymond had spoken to him on his last day in life, a promise of a visit to this place and of the disclosure of some special information, something secret, that Raymond had planned to discuss with him. Raymond's death had prevented that revelation, and now Geoffrey stood at Senlac Hill wondering what his father had meant to tell him, that needed to be divulged here and nowhere else. Had Raymond simply intended to show Geoffrey where he had fought beside his Duke, now their King, at the battle which had taken place here in Geoffrey's infancy? Had his purpose been to merely reminisce over the history-making experience? It seemed that there had been something more in Raymond's intent, something specific he had wanted to impart to his son, something that had to do with this place and what had occurred here.

Geoffrey left his men at arms waiting outside, but requested his new squire Henry to accompany him into the church that the King had ordered constructed upon this site, in thanks for his victory which had brought him the crown of England. Henry, still awed and unfamiliar with his new lord, trailed a bit behind him as they entered, genuflected, and knelt before the altar.

After a moment's reflection, Geoffrey said to Henry, "My father spoke of this place, this abbey, the night before he died. This is where our King defeated the usurper Harold Godwinson to claim the throne of England. My father fought in that conquest, and his efforts gained him our lands."

Geoffrey glanced at Henry, who was hanging on his every word. "He said we would come here together and that he had something important, something secretive, to tell me that should be revealed here and nowhere else. But he was unable to fulfill that wish, thanks to the successful aim of a French arrow." He reflectively touched the base of his throat, recalling the obscene sight of his father's body with the arrow protruding from that spot. "I shall never know now what his intent was, of course, but I felt I should at least honor his desire to visit the place."

Henry was respectfully silent, gazing at the cross upon the altar and silently offering a prayer for the soul of a man he had never met.

"If nothing else, it is a place of great importance, a place of history," Geoffrey said, rising to his feet. Though he could not imagine the important subject his father had wished to impart to him here, he did at least light candles in his memory, as well as for his mother and Milesenda.

He clapped Henry on the shoulder as they left the church, and with a last glance at the site of the Battle of Hastings, they mounted their horses and turned towards home.

*****

As soon as they arrived in Lydford and Geoffrey had greeted his family and introduced Henry, the two of them went to the stable to consider horses.

Actually, there were three of them, for Geoffrey still carried Tamsin in his arms, explaining to Henry, "She doesn't like it when I leave her." Tamsin looked at Henry for a moment, then flung her arms around her father's neck in a proprietary gesture.

"My da!" she insisted, as if afraid this new person was going to try to take him away from her.

"Of course, my lady," Henry replied with a small bow, and Geoffrey suppressed a smile. Obviously, Henry understood how important it would be for him to stay in Tamsin's good graces.

At that moment, young Ulric popped out from the stall he had been cleaning, and bowed to his employer, smiling happily.

"Welcome home, my lord," the boy said.

"Good day, Ulric," Geoffrey said. "This is my squire, Henry de Lessay."

"My lord," Ulric bowed again to Henry. Meanwhile Tamsin was bouncing on her father's hip, demanding attention.

"Me too!" she insisted. The two boys laughed and even Geoffrey smiled slightly as Ulric bowed so low to his lord's daughter that he came perilously close to toppling over. Tamsin beamed. Then she looked around for her father's horse and demanded, "Ride, Da!"

"Not right now, sweetheart. Henry and I must choose him a horse. Is it not time for your nap?" he asked, when she began to pout.

"No!" she cried, flinging her arms around her father's neck, and Geoffrey knew he could not send her away. "I want to ride!"

"Soon, sweetheart, I promise," Geoffrey assured her.

Henry was staring at his lord. He had never seen a man spend so much time with or show so much affection towards a small child. Certainly his own father had never treated Henry like that. Henry had been in England at the de Meules castle for five years before entering Geoffrey's service, and he suspected that his family had forgotten he existed. Ulric seemed to regard Geoffrey's treatment of his daughter as a normal everyday occurrence, as he returned to his work.

Geoffrey kept Tamsin in his arms as he began to stroll along the row of stalls, considering the various occupants, and Henry followed quickly behind him, until Geoffrey stopped at the second to last stall.

"This one will be a suitable steed for you, I believe," Geoffrey said. He stepped back so Henry could see the young stallion inside, and the boy's eyes went wide.

"He looks just like your horse, my lord!" Henry exclaimed.

"He ought to," Geoffrey replied. "That is his son." The golden stallion tossed his head proudly, as if he knew Geoffrey was talking about him. "He is a proud and spirited steed, like his sire, but responds well. I think you two will get along just fine. Why don't you get acquainted while I take this little lady for her ride? I did promise her, and a knight must always keep his promises to a lady. Remember that, Henry."

Henry responded, "Yes, my lord," and reached into the stall to pat the horse's nose, as Tamsin suddenly looked at him and advised, "Scratch his ears!"

With a grin Henry turned to her and bowed, saying, "Your wish is my command, my lady," which set the little girl to giggling, and she said to her father as he carried her towards his own horse, "I like him, Da."

Over his shoulder Geoffrey called back, "Well, Henry, I guess that means you can stay," and Henry smiled, with his place at Belvoir assured.

At that moment, Ulric returned and asked, "Is there anything I can do for you, my lord?"

The boy was so eager to please. "Yes, there is something," Geoffrey replied. "Please show Henry where the saddles and tack are stored while I take my girl for a ride. Henry, I'll be back in a few minutes, and we will get to work."

"Yes, my lord," Henry and Ulric both chorused in unison, then looked at each other and grinned boyishly.

When Geoffrey returned from taking Tamsin for her ride, after which he returned her to the nursery for Maud to deal with in terms of less desirable pursuits such as bathing and naps, Henry had his new horse saddled and ready. With an approving nod, Geoffrey mounted his horse again and he and Henry rode out to put Storm's son through his paces.

As they were brushing the horses down afterward, Henry said, "Your daughter is a most adorable child, my lord." He couldn't help being curious, and asked, "Where is her mother?"

Geoffrey stopped his work for just a moment, but long enough that Henry perceived the tightness that had invaded his master's stance. Geoffrey couldn't quite manage to keep his voice even. "Tamsin's mother died in childbed," he said, and the manner in which he looked away and refused to elaborate on the subject told Henry it would be wise to ask no more questions for now.

*****

While Geoffrey had been in Exeter enrolling his brother at the Priory, Alyssa had moved her possessions out of the lord's bedchamber and into a smaller chamber, insisting to Geoffrey upon his return that his status as Baron de Graville meant that he should be the one to occupy the larger bedchamber. Geoffrey stood in the room with his saddlebag in his hand, looking about at the large bed hung with its fine linen curtains, the heavy tapestries on the walls which not only looked elegant but also suppressed drafts, the large carved chest for holding clothes. It was a lord's abode.

He was half tempted to insist that his stepmother keep the room. It was, after all, her bedchamber, the room she had shared with his father for twelve years, where she had borne Stephen and Isabel. He felt uncomfortable taking it away from her. However, he reasoned, it might be good for him to vacate the tower room he had occupied since childhood. Although he no longer had nightmares about Milesenda and her death, the room where they had first loved was still full of memories of her. Sometimes in the morning when he first awoke, he still expected to see her beside him and his heart broke again when he came fully awake and realized it was only wishful thinking. He wondered if his stepmother felt the same way about the memory of his father, and it was with that thought in mind that he agreed to the new arrangements. With Henry's help, he moved his clothes, armor and other possessions into the lord's bedchamber, but he did not, as many other knights did, require that his squire sleep on the floor in his room. If Geoffrey woke during the night and was thirsty or hungry or needed the chamberpot, he could take care of himself. Henry was given a room of his own to sleep in.

No squire, no wife, not even his hounds accompanied him when the door closed behind him. The new bedchamber and large curtained bed were vast and lonely, but Geoffrey would not admit this to his stepmother when she asked him how he had slept, knowing very well what she would suggest to fill the loneliness. Several times she had gently suggested that he reconsider the notion of a marriage. He knew that if he wished he would have no difficulty finding a bride. He was titled, wealthy and handsome, and could be charming if he chose to be. Several fathers of well-dowered young ladies had approached him recently, but he resisted the offers and changed the subject whenever Alyssa mentioned it.

Very soon after the arrival of Geoffrey's sister Isabel, his friend Edmund married Carys, the midwife's daughter, and within an embarrassingly short time found himself the father of a squalling, red-haired son who was suspiciously fat and healthy to have been born so prematurely. As Geoffrey stood godfather while the boy was given the old Saxon name of Cerdic, he had tried desperately to suppress his jealousy at the sight of Edmund's beaming happiness. Edmund had his heart's desire, the woman he loved and their child, both alive and healthy. Geoffrey knew his envy was irrational, but he could no more squelch it than could he change the color of his eyes.

It was another irony in a life full of ironies that Baron de Graville, who had wealth, lands and the power that went with them, should be jealous of his bailiff, whose only possession of value was his horse, which had been a gift from Geoffrey. Baron de Graville lived in a castle and Edmund lived in a two-room cottage in the village, but Edmund lived in that cottage with his wife and son.

Though if pressed to put a name to his condition, he would have been unable; the truth was that Geoffrey was lonely, despite the fact that he was surrounded by people. He enjoyed the adoration of his daughter, the maternal love of his stepmother, the friendship of Edmund, the respect of his tenants and the loyalty of his retainers, yet those relationships did not fill the empty space in his soul which haunted him in his lonely bed.

Henry proved to be a diligent and hardworking squire, eager to please and basking proudly in Geoffrey's praise when he did well. Geoffrey enjoyed teaching the boy, enjoyed his company and admiration; and Henry's English improved rapidly. Briefly, as he instructed Henry how to hold a shield and wield a sword, picked him up and sympathized inwardly with his bruises when the quintain knocked him off his horse; Geoffrey wondered what it would be like to have a son of his own to teach. He knew that, had Milesenda given him a son, he would never have been able to foster the boy out even though it was customary.

Henry had not seen his family since the age of ten, when he had been sent to England to train at Lord de Meules's estate. Geoffrey knew that keeping one's sons at home for their training tended to spoil them, thus the reasoning for fostering. Perhaps that was why Raymond had been so strict with him. For his part, Geoffrey was certain that he could never send any child of his away from home.

20

It was not long before another opportunity to prove his fighting skills was presented, as the threatened invasion by King William Rufus's brother, Duke Robert, came closer to reality. In anticipation of Robert's arrival, a number of Norman barons in England declared their support for the duke, in rebellion of King William. Baron de Graville was one of those whose loyalties remained firmly with William Rufus, in spite of those of his fellow barons who proclaimed allegiance to Robert. Geoffrey had been knighted at the hand of Rufus's father, and if King William had chosen to pass the crown of England to Rufus rather than to Robert, then that was all the convincing Geoffrey needed to proclaim his loyalty to the second William.

King William Rufus, whose father had conquered England as Duke of Normandy, now called for an army of Englishmen to defend it against another Norman invasion, and Geoffrey, Baron de Graville, whose father had been part of the first invasion, answered the call to defend his country against the second. There was no hesitation in Geoffrey's mind this time as he prepared to fight, although it concerned him to leave his family behind at Belvoir with the possibility of a full-fledged civil war erupting at any time. He hoped that their fairly remote location in Lydford would keep them out of harm's way, with the garrison knights off to fight with Geoffrey and only the household guards left at Belvoir for protection.

The main strength of the rebelling barons was in the southeast, where they held the Conqueror's landing place at Pevensey as a base for the expected reinforcements from Duke Robert in Normandy. It was here that William Rufus's army of Englishmen, including Geoffrey de Graville and his squire Henry, gathered to defend their coast against Robert's advance scouts.

Robert of Normandy was not the forceful, awe-inspiring leader that his father had been, nor was he a match for the determination of his brother, William Rufus. When it became apparent that Rufus's English army was a force to be reckoned with, many of those castles supporting Robert realized their mistake and switched their allegiances back to their King. Among the last places to fall was Pevensey itself. It had held out for six weeks when the English army arrived.

Geoffrey did not allow Henry to participate in this battle, but insisted that he stay back with the other squires, holding his lord's other horse. It was a quick and decisive confrontation, as Robert's advance scouts attempted to get ashore, and were subsequently slaughtered by the English.

Geoffrey had long ago decided not to wear chausses on his legs in battle, and it was almost his undoing. On horseback, he needed the mobility afforded by not wearing the heavy chain mail leggings to compensate for the deficiency in his left hand, which was now clad in a custom-made gauntlet with only two and a half fingers. So when he took an arrow in the upper part of his right leg during the battle at Pevensey, it penetrated deeper than it might have had he been wearing chausses.

Just my luck, he thought irritably, glancing down at the arrow shaft protruding from his thigh, through the fabric of his braies. The bottom of his hauberk had flapped back and left his leg completely exposed for just a moment, but it was long enough. He was tempted to pull the arrow out but thought better of it. It didn't hurt very much just yet, and it was bleeding only a little. If he pulled it out now, it would only bleed heavier and he could not stop to have it bound up just yet; they had not quite finished dispatching their foes.

A minute later, the man just to his right was killed and as he went down, his horse slammed against Geoffrey's, breaking off the shaft of the arrow and driving the point deeper into his leg. Now it really hurt.

This time, when the battle was over and a barber summoned to tend to Geoffrey's wound, there was no tent, no cot, and no cousins; just his saddle, which an anxious Henry had removed and laid on the ground under a tree. Geoffrey sat on the ground, cold and wet from recent rains, grimacing with pain, and leaned against the saddle like a pillow. He gratefully accepted the cup of wine Henry brought him but refused another when he had finished it.

The barber-surgeon, who now cut open the fabric of Geoffrey's braies to examine the wound, was a short, fat man, and, thankfully, an Englishman-someone Geoffrey could understand. He looked up at his patient's face as Geoffrey waved away Henry's attempt to refill his cup, and wiped his pudgy face before speaking.

"My lord, I am going to have to dig this thing out of your flesh, and it is quite deep. I can see that you are no stranger to pain." Geoffrey had pulled off his gloves and thrown them aside, along with his helmet and hauberk. He saw the surgeon glance at his left hand. "It will be better for you to be very, very drunk before I do it."

"No." Geoffrey's reply was brief but firm. He remembered what the combination of too much wine and pain had done to him in Normandy, and he would not embarrass either himself or Henry by vomiting here like a breeding woman. Of course, back then in Normandy he had been a green boy in his first battle, with the sight of his father's dead body fresh in his mind. But Geoffrey intended to take no chances. He continued to refuse the wine his squire was trying to press on him.

"My lord," the barber began to entreat, but Geoffrey would not be swayed.

"Master Barber," he said in his most lordly voice, "I appreciate your concern, and I have no doubts as to your skill, but I will take no more drink. Just give me a piece of leather," he commanded, and although the barber looked at Geoffrey as if he were insane, he reached into his saddlebag, and with a look of reluctance, handed Geoffrey a thick leather strap, which Geoffrey put in his mouth, trying to ignore its horsy taste as he clamped his teeth firmly in the leather.

The barber-surgeon shook his head, muttering about gluttons for pain. "If this wound was much further to your left, my lord, you might have lost the ability to, um, become a father. It could have been the priesthood for you."

Geoffrey did not dignify the rotund little man's comment with a response. From the corner of his eye he noticed Henry kneel down next to him, whether to pray or to assist the surgeon, he was not sure. He held up his hand for the surgeon to wait a moment, and removed the leather piece from his mouth.

"Henry, there is no need for you to be here," he said, wanting to spare the boy from this gruesome sight, but to Geoffrey's surprise, Henry shook his head.

"I would like to stay if I may, my lord."

Geoffrey looked at his squire sharply; looked at his eyes and saw strength there. He nodded, giving Henry a look that said, *very well, you may stay but it will not be pretty*. With the leather strap replaced between his teeth, he gave another nod to the surgeon to begin his work.

It was not quick, it was not easy, and, as he had surmised, it was not pretty. The arrowhead had been driven deep into Geoffrey's leg. Ordinarily it would have been removed by pushing the arrow through in the direction in which it had entered him, but with the shaft broken off, it was not possible to do so in this case. By the time the barber-surgeon had it dug out of his flesh, the leather strap had been bitten almost in two with the pressure of Geoffrey's teeth, and the horsy taste of it was mingled with the salty taste of the sweat that ran freely down his face and into his mouth. His hands were black with dirt from digging his fingers into the ground next to him as the surgeon dug into his leg with his knife. But the important part was that he had not thrown up nor had he cried out in pain this time.

The area of the wound was a bloody mess, and Henry was staring at his lord's blood-stained leg, not with revulsion but with a look of revelation. *Poor boy*, Geoffrey thought, *his illusions are shattered. He must realize now that I am human after all.*

The surgeon wrapped a cloth around Geoffrey's leg to bind the wound, explaining as Geoffrey spit out the strap which now had the imprint of his teeth firmly and deeply embedded in it, "The wound is too deep to cauterize, my lord; it would do no good. You should keep a binding on it, but not too tight or your leg will wither and die. It has bled quite a bit but I have staunched it for now. You must, my lord, stay off the leg and rest until it heals. It would not take a great effort for the wound to burst open and begin to bleed again, and you would be in danger of bleeding to death in that case."

Geoffrey nodded, and now that his surgery was over, accepted another cup of wine from Henry, but only one. "You look as if you have never seen blood before," he said to his squire.

"I have, my lord, but never so much at one time," Henry replied with a shudder. His face was pale.

"You aren't going to be sick on me, now are you?" Geoffrey asked suspiciously, relieved when Henry shook his head firmly.

"Good," Geoffrey replied, leaning back against his saddle and closing his eyes for a moment. "When I was about your age," he went on, thinking, *God, it makes me feel old to say that,* "I had my first sight of a large amount of blood, when my father made me put down a horse that had destroyed itself. I wanted to refuse to do it, but of course I had no choice."

"What did you do?" Henry asked.

"Slit the poor beast's throat, then went behind the barn and puked like a dog."

Henry shuddered in sympathy, and then the barber-surgeon asked Geoffrey, "Is your home near here, my lord?"

Geoffrey shook his head. "Devon."

"Then my advice to you would be to seek lodging somewhere nearby for several weeks before attempting to travel back to Devon. Not only to allow your leg to heal, but also for your safety."

"Safety?" Geoffrey asked sharply.

The barber nodded as he tucked in the end of the binding on his patient's leg. "I have heard from some of the others that the fortress at Bickleigh still holds for Robert of Normandy. Although perhaps they will change their minds and give up when word reaches them that the invasion has been repulsed. I do not think - my lord, what are you doing?"

Geoffrey climbed awkwardly to his feet, calling for Henry to saddle their horses. Bickleigh! Bickleigh was only a day's ride from Lydford. A day's ride from his family, his daughter, with only a small contingent of guards there to protect them. God, if he'd known about Bickleigh he would have never left home. He had to get back, now, today, to make sure they were safe; to defend the castle if necessary, and hang his wounded leg. "We are going home," he announced, limping about as he picked up his helmet, his gloves and his sword.

"Home!" Henry exclaimed with surprise, but nevertheless obeyed his lord's curt commands and began saddling their horses, while the chubby barber-surgeon followed Geoffrey, protesting.

"My lord, your leg! You must allow it time to mend before you attempt to travel. You don't seem to understand how serious this is. If the wound opens, you could bleed to death." He caught hold of Geoffrey's sleeve. "My lord, listen to me. You cannot -" He stopped talking as Geoffrey turned to him with a scowl that could have made rocks tremble. The barber's hand dropped away from his patient's arm, and he took a step backwards.

"Do not," Geoffrey said in a cold voice, "tell me what I can and cannot do. I am going home to Devon, and I am going now. Henry!" he called out to his squire, "you and I will go alone. We can move faster and attract less attention if we travel alone, and the others will be needed here for a little longer anyway to make sure the coast is secure." He reached into his saddlebag and withdrew a gold coin, which he handed to the barber-surgeon. "Thank you for your services, and your advice," he said, dismissing the man, who had no choice but to walk away, muttering, "Don't say I didn't warn you!"

But Geoffrey paid him no heed. He pulled off his torn and bloody braies and quickly donned a fresh pair, then swung up into his saddle. The stab of pain from the wound made him see white, but it didn't break open. Henry scrambled up onto his horse's back as well, and Geoffrey looped his sword belt around his pommel. The rest of his armor would be left behind for his knights to bring with them. He didn't want the weight of it to slow him down. An hour after Geoffrey had limped from the battlefield with an arrow in his leg, he and Henry set off toward Lydford, and home.

*****

They almost made it. By stopping only to rest the horses when necessary, they made good time, heading due west after passing Forde Abbey, with Bickleigh to the north. They did not turn towards Bickleigh. It was not Geoffrey's intent to take the fortress or even to determine if it was still held by Robert of Normandy's supporters, but only to get to Lydford without being observed by any who might be supporting Robert. A day and a half, if they pushed hard, and they would be there.

Both Geoffrey and Henry, as well as their horses, were becoming exhausted as they rounded a bend, passing out from the shelter of a copse of trees, and came face to face with twenty armed men on horseback. Instinctively Geoffrey reached for his sword, but stopped himself before drawing it. They were hopelessly outnumbered, and Henry had no sword at all, only a dagger. All hopes of a peaceful encounter were dashed as the troop surrounded Geoffrey and Henry, swords drawn.

Geoffrey decided to brazen it out.

"Who are you," he demanded, "and what right do you have to interfere with peaceful travelers?" Out of habit, he had spoken in English, and the obvious leader of the group, a swarthy Norman with a long, diagonal scar across one cheek, raised his eyebrows in surprise. The Norman leaned his arm across his pommel, but kept his sword to hand and replied in Norman French.

"I might ask you that question, my bold fellow. Your horse, and that of your young friend here, and that fine saddle and sword, are definitely

Norman. But your speech and looks say otherwise. I would venture that the horse is stolen, and the sword as well. Get down."

"Now see here," Geoffrey protested. "We have stolen nothing, and we have no intention of attempting to hinder you or your men in your journey to wherever you may be going. Sheath your swords, and we will be on our way, and you on yours, none the harm."

The Norman knight sneered. "I am afraid it is not that simple, young man." Geoffrey flushed angrily at the man's rude tone. Young man! He knew that his fair coloring and blue eyes made him appear younger than he was, despite his size.

"I am a knight and a baron," he muttered, but the Norman either did not understand Geoffrey's English, or chose to ignore him.

"You see," the man continued, "you have seen us, and that puts us all in a predicament."

"So I have seen you," Geoffrey retorted. "Not a pretty sight, but I shall survive. Let us pass."

"I would not be so certain if I were you, about surviving this encounter, that is. We have taken great pains to travel unobserved, until the two of you surprised us."

Suddenly Geoffrey understood. These men had to be supporting Robert of Normandy, on their way to Pevensey to join the rebellion. He almost laughed at their tardiness.

"You are too late," he informed them. "Robert of Normandy's little rebellion has been quashed. If you are traveling to Pevensey, you can spare yourself the effort. The advance force has already landed, and has been destroyed. I should know; I was there, and personally did away with a fair number of the bastards." His temper was starting to get the better of him.

The look of surprise on the Norman's scarred face told Geoffrey that his assumptions about this group had been correct. The man quickly composed his features, but did not deny his loyalties. "Why should I believe you, Englishman?" he asked.

"I don't really give a damn if you believe me or not, but what I say is true. Allow the boy and me to go, and if you travel quickly, you can make the coast and take ship for Normandy before your treachery is discovered. I would suggest Corfe; to sail from Exeter or Pevensey would be too dangerous for those who support a man who attempts to usurp his brother's throne."

"Treachery, is it!" The Norman leaders face became mottled in anger, and Geoffrey was suddenly aware of the twenty drawn swords, all held in hands that appeared to be itching for a fight. If he drew his own sword now, how many of them could he down before they sliced him and Henry to pieces? Not even Geoffrey de Graville could win a fight when outnumbered twenty to one. One of the soldiers leaned from his saddle to speak to the leader, in a low voice but not so low that Geoffrey did not hear what he said.

"My lord Banyard, what if what he says is true? If Duke Robert's cause is indeed thwarted, we are branded traitors. Perhaps we should heed his advice and hasten to Corfe and on to Normandy. If de Poilley has sent forces after us, we are dead men."

Geoffrey knew who William de Poilley was, the lord of the fortress at Bickleigh. So Bickleigh had changed its allegiance to William Rufus. Good news, but not for the Norman leader. His face flushed with such anger that the scar on his cheek flamed and pulsed. He pushed the other man away from him.

"You are a fool, Raoul, and a coward as well, if you believe the word of this English dog." Chastened, Raoul turned away, and the leader, Banyard, turned back to Geoffrey. "I believe I gave you an order. Dismount."

"I will not." Geoffrey's pride was pricked.

Banyard gave a nod to the man he had called Raoul, who casually nudged his horse forward until he was directly in front of Henry's horse, then lifted his sword and rested it against Henry's chest, gently, not saying anything, but the threat was implicit. Henry sat in his saddle like a rock, and Raoul glanced at his leader, then at Geoffrey.

The Norman gave Geoffrey a mocking look. "Will you allow your pride to kill the boy? One word from me and he will run him through without a moment's hesitation." Raoul nodded in confirmation, and the others all grinned. Without another word, Geoffrey dismounted, and Raoul backed off enough to allow Henry to swing down as well. Banyard looked around until he saw a man at the edge of the group, a man Geoffrey had not noticed before. He was the only one of them who did not have a sword in his hand, and he was an Englishman, apparently a servant. "Take their horses," the Norman ordered, and the man quickly took the reins of Geoffrey's and Henry's mounts and tied them to a tree branch.

"Tie them up," he then ordered, and several of his henchmen dismounted and pushed Henry and Geoffrey roughly to their knees. As his knees hit the earth with a thud, Geoffrey felt the wound in his leg open with a sickening popping sound, and he didn't need to look to know that it was bleeding steadily. Several of the soldiers pointed and exchanged words as the blood began to seep through the fabric of Geoffrey's breeches. Quickly, men stepped behind them to bind their wrists behind their backs, and there were gasps of shock as Geoffrey's leather gloves were pulled off and they saw his maimed hand while tying leather cords tightly about his wrists.

He glanced at Henry kneeling next to him, receiving the same rough treatment, and Geoffrey cursed himself for his stupidity in putting the boy in such danger. He felt a thousand kinds of fool, and now it appeared that they would both pay for Geoffrey's recklessness with their lives. He should have waited, he realized with the clarity of vision that comes with hindsight, should have waited until the rest of his men were ready to accompany them. But no, he had rushed off, with a fifteen-year-old boy and a fresh wound that was now reopened, thinking that the two of them could reach Lydford without incident. When it came to his family, he tended to think with his heart rather than with his head.

The scarred Norman dismounted and sheathed his sword, now that his captives were subdued. "Now," he said with a fearsome scowl, "who are you? You speak excellent French, despite your accent, but damn if you don't look like an Englishman."

Geoffrey's hair was hanging in his face in a most undignified manner, and with his hands bound behind him he could not push it back.

For the first time in his life, he wished he had cut it short in the Norman style. An attempt to shake it back from his face was futile. He looked up at his captor from between the tangled strands as the man demanded again, "Who are you?"

Geoffrey hated to use his title. When he met people under normal circumstances he preferred to introduce himself simply as Geoffrey de Graville. But these were not ordinary circumstances. With as much dignity as could be mustered by a man on his knees, he spat out the words, "I am Baron de Graville."

"I do not believe you," Banyard the Norman replied. He looked at Raoul. "Kill him."

In an instant, Raoul stepped behind Geoffrey and grabbed his hair, pulling it hard and forcing Geoffrey's head back until he was looking at the sky, and a very sharp dagger blade was pressed against his throat. Geoffrey didn't flinch, didn't blink, didn't even breathe, just prayed for the courage to die with dignity as he felt the cold kiss of the knife against his taut skin.

Two things happened at once. Henry, stoically silent since their capture, screamed, "Nooooooh!" and struggled futilely against his bonds; and the English servant who had tied up their horses came rushing forward, shouting at the Norman, "My lord, he is who he says he is! He is Baron de Graville."

Banyard held up a hand for Raoul to wait, and the blade was moved an inch away from Geoffrey's throat and the grip on his hair slackened. Geoffrey allowed himself one small breath as the Norman asked the Englishman, "How do you know who he is?"

"I have seen him before," the man replied. "It was years ago, and he was only a boy when I left... when I came to live at Bickleigh, but I recognize him. He is Baron de Graville."

Geoffrey stared hard at the man whose confirmation of his identity had granted him a temporary reprieve, wondering if he should know him. He did look vaguely familiar, but Geoffrey could not remember where he might have met him. Geoffrey was also grateful that the man had not mentioned that Geoffrey's home was at Lydford. Better that this Norman, Banyard, did not know where he lived.

The scar-faced Norman stepped in front of Geoffrey who glared defiantly up at his captor. "Well, I suppose this changes things," he said. He waved his hand for Raoul to step away from Geoffrey. "A baron, and one who follows William Rufus. How convenient. A pretty ransom can be had for you, but I wonder if the boy is worth keeping alive?" He looked over at Henry, kneeling in the dust with huge eyes.

Geoffrey thought quickly. These Normans were keeping him alive only because he was worth something to them. How long would Henry live if they learned he was a third son with no inheritance? "He is my brother and my heir," Geoffrey stated, mentally willing Henry not to dispute the lie, and hoping desperately that the English servant who appeared to know who he was did not know that much about his family. If the man had lived away from Lydford for years, perhaps he would not realize the age was wrong, and would think that Henry was Stephen.

The Norman looked down at Geoffrey as if trying to determine whether or not to believe him. Perhaps, Geoffrey thought, if he was lucky, a few more lies might be to his advantage. "My men are an hour's ride behind me," he said. "If you and yours wish to travel unscathed, untie us and you can be gone before they arrive."

"Am I expected to believe you, Baron de Graville?" Banyard asked incredulously. Geoffrey shrugged as if unconcerned, trying to appear confident.

"I never lie," he said. *Unless my life is at stake.*

Banyard smiled evilly. "Very well, for the sake of conversation, how many men ride with you?"

"Forty." *Continue to keep your mouth shut, please, Henry,* he prayed. Even if his men were nearby, which they weren't, they were only fifteen.

"And why do you ride so far ahead of them?"

"I had personal matters to discuss with my brother here," Geoffrey nodded towards Henry, "so told them to hold back to give us privacy." It was a weak excuse, but the best he could think of at the moment.

Raoul had now stepped from behind Geoffrey to look in the direction he and Henry had come from, as if expecting horsemen to descend upon them at any moment. He glanced at Banyard with a worried look, and the scarred man said, "I suppose there is a possibility he could be telling the truth." He motioned for his men to gather round. "To be on the safe side, we will take what he says as truth. If he has forty men following him, we can either take another route, or ride now and surprise them. But in either case, we take them," he nodded towards Geoffrey and Henry, "to Normandy and hold them for ransom. Duke Robert can use the funds."

"But if there are forty men in his troop, we are outnumbered," Raoul observed.

"True," Banyard replied. "But we will have surprise on our side. That will compensate for the numbers. Suit up," he called out to the troop in general, and the men reached for the rolled hauberks strapped behind their saddles and began to pull them over their heads, along with their helmets. Banyard looked at Raoul. "I want you to stay here to guard our friends. When we have dealt with his soldiers, we will return here to retrieve them and then set out for Normandy. Do you think you can handle them both?"

Raoul grinned and walked over to stand in front of Henry and Geoffrey. "A wounded man and a boy? Of course I can." To prove how competent he was to handle them, the Norman put one booted foot on Henry's shoulder and pushed him over.

Unable to balance himself with his hands bound behind him, Henry fell to the earth with a thud and was still. The unwarranted cruelty infuriated Geoffrey. "Leave the boy alone, you filthy whoresons!" he shouted, trying desperately to pull his hands free from the tight leather cords bound about his wrists.

Raoul's dagger flashed out again, dangerously close to Geoffrey's eyes as he jerked his head back. Banyard laughed from atop his horse, the sun glinting from his helmet. "Behave yourself, Baron. You wouldn't want Raoul to mark that pretty face of yours. He might make you look like me." He fingered the scar on his cheek.

Geoffrey tried to ignore the dagger waving mockingly in front of his face, and said, "Did an Englishman give you that scar?" His voice was hopeful.

"No," Banyard replied. "Though I am ashamed to have to admit it, an English girl did this. She was unwilling, and I did not realize she had a knife until it was too late."

"Good for her," Geoffrey said, and Banyard frowned.

"Enough of this idle chatter! Raoul, keep a close eye on these two. If his men are an hour's ride back, we should be back here well before dark. We will take care of his little troop, and then retrieve you and take ship for Normandy. Keep them bound until we return," he instructed Raoul. "We'll be back as soon as we can. Don't hurt them any more than you have to. We need them in one piece when we seek their ransom."

With that, Banyard and the rest of his men turned and rode off in the direction from which Geoffrey and Henry had appeared, to look for knights they would not find. Geoffrey wondered how long the Normans would look before they realized he had been lying, and whether they would continue holding him and Henry captive when they discovered his deception, or just kill them on the spot. About three hours should give him the answer.

He looked over at Henry, lying on his face on the ground, hoping desperately that the boy was alive, knowing he would never forgive himself if his squire died because of Geoffrey's impetuosity. To his immense relief, Henry stirred slightly, but Geoffrey could not discern if the boy was conscious or not.

Raoul seemed to be enjoying his guard duty, walking around behind his captives and waving his dagger tauntingly at Geoffrey. He stared unashamedly at Geoffrey's bound hands and after a minute stepped around in front of where Geoffrey knelt and asked, "So how did you lose the fingers?" Geoffrey tried to ignore him, but Raoul squatted down in front of him so that their eyes were level. "Come now," he cajoled, "we are going to be in each other's company for quite some time. We might as well have some friendly conversation, and I admit I am curious to know where you left the rest of your hand."

Geoffrey looked at the man with hatred blazing from his blue eyes.

"Believe it or not," he spat out the words from between gritted teeth, "I lost those fingers in defense of Normandy. I was not a willing participant, to be sure. If it had been my choice to make, I would have let the French have the place and be damned."

Raoul leaped angrily to his feet, exclaiming, "You insolent English dog! I should slit your throat here and now and forget Lord Banyard's plans for you. We can ransom your brother there instead, since he is your heir."

"Oh, you can be very brave when your opponent is bleeding, bound and helpless," Geoffrey retorted. "Untie me and let us see how brave you are then." His horse was still tied to the tree, his sword belt still hanging from the pommel. If he could goad Raoul into a fight, he knew he could best him. This scruffy, brutal Norman would be no contest for him, no contest at all. If he could taunt Raoul into untying him and fighting, he could kill him and he and Henry could be gone in minutes. "Come now, Norman, can you fight like a man, or are you afraid to try me?"

Too late, Geoffrey realized the folly of taunting Raoul. This man was not interested in a fair fight. With a growled, "Damn you!" Raoul lunged at him again with his dagger, again swiping towards Geoffrey's eyes. He jerked his head back again, but the dagger's needle-sharp point caught him on the cheekbone and opened a stinging red line across his face, narrowly missing his eye. Raoul had obviously intended a more solid contact, and the force of his lunge caused him to stumble. He caught himself and turned again to his victim.

"You are a coward," Geoffrey said.

A feral grin crossed Raoul's face. "And you are a dead man." He raised his dagger again, and Geoffrey could read in the man's eyes that he intended to bury it in Geoffrey's heart. *Your lord Banyard will not be happy if you kill me,* he thought absurdly, but the blow never came. Raoul froze for a moment with his knife held poised to strike, then with a small groaning sound sank slowly to his knees, and the dagger fell from his hand. He stared at Geoffrey disbelievingly for a moment, then slowly crumpled to the ground in front of him, and Geoffrey then saw the second knife, protruding from Raoul's back.

It must have been thrown from behind him, but by whom, and why? The question was answered when a man stepped from the trees, the English servant who had known Geoffrey. *Where have I seen this man before?*

The man darted quickly over to Raoul's inert body and pulled his dagger from the man's back, then quickly stepped behind Geoffrey and cut the leather cords away from his wrists. Geoffrey immediately went to Henry and turned the boy over, breathing a sigh of gratitude that the boy was alive and conscious, but with a huge bruise purpling his cheek from the rock he had fallen on. The other man cut Henry's hands free as well. They both sat and rubbed their wrists to massage away the numbness from being tightly bound, and Geoffrey told Henry, "Your face looks awful, but as you can see, the other man got the worst of it." He nodded at the deceased Raoul.

"You have looked better yourself, my lord," Henry replied shakily, looking at the cut on Geoffrey's face. Geoffrey wiped the sticky blood on his sleeve. The hurt was minor; the hole in his leg was of more concern. He turned to the man who had saved his life.

"Thank you, my friend," he said to the man. "I shall be eternally grateful that you chose to return here at that moment."

"I slipped away from the others as soon as I could," the man replied. "Hopefully they won't notice I have gone." Geoffrey was perplexed about this man; he looked so familiar. And why had he risked his life to save Geoffrey's?

"Have we met?" he asked. "You look familiar to me, but I cannot recall making your acquaintance. Who are you?"

The man hesitated, looking at the ground for a moment before looking back at Geoffrey, who was helping Henry to his feet. "I heard you were kind to my sister," he said softly, "and were sorely grieved when she died."

Milesenda's brother! That was why he looked familiar to Geoffrey; the color of the hair, the placement of the eyes and the shape of the mouth, all showed a familial resemblance. What a stroke of fate that of all the men these Normans could have hired, it had been this one.

"Her brother! Of course, I see the resemblance. She told me you had moved away from Lydford. I owe you my life. What is your name?"

"Kenelm, my lord," the man replied, bowing.

"Geoffrey de Graville." Geoffrey held out his right hand in a gesture of friendship. Kenelm stared at him. This tall blond man was a lord, a baron. Such men did not shake the hands of low-born Englishmen, even in gratitude for their lives. But Geoffrey continued to extend his hand, and after a moment Kenelm grasped it. "How did you come to serve those brutes?" Geoffrey asked, nodding in the direction the Normans had taken.

Kenelm shrugged, embarrassed. "They promised me a fine reward if I would accompany them to care for the horses. I wasn't at all sure I could trust them, and when I saw you, my lord, and realized who you were, I decided to forgo their promises of payment and returned back here. I am glad I didn't get here any later. That Raoul looked as if he was about to skewer you."

"I am glad as well," Geoffrey said, "because skewering me was exactly what he had in mind."

"My lord," Kenelm began to say.

"Geoffrey." But Kenelm could not seem to bring himself to call Geoffrey by name.

"My lord, I think it would be wise for you and your brother to get yourselves away from here quickly. They may be back soon."

Geoffrey nodded. "They will be back in a fury when they realize they have been on a wild goose chase." He limped towards his horse, untying the reins from the tree and grasping the pommel to pull himself into the saddle. The movement invited a fierce stab of pain from his wounded leg, but he tried to ignore it. "Have you a horse?" he asked Kenelm.

"Yes, my lord." Kenelm nodded towards the trees.

Geoffrey looked down from atop Storm's back, and nodded to Henry to mount as well. "I owe you more than I can ever repay you," he said to Milesenda's brother. "Not only did you save my life, but my squire's as well. He is not really my brother, by the way, but I value him just as much." Henry smiled in proud surprise at Geoffrey's words as he continued, "and you sacrificed your payment for your services from those knights. Return to Lydford with me so that I can reward you." Kenelm started to shake his head. "You have a niece," Geoffrey said. "She is the image of her mother. I am sure she would like to see her uncle."

"I would like to oblige you, my lord," Kenelm replied, "but I have a family waiting for me in Bickleigh. Knowing that my sister's child is not orphaned is all the reward I need."

Geoffrey nodded. "Then we should all get us gone with haste. I would like to be far from here when Banyard and his troop return." Kenelm turned and grabbed the body of Raoul by the arms, dragging it into concealment in the bushes.

"They will find his body, but the looking will delay them a little." He walked towards his horse, tethered across the roadway.

"Kenelm!" Geoffrey called. Kenelm turned. "If you ever need aid of any kind, or a friend, you have one in Lydford. I am in your debt." From his seat in his saddle, he bowed. "Another thing," he added. "I don't know what you heard in Bickleigh about...about your sister and me, but I loved her. She was not loose with her favors. I wished to marry her but my father prevented it. Believe me, part of me died with her. I would not want you to think badly of her for laying with me, for we did truly love each other."

Kenelm's eyes widened at Geoffrey's bow. "I shall remember that, and pray that you reach Lydford without further incident. Please kiss my niece for me, my lord. Perhaps I will be allowed to visit her someday?"

"Any time you wish," Geoffrey replied.

"Godspeed!" Kenelm called. He quickly mounted his horse and turned it north, to Bickleigh.

Geoffrey and Henry turned their horses west, toward Lydford. "Godspeed!" Geoffrey called back. Henry had been anxiously looking out for the possible return of Banyard's men, and not really paying much attention to Geoffrey and Kenelm's conversation. Now he turned to his lord.

"Who was that?" he asked.

Geoffrey glanced back in the direction Kenelm had taken. "My brother-in-law," he said simply.

Henry looked surprised, and then his glance took in Geoffrey's bleeding leg. He reined in his horse. "My lord, your leg! We should stop and bind it, perhaps wait until the bleeding stops."

"No, we cannot wait and chance Banyard's return." The steady bleeding was beginning to make him feel light-headed, but he fought against it. Reaching out his hand, he grasped Henry's arm tightly. "I mean to get home to Belvoir, no matter what. If it means tying my hands to the saddle, or slinging my dead body headfirst over the horse's back, we will return to Lydford. Do what you must do. Is that understood?"

Henry swallowed with trepidation, but pulled himself erect in the saddle and affirmed, "Yes, my lord. Belvoir, no matter what." They both put their heels to their horse's flanks and hurried toward home.

21

They did not arrive in Lydford with Geoffrey's body headfirst over the horse's back, but it was a near thing, and Henry did have to resort to tying Geoffrey's hands to the pommel of his saddle as the loss of blood threatened his ability to remain upright. But as they reached the last hill just before the village, Geoffrey roused himself enough to insist that his squire undo the bindings. He would not arrive at his own castle trussed up like a prisoner.

The portcullis remained down until the two of them were close enough to be identified, in compliance with the instructions Geoffrey had left with the guards to open it only to those known to them. As they waited for the gate to rise, Geoffrey looked at it and it seemed to waver, as if it were not quite solid. What the...? He blinked, and his eyelids felt heavy and his vision became white about the edges. Vaguely he heard Henry gasp, and followed the boy's horrified gaze to look down at his leg, crimson with blood from thigh to toe, with sinister red droplets dripping from the toe of his boot to puddle in the dust below him. As if from very far away, he heard a shout, looked up and saw Edmund running toward him, looking terrified. *What is the damn hurry*, he thought irrationally. Geoffrey's head swam, his stomach began to rebel almost as if he were seasick, and the world began to tilt and sway as a roaring filled his ears. Then it all went black, and he pitched unconscious from the saddle.

*****

Geoffrey was dead. He knew it, knew he had to be, because for the first time since he'd left home he was warm, dry, clean and comfortable, all at the same time.

It was not at all what he had expected purgatory to be. He had rather imagined it to be a cold dark place where one could not see or hear or feel. It was true that he could see nothing-it was as black as midnight, but he could definitely hear. To his right he could hear the murmured prayers of angels, praying for his soul. *I'll need all the prayers you can spare.* And he could feel, oh, yes, he could feel; a sharp, throbbing ache in his leg, from the wound that had killed him. Unfair, that he should feel the pain of it still, now that he was dead.

Dead. Oh, God, he'd failed, failed when he'd been so close. Who would care for and protect his family now, with his estates forfeited to the king? Alyssa, Isabel...Tamsin, an orphan. *I've failed you all.*

Tamsin, my darling sweet child. I promised your mother I would protect her, but I couldn't, and she died. I promised you I would never neglect you, but I have, in the most permanent manner imaginable. My baby, I'm so sorry...

It was unfair, ironic, unconscionable that he should come so far, endure so much, and then bleed to death at the gate of his own castle. The desolation he felt at the thought of it made him so angry and miserable that his whole body twitched, sending the pain in his leg shooting through his gut with such intensity that his eyes flew open.

Damn. He wasn't dead after all. He wasn't in purgatory either, but ensconced comfortably in his father's bed. No, in his own bed; his father really was dead. Geoffrey had only been unable to see because his eyes had been closed in unconsciousness. He was alive. Damn. What a relief.

He turned his head-it was an effort, but decidedly preferable to the alternative-towards the sounds of the angel's murmured prayers he still heard, until he saw the two figures kneeling next to his bed, heads bowed in prayer. Not angels, but the next best thing, he thought, as he gazed down at the smooth auburn braids of his stepmother, and Henry's unruly mop of brown curls. He was letting it grow long, like an Englishman, Geoffrey noticed.

He opened his mouth to speak, to tell them he was alive, but nothing happened at first. His power of speech seemed to be stiff and rusty from lack of use, and it required several attempts to produce even the small croaking sound he made.

"I..." Both heads flew up, eyes wide. "I'm not dead. Yet."

Henry and Alyssa both sprang to their feet; Henry exclaiming, "My lord!" and Alyssa, "Geoffrey, oh, Geoffrey!" as she surprised her stepson completely by throwing herself across his chest with sobs of relief. The only other time he had ever known her to weep was the day he had told her his father was dead; to have her crying over him now unnerved him completely.

"If I had known my awakening would upset you so, Mother," he said, "I would have tried to remain unconscious."

Alyssa stood up and wiped her eyes. "Oh, Geoffrey," she exclaimed. "Please forgive my childish blubbering. We were so very worried that you would never awaken."

"How long have I lain here insensible?" he asked.

"Three days."

"Weeping Jesus. Oh, your pardon, Mother," he said quickly, contrite for cursing in her presence. Three days. He must have been near death. He still didn't feel very far away from it. No wonder his body felt stiff and creaky and his mouth dry. This presumption was confirmed when Henry, looking extremely relieved to see him awake, said, "Father Mathieu gave you Last Rites this morning, my lord, in fear you would never return to consciousness." The bruise on Henry's cheek was half healed, another indication of how long Geoffrey had lain unconscious.

"Not again," Geoffrey groaned. "When I do die, I shall surely be the most shriven man in Christendom." Henry and Alyssa both looked confused, and Geoffrey was about to enlighten them concerning the circumstances of his first sea voyage, when a commotion at the door captured their attention.

"There is someone who has been most anxious to see you," Alyssa said, and it was not necessary for her to tell him who that someone was, as he heard Tamsin's indignant voice even through the stout door.

"I want my Da!" she demanded. "Put me down, Mun!" The second demand was followed by a grunt of pain that sounded like it came from Edmund. If he was trying to restrain his goddaughter, he was sorry for it now, Geoffrey thought, as he struggled to sit up in the bed. The effort made him feel giddy and light-headed, and Alyssa turned to him with concern as his vision blurred.

"Geoffrey, you are still weak. You lost a great deal of blood, and you were feverish until just a few hours ago. You should be resting. I do not believe it would be wise to bring Tamsin in here until you are stronger."

"I want to see Tamsin," he said mutinously, hating the petulant tone of his voice but unable to suppress it. He looked at his stepmother. "Mother, I have bled across half of England in order to get home and I...will...see...my daughter." The effort to speak and his anxiety made him feel hot and feverish, and he started to push the bedcoverings off himself until he realized that he was naked beneath them. Yanking the fur blanket over his chest and flushing with embarrassment, he glared at his stepmother, having a distinct feeling that he looked more pathetic than intimidating.

Alyssa put her hand on his forehead. It felt cool and soothing. "Very well, Geoffrey," she agreed. "I shall allow Edmund to bring her in but I insist that you stay in bed. Is that agreed?"

"Yes, Mother," Geoffrey said obediently. It was an easy promise to make, because he knew he was too weak to get up. Alyssa nodded at Henry, who went over and opened the door to admit Edmund and Tamsin.

Again Geoffrey tried to sit up, but weakness and a glare from his stepmother kept him prone, so he had to satisfy himself with holding his arms out to his daughter. Edmund carried her over and set her on the edge of the bed, saying to Geoffrey, "Your child nearly unmanned me, Ge - my lord," by way of greeting.

"I am glad to see you too, Edmund," Geoffrey retorted, as Tamsin clambered up to sit squarely in the middle of his chest.

"Da!" she demanded, bouncing on him. "Where were you?"

"Why, I was off slaying a dragon just to keep you safe, sweetheart. Do you have a kiss for your Da?"

She covered his face with grubby kisses, and Geoffrey knew that all of the pain and suffering he had gone through to get home had been worthwhile. Alyssa stepped forward as if to remove the child from her rough affection, but Geoffrey caught his stepmother's eye and shook his head at her. He wouldn't care if Tamsin chose to dance a jig right on his wounded leg. He was alive, thank God, and reasonably certain he would remain so, and he could hold his baby in his arms and kiss her back, and that was all that mattered right now.

She patted at his stubbled cheeks and said, "Don't like it, Da." He had to agree with her. The unshaven beard itched.

"I shall shave it off, my darling, I promise," he assured her, "as soon as I have the strength for it." He glanced at his stepmother. "Perhaps by the time she is wed?" At that, Alyssa reached for Tamsin to take her away, fearing that this was too much excitement for him in his weakened condition, but Geoffrey shook his head again and petted his daughter's hair. Then Tamsin reached out and touched the scar across his cheek that Raoul's knife had left behind. He'd forgotten about that until now, but he winced when Tamsin touched it, for the area was still sensitive.

The little girl's face was concerned and sad. "You got hurt, Da. Did the dragon scratch you?" she asked, and Geoffrey closed his eyes for a second and prayed that Tamsin had not seen him fall from his horse, covered with blood. She must not have, if she was only concerned with the scratch on his face. She leaned forward and gave him another kiss, smack on the scar, and asked, "All better now?" just the way he kissed and soothed her little hurts.

"Oh, yes," he assured her. "It's all better now." Tamsin smiled and said "Good!" and laid down on top of him, cuddling her face into his shoulder.

"I love you, Da," she murmured, then put her thumb in her mouth and with all the artless aplomb of a four-year-old, promptly fell asleep.

Geoffrey held her and whispered, "I love you too, sweeting," as she slumbered against his shoulder. He looked up at Alyssa, Henry and Edmund standing at his bedside.

He'd made it after all. He'd made it home and his loved ones were safe. *Thank you, God.*

He smiled. "I'm home," he said.

* * * * *

In his weakened state, the brief period of consciousness exhausted him, and it was not long before Geoffrey fell asleep as well, with Tamsin held against his shoulder. When he woke again, it was morning and someone had taken Tamsin away. As if she somehow sensed that he had woken up, the door opened and his stepmother walked in, followed by a servant, the girl Moll, the one who used to tremble and stutter whenever she saw him. He smiled briefly at Moll; he had made a habit of being friendly toward her, just to prove to her that he was not the big bad monster she had apparently at first believed him to be.

"How are you feeling, Geoffrey?" Alyssa asked.

"Hungry," he replied, and his stomach confirmed it by grumbling loudly.

Alyssa smiled. "I will have some breakfast sent up for you shortly, but first we will change the binding on your leg." She reached for the blanket covering him, but just in time, he clamped his arms down and pinned it over his body.

"No!" he insisted modestly. Weeping Jesus, was she going to strip him naked before the entire world?

Startled at his vehemence, Alyssa stepped back a pace. "But Geoffrey, the binding needs to be changed and I have some salve to put on the wound that will help it heal." She reached for the blanket again and he had to restrain himself from slapping her hand away. Pulling back from his stepmother's hand, he blushed to the roots of his hair and whispered, "But, Mother, I'm ... naked."

Was it his imagination, or did Moll's eyes brighten a bit at that moment? He had tried to keep his voice low enough for just is stepmother to hear but had apparently been unsuccessful.

Infuriatingly, Alyssa just smiled. "I know that, Geoffrey. Who do you think it was who cut those horrible bloody clothes from your body, cleaned you up and bound your wound after Edmund and Henry carried you up here? They needed considerable help just in getting you up the stairs, but that is beside the point. Who do you think cleaned you and bathed you with wet cloths when you were burning with fever? There is no need for you to be modest with me now; you don't have anything I haven't already seen."

Nonetheless, Geoffrey refused to loosen his death grip on the blanket. He was embarrassed that his stepmother had had to clean him like a helpless baby. "I can change the binding myself. Or send for Edmund to do it," he suggested. Alyssa shook her head.

"You are still too weak to do it yourself, and Edmund is busy overseeing the threshing. And besides, those big clumsy hands of his would do you more harm than good."

"Henry, then."

"Henry is down at the stable, talking to the horses."

At least his squire was engaged in a worthwhile pursuit. "I shall wait."

She became exasperated. "Geoffrey de Graville, stop this prevarication this moment. I am merely going to treat your wound."

"Mother, please!" he begged, glancing at Moll who stood behind Alyssa holding her supplies. Moll had apparently gotten over her fear of him because she was smiling at him. His face went even redder. Damn, he thought he'd outgrown this embarrassing habit of blushing like a child. Perhaps it was because his stepmother was treating him like a child. He looked at Moll again. "At least send her away," he insisted, when he realized that Alyssa was not going to be swayed from her purpose.

"Very well." With an exasperated sigh, Alyssa took her basket from Moll's hands and dismissed her, and the girl dropped a quick curtsy and left. Still furiously embarrassed, Geoffrey suffered his stepmother to pull the covering down, but insisted on arranging the edge of the fabric to cover his privates as she removed the binding around his leg and smeared honey onto the wound which would inhibit both bleeding and infection, then bound it with a clean cloth.

"There!" Alyssa announced when she was finished and Geoffrey was allowed to pull the blanket back up to his neck. She patted his cheek. "You have been a very good boy. I shall allow you something to eat and a visit from Tamsin if you continue to behave," she teased.

"You are enjoying this," Geoffrey accused his stepmother with narrowed eyes. Instantly she became serious.

"No, Geoffrey, I am not enjoying this. I did not enjoy being called to the gate to see you laying there covered with blood, and fearing the worst. I would not enjoy the prospect of having to tell Tamsin that her father was dead. And I most certainly did not enjoy spending three days watching and praying while you laid here unconscious and delirious, not knowing if you would ever awaken."

"I was delirious?" he asked, curious.

Alyssa nodded. She turned away and began to replace things in her basket as she spoke. "You thrashed about and mumbled for hours. Most of what you said during that time was incomprehensible, but at other times you spoke clearly. You called out for people."

"For whom?" he asked, though he had a feeling he already knew.

"For Milesenda. You kept saying how sorry you were. And you called out for your father, and your mother. And someone named Solange." She looked at him questioningly, and he looked away, embarrassed again, and tried to sound nonchalant.

"Solange is a girl I met in Exeter," he explained. "Baron de Meules's daughter. I guess that would make her Henry's cousin. She is only a child," he added quickly, before his stepmother got the wrong idea. Why should he call out for her in his delirium, he wondered. Not only was she but a child, she was a child who exasperated him. To cover his discomfiture, he asked, "so I called out for you and my father?"

"No, not for me, for your real mother, Nicolette." Geoffrey was surprised, and the thought that he had called out for his real mother, whom he barely thought of anymore, made him feel slightly guilty, as if he'd been disloyal to Alyssa.

"Surely you must be mistaken," he said. "I must have meant you."

Alyssa shook her head. "No, I knew you were speaking to your real mother, because when you did, you spoke in Norman French, as you must have done when she was alive."

"If I spoke in French, then how do you know what I said?" he challenged.

"I understand Norman French," Alyssa replied with dignity. "Your father taught it to me. There were times, moments..." now it was Alyssa's turn to blush, "when he quite lost his command of English." From the quick glance she gave in his direction, Geoffrey guessed that the moments she referred to must have occurred in this very bed. Although Steven and Isabel were living proof, still it was hard for him to imagine his father doing *that*.

"I am sorry, Mother," he said, and Alyssa looked at him with surprise in her eyes.

"What are you sorry for?" she asked.

"Well, firstly, that I frightened and worried you with this," he swept a hand toward the wound that had almost killed him, "and also, that I called out for my other mother and not for you."

His other mother. That was how he thought of his real mother now. He should consider himself fortunate to have had two loving mothers; not many men were so blessed.

Alyssa's smile returned. "There was no need for you to call for me," she said, smoothing his hair away from his face. "I was right here all the time." She paused and looked away. "I pray to her sometimes, you know."

"To my mother?" he asked with great surprise. "Why would you pray to someone you never met?" And why, he wondered, would she pray to her husband's first wife?

"I pray to her to thank her," Alyssa replied, looking back at her stepson. "To thank her for allowing me to raise her son, and to thank her for the time I had with..." Her voice trailed off, and Geoffrey knew, just knew, that she was thinking of his father. Her eyes misted. "Oh, Geoffrey," she whispered. "I still miss him."

"I know," Geoffrey replied. "I know what you feel. I still miss ... her." He took a deep breath. "Milesenda." Though it saddened him to think of her, at the same time he felt slightly proud of himself that he had said her name without faltering.

To cover the awkward, melancholy moment, Geoffrey tried to smile and demanded, "I believe I was promised breakfast. Did you care for me just to starve me to death? Must I go and fetch my own food?" He sincerely hoped that Alyssa did not call his bluff, because just the effort of sitting up in the bed made him feel as if he were about to faint. Walking a few steps just might kill him. Alyssa turned to him with stern eyes.

"Yes, I will have some food sent to you but you are to stay in bed until your wound has healed and your strength returned."

"Very well," Geoffrey grumbled. "But then I wish to see Tamsin, and Isabel, and Henry. Yes, I most definitely must speak to Henry."

* * * * *

Henry must have been waiting outside the door as Geoffrey ate. He had glared away Alyssa's attempt to feed him herself, though his hands shook weakly as he lifted the spoon and cup. As his stepmother left with the tray he heard her say, "Don't stay too long, Henry, he needs his rest."

"Yes, my lady," Henry replied earnestly as he came in and shut the door behind him. He looked concerned and serious as he approached the bed and bowed to Geoffrey. "How are you feeling today, my lord?" he asked.

"I can sit up," his lord replied, "but don't ask much more of me just yet. How is your cheek?" He glanced at the healing bruise on his squire's face.

Henry touched the bruise as if he'd forgotten it was there. "It's fine," he muttered. "Lady Alyssa put some ointment on it. Thank you for agreeing to see me, my lord."

What was he talking about, Geoffrey wondered. He had sent for his squire, but here the boy was looking anguished and wringing his hands like a supplicant. Clearly something was bothering him, and it was obviously more than concern for Geoffrey's condition.

Suddenly the boy threw himself to his knees next to Geoffrey's bed with his hands clasped before him and begged passionately, "Please, my lord, please don't send me back to Normandy, or back to Exeter. I couldn't bear to leave here. I will do anything if I may stay at Belvoir. I'll clean your stables, I'd be your servant, your slave, anything, but I beg of you not to send me away, even though..." Henry's voice wobbled suspiciously, and he broke off and lowered his gaze quickly to the floor, his tousled curls bouncing with the movement of his head.

Geoffrey stared at the top of his squire's head in complete and utter astonishment. Whatever in the name of heaven was the boy babbling about? Had something disastrous, such as instant insanity, happened to him in the time Geoffrey had been unconscious? Derangement could be the only explanation for Henry to think Geoffrey would even consider dismissing him from his service. He had called the boy here to commend him on his stoic courage during their ordeal, not to banish him.

"For the love of Christ, Henry, get up. Save your knees for the chapel." Henry obeyed but wouldn't meet Geoffrey's eyes. "Now tell me just what this demented notion of yours is all about. What in the name of all that is holy makes you think I wish to send you away? I will, however, not deny you your wish for stable cleaning. It is my firm belief that no man should be above cleaning up after his own horse. If it is truly your wish to leave my service I will not hinder you, but I would know the reason."

Henry paced back and forth across the room several times before answering. Watching him made Geoffrey's head ache, and he was relieved when the boy stopped. Henry's voice was very small and filled with shame.

"My lord, I am unworthy to be your squire. I am undeserving of your consideration; unfit to so much as touch your boots."

"For the sweet love of Christ and all the saints, what the hell are you talking about, Henry?"

Henry finally looked at Geoffrey, his expression struggling for composure. He spoke just above a whisper. "I was afraid. I was a sniveling, terror-stricken coward, and I am unfit for knighthood, or to serve you."

"When were you afraid?" Geoffrey asked, not condemning or even chastising, merely curious.

"When that man, that Norman," Geoffrey had to smile at the way Henry said 'that Norman', as if he wasn't one himself, but forced himself to keep a serious face and pay attention as Henry went on, "when he put that knife to your throat and I thought he was going to kill you, and that I would be next, I was so afraid, I almost wet myself! I am ashamed. And then when we finally got home," Geoffrey did not fail to notice that Henry had referred to Belvoir as home, "and we thought you might still die, I was afraid again. I prayed and prayed, not only that you would live, but that you would keep me as your squire. But I know that I am unworthy for that honor, unworthy for knighthood. I'm a coward."

"Henry, you are not a coward." Henry shook his head. He did not believe Geoffrey's words.

Poor boy, Geoffrey thought. He could almost pity his squire for the anguish he was feeling. The events of their encounter with Banyard and his men had thrust Henry abruptly into the harsher aspect of manhood and he hadn't been ready. One was never really ready, as Geoffrey knew from the night of his own precipitous and terrifying jolt into despair; the night of Milesenda's death. He had cried like a baby on his stepmother's shoulder at the dreadful prospect of facing the rest of his life without the woman he loved. Facing death had been less difficult.

He looked up at Henry, searching for the right words to put the boy at ease. "Henry," he said, "to look at you I must wonder if I was unconscious for much longer than three days, perhaps for a year or two. I swear you have grown a foot. Find a stool and sit down so I can talk to you face to face."

Henry retrieved the three-legged stool from the corner and drew it up next to his master's bed. He sat down and rested his elbows on his knees and his chin in his hands, studying the toes of his boots. "Henry, look at me," Geoffrey said.

The boy raised his eyes. He was growing into a comely young man, with those outrageous curls framing a handsome face and big, long-lashed dark eyes. The local girls would surely soon be taking notice of this well-favored youth, as soon as the rest of his body caught up with his feet, which were almost as big as Geoffrey's.

Geoffrey sat up straighter in his bed, trying to look dignified, which was difficult when all he was wearing was the fur coverlet. He pulled the blanket up to his chest.

"Let me tell you something that my father told me, the night before he died." His mind took him back to that stifling hot August night in a tiny tent in Normandy. It had been a year and a half now since his life, and his body, had been so drastically changed by an arrow and an axe. "Every man fears something at some time and it is not wrong to feel fear. Even my father, believe it or not, felt fear and his fear was for me. Don't be ashamed to fear death, Henry, though you needn't shout it to the world." Henry was staring into Geoffrey's eyes and he opened his mouth as if to say something, but Geoffrey forestalled him, and amazed him, by saying, "I was afraid too, Henry. You aren't the only one who came close to disgracing himself at that moment." Henry's mouth rounded in disbelief as Geoffrey added, "but that can be our secret, one soldier to another. Do close your mouth, Henry, flies may get in."

Henry's mouth snapped shut, but opened again quickly to say, "Your father was afraid for your sake?"

Geoffrey nodded. "And yet, he was the bravest man I ever knew. The day after we spoke of that, he was killed and this happened," he lifted his left hand slightly, not embarrassed for Henry to see it. Henry had seen Geoffrey's disfigurement enough times that it no longer bothered Geoffrey for the boy to be aware of the imperfection.

"Your father must have been a remarkable man," Henry said reverently. "I wish I had known him."

"So do I," Geoffrey replied. "I wish I had known him better. But that is all in the past, and now we must deal with the present. Henry, feeling fear does not make you a coward, as long as you do not allow what you fear to destroy you. As a matter of fact, my intent in calling you here was to commend you on the courage you displayed, and also to apologize to you."

"Apologize?" Henry looked puzzled.

"I was foolish and reckless, to come dashing home like that and putting you in danger as I did. If I had waited until the rest of the men were ready, none of that nonsense need have happened. I ask your forgiveness for putting your life needlessly into danger."

Henry was so astounded, he stuttered. "You wish m-me to forgive you?" Geoffrey nodded. "But my lord, there is nothing for you to forgive. It is I who should beg your forgiveness."

"Very well, we shall forgive each other." To Geoffrey's relief, Henry smiled. "Now," Geoffrey continued, "I have absolutely no intention of dismissing you from my service or sending you away." Henry's relief was obvious. "You're a brave boy, and I have a very important task to assign to you, one that I trust only to someone with great courage."

Henry leaped to his feet. "Anything, my lord!"

"Good. I wish you to go to the nursery and fetch Tamsin here to me, even if you have to steal her out from under Maud's nose. That is the part which will require courage."

"But, my lord," Henry protested doubtfully. "Lady Alyssa said you were to rest."

And here I believed that I was the lord of this demesne, Geoffrey thought. "I cannot rest unless I see my daughter," he insisted.

"In that case, I shall fetch Lady Tamsin immediately," Henry said with a bow.

As he turned to go, Geoffrey called out, "Just one more thing before you leave, Henry." He pointed to the chest against the wall where his clothing was kept. "Fetch me a pair of trews."

22

As if Henry's misguided notions of cowardice had not been surprising enough, three days after awakening from his coma, Geoffrey was even more astounded when just before dark, Stephen bounded into his room, grimy and breathless.

Geoffrey could only stare.

"Stephen!" he exclaimed, as his brother strode to the bed and the two of them grasped each other's arms. "What are you doing here?"

Stephen looked at Geoffrey and blinked as if his brother had said something incredibly stupid. "Mother sent word that you were wounded and near death," he said, as if that explained everything.

While it was true that Geoffrey could neither read nor write, he could count. If he had lain unconscious for three days, and been awake another three, that made six days since he had arrived home to fall in a bloody heap at the castle gate. Traveling light, a man could make the trip from Exeter to Lydford in four days if he pushed his horse. If Alyssa had sent word to Stephen in Exeter after Geoffrey's return, he couldn't have made it back to Lydford so soon.

"But how did you get here so quickly?" It was true that Stephen was an excellent rider; he was, after all, a de Graville, but he was also barely twelve years old.

"The horse you left for me at Rougemont came in handy after all," Stephen replied. "I pushed him hard, and he took the punishment without complaint. But more importantly, how are you, Geoffrey? What happened to you?"

Briefly Geoffrey explained to his brother about the battle at Pevensey, his arrow wound, and the encounter with the Norman knights from Bickleigh. "You did not encounter anyone suspicious on the way from Exeter?" he asked his younger brother.

Stephen sat on the edge of Geoffrey's bed and shook his head, breathing heavily with exertion. "No, I traveled directly across Dartmoor and I saw no one."

"You rode across Dartmoor alone?" Geoffrey was astounded, and a little angry. Dartmoor's bogs were dangerous and usually avoided, but it explained how Stephen was able to make such a swift journey.

Stephen smiled and wiped his sweating face on his sleeve. "The messenger that Mother sent to Exeter did accompany me home, but I left him behind some ways back. He should arrive shortly. I hope he is not angry with me for abandoning him, but his horse was slower than mine and I had to get home as soon as possible. Thank God that you are alive and recovering, Geoffrey."

"I am glad of that myself," Geoffrey replied. "Though it was a foolhardy thing for you to cross Dartmoor alone, and risk killing your horse with such a fast pace, I of all people cannot fault you for it. Apparently, the desire to reach home at any cost is a trait common to the de Gravilles."

At that moment, Lady Alyssa, having been informed of her son's arrival, hurried into the room. Stephen was reluctant to hug his mother in his filthy condition, having come straight from his horse to see his brother, but Alyssa cared nothing for the dirt. "Stephen, Stephen, what are you doing here? How did you get here so quickly?" Behind her back, the two brothers smiled at each other at the way Alyssa unknowingly echoed her stepson's words.

"Why, Mother," Stephen said, "you do not think I would remain in Exeter with Geoffrey in a bad state, do you? I had to get home to see him myself. I hope the brothers at St. Nicholas's forgive me my disobedience in leaving so precipitously, but I assured them I would be back."

"Oh, Stephen." Alyssa hugged him harder. "You are a silly boy, but I am glad to see you. Come along and get cleaned up and have some dinner. You must be famished."

"But, Mother," Geoffrey protested as Alyssa started to lead Stephen from the room. "Stephen came home to see me. Let him stay." Convalescence was becoming damn boring and he wanted to talk to Stephen. He wanted to know if there had been any attempted rebellion in Exeter by any who followed Robert of Normandy, though he doubted there would be with Exeter under the domination of Lord de Meules who, like Geoffrey, was a King's man. He wanted to ask Stephen if he was enjoying his studies at St. Nicholas Priory, and he was curious to know if, while fetching his horse from the de Meules stables, his brother had noticed a petite, black-haired little girl with an inclination for frequenting stables.

"You," Alyssa informed him sternly, "should be resting. It is late. Stephen will still be here tomorrow, and he needs a bath and food now. You need sleep." To enforce her point, she blew out the candle on the table by his bed, leaving Geoffrey in the semi-darkness as she took Stephen away, without even giving her stepson an opportunity to argue the point.

Resting! That was all his life consisted of now. Though he was still weak, he was tired of resting. The only time Alyssa allowed him out of his bed was to utilize the chamber pot, and then only with assistance from Edmund or Henry, lest he fall and reopen his healing leg wound.

He punched the pillow into submission and when he had it properly subdued he laid down, certain that the surprise and excitement of Stephen's arrival would keep him awake for hours. However, he was asleep in mere minutes.

*****

Geoffrey balanced the tiny mirror on his knees as he shaved, steadying it with the remains of his left hand and being careful to avoid the scar on his cheek. The mirror had been a gift from his father to Alyssa, and had been hideously expensive. He handled it carefully, certain that if he broke it, he would wish he had died under Raoul's knife, compared to what his stepmother would do to him if he shattered her precious mirror. Alyssa had shaved him a few days ago, and had offered to do the job again today. She had a gentle but steady touch that was soothing, efficient and maternal, but pride made Geoffrey insist on doing the job himself as soon as he had enough strength to hold the knife steady.

I am becoming a scarred old warhorse, he thought as he put down the knife and studied his face. Fortunately, the fresh scar across his cheekbone was straight and thin, and would most likely become less noticeable once he had a chance to get outdoors and his skin regained its usual healthy tan. If he ever got outdoors again.

Mentally he cataloged his other scars. There was of course the tiny mark on his forehead from his childhood accident on the battlements. His hair covered it most of the time. The arrow wound in his leg that had almost caused his death was an ugly, puckered indentation. He had tried not to look at it when Alyssa changed the bindings, as she still insisted on doing every day to keep it clean as it healed and to avoid infection, but some kind of morbid fascination drew his eyes unwillingly.

And then of course there was his hand, his most obvious and distressing feature. He had almost gotten to the point where he could bear for those here at Belvoir to see it. There was after all little point in hiding from his family what they all knew perfectly well existed, and they were all tactful enough to behave as if he was no different than he had been before. But he still always wore gloves in public, away from Belvoir and when on horseback, and he studiously avoided the archery butts, still feeling jealous and left out from the sport in which he could no longer participate.

It had been two weeks now since his return, and the interminable resting was about to drive Geoffrey mad. He even found himself looking forward to Father Mathieu coming to his bedchamber to hear his confession, he was that bored. Most of his confessions dealt with uncharitable thoughts.

His strength was returning, but it was a frustratingly slow process.

The unaccustomed idleness made him cross and irascible, especially when Alyssa constantly shooed his visitors away. Just yesterday she had scolded him soundly after discovering both Isabel and Tamsin crawling around on his bed, giggling madly from his tickling. He thought he had been rather clever in charming Maud into leaving both little girls with him to relieve his boredom, but Alyssa hadn't thought him clever at all. She swept both children away and told him for the thousandth, or millionth, time that he should be resting. If he never heard that word again in his lifetime, it would be too soon. At least Tamsin had clung loyally to her father's neck and begged to stay with her Da, but only until Alyssa had told her that if her Da did not get enough rest, he might become ill again. At that, Tamsin had kissed him quickly, said, "Goodbye, Da! You rest now," and left holding Alyssa's hand.

"Traitor!" Geoffrey had muttered to her back.

Now he was determined to get up and rejoin the human race. He would go berserk from the boredom if he had to spend one more hour resting. He wanted a bath, but the large oak tub was too big to bring up to his bedchamber and Alyssa would not allow him downstairs to the garderobe. His washing had to be done in pieces from a basin. He wanted to ride his horse and feel the wind and sunshine on his face. Storm had probably forgotten him by now. He wanted to see if Henry had mastered the quintain yet. He wanted to shovel manure, teach Tamsin to swim, scratch the bellies of the hounds who frequented the great hall. He wanted to get out of this bed, even if he had to crawl on his belly.

He flung the covers aside and swung his legs over the edge of the bed. His wounded right leg protested the quick movement with a stabbing pain, and he wondered briefly if he should wait until Edmund or Henry came to lend him a shoulder to lean on. No, he was going to do this on his own, he told himself. He put his bare left foot on the floor, leaning his weight on the uninjured leg until he determined how much strength was in the wounded one. So far, so good. Ignoring the throbbing darts of discomfort from his injury, he placed right foot next to left and shifted his weight forward, fighting back a wave of giddiness.

He was concentrating so heavily on his legs and whether they would support him that he didn't hear the door open until Alyssa said sharply, "Geoffrey de Graville, whatever are you doing! Get back in that bed this instant. You should be..."

"I am sick of resting!" he bellowed, sitting on the edge of the bed and glaring at his stepmother. "I shall go insane if you force me to stay in this bed for one more minute. I am a grown man, and I am going to put on my clothes and go -" he waved his hand toward the window, "outside."

"It is raining outside," Alyssa informed him.

"I don't care."

"But I do care, and I am telling you that you are not ready to go traipsing about the countryside and doing Lord only knows what kind of damage to yourself. Geoffrey, you almost bled to death and it takes time to recover from that."

"I have recovered," he insisted, hobbling to his feet, leaning his weight on the good leg and holding the bedcurtain for support, hoping he didn't look too pathetically pale. Alyssa stepped in front of him, put one hand on his chest, and pushed. He was so surprised at her laying hands on him in that manner, that he actually did fall back onto the bed, where he sat glaring at his stepmother. He didn't like to think that it was most likely his weakness as much as surprise which collapsed him so easily.

"You have not yet fully recovered, young sir!" Alyssa stated firmly. "You can get up when I say you are strong enough, and that is not today. And if you try to sneak out of here again, I shall send Edmund up here to stand guard and make sure you stay in bed."

"Edmund wouldn't do that," Geoffrey countered. Not if he knew what was good for him.

"Very well, I shall send Henry. He will do it if I ask him to."

Geoffrey fell back against the pillows with a groan, knowing he was out-maneuvered. Even in the short time he had been at Belvoir, Henry's mute, puppy-like adoration of Geoffrey's stepmother had become obvious. If she asked him to jump to his death from the battlements of the castle for her sake, he would do it without hesitation. If she smiled at him, he'd do it twice. But, Geoffrey realized with a flash of inspiration, Henry was only a boy, and Geoffrey had considerable size on him. "Henry is not strong enough to keep me here if I wish to leave," he said.

"Ha!" Alyssa countered. "I just pushed you down, and I am certain that even as young as he is, Henry is much stronger than I am."

"I allowed you to push me."

Alyssa sighed. "Geoffrey, my intention is not to vex you but only to ensure that you have completely recuperated before you attempt anything strenuous. It is no more than the concern you lavished upon me when I was carrying Isabel, but in your case the danger is much greater." She looked down and sighed deeply. "You are so brave, Geoffrey, that you don't understand how frightened we were here while you were gone, and then how terrified I was when you arrived home more dead than alive. Surely you do not wish to frighten me so again." Now he didn't know whether he should be sorry for being so cross with her, or if he should suspect she was using feminine wiles to get her way. While he hesitated, she pressed her advantage. "So I am going to have to insist that you stay in bed a few more days until I am certain that you are strong enough to be up and about."

Peeved beyond words, Geoffrey turned away and refused to acknowledge his stepmother, angered into uncharacteristic rudeness. He had never been able to out-argue her and obviously wasn't going to begin today. He didn't turn to look at her until she said, "Very well, Geoffrey. I was going to sit and talk with you a while because I knew you must be bored, but if you are going to behave childishly, I shall leave."

He almost shouted out apologies and promises of good behavior at that point, but pride made him hold his tongue. As she opened the door to leave him to continued tedious monotony, Edmund came in and before Geoffrey could enlist his friend's support, Alyssa told him sternly, "Geoffrey is to stay in bed until I say otherwise, Edmund."

"Yes, my lady," Edmund replied with a bow as she swept from the room.

Geoffrey crossed his arms over his chest and glared after his stepmother. "She is treating me as if I were a baby in swaddling," he grumbled. "Just who does she think she is?"

As usual, Edmund refused to be intimidated by Geoffrey's ill humor. "I believe," he said with a grin, "she thinks she is your mother."

"You are on her side!" Geoffrey accused, feeling betrayed.

Edmund looked puzzled. "But Geoffrey, it is not a matter of choosing sides. Lady Alyssa is merely concerned for your welfare, and I am certain she knows what she is doing."

"Get out."

"Get out?" Edmund repeated in confusion. "But, Geoffrey, I thought you wanted to discuss…"

"Get out! Go away! Leave! Shall I repeat it in French? Just go away and leave me alone. You annoy me. You all annoy me."

Edmund shook his head. "Very well, my lord. If you wish to sulk in solitude, I shall leave you to your rest. However, I would be remiss if I did not remind you of your orders to stay in bed." He ducked towards the door as he saw Geoffrey's hand reaching for the small metal cup on the table next to his bed, and slammed it shut behind him as the cup became a missile aimed at his red head, then bounced off the door and clattered harmlessly to the floor.

Geoffrey laid down, fuming at the world in general. He knew that sulking was exactly what he was doing and that it was stupid and childish. Tomorrow, or maybe the next day, he would apologize to his stepmother and to Edmund for his discourtesy, but for now, he preferred to sulk.

*****

He was still irritated and moody when he heard a knock at the door, so he ignored it, closed his eyes and pretended to be asleep. When he heard the door open despite his lack of response, he opened one eye to see who would dare to enter his room without permission.

It was Moll. He quickly squeezed his eye shut before she saw he was awake and lay still, wondering what she was doing here. He heard her footsteps approach the bed, sounding soft, as if she were barefoot, and stop, then heard no sound but her breathing for several minutes. She was watching him, he realized, just standing there watching him.

"How do I look?" he asked without opening his eyes.

She squeaked in surprise, and he opened his eyes then to see her clutching a goblet in both hands. He considered himself fortunate that she had not dropped it on him. "Well, Moll, I asked you a question. How do I look?"

"You look very well, my lord." At least she no longer shook and stammered, he thought, just seemed surprised that he was awake.

When that was all she said, he asked patiently, "And why are you here, Moll?"

She held up the goblet she had in her hands. "I brought you some wine, my lord. Red wine," as if that made a difference, "It is said that red wine restores strength lost from bleeding."

"Is that so?" he asked, pulling himself up on his elbows and taking the cup. "My lady stepmother sent you to bring this?"

"No, my lord, it was my idea."

He looked at her in surprise, the cup halfway to his lips. "Your idea?" She nodded, looking at her feet shyly. "I thank you for your thoughtfulness, Moll." He paused. "You must stay while I drink it, however, just in case it does not have the desired effect and the goblet drops from my weak fingers." She recognized the teasing tone in his voice and looked up at him, smiling, and watched as he drained the cup. In fact she seemed fascinated by the movement of his throat as he swallowed.

When he had finished he handed the cup back to her and said, "This is certainly much more pleasant than the horrible willow-bark stuff my stepmother makes me drink. I believe I do feel stronger now." It was true, he did, but it seemed to have more to do with Moll standing so close to his bed than the effects of the wine. She set the wineglass on the table but made no move to leave.

"Tell me something, Moll," he said with curiosity, pushing his hair back from his face.

"Yes, my lord?"

"When you first came here, you stuttered and trembled every time I saw you. Why were you so afraid of me? I do not believe I have a reputation for cruelty."

She looked at her feet again, but only for a moment, and he thought he saw her gaze rest for a moment on his bare chest as he sat up in the bed. "When I came here to work," she explained. "You were away." He nodded. He had been in Normandy. "I asked some of the other girls what Baron de Graville was like. They said he was fierce and stern, and impatient. I was frightened of you, my lord."

"They said that, did they?"

"Yes, my lord. And..." He nodded, giving her permission to continue. "I was told that Baron de Graville was a dark, bearded Norman. When Lady Alyssa sent me to bring you the food, and you opened the door, I thought I had gone to the wrong room. You..."

"I do not appear to be a Norman, but an Englishman?" he supplied hopefully. She nodded. "An impression I take care to cultivate," he said with a grin. When she looked confused, he realized that politics and the cultural differences between Normans and English were beyond her grasp.

"That was not me the other girls spoke of," he told her. "That was my father."

"Your father, my lord?"

"Yes. My father was killed in Normandy, so you never saw him, and I returned to England without him." He looked intently at the girl, and she looked intently back at him. She was very pretty, blond-haired, though of a somewhat darker shade than his, and big soft brown eyes, like a doe's.

"There is no need to be frightened of me, Moll," he said softly. She was standing very close to the bed, her knees touching it. "I am not fierce, or stern. Or impatient." He reached out his arm and put it around her waist, drawing her to sit on the bed next to him. "I am gentle, and kind." She made no move of resistance as he drew her nearer to him. "And patient."

It had been a long time since he had been with a woman, and this one seemed willing enough. In fact, her acquiescence made him wonder if that had been her intention in coming here, under the guise of bringing him wine.

He caressed her neck with the back of his hand, and asked, "Are you a virgin, Moll?"

"No, my lord," she answered honestly.

"Good." He said the word softly, and his arm tightened around her waist. It was his left arm, with his hand behind her back, where it was not so obvious, although he knew she had seen it. His right hand went to the neck of her gown, teasing at the ties that held the front closed. She sat very still, her eyes wide and intent, her mouth slightly open.

The top loop came open. "Are you married, Moll?" he asked, tugging at the next section of the lacing. She shook her head, and the tie came through another loop. "Betrothed? In love?" To each of these she shook her head, watching his eyes as the laces came undone.

"You realize, Moll, that I offer you none of those?"

She looked straight at him, her head slightly tilted. "Yes, I understand that, my lord." Her expression conveyed the thought that she not only understood; she didn't much care.

Forgetting his bad hand, Geoffrey spread the fabric of her gown apart with both hands, baring her shoulders and revealing full, firm breasts. He cupped them in his hands. She wore no shift under her plain gown, and he wondered if she did not own one, or if she had left it off for his convenience.

He looked at her eyes to see if she was going to try to flee, but she didn't move. Slowly, he lowered his head and placed his mouth over her breast, tugging gently on her sweet flesh and flicking his tongue over the puckered little nipple. She tasted good. It had been so long. Moll trembled, and clutched at his hair.

"Are you still afraid of me, Moll?" he asked, raising his head.

"No, my lord."

"Then why do you tremble?"

"Because..." Instead of finishing her answer with words, she pulled her arms out of the sleeves of her gown, put her hands on his shoulder, the first time she had touched him, and leaned towards him. Her lips brushed the smooth skin of his chest, and then closed on his own flat nipple, as she in turn tugged on it with her tongue. No one had ever done that to him before, and then he knew why she had trembled, for the feeling of her mouth on him like that caused a sensation to flow through him that made him shudder as well.

"Jesus, Moll, you are a tempting little witch," he muttered, pulling her to him and kissing her roughly. She put her arms about his neck and willingly pressed herself against him.

When he released her mouth he suddenly remembered how she had walked unbidden into his bedchamber, and realized the distinct possibility of someone else doing the same thing. Her eyes were closed, her lips slightly parted and swollen from his assault. "Go and bolt the door," he ordered hoarsely. She looked up at him with a little surprise, but slipped from the bed and darted across the floor to do his bidding. Geoffrey felt a sudden gratitude to his father for designing Belvoir with doors of stout English oak, rather than the leather curtains which enclosed most bedchambers. Wood doors provided far more privacy.

For those few moments, he closed his eyes and leaned back, feeling guilty. What was he doing, seducing a poor serving wench? He was the lord here, and she must feel compelled to obey him. But, he reasoned, she was apparently doing as much of the seducing as he was, if not more. By her own admission, she had no maidenhead to protect. Her unbidden entrance into his bedchamber under the flimsy excuse of conveying restorative wine, the fact that she had arrived barefoot and with no shift under her gown, and her unhesitating acquiescence to his advances all pointed to premeditation.

When she had set the bolt in the door and returned to stand again at the side of the bed, he opened his eyes and sat up, looking at her standing there with her gown hanging from her hips. He couldn't help but stare at her full breasts and large brown nipples, but he reached out and took her hand in his, holding it gently.

"Are you willing, Moll?" he asked in a gentle voice. "I will not force you. If you wish to leave, you may, and nothing more will be said on the matter. Your employment here will not be jeopardized, I promise." He let go of her hand, in case she chose to go.

But she stayed where she was. "I am willing, my lord," she said, her voice even softer than his. "I do not wish to leave."

"Then, in that case," he replied, "come here."

Before she obeyed him, she pushed her gown down from her waist until it fell to the floor, then, with neither clothing nor uncertainty, lifted the blanket and climbed into his bed. There was no need for him to get undressed; he was wearing only his trews and they were easily disposed of. All that was left on him was the white cloth binding around his thigh.

He pressed her down in the bed, caressing her breasts first with his hands and then again with his mouth. He reminded himself of his promise to be gentle and patient, but she seemed to want neither gentleness nor patience, kissing him and touching him boldly with eager abandon.

When he rolled to position himself over her he tried to put most of his weight on his uninjured leg, because the wounded one did still throb somewhat uncomfortably. But other parts of him were throbbing even more, making the discomfort of his wound seem minor just now.

She lay beneath him panting and eager, but before he went any farther, he held her chin in his right hand and forced her eyes to meet his. "Tell me, Moll," he said, "Why did you really come here? Merely to bring me wine?" She was wide-eyed in anticipation, and did not answer, biting her lip.

"I want the truth," he demanded, "Was it only the wine? Or did you come here for this?" He let go of her chin and kissed her vigorously, his tongue demanding an answer from hers as his hands pinned hers above her head. "I said I was a patient man, Moll, but not with liars. Isn't this really why you came here?"

"Yes," she admitted. "I came here for this. The wine was merely..."

"An excuse?"

She nodded and smiled saucily.

"Why?" he asked.

"Because I wanted to." He released her hands to slide his own hands beneath her shoulders and draw her up to him. Her tongue touched her lip, and she added, "May I ask you something, my lord?" He nodded.

"Are you going to ask me questions all night, my lord? Or…"

"Weeping Jesus," he said with a moan. "I have no more questions."

He was completely stunned when suddenly Moll squirmed away from him, sliding her body sideways until she was next to him rather than beneath him. Jerked too quickly from concupiscence, he could only stare stupidly as they knelt on the bed facing each other.

Moll smiled, an absurd gesture if she meant to deny him at this point. But instead of leaving Geoffrey's bed, she put her hands on his shoulders and urged him onto his back. She pushed his chest and hips down until he was prone, then, kneeling next to him, slid her hand over his hip and grasped his straining manhood, her fingers encircling him as she stroked slowly up and down, making him gasp like a landed fish as Moll explored and tormented.

"It is true then what they say, my lord," she said in a husky voice, her eyes half closed.

The very slowness of the movement of Moll's hand on him in such a barbaric manner was driving Geoffrey crazy. "What?" he moaned, finding it difficult to think, much less speak through his fragmented senses. "W-what is true?"

"I have heard," Moll replied, "that men who are very tall are also very large … here." She squeezed, and he groaned. "You are a very … tall man, my lord."

"Oh, God," was all he could say as he lay back and gave himself up to her mercy.

Moll had another trick with which to amaze him. She swung her leg around and actually straddled him, one knee placed on either side of his hips, and the hand which had been stroking now guided him into her as she settled herself on him as if he were a horse about to be ridden. She confirmed the comparison by murmuring, upon seeing his look of impassioned surprise, "This is called riding the stallion, my lord."

Riding the stallion, indeed. Surely this was unnatural, to have the woman on top like this. Unnatural perhaps, and sinful most definitely, but it was the most erotic experience Geoffrey had ever known. She rose up on him until he almost came out, then sank back down, her large breasts with their dark nipples jiggling in front of his face and her braids swinging between them. He grasped her hips in his hands and surged within her, held within her pulsing grip.

Despite the tremendous pleasure, it frightened him how closely he trod the borderline of control. When she rose up one more time, his hands on her hips pushed her upward and off him, flinging her down on her back almost roughly. She didn't seem to mind.

He parted her thighs with his knee, and she opened herself willingly to him. Common sense fled and he pressed himself into her in a single deep motion, all thoughts of the gentleness he had spoken of earlier forgotten. She responded with a deep-throated, "Aaah," and arched her hips up to meet his thrusts, her fingers locked tightly behind his neck as he drove himself deeper into her.

Their momentum increased and intensified, as her hands raked his back and his teeth scored the tender skin of her throat. He suddenly needed her desperately, though he didn't even know her. He only knew that she was a woman, soft and warm, willing and passionate, and he was a man who had come close to death, and God, he was glad to be alive, able to take comfort in the arms of a seductive woman. *I was afraid to die*, he wanted to say, but didn't, as they used each other with the blind, thoughtless urgency of need and lust.

The constraints of war and recuperation from his wounds had kept him celibate long enough that he almost lost himself now too soon, but Moll was experienced, and knew just what to do, and what not to do, to prolong the pleasure until they both reached the highest plateau of desperate, demanding need. An animal passion drove them, a lust which raged through Geoffrey's veins and heated his skin.

At the moment of climax, she lifted her legs to wrap them tightly around his hips. Completely oblivious now to either his wounded leg or his maimed hand, he plunged himself into her again and again, dimly hearing her cries of satisfied release echoing his own, until they both convulsed and collapsed, drained, sweat-drenched and trembling from exertion.

*****

Geoffrey sat up, leaning back against the wall and pushing his hair back from his face, watching Moll tie the laces of her gown. Observing her nimble fingers do up the laces, he was aware for the first time since she had entered his bedchamber of his disfigured hand, which he now discreetly slid under the blanket. It would have been difficult and time-consuming, perhaps impossible, for him to tie those slender bits of cloth without having all the usual fingers, and he was glad he had not been required to do so. However, he had had no difficulty in undoing them, and, he realized with something of a start, not once had Moll cringed from his touch, not even from the touch of his bad hand. Apparently, it hadn't mattered to her at all.

Moll saw him watching her, and as she finished fastening her gown, she smiled, moved forward and kissed him, then stepped back and for the first time, she blushed.

"What, blushes now, Moll?" Geoffrey asked with amusement. "A bit late, I believe."

She patted loose tendrils of her hair into place, and reached for the empty wine goblet on the table. Before her hand reached it, however, Geoffrey took hold of her arm and drew her back towards him.

"The wine you brought me was very beneficial. However, I think that you had better bring me another cup tomorrow, just to make sure I make a complete recovery. I do wish to, ah, regain all of my strength."

"I found nothing amiss with your strength, my lord," Moll said mischievously.

"That may be, but we do wish to be certain, do we not?" His eyes gleamed. "Tomorrow, Moll? Another cup of red wine?"

She nodded and picked up the goblet. "Tomorrow," she agreed, "I will bring you another cup of wine, my lord."

After she left the room, he lay back down in the bed, his hands behind his head, stretching out his legs and smiling to himself. Perhaps, he thought, he would not object too strenuously to his stepmother's coddling; the way she endeavored to keep him idling in bed until she saw fit to allow him up. Just for a few days, he conceded, he would allow her to have her way. Although the inactivity chafed at him and made him restless and edgy, there were, he reflected, compensations. Perhaps, just perhaps, he would not insist that strongly on ending his convalescence. Not just yet.

23

Finally, the day came when Alyssa determined that Geoffrey was strong enough to leave his bed and resume his work. He was embarrassed to find that his leg wound had left him with a slight limp, especially when he was tired or the weather was wet, but he was determined to conquer that flaw, and after several weeks of hard work it was barely noticeable. Edmund had offered him the use of a stout stick to aid his walking, but took it away when Geoffrey threatened to use it over his friend's head.

When the knights that Geoffrey had left behind at Pevensey returned to Belvoir, they had no reports of encountering anyone fitting the descriptions of Banyard and his men. A search party was sent out to trace Geoffrey and Henry's route, and upon their return reported finding the clearing where they had been attacked, with a shallow unmarked grave nearby that must have been Raoul's. But no other evidence of the rest of the troop was found, and Geoffrey could only surmise that when they had returned to find Raoul dead and Geoffrey and Henry escaped, the Norman rebels must have heeded Geoffrey's advice and beaten a hasty retreat for Normandy.

He also sent one of his knights with a message to Bickleigh. If the man assigned to this duty wondered at why Baron de Graville was inquiring after the well-being of a mere peasant in a village miles away from Belvoir, he knew better than to ask. In their loyalty, Geoffrey's retainers kept their curiosity about their lord's eccentricities to themselves, and the man merely dutifully reported back that the villein Kenelm of Bickleigh, as well as his family, was in good health and spirits and sent his regards to Baron de Graville and his daughter.

Geoffrey insisted on escorting Stephen back to Exeter himself when the boy returned to resume his studies at the priory. He knew that Alyssa would have liked to protest his undertaking the journey so soon after his recovery, but Geoffrey would have none of it. He was back in command of his life now, and his stepmother would just have to understand that he considered some things to be his personal responsibility.

After seeing Stephen safely reinstated at St. Nicholas Priory with gruff orders to stay put, Geoffrey again paid a call at Rougemont Castle to thank Baron de Meules for maintaining the horse he had left for his brother, and to install a fresh horse for Stephen's use in Rougemont's stable.

It was while he was seeing to the comfort of that horse that he heard the stable door creak open behind him, and he had a distinct feeling that he knew who was there.

"Good afternoon, Lady Solange," he said without turning to look at her.

"Good afternoon, Baron de Graville," she replied as she walked past him with her nose in the air. "Are you pretending to be a groom again?"

"I never pretended anything," he countered. He leaned over the stall door and watched her as she went to the stall across from him where her pony was kept. "However, some people make assumptions before learning the truth."

"Oh, you are a vexatious boy!" she retorted.

He laughed. "Vexatious I will admit, but hardly a boy."

She turned around and walked toward him, another cutting remark about to spring from her lips, but as she stepped close and saw his face, she suddenly went pale and put her hand over her mouth with a horrified gasp. "What have they done to you?" she whispered when she saw the fresh scar on his cheek.

For the most part Geoffrey barely thought about the mark on his face; it didn't bother him nearly as much as his hand did. It surprised him, and yet at some level also gratified him that she was so concerned about him.

"'Tis naught but a scratch," he assured her, stepping out of the stall, "and the man who did it is dead."

"I am glad of that," she said. "That is, I am glad you killed the man who did that to you."

What a blood-thirsty little wench, Geoffrey thought. He really ought to tell her the truth, that he himself had not killed the man who had marked him, but then she might ask who had, and then what would he say? That his attacker had been slain by the brother of the woman he had loved, who he still loved despite her death, the mother of his child? Something told him she would not like to hear that his heart was en-thralled, but another part reasoned, what would it matter? What was she to him, but the daughter of a friend? What was he to her, but merely a friend of the family. She wouldn't be jealous, would she? There was no reason for her to be. He almost opened his mouth to explain, but then she turned those big, deep, dark eyes on him, looking at him with an expression he might expect to see if he had slain a fire-breathing dragon and laid it at her feet.

He kept his mouth shut.

"Does it hurt?" she asked in an awed voice. Geoffrey shook his head and smiled slightly. He had to admit, he rather enjoyed having a pretty girl swooning over his injuries. Though the maternal look she gave him when she asked if his face hurt did make him glad she hadn't been at Belvoir when he'd arrived home with half his blood spilled about the countryside. In company with his stepmother, the two of them most likely would have conspired to keep him lingering in bed until he was thirty.

"Were you wounded in the uprising?" she asked and he nodded in affirmation.

"But it is all over now," he assured her. "You need not fear an inva-sion." He wondered if she would be impressed or revolted if he told her about his other wound, the more serious one. Perhaps it would be better if he said nothing, as she frequently refused to believe what he told her and she might demand to see it in order to confirm its existence.

"Tell me about it," Solange entreated, looking up at him with big eyes.

He hesitated. "It was a battle," he said. "It was bloody and violent. I don't think it is something you would like to hear about."

"Yes, I would," she insisted.

"Very well," Geoffrey sighed, and gave her the edited version, skimming over the details and making light of his leg wound. He managed to convince her it was just another scratch, and he completely eliminated mention of the deadly encounter with the Norman troop on the way back to Belvoir. Still, she seemed impressed.

"Are you planning to go for a ride?" he asked, looking at her pony. If she was, she would have to wake the beast up.

"No," she said with a sigh. "I am going nowhere. My father has forbidden me to leave the keep alone and has conveyed those orders to the guards at the gates. Even the postern gate is guarded. I am not even supposed to be in the stable alone at all, but I wanted to make sure she was being well cared for." She petted the somnolent pony's nose. "Sometimes those churlish stable hands ignore her."

Not only was she blood-thirsty, but disobedient as well. Baron de Meules must have discovered his daughter's solitary sojourns about the countryside. Geoffrey couldn't resist teasing her. "You are not allowed out even with that wicked knife to protect you?"

Solange pouted. "My brother returned from Hereford and took it away from me."

"Smart man," Geoffrey observed. "I should like to make his acquaintance."

"He is not here now. He has gone to court," Solange replied.

"Tell him to watch his backside," Geoffrey muttered below his breath.

"What did you say?" Solange asked.

"Nothing, nothing," he replied quickly. It would most definitely not be proper for him to tell this gently bred young girl that rumor had it that their bachelor king preferred the company of pretty young boys over female companionship. Geoffrey would fight, would lay down his life if necessary for king and country, but if he were ever called upon to go to court, he would avoid the king and darkened corridors as he would avoid a leper.

"How old is your brother?" he asked Solange, just to change the subject. He hadn't yet met the man.

"I am not sure," she reflected. "He is the oldest in our family, and then came Judith."

Judith? Ah, yes, Judith. The older sister. His almost-betrothed.

"I am the youngest. So my brother Gilbert must be very old. Older than you, even."

Oh, thank you, Geoffrey thought sourly. She made it sound as if anyone older than him bordered on decrepit.

He stalked out of the horse stall, fully intending to walk away from her, but then he saw her eyes twinkling with mischief, and he suddenly recalled the day last year when they had first met and had lied outrageously about their ages to each other. She laughed at his offended expression.

"You are an impertinent little chit who should have more respect for your elders," he informed her. He paused, feeling suddenly shy, then said, "If you are not allowed out alone, perhaps it will be acceptable if I escort you for a brief ride. I would like to get out into the fresh air for a little while. That is, if you don't think me too ancient to provide adequate protection."

She apparently liked that idea very much, for her eyes sparkled with pleasure. "That would be wonderful!" she exclaimed childishly. "My father would certainly consider you to be an adequate escort. He likes you."

Geoffrey was gratified to hear that Baron de Meules liked him and considered him to be a suitable companion for his daughter. He stepped towards Solange's pony to saddle it for her, but stopped when she tugged on his sleeve. It was his left sleeve and although he was wearing his gloves he still had to suppress the urge to snatch his arm away and hide it from her view.

"My Lord de Graville?" she asked hesitantly. "May I ride on your horse with you?"

It was not an outrageous request, in fact it was quite common for ladies and girls to ride pillion with their escorts. He mounted Storm, walked the stallion to the mounting block, and helped Solange up behind him. As she arranged her skirts over her legs, Geoffrey tried very hard to banish from his mind the memory of Milesenda riding behind him in the past, with her arms around his waist and her cheek leaning against his back as they sneaked off to their trysts at the lake in the clearing. Fortunately, Solange did not cling to him so intimately as they passed through the gate and acknowledged the guard's respectful salute, but he was still very much aware of her small hands on his hips as they rode.

They did not stay out long as it soon grew cold and windy, a premonition of approaching winter which in this part of the country promised coastal gales and bone-chilling mists. As Geoffrey brushed Storm down after their return, Solange waited patiently for the promised opportunity to feed him apple pieces, a transaction for which his horse seemed to be becoming quite greedy.

"My lord de Graville?" she said in a questioning voice as she wiped her hand on the skirt of her gown after Storm took his treat from her. "May I ask you something?"

"Of course you may," he replied. "What is it?"

"That day I first met you, in the stable, when I thought you were a groom. Why did you not simply tell me then that you were the son of Baron de Graville? Then I would not have been angry with you the next time I saw you."

"I mean you no offense, my lady," he replied, "but at that moment I did not believe it was any concern of yours who I was. Besides, the clothing I was wearing that day was dirty, worn and completely unsuitable for the heir of a Norman baron. If I had told you that Lord de Graville was my father, you would never have believed me."

"I took no notice of your clothing that day," she said. She looked up at his face with an intent expression that unnerved him. "I only noticed ..."

He averted his eyes, feeling a bit disquieted at her gaze, and brushed an imaginary piece of dust from his horse's flank. "You noticed what?"

How could she have not taken note of the clothes he'd been wearing? She'd sat on his lap, wiped her tearstained face on his sleeve. His dirty sleeve, attached to a tunic that was old, smelly and ripped in places. Even the actual grooms had been more presentable than he'd been that day, not that he'd cared at the time what he looked or smelled like.

"I noticed your arms," she said. "How strong they felt, and yet at the same time, how gentle. And I noticed your eyes. I have never before seen eyes so blue. Nor so sad. I had never seen such sad eyes in my life."

Geoffrey was surprised, and glad he was facing towards his horse so that Solange could not see his sad blue eyes at the moment. He thought he'd succeeded in hiding his melancholy and grief, keeping it off his face and hidden behind ice.

"Why were you so sad, my lord?"

He couldn't tell her. He couldn't tell anyone, especially not this pretty young girl, about the despondency and unhappiness which controlled him still, even five years after Milesenda's death. He continued to stare at Storm's side, searching his mind for another reason to give her.

"It was the first time I had been away from-"

He stopped himself before saying, my daughter. Surely this noble girl would disapprove of him having an illegitimate child, so he revised his words.

"The first time I had been away from home for a long time, and we were leaving for war."

That seemed to appease Solange. The reasons for his sadness should have been none of her concern, this silly young girl he barely knew, and yet, he enjoyed having someone to talk to.

"When do you return to your home?" she asked.

"Tomorrow. We leave at first light. I wish to depart for Belvoir before the weather becomes foul."

"Your Belvoir must be a lovely place. You always seem eager to return there," Solange observed. Geoffrey agreed with her and found himself telling her how lovely his home was for such a long time that he suddenly realized he must be boring her.

"I shall be returning here in the spring," he said, as if she would care. Did he want her to care? He wasn't sure. "Your father wishes to have some of his mares bred, and I will be bringing several of our stallions here in the spring to service them." He knew this was a task he could easily have delegated to others, but something seemed to make him wish to travel to Exeter himself, more than just his wish to visit his brother. If he were to be honest with himself, he had to admit that it was at least partially that he enjoyed Solange's company.

That was not so unreasonable, he told himself. After all, she was a child and he liked children. All children, even Edmund's son Cerdic, despite the fact that the last time he had held his godson, the boy had rudely wet on him, and had come away with a handful of Geoffrey's hair in his fist as well. Solange made him laugh with her childish antics, even though she also irritated him with her tempers as well. He just wished she wouldn't continue to turn those big dark eyes to him, eyes that held a constant reminder that every day she became less a child and more of a woman.

24

That winter, Geoffrey's sister Isabel had her first birthday, and as soon as she began to walk, she attempted to follow Tamsin around everywhere. Tamsin, in turn, attempted to follow her father around everywhere. Geoffrey felt it somewhat demeaned his dignity as lord of Belvoir to have two toddling little girls constantly treading his heals like eager puppies, so he frequently scooped them both up and carried one on each hip, which they both enjoyed immensely. It also silenced Tamsin's constant shrill cries of, "Da! Wait for me and Bell!"

Bell was what Tamsin called her aunt Isabel. She had developed a habit of calling people by the ending of their names. Edmund was Mun, Isabel was Bell and Henry was Ree in Tamsin's childish vocabulary. But problems arose when little Isabel learned to speak her first lisping words. Geoffrey then found it necessary to inform his daughter that she was not to address Lady Alyssa as Mama, even though Isabel did. The confusion evident on Tamsin's face as her father instructed her to address his stepmother as My Lady rather than Mama, hurt Geoffrey to the quick, but he found he lacked the courage to really explain to Tamsin about her mother and what had happened to her. She didn't need a mother, Geoffrey tried to tell himself. She had him, and his love would have to be enough.

The same applied when Isabel, imitating Tamsin, looked at her brother Geoffrey and said, "Da!" Then it was Alyssa's turn to try to explain to her bewildered baby that Geoffrey was not her Da, and that she should address him by his name or as My Lord.

As for Alyssa, her heart nearly broke as she watched her stepson tearing himself apart to be both mother and father to Tamsin. It was obvious as the little girl grew and became more aware of the world around her, that she noticed that almost everyone she knew had a mother, except for Tamsin, although no child at Belvoir or in Lydford had a more loving or more attentive father than Geoffrey.

Being Geoffrey's offspring, she began at a young age to find trouble and get herself into childish scrapes, but she also learned young that she could redeem herself utterly in her father's eyes with a few kisses and hugs.

As much as he could, Geoffrey kept his daughter with him when he was at Belvoir, perched in front of him on his horse or carried about on his hip. Those days when he was forced by circumstances to leave her at home, when he returned the first place he went was to the nursery to see her. One afternoon, he walked into the room to the distinct feeling that he had interrupted something.

Lady Alyssa and Maud were both there, hands on hips, glaring down at Tamsin who stood her ground with a combined expression of guilt and defiance on her face. As usual, her smock was dirty. Like her father before her, she defied Maud's efforts to keep her clean. At that moment, she no longer appeared to resemble her mother quite so much, but with her eyes dark with rebellion, she was every inch Geoffrey's child.

Geoffrey halted at the sight of this frozen tableau and glanced from Tamsin to Maud, then to Alyssa. "What is it?" he asked. "What has she done now?"

Alyssa turned to him, her expression carefully guarded. She said only one word, but it was enough.

"Frogs."

Tamsin had been about to throw herself on her father's mercy, a tactic which was always successful in forestalling his anger. But she never got the chance. Her little mouth rounded in amazement and astonishment when, with a strangled sound, her father quite suddenly stuffed his fist in his mouth, turned and fled from the room.

He dashed down the corridor to his bedchamber and once he had gained the room, sagged weakly against the wall, gasping with gusts of unhinged laughter. He laughed until he cried, hysterical tears wetting his cheeks as he slid down the wall to sit on the floor, resting his forehead on his knees as he laughed some more.

Frogs! Tamsin was only five years old. He himself had been eight when he had discovered the amusing effect the sudden appearance of a few wet frogs had on some people. Tamsin no doubt thought he had gone insane to flee as he had, when she had most likely expected to be punished, although they all knew full well that Geoffrey had never administered any punishments to his daughter other than a few stern words. Though his own father had beaten him severely for tormenting his stepmother with frogs, Geoffrey had never so much as spanked his child and he never would, but he couldn't let her see him doubled over helplessly at the thought of her antics. It would completely destroy his fatherly authority and what was left of his dignity.

He looked up quickly at the sound of footsteps. *Please, not Tamsin,* he thought. He couldn't face his daughter just yet; he needed more time to compose himself. But it was Alyssa standing over him, laughing as well. He gulped and swallowed, wiping his face on his sleeve.

"Oh, Geoffrey," his stepmother giggled. "You should have seen your face. I thought you were about to die on the spot."

"Where," he could barely speak, the laughter again threatening to bubble up through his throat, "where did she put the frogs?"

"In Maud's bed."

"Oh, lord..." He pressed his forehead back to his kneecaps. "How did she know? You didn't tell her, did you?"

"Of course not! It seems that de Graville children have a natural affinity for frogs. I just wonder how she got them."

"Most likely she charmed one of the servants into bringing them up from the river," Geoffrey mused. "Or perhaps she asked Henry to get them for her, without bothering to tell him what she intended to do with them." Henry's unwitting complicity was a very plausible possibility. The boy's devotion to his lord's daughter was second only to his devotion to the lord's stepmother. If any females were deserving of devotion, it was Alyssa and Tamsin, but still...

"I know she needs a spanking," Geoffrey stated, "but Lord help me, I just can't do it."

Alyssa looked down at him and said, "What that child needs is a mother."

Geoffrey's laughter died a sudden death. Cold seeped through him, ice stiffened his veins, and it was a secure feeling far preferable to the unruly laughter in which he had almost lost himself. He bounded to his feet, all traces of amusement disappearing from his face. "Tamsin has all she needs right here," he said grimly, flattening his hand on his chest.

"Geoffrey, she is becoming hopelessly spoiled. She needs a woman's guidance," Alyssa insisted. "You cannot be both her mother and her father, much as you may strive to."

"She has you, and Maud, for feminine influence," Geoffrey replied, turning away and studying the toe of his boot. His mirthful mood disappeared as if it had never been. He knew what his stepmother was leading up to, and he didn't want to hear it.

But he was going to hear it regardless.

"Geoffrey, dear," Alyssa said to his back. "It has been over four years now since Milesenda died. You have grieved for her, but you will not be unfaithful to her memory if you were to marry. Not only does Belvoir need an heir, but your daughter needs the influence of a mother, more than just myself and Maud. Let yourself live, Geoffrey. It would not be a sin."

Geoffrey leaned his forehead against the wall, feeling the memories of Milesenda slicing his heart to shreds. And he also heard an echo of his father's voice announcing his upcoming marriage to Alyssa. *Your mother has been dead for three years*, Raymond had said. *It is no sin for me to wed again.* But that had been different. His father had not loved his mother. Theirs had been a marriage of convenience. Geoffrey still loved Milesenda; he had to. He had sworn an oath to love her forever, and a knight did not abandon his oath. His stepmother should know that. They had been over this ground before.

"Mother, how can I allow another woman to raise Milesenda's child?" he asked, anguished, and still not facing her.

"Another woman raised your mother's child, and he seems to have survived the experience," Alyssa replied tartly. Then her voice softened. "Milesenda would not want you to live alone for the rest of your life for her sake," she said. "She would want you to be happy."

Happy! The only thing that would make him happy would be to have time reverse itself to before Milesenda's death, and then for him to find some way to prevent it. He turned around and faced his stepmother, suddenly consumed with affection for her because he knew she had only his and Tamsin's best interests at heart, and because he could see in her eyes how she hated hurting him by mentioning the subject of another marriage. Part of him wanted to kneel at her feet and promise to do whatever she wished him to, just to see her smile, as he knew Henry would do, given the opportunity. But that part of him was overwhelmed by the reluctance he still felt about marriage, although he knew perfectly well his obligations in that direction. He was afraid to give his heart to another woman. They died too easily.

"Mother," he said softly, and his eyes were filled with pain. "I promised, I swore an oath to Milesenda, on my honor, that I would never love nor marry anyone but her. I cannot go back on my word."

"But Milesenda died," Alyssa countered. "It is not the same as it would be if she were still alive."

"I know," Geoffrey interrupted. "If she were still alive, we would be married and this conversation would be unnecessary."

Alyssa had her own theories where Milesenda was concerned, although she would never distress her stepson by speaking of them to him. She had been quite fond of Milesenda and had been genuinely saddened by her death, for her own sake and not only because it had destroyed Geoffrey. But in her heart, she did not believe that Milesenda was the right woman for her stepson. Not because of her low birth, although that would have caused problems for Geoffrey among the other nobles of England had he truly married her. She knew that had Milesenda lived, Geoffrey would, regardless of anyone else's opinion, have wed her legally when his father died, because Raymond would never have given his permission while he was alive. But Alyssa believed in her heart that Geoffrey's great love for Milesenda had not really been more than the romantic attachment of a passionate young man for his first lover, and that eventually he would have become bored with her. She had been sweet and adorable and biddable, and utterly devoted to Geoffrey, but in Alyssa's opinion, Geoffrey needed someone with more fire and wit and spirit, someone strong-willed like himself, who would not merely be his shadow and agree with his every word. Milesenda had not been that someone in Alyssa's opinion, but her sudden and tragic death had transcended the incompatibility that had yet to evolve and had burned her memory indelibly onto Geoffrey's heart, rendering forever unknown the issue of whether or not their love would have endured. Alyssa knew that her mentioning Geoffrey's responsibility to marry and father an heir grieved him by bringing up painful memories, and she hated to hurt him, but she felt that what she was doing was for his own good.

"But Geoffrey, Milesenda's death released you from those vows and you should know that. When you were knighted you swore a vow of loyalty to King William, but at his death you transferred that loyalty to William Rufus, did you not?"

"Yes," Geoffrey admitted reluctantly. "But my oath to the king was to him and to his heirs after him. I did not abandon it at his death; I merely fulfilled the additional portion of it." He raked his hair back from his face and gave his stepmother a look that said, counter that if you can!

But to Alyssa, this was not a contest of logic between herself and her stepson, but a very real attempt to secure his happiness and security for his family. She put her hand on his arm.

"If Milesenda had known that she was going to die," Alyssa said softly, "I am certain that she would have wished for you to marry again, for Tamsin's sake as well as your own. Your happiness was always para-mount to her, Geoffrey." The pain evident in Geoffrey's eyes as his step-mother spoke of Milesenda was terrible to see. "Is there no one you have met with whom you might be happy, with whom you might find a contented marriage?" she asked.

"Even if there was," Geoffrey said evasively, "there is still this." He lifted his left hand slightly, and Alyssa looked at him with surprise.

"What does your hand have to do with whether or not you marry?" she asked.

"Mother," he said patiently, "no woman would be willing to marry a man with such a ... deformity, and I will have no reluctant bride being compelled into a marriage she would find repulsive."

Alyssa didn't know if she should laugh or cry at her stepson's words, but to spare his feelings, she did neither. Instead, she reached for his hand and when he put it behind his back, she assumed her most maternal expression. "Geoffrey, give me your hand. Now!"

Reluctantly, wishing he had his gloves on, he dragged his left hand from the folds of his tunic and his stepmother took it in both her hands, touching the scars and the stumps where he should have had fingers. *How could she touch it without being sick*, Geoffrey wondered.

"Geoffrey, your hand has been injured but it is an honorable battle wound. It is not repulsive nor disgusting, and there is no need for you to hide it in those gloves you wear." She tightened her grip on his hand when he tried to pull it from her grasp. "You should not let this hinder you from marrying. Only a silly, vapid, foolish girl would allow something like this to be an impediment, and such a girl would not be worthy of you in any case. Geoffrey, it is terrible that this injury had to happen to you but it is not as bad as you seem to believe."

Geoffrey wanted to believe what his stepmother was telling him; the sensible part of him said she was right, but his gut instinct still considered it a hideous deformity. As soon as she loosened her grip on his hand he folded it back in the fabric of his tunic. He had no logical answers for his stepmother and after a minute she sighed, discouraged, and left him alone with a sympathetic pat on the shoulder.

He returned to the nursery to explain gently to Tamsin that it was most discourteous to place frogs in anyone's bed, but as he did so his stepmother's words about his knowing anyone he might be happy with echoed in his head. A memory flashed through Geoffrey's mind then, an image of a small, spirited, black-haired girl who had sat on his lap and cried, kicked his leg, pointed a knife at him. Why should he think of her when his stepmother was urging him to marry, he wondered irritably. She was only a little girl, more suitable as a playmate for Tamsin than as a wife, even if he were interested in a wife, which he wasn't.

However, his brush with death after the battle at Pevensey had scared Geoffrey, bringing back the worries about his mortality and his family's future, worries that chased each other around his head like pups after their tails. His obligation as lord of Belvoir was to produce a legitimate male heir. His oath of eternal devotion to his love, his Milesenda, contradicted his responsibility. He wanted, needed, to fulfill his obligations but his heart refused to allow him to do what ought to be done. And he was terrified, petrified to the bone, of the possibility of killing another woman by the bearing of his child. He thanked God that his mistress Moll had never conceived during their liaison.

They surrounded him like enemy soldiers, and twice as menacing. Responsibilities. Vows. Fears. Whatever way he turned, he was damned.

Tamsin's favorite place in the universe was in her father's lap, and Geoffrey held her there, thinking about Milesenda, but the memories were becoming intermingled with thoughts of Solange de Meules, in spite of his efforts not to think about her. It confused him and made him feel vulnerable, and that was something else he had vowed to avoid. So to keep the confusing, troublesome emotions at bay, he took Tamsin down to the stable for a ride with him on Storm. If his daughter's favorite place in the world was in his lap, her second favorite place was on his horse's back, and for a while at least Geoffrey was able to lose himself in the little girl's delight.

25

One of the lordly responsibilities that Geoffrey now held was that of presiding over hallmote, the manor court, where disputes were aired and settlements attempted; the few petty crimes that occurred tried. Before Raymond's death he had allowed Geoffrey to observe this procedure, held in Belvoir's great hall, until the day he had noticed that the two villeins standing below the dais to discuss grazing rights had stopped speaking and were staring past Lord Raymond's shoulder. Baron de Graville had turned around to catch Geoffrey and Edmund, finding this whole proceeding quite boring, standing behind him making comical, contorted faces at the amazed villagers who were now struggling to retain their composure in their lord's presence. Raymond had banished the pair with a single growled word, "Out!" and a look to Geoffrey that had plainly said, *I shall deal with you later*, and the two boys had scampered off to more interesting adventures. Geoffrey had been fourteen years old then; now, at the advanced age of twenty, he wondered if those gathered today in the hall would remember that incident, as he took his place in his father's chair on the dais. Not his father's chair, he reminded himself, again, but his chair. His demesne. His responsibility. Remember that, Geoffrey.

He turned to Father Mathieu, standing to his right as he had stood with Raymond. It had been Dunstan's duty to stand at Lord de Graville's left during hallmote, and now red-haired Edmund took his place. Geoffrey didn't dare look at his friend's face; he was afraid Edmund

297

would recall their childhood disgrace at a similar gathering and he was not at all certain either of them would be able to restrain a childish fit of giggling.

"Well, Father," he asked the priest quietly, "what is the first order of business?" What excruciatingly fascinating subject shall we discuss today? One of the tenant's rights to graze his swine in my woods, or perhaps grain allotments, or a case of petty theft for which to mete out punishment?

Father Mathieu gave his cousin a look that admonished, take this seriously, Geoffrey, cleared his throat and said, "My lord, there has been a charge of rape brought against one of the villeins."

Oh, lord, couldn't we start with something simple and boring, Geoffrey lamented silently. He sighed. "Very well, bring in the accused."

Father Mathieu nodded at the guard at the doorway, and at his gesture, two more men led in the accused man, his hands bound tightly behind his back, eyes fixed firmly on the floor. The man's clothing was ripped and dirty, his light brown hair hanging over his face. When the two guards had their prisoner before the dais, one of them prodded him in the back with a wooden club until he fell to his knees. Geoffrey wanted to call out, no need to treat him so viciously. He knew well the humiliation of being bound and forced to his knees. But this man was accused of rape. Geoffrey kept silent, until the rougher of the two guards pulled the young man's bowed head by the hair, forcing it up until Geoffrey saw his face.

"Oh, my God, Dewi!" Geoffrey rose to his feet, a sudden memory assailing him, a youthful memory of flinging mud at that same face until it was unrecognizable. It was almost unrecognizable again today, but this time because Dewi had been so severely beaten. Both eyes were blacked and swollen shut, his face and lips bruised and battered, the nose broken. Geoffrey had never seen anything so pitiful.

"Merciful Christ, who did this to you?" he demanded.

Dewi didn't speak, it was probably impossible. There were bruises across the front of his throat as if whoever had beaten him had tried to strangle him as well, but Dewi's head moved ever so slightly towards the man to his right, the one with his hand still tangled viciously in his hair.

Geoffrey's first impulse was to have the other man imprisoned and fined for assault, but he reminded himself that Dewi was the accused here. He willed himself calm, sat down in his chair, and tried to think impartially. "Let go of his hair, Osbert, he is not going anywhere," he said to the rough guard, and with a look of reluctance, Osbert unhanded Dewi and stepped back a pace. Dewi's head went back down, ashamed of his situation and appearance.

This wasn't right, Geoffrey thought. He had known Dewi since childhood, and a less likely rapist could not be imagined. They were close to the same age, and Geoffrey knew Dewi to be a serious, thoughtful and courteous young man, hard-working and honest. He was tall and lithe, and had been good looking until he'd been beaten half to death. He was known to be a reserved, quiet man who spoke little but whose feelings ran deep, a man Geoffrey could relate to. Geoffrey knew he couldn't allow his pity for Dewi's current condition to cloud his judgment. The young man had been charged with a serious crime, and if found guilty, would have to suffer the punishment for it, a thought that made Geoffrey shudder inwardly. He looked at Osbert.

"Do you bring the charge of rape against him?" he asked, nodding towards Dewi and recalling that these hearings had been conducted in Norman French in his father's day, with Father Mathieu or Dunstan supplying names and translating if necessary. Now, with Geoffrey as lord, no translations were necessary because they all spoke in English, and Geoffrey knew the names of everyone at Belvoir and in Lydford.

Osbert nodded. "Yes, my lord. I bring the charge."

"What proof do you have?" Geoffrey tried to sound dispassionate.

"My own eyes have the proof, my lord. I caught him myself, caught him in the act, the animal, in the shed behind the miller's house, defiling..." Osbert's voice trailed off.

Geoffrey looked at the accused. "What say you, Dewi? Is this true?" Silently but firmly, Dewi shook his head, not lifting his gaze from the floor.

"He lies!" Osbert shouted, his face going red with anger. "He raped her, my lord. He should be hung by his..."

Geoffrey held up his hand. "Hold, Osbert. I shall decide the punishment here, if the crime is proven." His stomach lurched at the thought of the punishment that a proven case of rape demanded. What would his father have done in this situation? He would have heard all sides before making any judgments, Geoffrey determined. He looked at Osbert. "What of the girl? What does she say? Does she accuse him of rape?"

Silence reigned. Osbert's gaze shifted nervously, and Geoffrey thought he saw Dewi tremble slightly. "Well?" he demanded. "Who is the girl, and what is her assertion?"

Something in the way neither accused nor accuser would identify the victim set off a warning for Geoffrey. He looked around at the twenty or so spectators, all listening avidly. No girl deserved to have her shame made public like this, he thought, but he could neither condemn nor acquit Dewi without hearing what she had to say. His decision made, he stood up once more.

"We will conduct this inquiry in private," he said to the assemblage, most of whom looked disappointed at having this scandal removed from public display. "Only the accused, accuser, myself and Father Mathieu as witness. In there," he nodded towards the small office off at the side of the hall. The assembled villagers began to buzz with speculation as Geoffrey continued, "But first, Edmund, unbind his hands." At Osbert's sputtered protests, he stated firmly, "He is unarmed and half dead. We shall all be quite safe, even if he is untied. Edmund!"

Edmund sprang quickly to do Geoffrey's bidding, shouldering Osbert aside as he worked at the leather lacings tied tightly about Dewi's wrists. The young man lifted his face for a moment and despite his battered visage, gave Geoffrey a look of gratitude. The cords were snug and twisted, seemingly unwilling to loosen their stranglehold on Dewi's wrists. Frustrated as he pulled and worked at them, Edmund exclaimed, "God's feet, these things are tighter than a virgin's... Geoffrey, give me your knife!" He held out his hand impatiently towards his friend, but looked up at the collective gasp that arose.

Too late, Edmund realized his blunder as all eyes focused on him. He had forgotten himself and called his friend by his Christian name in public, in front of the other tenants who would never dare to address Baron de Graville as anything other than "my lord", and he had virtually ordered Geoffrey to loan him his dagger.

If the situation hadn't been so deadly serious, Geoffrey would have laughed at the stricken expression on Edmund's face, as he realized his error and blushed and stammered, "Um, my lord, if you would be so kind as to allow me the use of your knife to cut these bindings, my lord..." His voice trailed off in hideous embarrassment.

Not trusting himself to speak, Geoffrey wordlessly stepped down from the dais and handed his dagger to Edmund who sliced through Dewi's bonds and let them fall to the floor. As Geoffrey slid the returned knife back into his belt and Osbert glared furiously, Dewi rubbed his abraded wrists, chapped raw by the rough leather. *I know how that feels*, Geoffrey thought.

His position as impartial judge would be compromised if he helped Dewi to his feet and escorted him to the office, so he nodded at Edmund, who understood his intent and tugged Dewi upward, wincing at the close-up view of his bruised face.

With a jerk of his head for the others to follow him, Geoffrey led the way to the small office, and when Edmund closed the door behind him, leaving the four of them alone, Geoffrey sat in the chair, with Father Mathieu standing silently behind him, and looked at the two men standing across the table.

"Very well, Osbert, I need to know the name of the girl you accuse Dewi of defiling. We must bring her here and ask her if rape was done." He glanced at Father Mathieu and the priest nodded in confirmation. It was the correct course of action.

Dewi glanced once at his accuser before again turning his eyes to the floor, but his now unbound hands were clenched into tight fists. Osbert hesitated, clearly unwilling to name the victim, but under Geoffrey's demanding glare finally burst out, "It was my daughter, my lord! My little girl, my..."

"Little Kerensa?" Geoffrey was incredulous and horrified. "But she is only..."

"Sixteen." The word slipped out from between battered lips, the first utterance Dewi had made in this whole ordeal. Geoffrey hadn't realized that Osbert's daughter was so grown up. Dewi looked up now, turning away from Osbert's angry glare to look at Geoffrey. Despite the obvious pain it caused him to speak, he said in his defense, "It was no rape, my lord. I swear it."

Quickly Osbert stepped threateningly toward Dewi, his hand raised to strike. "How dare you, you filthy swine, how dare you deny it!"

Geoffrey stood and leaned his gloved hands on the table. "Osbert!" he said, loudly enough that the man's attention was diverted. "He has a right to speak in his defense. I think you have damaged him enough as it is. You are the one who beat him, are you not?"

"Yes, my lord, I admit that." Osbert's chin came up, defiant. "But, my lord." he entreated, "think how you would feel, were it your daughter."

The thought of any man ever laying hands on his daughter, or his sister, made Geoffrey feel murderous, but he had to keep this hearing in hand, had to know the truth of the matter. He waved his hand at Osbert to indicate he should back away from Dewi, and said, "Tell me what you know, then Dewi may defend himself, and then, I will speak with Kerensa."

Osbert looked as if he wished to argue with Geoffrey's last statement, but the baron's scowl forestalled him. Swallowing nervously, he began his tale.

"I went to the mill to take my wheat to be ground," he said. "To make a shorter walk home, I went behind the miller's house, and when I passed the shed there I heard it...heard...sounds. It sounded like my Kerensa's voice. I went in and found him, he was on her, her clothes were ripped off, they were, that is he was...it was rape!" he finished vehemently. His voice lowered. "I pulled him off her, struck him to keep him away from her, my little girl..." He looked away

Geoffrey let Osbert's words sink in, and somehow it didn't ring true. He wondered how it was that the man would just happen by at that exact moment. Turning to Dewi, he said, "Tell us your side," with a quelling look at the outraged father to keep him from interrupting.

Dewi tried to lick his lips, the effort obviously paining him, and turned his back on Osbert to look directly at Geoffrey. Geoffrey couldn't help but wince as the bruised face turned to him. The young man's voice was soft and strained with the effort to speak through swollen lips and a bruised throat.

"My lord, it was no rape. She was willing. We-" he broke off as Osbert lunged towards him again, to be stopped by Geoffrey's frown. "My lord," Dewi's voice was coming a little stronger. "I love Kerensa. I would never hurt her. I wished to marry her, and I never would have touched her without the blessing of marriage, but... I asked her father for her hand in wedlock, but he refused me."

"Why did you refuse Dewi's suit?" Geoffrey asked of Osbert.

"She is already betrothed to another," Osbert said. "Though if her betrothed finds out she has been sullied, he most likely will not have her."

"To whom is she promised?" Geoffrey asked.

Again, Osbert hesitated, unwilling to answer, until Geoffrey became impatient. "The man's name!" he demanded.

"Leofric," Osbert finally admitted.

Geoffrey was stunned. Leofric had to be the oldest living man in Lydford. "But he is old enough to be the girl's grandfather!" he exclaimed.

"And he has no teeth," Dewi put in.

Shaking his head in amazement, Geoffrey said, "Leofric has no need for a wife; what the man needs is a nursemaid. Surely you did not seriously intend to give such a young girl to him."

"He was my choice for her," Osbert insisted. "He will care for her well."

"He cannot even care for himself, much less anyone else," Geoffrey muttered. "Why would you wish to wed your daughter to him?"

Again, Osbert hesitated, as if he wished to avoid disclosing everything. Had the man thought that Geoffrey would merely take his word without elaboration that Dewi was guilty of rape? "Osbert," he said sternly, "it does your case no good if you are unwilling to answer what I ask."

Reluctantly, looking embarrassed, Osbert told him, "I have nothing with which to dower her, and,"

"I would have wed her dowerless," Dewi interrupted.

"Then why did you refuse him?" Geoffrey asked again, nodding at Dewi.

"Because..." again Osbert hesitated, and again Geoffrey had to use his scowl to induce him to finally blurt out, "Leofric offered me a bride price, a payment, if I would allow him to wed her."

"Weeping Jesus!" Geoffrey shouted, too shocked to notice Father Mathieu's scolding glare. "You were going to sell that sweet young girl to a toothless old man! I will not have slavery on my demesne, Osbert. You may call it a bride price if you wish, but it is nothing more than slave dealing. You will tell Leofric his suit is denied. I will not allow him to marry your daughter. You forget," Geoffrey echoed what his father had said to him, "as the overlord here, no marriages can be performed without my approval."

Under Geoffrey's righteous anger, Osbert subsided in sputtering protest, and Geoffrey turned then to Dewi. "Did you know about this...arrangement?"

Dewi nodded. "Yes. She told me about it, after he refused my plea to marry her. So she said, that is we decided," He hesitated, took a breath, then spoke in a rush, "We thought if she got with child, if I got her with child, he would have to allow us to wed." Geoffrey sensed that somewhere under the bruises, Dewi was blushing. Meanwhile Osbert was red also, but in his case, it was caused by fury.

Jesus, what a coil. He was certain now that Dewi had not forced himself on the girl, but he also knew he could pass no judgment without hearing her testimony as well. He wanted to say to Dewi, it didn't work with me, when he had entreated his father to marry Milesenda when she became pregnant.

"Is she with child?" he asked Dewi.

The young man lifted his shoulders helplessly. "I don't know. I have not been able to speak with her since..." He gave Osbert a sideways glance.

"My lord, don't believe him," Osbert entreated. "It was rape."

"And that," Geoffrey retorted, sweeping an angry hand towards Dewi's broken nose, "is assault. I will make no judgments, however, until I speak with Kerensa, and hear from her own lips if she was forced or willing. I order you, Osbert to bring her here. It is late now, bring her tomorrow, to this room, and we will hear what she has to say."

Osbert obviously wished to protest, but didn't dare. Instead he asked, "And what of him? Is he to be allowed free?"

"No, he will be locked up until this case is done," Geoffrey affirmed. "Now go, but be back tomorrow with your daughter."

Slinking snake-like under Geoffrey's ire, Osbert left the room with a reluctant bow, and Geoffrey turned to Dewi.

"You understand, Dewi, I will have to detain you here tonight." Dewi nodded, looking miserable and embarrassed. He studied the floor again, but his words were firm. "I swear to you, my lord, it was not rape."

"I want to believe you," Geoffrey said, "but I must hear it from Kerensa as well." He paused. "God, you look awful. Does it hurt?"

Dewi nodded again, and Geoffrey went to the door, calling for Edmund. "We shall have to lock him in one of the storerooms in the donjon until tomorrow," he told his friend. "Have someone take down blankets and food. And, please, fetch my stepmother and ask her to bring her medicine basket to see if anything can be done for him." He jerked his head towards the silent Dewi waiting in the room behind him under Father Mathieu's watchful eye.

"Geoffrey," Edmund said urgently, "surely you don't truly believe that Dewi would rape anyone."

"No, I don't believe it," Geoffrey replied, "but tomorrow will tell."

He dismissed Father Mathieu and waited with Dewi, neither of them having much to say, until his stepmother arrived. She paled at the sight of the battered face, and, her maternal instincts aroused, ordered him to sit on the bench against the wall so that she could treat his hurts. Dewi hesitated, knowing he should not seat himself without permission in the baron's presence, but Geoffrey waved a hand at him and said, "Lady Alyssa is chatelaine here. We all do her bidding. If she says sit, you must sit." Dewi complied with a weary sigh as he collapsed gratefully on the bench, and Alyssa sat next to him and reached into her basket for a healing ointment to smooth onto the bruises and lacerations.

"This may sting," she said apologetically, and Geoffrey chuckled as he recalled her ministering to his childhood hurts.

"That stuff will make you feel better," he assured Dewi, perching one hip on the table as he watched the treatment, "but mostly because it smells so bad, it will make you forget the pain."

"Fie, Geoffrey, you should not tease the poor boy," his stepmother scolded as she gently dabbed at Dewi's injuries. "Whoever did this to him should be whipped. You poor thing," she crooned, "Your nose is broken. Geoffrey, come here, it takes a strong hand to set it straight." Geoffrey tried to object; the thought of causing Dewi more pain made him feel sick, but Alyssa gave him a look that gainsaid any protest, and obediently Geoffrey sat down on the other side of Dewi and, under his stepmother's guidance, put one strong hand on either side of the crooked nose.

"I am sorry," he said, in much the same manner he had apologized to the first horse he had had to destroy, and quickly pressed the broken pieces of cartilage together. Even through the bruises, Dewi went quite pale and came close to fainting, and a thin trickle of blood seeped out from one nostril, which Alyssa quickly wiped away. Geoffrey studied his handiwork. The nose would always be slightly disfigured, but it was decidedly improved. As Alyssa finished up her treatment and returned her ointments to her basket, Geoffrey asked Dewi, "How is it that you allowed Osbert to beat you so badly? You are no weakling, and he is twice your age."

"He had help, my lord," Dewi replied. "Two strong men who held me fast, and he made Kerensa watch while she screamed for him to stop. This," he indicated his nose, not quite touching it, "he did with the leg of a stool."

"It sounds as if he planned it," Geoffrey mused, and Dewi nodded in agreement.

"I believe that he followed her." Then Dewi slipped from the bench to his knees on the floor, his hands clasped in supplication. "Please, my lord," he begged, "do not allow him to marry her to that disgusting old man. I swear to you, on my life, that I did not rape her, that she wanted to get with child so that her father would have to let her wed me. Even if I cannot have her, she does not deserve to be sold by her father to an old lecher like Leofric."

To Dewi's surprise, Geoffrey reached down and pulled him to his feet. "Do not worry," he said, "one thing I am certain of, and that is I shall not allow such a marriage to take place. Now, I shall have to have the guards take you down to the donjon for tonight. There should be blankets and food for you there, but a guard will be posted outside the door." He went again to the office door, and motioned for one of the men-at-arms to escort Dewi away.

After they had gone, Alyssa came to stand beside her stepson. She had not been present during the proceedings and was ignorant of what had transpired. "Geoffrey," she protested, "why is Dewi being imprisoned? Should you not be locking up those who attacked him?"

Wearily, Geoffrey turned to his stepmother with a sigh. "Mother, Dewi has been accused of rape."

"Sweet Mary, no." Alyssa put a fluttering hand on Geoffrey's arm. "But the punishment for rape... It is too hideous to imagine."

"I know," Geoffrey said. His eyes were troubled. "The punishment for rape is castration."

<h1 style="text-align:center">26</h1>

Father Mathieu did not quite agree with Geoffrey's plan for his interview with Kerensa the next day when Osbert returned at the appointed time with his daughter, but Geoffrey insisted.

"I want to see how she reacts to him, without influence or hindrance." When the guards had brought Dewi up from his night spent below ground, Geoffrey insisted that he stand in front of the table in the small office so that he would be the first person observed by anyone entering the room, while Geoffrey stationed himself and the priest against the wall behind the door, out of immediate sight. Someone, most likely Lady Alyssa, must have sent water and soap to Dewi's cell because he was much cleaner than he had been the day before.

Geoffrey instructed Edmund to send Kerensa in alone and watched unobserved as she hesitantly pushed open the door and entered the room. She was a petite, dark-haired girl and for a moment Geoffrey was reminded of Solange de Meules. Her face filled with dismay when she saw Dewi, and she ran to him, weeping, oblivious to the presence of Geoffrey and Father Mathieu.

"Oh, Dewi, my love!" she cried, throwing herself against his chest as his arms enfolded her hungrily. "I hate my father," she said vehemently. "I shall never, ever forgive him for doing this to you. My poor darling, I am so sorry that you had to suffer so for me." She circled her arms around Dewi's waist and laid her head against his chest.

Dewi touched her chin with his hand and turned her face up.

Kerensa had a bruise on her face as well, a fresh one on her cheek that looked as if it had been caused by a hard slap. "Did he strike you too?" he asked angrily.

Kerensa nodded. "He was so angry, but all he would say was that Lord de Graville had ordered him to bring me here. But... where is he?"

"Here," Geoffrey said, stepping forward. Startled, Kerensa moved away from Dewi and curtsied deeply. "I think my questions have been answered," he said. "Father Mathieu, bring Osbert in here."

In a moment Osbert was with them, reaching angrily for his daughter when he saw her standing with Dewi, to be stopped by Geoffrey's hand on his arm. "Stand away," he said in a threatening voice, and Osbert obeyed him.

Geoffrey sat down in his chair and looked at the group before him. "This is my judgment," he began. "There has been no rape done here. Kerensa was not forced into anything; her actions have told me that more than any words could. You, Osbert, are a fool on two counts. One, that you would think I would be so rash as to convict Dewi, or anyone, of rape, on no more than your word alone. Two, that you would think for a moment that approval would be forthcoming for such a marriage as you have attempted to contract for your daughter.

"The only crime committed has been your assault upon this young man, and on your own daughter, and you should be grateful that I don't have you flogged for it. If I ever, ever, hear of you even considering such actions again, you shall answer to me. Is that understood, Osbert?"

Osbert nodded miserably, knowing his plans were undone and he had no recourse. Geoffrey turned to the young couple holding hands, and saw the relief flood Dewi's face as Geoffrey pronounced his acquittal. "Now, Kerensa, Dewi has told me of the plan to, um, get you with child in order to persuade your father to allow you to wed. Were you successful? Are you with child?"

After a moment's hesitation, Kerensa nodded shyly, at which both Dewi's and Osbert's eyes widened, Dewi's with wonder and Osbert's with anger. Kerensa turned to Dewi. "I did not wish to tell you until I was certain, but now I am sure." Her hand covered her stomach protectively in the age-old gesture of motherhood. Dewi put his arms around her and laid his cheek against her hair, murmuring something too soft for the rest of them to hear.

"Well, then," Geoffrey said. "The only remedy now is that you must marry her, Dewi."

Dewi was so startled at Geoffrey's friendly tone of voice that he jumped, and then stared, unable to quite believe in his good fortune, acquittal from the charge of rape and Kerensa's hand, which he now held tightly. Geoffrey looked at Osbert and said, "Do you give your blessing to them?" He nodded towards Dewi and Kerensa but kept his eyes on Osbert with a look that clearly said his blessing was merely a formality. The wedding would take place regardless by Baron de Graville's command.

Defeated and helpless, Osbert said heavily, "Yes, my lord, I give my blessing." He looked at his daughter but she spared him only one quick, unforgiving glance before turning back to Dewi. Geoffrey wanted to draw Kerensa aside and tell her, *you should make amends with your father, for you never know when it will be too late.* But he held his tongue, knowing that if anyone had advised him thusly about his estrangement from his own father, he wouldn't have heeded their counsel either. Such a reconciliation had to occur of its own accord if it was to happen at all.

"Very well," Geoffrey said with forced cheerfulness. "It is decided. The marriage shall take place here, today, in the chapel. I shall provide a dowry for the bride." He felt an urge to have Dewi and Kerensa's marriage made official immediately, and not only because of the bride's pregnancy. He saw something of himself and Milesenda in the young couple, in love and desiring to wed despite the opposition. He wanted their desire to be fulfilled as his and Milesenda's had not been, and he felt justified in insisting on an immediate ceremony.

He was getting rather good at it, he told himself only a few hours later as a small group gathered in the chapel for the wedding. He was becoming quite proficient at perfecting the lordly, intimidating scowl that compelled everyone to do his bidding. That scowl silenced Father Mathieu's objections and sent him scurrying to ready Belvoir's chapel.

It sent Edmund to tow the bridegroom home to change into fresh clothing and see him back to the chapel, and sent his stepmother to fetch flowers for the bride's hair, although in Alyssa's case the scowl was unnecessary. Alyssa went one step further and took the bride up to her own bedchamber to outfit her in one of her own gowns, with the hem hastily taken up to accommodate Kerensa's shorter stature. Kerensa cried at Lord de Graville's and Lady Alyssa's generosity, but Alyssa wiped her tears away and insisted the girl show only smiles on her wedding day.

Within a very short time the de Graville family, Osbert, Edmund and Carys and a few of the servants had gathered at the chapel to witness the impromptu wedding. Before they went in, Kerensa curtsied deeply to Geoffrey and said, "My lord, I don't know how to thank you for all you have done for us. I wish there was something we could do to show our gratitude." Dewi, standing with her, bowed and echoed the girl's words. His happiness made the bruises on his face seem to fade.

Geoffrey allowed the lordly scowl to slip away. "There is something you can do for me," he said.

"Anything!" the couple exclaimed in unison.

"Name me godfather to your firstborn." Their faces wreathed in smiles at the thought of that firstborn, already on the way.

"It would be our honor, my lord," Dewi insisted, putting his arm around Kerensa's shoulder.

"Very well," Geoffrey said with a nod, then added, a little gruffly, "Go on. Go get married." Dewi and Kerensa did not require a second invitation to that order, and Geoffrey followed them into the chapel and sat beside Edmund.

It would be Geoffrey's third godchild, after his sister Isabel and Edmund's son Cerdic. At this rate he would soon be godfather to half the children in Lydford. Godfather to many, but father to only one illegitimate daughter, when he should have several sons to ensure his inheritance. Again, he felt his duties and his heart pulling him in opposing directions.

As they watched Dewi and Kerensa embracing happily after Father

Mathieu declared them husband and wife, Edmund leaned toward him and whispered, "So, Geoffrey, what are you waiting for? When are we going to see you at that altar?" Geoffrey had no answer but a frown for his friend, who merely smiled with the complacency of a happily married man.

Later in his bedchamber, Geoffrey undressed for another lonely night, feeling jealous and disconsolate at the thought of Dewi and Kerensa, at this moment ensconced, at Geoffrey's insistence, in one of Belvoir's guest chambers consummating their marriage.

I wish you were here, his heart said to Milesenda. *I am so alone.*

Of course there was Moll, always willing and eager to romp with him in diverting bedsport. A glance from him would have ensured her company whenever he wished it, but to be perfectly honest, he was becoming bored with her. Though she was all fire and passion in bed, he was beginning to realize that he wanted more. He wanted someone he could talk to afterward, and that was certainly not something he could do comfortably with Moll. While it would have been cruel to say that Moll was stupid, it would have been untrue to say she was terribly intelligent. Geoffrey had never invited her to spend the entire night with him.

He stood next to his too-large bed and felt almost reluctant to lay down on it. He knew he would be unable to sleep. Edmund's words came back to haunt him.

What are you waiting for?

It suddenly struck him that he knew exactly what he had been waiting for; the realization smiting him with such blinding intensity that his knees felt weak and he had to sit on the bed and grasp the bedcurtain for support. He knew with sudden, sickening clarity.

He was waiting for Solange to grow up.

27

Tamsin was becoming accustomed to the fact that there were times when her father had to go away from Belvoir and leave her behind, but that did not mean that she had to like it. On the day her father turned twenty-two, he took her up on his horse with him as he said his good-byes, and Tamsin fussed and complained and begged to come with him. He petted her hair, noticing that it was getting lighter in color, no longer showing any of the honey brown of her mother, but shaded with blond highlights almost like his own.

Alyssa was standing next to his horse preparing to take Tamsin when he left, as Geoffrey said, "Now, darling, I am sorry but I cannot take you with me. It is too far away."

"But I want to come with you!" the girl insisted. In her six-year-old mind, 'far away' was over the next hill. She could ride that far sitting right here, with her Da on his horse. "Please!" she entreated, twining her hands in the front of his tunic.

Over his daughter's head, Geoffrey gave his stepmother an agonized look. He hated denying Tamsin anything, and he hated being away from her, but he would not risk her safety on a journey as far away as Exeter. Alyssa reached up to take the child. "Tamsin, dear, come with me. You cannot go with your Da when he is going to court his sweetheart."

Geoffrey glared at his stepmother. How dare she make up such an outrageous fabrication! Alyssa only smiled sweetly up at him and said, "Henry tells me you spend much time in the company of his cousin

Solange when you are in Exeter. She is the same girl you called out for when you were unconscious, is she not?"

For a moment Geoffrey turned his glare to Henry, who stood next to his horse a few feet away, waiting to leave. The boy smiled innocently. *Damn his wagging little tongue*, Geoffrey thought irritably. Henry was not the sort to indulge in idle, or untrue, gossip, in fact bore a fairly reticent personality. But of course, with Lady Alyssa, he was different. He'd talk himself blue in the face if he thought it would please her.

Geoffrey turned back to his stepmother, cursing to himself. They were all blowing some unconscious ramblings far out of their proper perspective. He'd had no control over what he said in his delirium, and the fact that he had called Solange's name once or twice meant nothing. "She is not my sweetheart," he said with dignity.

Alyssa gave him a maternal look which said, *tell me another story*, and Tamsin asked brightly, "What's a sweetheart?"

"You are," her father replied quickly as he picked her up and kissed her little nose. Alyssa reached for Tamsin, who realizing that this was one occasion when she was not going to charm her father into taking her with him, reluctantly allowed herself to be handed down into Alyssa's arms.

"There's my good girl," Geoffrey said, leaning down to kiss the top of her head. "I shall bring you a gift when I come home. Would you like that?"

Tamsin nodded vigorously. "I want a kitten!" she demanded.

A kitten, her father mused. He could acquire a kitten from almost anywhere. There was probably a litter in the stable right now. But he had promised to bring her a gift from Exeter. "A white kitten," his daughter qualified.

Geoffrey exchanged a look with Henry. "A white kitten," he said to his squire, and unspoken, they both knew a white kitten would be found if they had to scour every stable and alley in Exeter.

"Good-bye, my precious," he said to Tamsin, and to his stepmother, "Farewell, my lady."

"Hurry home, Da!" Tamsin called out. "Don't forget my kitten!"

Henry turned to mount his horse, then suddenly, as if inspired, turned back to Lady Alyssa, echoing Geoffrey's words, "Farewell, my lady," and to Alyssa's surprise, the boy took her hand and pressed a quick kiss to her fingers, like a gallant knight taking leave of his lady. As Tamsin giggled he kissed her little hand as well, and then, blushing, mounted his horse and hurriedly followed Geoffrey out the gate.

Geoffrey couldn't help but smile at Henry. The squire gazed straight ahead and refused to meet his master's amused glance. *What a lovesick young pup.* Perhaps, Geoffrey allowed grudgingly, he would, just this one time, forgive the boy's presumption in insinuating to Alyssa that Solange was his sweetheart, though nothing could be further from the truth.

He almost avoided Solange while they were in Exeter, just to prove to Henry that his assumptions were incorrect, and in truth he was very busy while he was there. As promised, he had brought several stallions, including his own Storm, to breed with some of Baron de Meules's mares, and the process kept him in the stable or the paddock most of the time he was there.

Still, he felt an unexpected and completely irrational wave of jealousy when he led Storm out of the stable and saw Henry leaning over the paddock fence talking to Solange. She was giving him a cup of water to drink. They were cousins, and close in age, and Henry was only taking a brief, well-deserved rest from assisting Geoffrey with the horses, but in spite of those rationalizations, he found himself shouting at his squire.

"Henry!" His bellow made both of them jump, startled. Good. "Take that mare over there to have her rear shoes removed. And quit dawdling about! I do not have all day to wait." The surprise Henry felt at Geoffrey's uncharacteristic surliness was evident on the boy's face as he scurried away from the fence and led away the mare Geoffrey had indicated. Mares were never sent to stud until their hind shoes were removed, to prevent injury to the stallion should they kick back during the mating process.

Solange found it necessary to pass near where Geoffrey was standing in order to return to the keep, but she did not stop to speak to him nor did she offer him a drink of water, even though it was he, not Henry, who was working up a sweat. "You seem to enjoy conversing with that pup," he grumbled at her. "Have you nothing to say to me?"

"You are correct, my lord," she replied haughtily. "I have nothing to say to you. Perhaps later, when you are in a better mood, and have bathed."

She tossed her head and walked away, waving her hand in front of her nose as if she detected a foul odor, leaving Geoffrey to stare stupidly after her. He thought he heard a snicker from behind him but when he turned around he saw no one. *Why do I bother speaking to her at all,* he wondered, as he stalked over to the bucket of well water she had left on the ground and poured his own cooling drink. Surreptitiously he sniffed at his armpit. If he did bear a stink, it was from no more than the sweat of honest labor. Still, he had no wish to offend Lady Solange's delicate sensibilities. Perhaps he would bathe.

They were both in a better mood when he joined the family for the evening meal, though Solange seemed preoccupied and left the hall immediately after she finished eating. She didn't even seem to notice that Geoffrey had not only bathed and shaved, but had also washed and combed his hair as well as donned clean clothing that even his father would have approved of. In fact, Solange barely seemed to notice Geoffrey, and he found, against his will, that he wanted her to notice him, since he had gone to so much trouble to improve his appearance for her sake. But she left the hall with merely the briefest of goodnights, obviously offered for the sake of courtesy only.

Henry found a couple of boys his own age with whom to amuse himself, and Lady de Meules retired early also, to leave Geoffrey and Baron de Meules sitting in the hall drinking wine until both were yawning and nodding.

"I am off to find my bed," Lord de Meules declared with a half-drunken slap at Geoffrey's knee. After he had left Geoffrey finished his own cup and was gathering up his gloves to go to bed himself when he heard a small voice coming from the direction of the doorway.

"Baron de Graville?" the tiny, disembodied voice inquired, but though he looked in the direction it came from he saw no one. He could have sworn it was Solange's voice he heard, but she had gone to bed long ago. *I've drunk too much tonight and I am hearing things*, he thought as he headed for the doorway.

It was dark in the unfamiliar corridor and he was groping to find the stairs when something small and soft touched his arm. "Jesus!" he shrieked, startled, as he swung around and heard someone jump away from him.

"Don't be afraid, it's only me," Solange said, and as his eyes adjusted to the darkness he saw her standing against the wall.

"I am not afraid, you merely startled me," he said with dignity. "What the hell are you doing, creeping about the hallways in the middle of the night?" He knew it was rude to curse in front of her but she had surprised him more than he cared to admit.

"I was waiting for you. I need your help."

"What do you need my assistance with at this hour? You should be in bed."

"It is Drusilla. She is, she was my nursemaid when I was small, and she's ill. She's very ill, and I am afraid she may be dying."

"I am no physician," Geoffrey said.

"That is not what I need you for," Solange replied. "The physician has already tended her, and he says we can only wait and see if she will live or not. But she wants to see her sister. They are very close, and Drusilla wants to see her now. If she is to die, it will be her last opportunity. I want you to help me fetch her sister."

"Why do you need my help?" Geoffrey asked suspiciously.

"Because Drusilla's sister lives in Exeter, on the other side of the city from the castle. I need you to escort me there. I don't think it is safe to go there by myself at night. You will take me, won't you, my lord?" She stepped towards him and even in the dimness he could see her face turned up to him.

"Me?" he protested. "Why me?" He was tired and his head was ring-ing, and here this naughty little girl was making unreasonable demands on him. "You are correct that it would be a dangerous errand for you to venture out into the streets at night. Why don't you send a servant?"

"Because the guards at the gate will not let anyone in or out at night without my father's orders. Not even my mother has authority over them."

"Very well, then, ask your father to send someone. If the nursemaid means that much to you, I am certain he will send for her sister." Even with as much as he had drunk tonight, he could still reason rationally, something Solange could not seem to do at all in this situation.

"I tried to ask him, but he is asleep. I could hear him snoring from out in the corridor. Even if I could gain access to his bedchamber, which I can't, I would have to set fire to the bed in order to wake him up, and even that might not be enough. You plied him with too much wine, my lord." Her voice took on an accusatory tone, and Geoffrey bristled.

"I held no knife to his throat to force him to drink," he defended himself. He still didn't understand why she needed him for this errand.

"My Lord de Graville," her voiced switched to pleading. "You are a guest here, and my father's friend, and equal to him in rank. You would be allowed to come and go as you please, and I am certain the guards would know who you are." That much he had to concede; his height and long fair hair made it difficult to be inconspicuous. "You can leave the castle if you wish. Please take me to fetch Drusilla's sister. You are the only one who can help us." She sounded almost like Tamsin in her wheedling, and lord knew he was seldom able to resist a little girl's pleading. But still, it was late and he was half drunk, though finding himself sobering quickly as Solange entreated his help.

"Why don't you wait until the morning?" he suggested. "Then it will be a simple task to send word to the sister that her presence is needed here."

"But Drusilla may be dying!" Solange cried heatedly. "It may be too late if we wait until morning." There was a pause and Geoffrey thought he heard a sniffle. Was she close to crying? His eyes had accustomed themselves to the dark enough to see that Solange had turned away and had her arms wrapped around her waist as if she were cold. Her voice was anguished. "She is my friend and I promised her! Were you never a child, my lord, or were you born a great oaf? Did you never have a nursemaid as a child, and would you not want to help her if she needed you? Why will you not do this for me? I thought you were my friend!"

Her friend? That was a new concept for him, a female as his friend. He had known women as mother, daughter, wife and mistress, but never as simply a friend. But it did put a definitive label on their relationship.

"Yes, I was once a child, and I had a nursemaid," Geoffrey admitted. Maud was like a member of his family, and if she were sick to dying he would be devastated, and would do anything in his power to ease her. Grudgingly he had to admit that Solange should be commended for her loyalty. Did she know how much the fulfilling of promises meant to him? Very well, he would go and fetch this all-important nursemaid's sister to the castle, despite the lateness of the hour and his sore head. Then let her call him a great oaf! He summoned up all his chivalrous courtliness.

"As always, your wish is my command, Lady Solange. Tell me where to find your nursemaid's sister, and I will fetch her here."

"I must go with you to direct you to her home," Solange insisted. *Oh, no,* Geoffrey thought. *You are not going anywhere.*

"No, you should stay here where it is safe. I promise to bring this sister here if I must kidnap her."

"You will never find her home by yourself," Solange insisted, taking the mile when she had been granted only an inch. "I know the direction we must follow through the streets. If we bring a torch I can show you how to get there. And Drusilla's sister and her husband won't know who you are. They know me."

Why was she doing this to him? "And just how do you propose escaping from the castle gates if you know the guards will not allow you out?" he countered.

"I can pose as your servant, and then they will take no notice of me. I have already dressed in some of Drusilla's clothes."

"Wait here. This I must see," Geoffrey said, and he turned quickly back into the hall and took a flaming torch from the wall sconce. When the corridor was illuminated by its glow he saw that she was indeed attired in a plain gown of coarse wool frieze, much too big for her, and a simple brown cloak with a hood. As he watched, she pulled the hood up over her head and forward so that her face was shadowed and hidden in its depths. Garbed so, she could indeed pass for one of many anonymous servants, if her imperious manner and speech did not give her away.

"Let's go!" she demanded, and turned to leave. But the light afforded by the torch in Geoffrey's hand had revealed a glaring oversight. When Solange's touch on his arm had startled him, he had dropped his gloves on the floor. Even in the dark of night, he wasn't going anywhere with her without them.

"I shall be with you in a moment," he muttered, looking about on the floor for the gloves and hoping he could pull them on inconspicuously.

"What do you need?" she asked, turning around. "We should leave now before any of the servants see me."

He located the gloves on the floor next to his feet but hesitated to pick them up. He was holding the torch in his right hand, and if he attempted to retrieve the gloves with his left the clumsiness would make his disfigured hand obvious. The same would apply if he attempted to hold the torch in his left hand. What to do?

He thrust the torch towards Solange. "Here, take this." Startled, she took it without question and he leaned down, scooped up the gloves and turned away from the torch's range of light to pull them on. That way, Solange was spared the hideous sight.

He took the torch back from her and strode toward the bailey with no explanation for his actions. "If you are going to pretend to be my servant," he told her, "walk behind me, keep your hood up, your head down, and your mouth shut!"

As Solange had assumed, the guards at the gate recognized Baron de Graville and allowed him passage without question, barely sparing a glance for the hooded servant accompanying him. Although he gloated secretly at her submissive demeanor, even if it was assumed only out of necessity, Geoffrey still walked in terror that Solange would break her silence or that her hood would slip down and that either her imperious voice or glossy black hair would give her away. He held his breath until they were safely on the outside of the gate, not wanting to even imagine the sort of trouble he would find himself in if he were to be discovered spiriting the lord's daughter out of his castle in the dead of night.

Once away from Rougemont's gate, he breathed easier and held the torch up to light their way as Solange guided him through the quiet streets. She obviously knew where she was going, causing Geoffrey to wonder how many times she had escaped her parent's supervision to make this excursion. He was relieved in one respect, that the route on which she led him took them away from the docks and the rougher areas of Exeter; environs in which Geoffrey would not fear to travel himself but to which he would not wish to expose Solange. He would have preferred riding to walking, but both he and Solange realized without voicing it that it would have been dangerous to attempt to take a horse from the stable, since there were grooms sleeping in the loft who might awaken and raise the alarm.

"Is this the same nursemaid who slapped your hand for blundering your embroidery?" he asked Solange, recalling the day he'd met her when she'd cried on his shoulder over that insult. "If it is, I am surprised you care so much for her condition." He patiently slowed his strides so that she could keep up with him.

"Yes, it is her. But I forgave her for that, and we became friends again. I did try her patience," the girl admitted. "I threw the workpiece at her feet when she told me to do it over, but she was correct in that it was a poor piece of work. I am afraid a skill with the needle is not my gift."

Geoffrey chuckled, and appreciated Solange's mature attitude toward the incident. He realized that she was seventeen years old now. Old enough to bear children, old enough to marry, an inner voice said to him, insidious as a snake hissing in the grass, and he suddenly disliked her maturity. He didn't want her to grow up just yet; he wanted her to remain a little girl so that he could resist her for a while longer.

After a walk of about an hour, Solange stopped in front of a building whose residual fragrance defined it as a baker's shop. She raised her hand and knocked but there was no response. "The occupants most likely are asleep," Geoffrey surmised, raising his own fist and pounding on the door with a knocking guaranteed to wake all but the dead. After another minute a fearful but still sleepy male voice called from the inside, "Who is there?"

"It is Solange de Meules," the girl called through the door. "Aidan, I must speak to Elsbeth. It is an emergency!"

The door opened quickly, and a startled man poked his head out and stared at Solange. "My lady!" he exclaimed. "What are you doing out alone at night? Tis fearful dangerous!" He opened the door wider for Solange to enter.

"I am not alone," Solange announced as Geoffrey followed her into the baker's house, ducking his head through the door as an automatic gesture required for one of his height. "This is Baron de Graville," she introduced Geoffrey to the startled Aidan, who bowed quickly, mouth and eyes round in amazement.

"I must see Elsbeth," Solange insisted. "Drusilla is ill and is calling for her." As if conjured up by Solange's words, a sleepy woman emerged from the back room, pulling a shawl around her shoulders.

"What is it?" the woman asked, then saw Solange. "Lady Solange!" she exclaimed, curtsying quickly. Without formality, Solange went to her and put her arm around the woman's shoulder.

"Elsbeth," the girl said gently, "Drusilla is very ill, and she wants you to come to her. You must get dressed and come with us now before it is too late. This is Baron de Graville," she repeated, with a glance at Geoffrey who waited patiently near the door. "He will escort us back to Rougemont."

Elsbeth's concern for her sister outweighed her astonishment at having Lady Solange and a strange nobleman appear at her home in the middle of the night, and quickly went into her bedchamber to dress herself, emerging moments later in clothing very similar to what Solange was wearing. Before he escorted the two women out the door,

Geoffrey turned to the husband and assured him, "I will see your good wife safely to Rougemont, and then see that she arrives safely home as well."

"Thank you, my lord," Aidan stammered, surprised at hearing this nobleman speaking to him in unaccented English.

The three of them walked quickly back through the dark streets toward Rougemont, Geoffrey breathing silent prayers of gratitude that they were not approached by ruffians of any sort. An advantage of his size. As they approached the gate of the castle, he turned to Solange and asked, a little sarcastically, "Did you devise a reason to give as to why I should leave the castle with one servant and return with two?" He heard Elsbeth gasp at his referring to Solange as a servant, but neither of them had any answer for the question he posed. Fortunately, when they presented themselves at the gate there had been a change in the guards and once Baron de Graville was again recognized he and his companions were again admitted without comment, although behind his back two of the guards exchanged amused glances as they watched him cross the bailey with the two silent women following him.

"Two?" one of the guards whispered to the other. "Lord de Graville must have stamina as well as size."

When they entered the keep Geoffrey breathed a huge sigh of relief that the whole crazy scheme had come off without incident, and the two women hurried to the stairs to ascend to the ailing Drusilla. Solange told Elsbeth, "She is in the first room on the left at the top of the stairway, on the third floor."

Elsbeth nodded and exclaimed, "Thank you for bringing me, my lady. And my thanks to you as well, my lord." she curtsied to Geoffrey and he handed her the torch he still carried.

"Take this to light your way," he said. "I hope your sister recovers." The circle of light ascended with Elsbeth's steps, and before she followed, Solange turned to Geoffrey. She had gone up three steps and so was now at eye level with him.

"Thank you so much for taking me to fetch Elsbeth, my lord," she said with sincerity. "It will mean so much to Drusilla to have her here. You are a very gallant knight, and a special friend."

With that eloquent appraisal, Solange quite unexpectedly leaned forward and kissed his cheek, just the merest, briefest brush of lips before turning away and following Elsbeth up the stairs.

Stunned by that fleeting kiss, Geoffrey stood speechless at the bottom of the stairs, a sudden glow permeating through his chest and an unexpected tug of desire stirring in his loins. It was only a chaste and friendly little kiss, an expression of gratitude for a favor, he told himself. Nothing more. But the sudden tightness he felt in his breeches seemed to disagree.

You are a fraud, Geoffrey de Graville, an inner voice told him. *You have been to war and killed men in battle. You are a strong, powerful man, a knight. And yet one innocent kiss from this pretty young girl and you are reduced to helpless, trembling lust.*

He forced himself to wait a long time before climbing the stairs to seek the chamber where he was to sleep. If Solange realized how her innocent action had affected him, he would die of embarrassment. It was a very long time before sleep accepted him.

<h1 style="text-align:center">2 8</h1>

The next day was very warm and sunny, and most of the horse breeding had been accomplished, so Geoffrey took advantage of the fine weather to take Storm out for a ride outside of Exeter's confines. He was curious as to the condition of Solange's nursemaid but felt reluctant to search the girl out to inquire about Drusilla.

He found himself directing his horse to the same hilltop Solange had first taken him to last year. It was a pretty place, he conceded, almost as pleasant as the lakeside clearing in the woods outside Lydford he had visited in his youth. Storm found the grass here to be to his liking and grazed happily, and Geoffrey found the same greenery to be soft to repose upon, and the gentle breeze and warm sunshine soon lulled him into dozing, to reclaim some of the sleep he had lost the night before. Being alone, he pulled off his boots, gloves and tunic, laid down on his bare back in the warm grass, and closed his eyes.

He dreamed, and in the dream he saw Solange in front of him, standing on the stairs as she had the night before so that they were face to face. Except that, in the dream, her hair was unbound from its confining braids, and he buried his hands in the thick silkiness of it. The soft tresses waved and curled about his hands and fingers, entrapping them in a glossy web. The hands that he threaded through her hair were both whole and complete. This was, after all, a dream. And in the dream she kissed him again, but this time it wasn't a quick kiss, and it wasn't on his cheek, but a lingering sensuous kiss full on the mouth.

The dream was interrupted by an inquisitive insect, a fly perhaps, flitting near his nose. He brushed it away. A minute later it was back, tiny insect feet tickling. Annoyed, he brushed it away again. "Go away," he muttered sleepily, but the persistent thing only returned to pester him, fluttering at his nose and skittering down his cheek.

"Damn!" he grumbled, slapping at it and accidentally slapping his own face in the process. A feminine giggle from nearby brought him to complete consciousness and his eyes snapped open to see Solange sitting next to him holding a long stem of grass, the "insect" that had plagued him.

He sat up quickly, very conscious of his bare torso and bare hands. "What are you doing here?" he demanded, embarrassed. He thrust his left hand quickly under his leg, and also shifted his hips uncomfortably, blushingly aware of the physical evidence of the erotic dream he'd been having. Fortunately, Solange either didn't seem to notice that (but how could she not?), or tactfully ignored it.

"I followed you," she admitted. "But I had to walk, so it took me a long time to get here."

"You followed me? And how, pray tell, did you slip past your father's guards without my assistance?"

She smiled. "I found it so successful to pretend to be a servant that I used the ruse again today. The guards didn't even glance at me. See!" She stood and twirled around, and Geoffrey's eyes rounded in horrified amazement.

She was wearing a boy's tunic, and he blinked his eyes, certain that they deceived him - she was wearing braies! Her feminine curves were however not at all concealed in the boy's clothing, in fact they were accentuated, and her hair, done today in one thick glossy braid hanging down her back, was like nothing he had ever seen on any boy. A man would have to be completely blind in order to mistake her for a male servant. He couldn't believe that Lord de Meules would have such incompetents in his service.

"You walked outside dressed like that?" His voice was strangled with disbelief. She stopped her little twirling dance and pointed to a hooded russet cloak lying on the ground.

"I wore that also, to cover my hair. But it is so warm, I took it off when I got here."

"And where, pray tell, did you get those...clothes?" he asked icily.

She looked down at herself and sighed. "I am afraid that my next confession will have to include an admission of committing theft. I took these clothes from Henry's bag when I saw him leave the keep. I intended only to borrow them," she said defensively, "and I would have planned to return them, but the arms and legs were so long on me that I had to cut them off. I don't suppose he will want them back in this condition."

Geoffrey tried to sound dignified and chastising, a difficult attitude to maintain when he was sleep-tousled and nude from the waist up, with all of his visible skin pink with embarrassment. As for the parts of him not visible because they were covered by his braies, well, he tried not to think about those parts. He cleared his throat.

"So, you steal and ruin my squire's clothes, and I shall be expected to replace them," he grumbled.

She sat down on the ground next to him. "Are you that poor, my lord, that you cannot afford to clothe those in your service?" she asked archly.

"I can afford it," he muttered.

"That is good," she countered, smoothing a sleeve that he now saw had been cut off crudely at the wrist, "because these were getting too small for Henry in any case."

He didn't like the fact that she took so much notice of Henry's body and the state of his clothing, and he also didn't like the fact that it bothered him.

"Do you care for him?" he demanded abruptly, recalling their meeting at the paddock and silently cursing the jealousy that crept into his voice.

"For Henry? Of course I care for him. He is my cousin."

"I don't mean as a cousin. I mean do you care for him as a man." *Man, my eye, he's a whelp.*

Solange looked surprised. "But Henry is not a man."

"He is the same age as you," Geoffrey countered, playing devil's advocate.

"I know," Solange replied with a touch of scorn in her voice. "But he is a skinny weed who does not even need to shave yet. He is a nice boy, not a man, though…"

She broke off with a glance in Geoffrey's direction, causing him to surmise that her unfinished words might have said that Henry was not a man, though Geoffrey was. He couldn't stop the small smile of triumph that softened his lips.

Solange's answering smile was dazzling, and very self-possessed. "My lord, I do believe you are jealous."

"I am not jealous. I am merely curious." He was furious with himself now for having brought the subject up, so sought to change it. "I am also curious as to why you decided to dress up as a servant, as a male servant, in stolen clothes, and to follow me out into the countryside in direct defiance of your father's orders and my advice. I realize that your nursemaid is ill, but I did not realize that I had been assigned as her replacement."

Her bright smile disappeared; his last remark had hurt, as he had intended it to. It was not his usual inclination to purposely offend anyone, but he would use offense if it was necessary to protect her from the folly of her own actions.

"You are cruel," she cried, then leaped to her feet and quickly strode away from him, obviously intending to return to Exeter in the same manner she had left, except that she left the disguising cloak lying on the ground at Geoffrey's feet.

"Wait!" he called out, immediately regretting his insinuation that she still needed a nursemaid. She was seventeen, he reminded himself, an age at which the greatest insult is to be thought childish. He ought to have realized that; he had felt the same in his teenaged years. He grabbed at his gloves and pulled the left one on as he leaped to his feet to follow her. She moved quickly despite her tiny stature, and Geoffrey abandoned his tunic, boots and right glove to follow her barefoot and bare-chested.

"Wait!" he repeated, covering the distance between them in a few strides.

She called, "Leave me alone," over her shoulder but he ignored her demand as he grabbed her arm and pulled her around to face him, arresting her forward movement.

"I'm sorry," he started to say, but she obviously didn't hear his apology as she glared up at him with a face flushed with anger. Tendrils of hair had escaped the confines of her braid and framed her face. Unbound, the hair was wavy, as it had been in his dream. She tried to pull her arm from his grasp, at which he muttered, "You stubborn little..."

"I shall tell you why I followed you!" she shouted, shaking with fury. "My intention was to thank you for your assistance last night. Drusilla's condition is actually improving, and I am sure it is due to her sister's presence. I was going to tell you that I was grateful that you made it possible. But you don't deserve gratitude! You wish only to insult me. You are rude, and mean, and heartless, and you enjoy tormenting me, and-"

Angered by her outburst, and driven by some other feeling he didn't understand, Geoffrey seized Solange's upper arms in his grasp, lifted her up off her feet, hauling her against his chest, and brought his mouth down on hers in a sudden and unexpected kiss.

He hadn't intended to enjoy it so much. It had been a reflex more than anything else, just something to make her shut up, and in that it was effective. But enjoy it he did, despite the fact that she kept her mouth childishly closed, and kicked and squirmed in his grasp, gasping with outrage when he finally set her on her feet. He could tell from her lack of finesse that she had never been kissed before, and for some inexplicable reason he enjoyed the fact that he was the first man to ever taste those sweet, soft lips.

She drew her arm back to aim a slap at his face, the black eyes flashing sparks, but he caught her hand easily in his own and held it tightly enough to prevent her from pulling away. Grinning, he lifted her hand to his mouth and pressed a soft kiss into the palm. A lover's kiss; even Solange knew that. A kiss on the back of the hand was insignificant, an ordinary greeting, but it was common knowledge a kiss on the palm or wrist was a portent of intimacy.

Solange gasped, stunned speechless by his action, and Geoffrey took advantage of her silence to say, "I apologize for offending you, Solange. I will make every effort not to do so again. And I am very happy that your friend Drusilla is improving. If there is anything further I can do to assist her recovery, you have only to ask it of me."

The girl put a finger to her lips; they looked bruised and he was sorry for that, but did not want to embarrass her by mentioning his impetuous kiss. He hoped she noticed that he referred to Drusilla as her friend, and not her nursemaid.

Something had happened to him when he had kissed her, a spark had flickered to life, unbidden but nonetheless real and exciting. He had been trying so hard to convince himself that Solange was still a child, so that he wouldn't have to admit to the attraction he felt towards her, but that impulsive kiss had banished that notion forever. It was not a child's body he had felt when he held her against his chest, but most definitely a woman's lush curves he felt through those ridiculous boy's clothes. Though he had only touched her lips for a few seconds, nevertheless he had felt an aliveness, a sentience that transcended mere lust, something that he had to admit he hadn't felt since Milesenda. Although outwardly he remained calm and dignified, inwardly his emotions were churning.

He also realized another feeling, a sudden panic of fear as he swept his gaze around them, sighing with relief that there was no one in the area to have witnessed him with his hands on Solange. If Baron de Meules had caught Geoffrey kissing his precious daughter, he would have had him hung from the castle battlements by his own guts, and asked questions later. At the very least, that is what Geoffrey would do to any man he ever caught even attempting to touch Tamsin.

He glanced at Solange; she was staring at his face, as speechless as he had been last night in the stairway. After a long moment she said, "Thank you, my lord."

Whatever reaction he might have expected, it certainly hadn't been to be thanked. He cocked his head in amusement. "The pleasure was mine, my lady," he said.

Solange blushed and looked away. "I meant, thank you for helping me to bring Drusilla's sister to the castle. I think she is going to recover."

"Oh," he replied heavily, disappointed. Silly of him to think she would thank him for kissing her. "How did you explain her sister's presence?" He turned from her and walked over to where he had left his tunic and boots, scooping the tunic up and pulling it on. As his head popped through the neck opening Solange replied, "By the time anyone noticed that Elsbeth was there, it was late enough in the morning to assume that she had arrived herself after daybreak."

"Very clever," Geoffrey murmured, sitting back down on the grass to pull on his boots. As he grasped the first boot he noticed his gloved left hand, mortified that he had forgotten himself enough to actually touch Solange with it. He had seen several emotions cross her face when he'd released her, but he hadn't seen revulsion or disgust. Thank God he had the glove on; perhaps she hadn't noticed it. Quickly he put on his other glove, pulling it over his wrist with his teeth since his left hand lacked the dexterity to manipulate it. He had to leave the lacings on the front of his tunic hanging open. With his missing fingers, he could pull the lacing tight but not tie it to secure them, so he usually just let them hang. Though tunics with front lacings were a peasant style, despite his handicap, Geoffrey still preferred to wear them. At home, his stepmother or Henry would frequently wordlessly step up to him and tie them neatly, never commenting on his need for their assistance and merely doing the small task as a normal part of the service a mother or a squire would render for son or master. Geoffrey couldn't help but wonder how badly he would disgrace himself if Solange were to tie his laces.

The charged moment was broken by the sound of Geoffrey's horse making a snorting sound. Solange looked over at Storm. "Did you think

I had forgotten you?" she asked, smiling. She picked up the servant's cloak she had brought with her and withdrew an apple, which she held out to Geoffrey.

"Why, thank you," he said, surprised. However, Solange snatched the apple away from him before he could take a bite.

"It is not for you to eat, it is for Storm!" she declared.

"But you gave it to me," he protested stupidly.

"I gave it to you to break in half for me, silly boy!"

Blushing again, he took the apple back and obediently broke it into two pieces. But he only gave one of them back to Solange. "I need nourishment too," he insisted, defiantly biting into the other half.

She gave him a rolling-eyed glance of amusement and walked over to Storm. Geoffrey followed her quickly; Storm was not tethered or hobbled and he didn't want Solange to make the horse nervous so that he might unintentionally hurt her. But the stallion stood absolutely still as Solange, remembering what Geoffrey had taught her, laid the apple portion flat on her palm for him to eat. Then she stroked his nose affectionately. "Did you like that, Storm?" she crooned. "You are the most beautiful horse, aren't you?" The girl continued to pet Storm and murmur compliments to him, putting the beast in great danger of becoming hopelessly vain, because of course he could understand every word.

So, Geoffrey thought, she now addresses my horse by his Christian name. I was a fool to think she followed me out here because she was attracted to me; it is the horse she really wanted to see. He didn't think it was possible for a horse to make cow eyes, but he could swear that was exactly what Storm was doing as Solange petted him.

"We had better return to the castle before your parents miss you and send out the guards to scour the countryside," Geoffrey advised. "I suppose you planned to ride pillion with me again."

She looked at him haughtily before retrieving her cloak. "I did not intend to walk back to Exeter," she said.

"What would you have done if I had not been here, after you walked all the way out here?" he challenged.

"Oh, I knew you would come here," Solange said confidently.

He arched an eyebrow at her. "And how did you know that?"

She smiled, that brilliant smile that took his breath away, and replied, "I just knew."

"Lord," he muttered. "Put on that cloak, and for the love of God pull the hood up over your hair." When she complied, he hoisted her up onto Storm's back and leaped up in front of her. He would have to assume that she was becoming accustomed to riding bareback.

As they started back toward Exeter, Solange said from behind him, "It is so much easier to ride wearing braies than skirts. Perhaps I will keep these."

Geoffrey glanced over his shoulder, and intoned in what he hoped was a paternal voice, "Solange, if I ever catch you wearing boy's clothing again, I swear by all that is holy that I will…"

"You will do what?" she challenged.

He hesitated. There were several things he wanted to do. He wanted to sit her at his feet and lecture her sternly on proper behavior. He wanted to put her over his knee and spank her into submission.

Jesus. He wanted to kiss her again, and this time he wanted to teach her to kiss him back.

All he could say to finish his threat was, "I shall be most annoyed."

Amazingly, she chuckled at him, and then she put her arms around his waist and leaned her cheek against his back. Geoffrey stiffened at Solange's innocent familiarity, and Storm stepped sideways at his master's unexpected pressure on the reins. Solange continued to snuggle comfortably against him, feeling so relaxed that Geoffrey guessed she must have fallen asleep. It had been a long walk for her from Exeter; he was touched that she had undertaken the journey to thank him for his assistance.

A few minutes later her voice floated up to him, "My lord, may I tell you something?"

"Of course, Solange."

"You are very pretty when you are asleep."

Geoffrey almost fell off his horse, but managed to contain the lustful feelings Solange's half-teasing words engendered in him. He turned his head around to look back at Solange smiling at him. It took a considerable amount of control not to grab her right there on the horse's back and kiss her until they were both dizzy, but he managed to contain himself and merely arched his eyebrows at her. "Pretty?" he said. "I am insulted."

"Very well," Solange replied. "Perhaps pretty is not the right word. Handsome. You are very handsome, my lord. Especially when you are smiling. You were smiling when you were asleep. You should do it more often."

"I should sleep more often?" he inquired.

"No, silly. You should smile more often."

If only it were that easy, he thought. To smile merely because it pleased a young girl. Yet, it was easy, with Solange. "You see?" she said happily. "That was not so very painful. You can smile if you try hard enough, and just as I said, you are very handsome. The most handsome man I have ever seen," she added, then blushed and looked away shyly, embarrassed by her impetuous, audacious words.

Geoffrey didn't even notice that he no longer despaired that Solange sometimes appeared to be infatuated with him. Now he enjoyed it, more than he cared to admit. He almost lifted his hand to touch her cheek but his leather gloves reminded him not to. "And you are very beautiful, Solange," he said with sincerity, and then added, "I had better get you home, before you get into trouble." *Before I get us both into trouble*, he added to himself, wrapping the reins about his left wrist and urging the horse into a trot. Before they had gone very far he felt Solange move behind him ever so slightly, and something - he was almost certain it was her hand - touched his hair. Then her arms went around his waist again and he heard her say very faintly, probably not intending for him to hear, "My golden knight."

He snuck her back into the castle, wondering how many more times he could do it before his luck ran out. This girl would give him gray hairs, he was certain. They went to visit Drusilla, who seemed to be recovering from her illness and expressed heartfelt gratitude to Geoffrey for bringing her sister to her side in her hour of need. The three of them,

Solange, Elsbeth and Drusilla beamed at him so, as if he'd single-handedly defeated an army to accomplish the deed, that Geoffrey hastened to leave their feminine company before they tried to kiss his hand. He and Henry were leaving for Belvoir early in the morning, and he still had to acquire a white kitten for Tamsin.

Fortunately, luck continued to accompany him, and a brief excursion back into Exeter yielded the discovery of a white kitten in a litter residing in a stable not far from the castle. The innkeeper whose stable housed the felines was only too glad to sell Geoffrey a kitten he had been about to drown, and they put the purring bundle of fur into a cloth sack for its journey to its new home.

Now, Geoffrey thought as Storm trotted through the streets of Exeter, all I need to do is figure out how to keep the damn thing alive once I get home and the castle dogs become aware of its existence.

He had barely left the inn behind him when his attention was captured by a merchant's stall with bright colored fabrics on display. Dismounting from Storm's back, he tied the squirming cloth bag to the pommel of his saddle and examined the length of green silk that had caught his eye. It was a shimmery, exquisite emerald piece that would complement nicely with his stepmother's auburn hair, and she deserved something nice.

"My lord has excellent taste," the cloth merchant said. "These are silks brought from heathen lands far to the east." Geoffrey was about to make a bid on a price for the green silk when he spied another length of fabric, also silk, but this one a vibrant, barbaric shade of crimson that would look stunning on a person with dark exotic coloring. The red silk fairly begged to be worn by someone with black hair and fair skin.

It would be completely inappropriate for him to purchase such a gift for a woman not related to him, and Geoffrey was well aware of the fact, but he couldn't help imagining how beautiful it would look on Solange. Quickly, before his better sense could ask him just how he intended to present her with the red silk without arousing her parents' suspicions, he negotiated with the cloth merchant and rode away with both the green and the red silk fabric, wrapped in pieces of cheaper cloth to protect them.

He spent that evening again in Baron de Meules' hall, though this night vowing to drink less and retire earlier, and hoping that Solange did not accost him for assistance in another outrageous excursion. Thinking of her, he allowed his mind to wander from his host's conversation, and started guiltily when he heard Baron de Meules mention her name.

"Solange tells me you were quite the hero at Pevensey," de Meules said, grinning at him.

Geoffrey flushed, and sent a scathing glance over at Solange, sitting across the room with her mother, tonight the very picture of a demure young lady, with her eyes modestly downcast. She didn't look at Geoffrey. "I was no hero," he said. "I merely did what had to be done. Your daughter tends to exaggerate."

"My son Gilbert was at Pevensey also," the older man said. "But since you have not met him yet, I suppose you wouldn't have known him if you had seen him."

"How did he fare in the battle?" Geoffrey asked politely.

He was relieved when de Meules answered, "Not a scratch. He is in London now but should return home soon."

Geoffrey held up his wine glass and looked into it as if the contents suddenly fascinated him. Lord de Meules took that as a sign that his guest wished his cup to be refilled, but Geoffrey waved away the servant who approached with a pitcher. He didn't want more wine and he wasn't really interested in Lord de Meules' son. Rather, he was gathering himself to talk seriously to his host.

"Solange is a delightful girl," he ventured.

De Meules chuckled. "I am not certain that delightful is a trait I would often apply to Solange. Her mother and I despair of her at times. She can be very willful, and has an annoying habit of not being where she is supposed to be most of the time."

Geoffrey used all of his willpower not to blush at that moment, knowing that many of the times that Solange was not where she was supposed to be was because she was with him. "Is she betrothed?" he asked.

"No," de Meules answered. "I had an offer for her recently, a very good one, but she rejected the man sight unseen. In fact, it was just after you were here last fall. Oh, I know I could have, and probably should have insisted that she accept the man, but she is my youngest and my only surviving daughter. Perhaps I spoil her."

"It is easy to spoil a daughter," Geoffrey mused, thinking on how Tamsin could wind him around her little finger with a glance. He looked again across to Solange, her face lit to glowing by the fire's light, and his heart danced with a bit of unbidden happiness at the thought that she had refused to marry the unknown suitor.

Following the direction of his guest's gaze, de Meules suddenly realized the bent in which Geoffrey's conversation seemed to be heading. He had a good opinion of the young Baron de Graville, finding him to be a serious and hard-working young man and not at all the feckless boy his late father had complained of. His friendship with Raymond de Graville had disposed Baron de Meules to consider betrothing his daughter Judith to Geoffrey, despite Geoffrey's youthful shortcomings. When Judith had died, de Meules had wanted to offer Solange in her place as a bride for Geoffrey, but she had been too young then for the marriage bed and Geoffrey's father had seemed to think the boy should be married right away, though obviously that had not happened.

"Geoffrey," Baron de Meules said earnestly, eagerness dawning in his voice, "Baron de Graville, are you asking-"

Geoffrey panicked. He couldn't do it. Though he wanted Solange with an intensity that burned inside him, he just couldn't bring himself to say the words that would make her his, at least not yet. He was not so completely consumed with lust for Solange that he could yet abandon his oath to Milesenda. In spite of the rudeness, he interrupted his host.

"I would like to invite you to come visit me at Belvoir," he said quickly, before Lord de Meules could finish his thought. "Bring your family, your wife - and bring Solange. We have had no guests since my father's death, and I am certain that my lady stepmother would enjoy having you visit. Now that Robert of Normandy is discouraged in his attempts at invasion, travel between here and Lydford should be safer."

De Meules smiled. He thought he understood Geoffrey. So, the boy was reluctant to make a commitment at this time; probably still sowing his wild oats. Let him prevaricate. De Meules had been that age once himself. Perhaps in the security of his own home, Geoffrey would be more amenable to the idea of a union of the de Graville and de Meules families. Lord de Meules had all but given up on matching Geoffrey with a daughter of his, but now it appeared that it might yet be accomplished.

"We would be delighted to come to Belvoir to visit you and your family," the older man agreed. "I haven't been there for years, since you were a small boy, before your father remarried. I seem to recall some sort of ruckus then involving the priest having his leg tied to the leg of his chair-do you recall such an incident?"

Geoffrey chuckled. "Yes, I recall it. Father Mathieu was caught unawares and nearly broke his neck when he tried to stand up. The result of that incident was that I ate my meals standing up for a week. But as you can see I am too big now to go crawling under the table. You shall all be quite safe from wayward boys, I assure you."

"In that case, we shall plan a journey to Belvoir without anxiety," de Meules replied. "My son Gilbert will be returning from London within a fortnight. When he arrives, we shall proceed to Lydford. You there," he beckoned to a passing servant, "inform my lady that her lord would speak with her."

The servant obediently proceeded across the room to inform Lady de Meules of her husband's summons, and as she left her seat by the fire and approached the two men, Geoffrey rose to offer her the chair he had been occupying. He was glad to leave Lord and Lady de Meules to discuss arrangements for the proposed journey to Lydford.

He wanted to talk to Solange out of her parent's hearing. All the times they had found themselves alone with ample opportunity for private conversation, and now he wished for it but could not arrange for it. Fortunately, the hall was large enough that he could speak to her quietly without being overheard while still observing the proprieties under her parents' eyes. She looked up, smiled and rose to her feet as he approached.

"How is Drusilla feeling?" he asked her.

"She is much better," Solange replied. "Thank you again for your assistance."

"I am glad she is improving," Geoffrey said. "Tomorrow morning we leave for Belvoir."

"I know," Solange replied with sadness in her voice. "I shall miss you."

He realized with a jolt that he would miss her too, though he did not say so. "I have arranged with your father for you and your family to come to visit me, to visit us, at Belvoir," he said. "When your brother returns from London, your father will bring all of you to Lydford. Would you like that?"

Her face lit up with that beautiful smile that made Geoffrey's breath catch. "We are coming to visit Belvoir? I should like that immensely!"

"I should warn you, Lydford is a rural village surrounded by farms and woodlands. There are no crowded city streets or smelly dockside quays in the area."

"That is precisely why I shall be glad to visit," Solange declared. "I much prefer the fresh air and open spaces of the countryside over the confines of the city. And of course, because it is your home. I am eager to meet your family."

His family. She wasn't aware of exactly whom his family consisted. He had never told her that he had a child, though he had known Solange for three years now. He was certain that Henry had not told his cousin of Tamsin's existence either, since Solange would surely have said something to him if she was aware that he had an illegitimate child. Geoffrey knew he was going to have to tell her about Tamsin, before she and her parents arrived at Belvoir. To surprise her without warning with an illegitimate daughter in his home would be most inconsiderate and a risk to their fragile relationship. Yet how would she react to the knowledge, no matter when or how it was presented? He couldn't risk it here, in her parent's hall and uncertain of her reaction. In addition, he desperately wanted a more private opportunity to say his farewells to Solange, and there was also the matter of the red silk fabric burning a hole in his saddlebag.

He wanted to touch her. She stood there before him with her face aglow at the prospect of visiting his home, and it took a concerted effort on his part not to sweep her into his arms and kiss her right there in the great hall, despite his bad hand and her parent's presence only a few feet away. But propriety prevailed and Geoffrey had to settle for turning himself so that his broad back was between Solange and her parents.

Their right hands crept towards each other, seemingly more of their own volition than from any conscious effort on the parts of their owners, and as he held her hand Geoffrey silently damned the deformity which required the leather gloves he wore. "I want to see you before I leave," he said, his voice almost a whisper. Though he did not speak the word *alone*, it was nevertheless silently understood.

Solange nodded. A tinge of pink colored her cheeks, and her voice was as whisperous as his. "There is a small walled garden behind the chapel. If you follow the wall to the left of the chapel you will find it. I can meet you there in the morning before Mass, if you like."

"Till morning then," he said. He raised her hand and presented the briefest of kisses to the back of it, the height of proper decorum. He strode quickly upstairs before anyone else had a chance to do the same. If he were to encounter Solange on that dark stairway again, he wasn't sure he could be responsible for his actions.

* * * * *

It was not difficult to find Solange's garden the next morning. It was a small space, and Geoffrey could not help but compare it to his stepmother's spacious gardens at Belvoir, where she grew a variety of herbs, legumes and flowers. However, here within the confines of a walled city, such space was limited to this tiny area, with a single pear tree, a few plants and a small bench.

Solange was not there when Geoffrey arrived, and he worried that she may have been unable to sneak away from her mother's supervision, or had been here already and left before he arrived. Or perhaps her parents had overheard them making plans for a clandestine meeting, and even now a contingent of Rougemont's stoutest soldiers could be searching for Geoffrey and preparing to beat him to a bloody pulp. He paced and worried until he realized he was destroying the plants beneath his feet, and sat on the small bench beneath the blooming pear tree to wait, clutching the package containing the red silk.

The wooden gate in the garden wall creaked as it opened, and Geoffrey tried to think of innocent expressions for a need of solitary contemplation, should the person entering be anyone other than Solange. But his fears were ungrounded, for it was Solange who entered, smiling when she saw him waiting for her. He rose to his feet as she approached, and it seemed quite natural for her to hold out her two hands and for him to take them in his. A tiny frown crossed her face at the touch of his leather gloves, though she kept her hands in his, and Geoffrey prayed that she did not detect how insubstantial the left hand was.

She was dressed to attend Mass, with a fine white veil completely covering her hair and falling in draperies around her face. It gave her a serene, almost nunlike appearance, and made her eyes seem even bigger and more luminous.

"I apologize if I kept you waiting," she said.

"I would wait for you no matter how long it might take," Geoffrey declared. It was true, he would have waited without complaint despite the fact that Henry and the rest of his men were even now assembling in the courtyard in preparation for leaving for Lydford.

They stood there just holding hands and gazing at each other's faces, until Geoffrey realized that what he was doing was memorizing her features to keep in his memory until he saw her next. "Come, sit down," he suggested, drawing her to sit beside him on the small bench beneath the pear tree. It was a very small bench, and Geoffrey was a big man. As a result, it was inevitable that their hips should touch as they sat together. The warmth of that small contact sang through Geoffrey's veins in a most uncomfortable manner.

"I am so eager to visit Belvoir," Solange said earnestly. "I could not sleep at all last night, anticipating it."

"I am looking forward to your visit as well," Geoffrey replied, a bit more formally than he intended. Inside his leather gloves, his hands were sweating. He looked at Solange for a moment, then turned his eyes to his knees. There could be no more prevarication, no more hesitation. He must tell her, and endure however she reacted.

"Solange, when you come to Lydford, you will meet my family. As you know, my brother Stephen is here in Exeter, at St. Nicholas Priory. At Belvoir there is my stepmother, Lady Alyssa, my baby sister Isabel," he paused, drew a deep breath, and prayed that Solange was as open-minded as he hoped, "and my daughter. I have a daughter, Solange. She is illegitimate, but I love her just the same, and she lives with me at Belvoir."

The silence hung heavy between them for a long moment until Geoffrey gathered the courage to look at Solange's face. She was staring at him, her expression unreadable. After a moment of unbearable tension, she said in a small voice, "You never told me you had a child, my lord."

It took a conscious effort of courage on Geoffrey's part to continue to meet Solange's eyes, still uncertain as he was about her reaction to his news.

"Well, are you going to tell me about her or not?"

With a start, Geoffrey realized that Solange had been staring at him, not with rage or rejection, but with curiosity. Hesitantly, he asked, "Do you wish to know about her?"

"Of course!" was the firm reply.

It was like having a huge weight lifted from his shoulders to be encouraged to speak openly about Tamsin. It had been his experience that most people disapproved, not that he had an illegitimate child, but that he acknowledged her and was raising her himself. "Her name is Tamsin," he began. "She ... she is the light of my life."

"Tamsin, what a pretty name. Tell me what she looks like."

Geoffrey warmed to the opportunity to talk about his beloved daughter. "She has blond hair and blue eyes..." he began.

"Like you," Solange interrupted.

"Not quite, her hair is a bit darker and her eyes lighter than mine, and she is much prettier. She is, after all a girl," replied Geoffrey, in whose eyes Tamsin was still the image of her dead mother, despite the assertions by everyone else at Belvoir that his daughter every day resembled more a small, female version of Geoffrey. "She is six years old," he said in answer to Solange's previous question.

"Six!" Solange said with surprise. "Then you were only sixteen years of age when she was born."

"Yes." Then with a weak attempt at humor, he added, "I had forgotten how adept you were at doing sums."

Solange did not seem to find anything humorous about his remark. She glanced down at her hands. "My sister Judith was sixteen when she died, and I recall my mother saying that you and she were the same age. Your little girl must have been born about the same time as Judith died."

"Some months later," Geoffrey admitted uncomfortably.

"But you were not married?"

He shook his head. "No, Tamsin is a bastard." Though he still hated to use that word, Geoffrey had by now come to realize that it was true. He had never been legally married to Milesenda, and in the eyes of the world and the Church, Tamsin was and always would be a bastard.

Then Solange asked the question that had put Geoffrey's stomach into knots. "If your daughter lives with you, where is her mother?"

Again Geoffrey gazed at his knees as he replied. "Tamsin's mother died giving birth to her. She was a woman from the village of Lydford near Belvoir, a little older than me though it mattered not. I wanted to marry her but my father would not allow it because she was a peasant. She died, but our child lived. My father suggested sending Tamsin away to live with strangers because she is illegitimate, but I refused to do it. She is *my* daughter, and no one will take her away from me merely because she was born outside the blessing of the Church."

No reply came from Solange, and Geoffrey was afraid his revelation of Tamsin's existence may have done irreparable damage to their budding relationship. His inner voice, the one that expressed his most passionate thoughts but which never allowed them to be heard by others, anguished, *please do not hate me for things that happened before I met you.* "Are you upset?" he was finally forced to ask.

Solange looked up at him then, her eyes wide. "Oh, yes, my lord. I am very upset."

Oh, Lord, no, the inner voice wailed.

"That poor precious little girl, to have no mother."

Relief and revelation swept through Geoffrey's soul. Solange wasn't upset that he had fathered a child, rather she was upset that the child's mother had died. Perhaps there was hope after all. He looked at Solange and was able to smile. "I thank you for your sympathy. I have tried to do my best to raise her myself, but she sometimes manages to elude me, and she is constantly getting into mischief. My stepmother says she is very much like I was as a child in that respect."

"I do not believe that, my lord."

"Oh, but it is true. Once she put frogs into her nursemaid's bed, and then there was the time she..."

"I meant, I do not believe that you were the type of person to get into mischief as a child. You are so correct and honorable."

Put in that manner, she made him sound like a boring old man. "You have my word on it, I was a most troublesome child. When you come to Belvoir, I am certain that Lady Alyssa, my stepmother, will be willing to tell you all about it."

"You can be certain I shall ask her."

He suddenly recalled the red silk he held on his lap. Placing the package in Solange's hands, he said, "I have a gift here for you."

"A gift for me!" Solange exclaimed. "My lord, you should not."

"Yes, I know that I should not, but I wished to anyway. As I said, I am a most mischievous boy. Go ahead, open it."

With excitement in her eyes, she unwrapped the plain cloth to reveal the bright shimmery crimson silk. Her eyes widened. "Oh, my lord, it is so beautiful!" She held the fabric to her face and rubbed her cheek against it. Geoffrey had to fight the urge to follow the cloth with his hand.

"I will understand if you wish to keep this a secret and not use this cloth to make a garment with. Your parents might be angry if they knew I gave it to you, and I would not wish to cause trouble for you with them. But when I saw it, I knew it was for you."

"This is the most beautiful thing I have ever seen!" Solange exclaimed, her eyes shining as if he'd given her the world. *No*, Geoffrey's inner, suppressed voice said silently, *you are the most beautiful thing I have ever seen.*

She looked up at him with that adoring gaze which was Geoffrey's undoing. "My lord, how can I ever thank you for such a lovely gift?"

"I can think of a way," Geoffrey muttered, putting his hands on her waist and pulling her onto his lap, to which she offered no protest. She opened her mouth as if to say something, but Geoffrey could not wait to hear it, so urgent was his need to kiss her. As he bent his head to her mouth, she flinched a little, and Geoffrey knew why. The first time he had kissed her, he had forced himself upon her unsuspectingly. It had been harsh and brutish, and had no doubt hurt her tender mouth. He was sorry for having hurt her, but not sorry he had kissed her. "I won't hurt you, I promise," he murmured, and trusting him, she relaxed and allowed him to touch his mouth to hers.

She had the softest, sweetest, most innocently arousing lips he had ever touched. The feel of them made Geoffrey giddy. The feeling of swirling desire was compounded as she hesitantly put her hands on his shoulders; the red silk fabric sliding from her lap to lie in a shimmering heap at their feet.

He parted his own lips to trace the outline of hers with his tongue, teasing at the center of her mouth to encourage her to open her lips for him, and when she did, slid his tongue inside to trace the surfaces of her teeth and the moist soft interior of her mouth. She gasped a little at the invasion, but he swallowed the small breath and continued to kiss her, holding her on his lap with hands which trembled on her waist, until she relaxed in his arms and allowed her arms to encircle his neck. The trust she was placing in him at that moment was infinitely endearing. In a very small space of time, she learned the lesson he was teaching her and moved her own tongue against his, causing Geoffrey to groan help-lessly against her mouth. The feel of her little derriere squirming about on his lap did dangerous things to the thin thread of his self-control.

A moment later the ringing of a bell penetrated the fog of concupis-cence which held them, and Solange suddenly jerked her mouth away and sat up straight, her face stricken but her arms still around Geof-frey's neck. "What is it?" he asked in a hoarse croak, devastated at the sudden termination of this intense pleasure.

"The chapel bell!" she gasped. "Mass is about to start. My mother will be looking for me."

"Will she look here?" Geoffrey asked, glancing fearfully around them.

"Oh, yes," came the reply, as Solange slid from his lap and stood be-fore him.

"Oh, no," Geoffrey breathed, dreading the thought of Solange incur-ring her parent's wrath on his account.

"I am sorry, my lord, but I must go now, before..." She did not finish her sentence, but Geoffrey discerned her thought. Before some-one caught her, Baron de Meules's virgin daughter, passionately kissing a man who was supposed to be her father's friend. Geoffrey couldn't blame her for panicking at the thought; the idea of the repercussions for both of them swirled panic through him as well.

"The last thing I would wish for would be to incur the wrath of your parents and to have you suffer for it," he said, then sighed with great reluctance. "Perhaps the best thing would be for you to hurry to Mass before your mother or father finds you here with me. I will see you in a few weeks when your family comes to Belvoir."

Solange nodded, breathing deeply, and Geoffrey couldn't help but wonder if it was the effect of his kissing her that caused her chest to rise so rapidly. God, she was beautiful. She stooped to gather up the red silk which lay forgotten at his feet, and wrapped it up in the coarse cloth covering. "Thank you again for the lovely gift," she said, her eyes still shining.

"You are most welcome, Solange," Geoffrey replied, still sitting in his place on the bench, knowing that it was going to take a few minutes to compose himself before he stood up and attempted to walk. "It was my unutterable pleasure to give it to you." She smiled sweetly. "Your veil is crooked," he noticed, and lifted his hand to adjust it for her, then saw his leather gloves. Oh, lord, he had forgotten himself so much that he had actually held her with both his hands, the good one and the maimed one. Quickly he dropped his hands into his lap and said, "Perhaps you should straighten it."

With a small frown Solange set the package in her hands on Geoffrey's knee and set her veils straight, then before retrieving her gift she leaned forward and flung her arms briefly about Geoffrey's neck again, pressing a brief but fervent kiss against his cheek. "My lord, I must tell you that I very much enjoy kissing you," she murmured, then scooped up the package of fabric and turned to hurry to the gate of the little garden.

Bemused and regretful at the sudden end to their enjoyable interlude, Geoffrey watched her push open the gate and glance outside to see if anyone was near. She turned and looked back at him just before slipping through the doorway. "Good-bye," she said with a small wave of one hand. "I shall count the minutes until I see you again at your Belvoir. I am looking forward to meeting your daughter." And with that she was gone, hurrying to the chapel to avoid being caught with him.

Counting the minutes, Geoffrey mused as he waited before leaving the garden himself. He would be counting the seconds.

* * * * *

When he arrived at the courtyard just inside Rougemont's gatehouse, Henry and the rest of his men were waiting with ill-disguised impatience. Henry held the reins of Geoffrey's horse, and exclaimed, "There you are!" upon seeing him.

Geoffrey offered no explanations for his tardiness, only flashed a quelling look at his insolent squire. Did the boy dare to chastise him? Or was he merely worried that Geoffrey had gone missing? In silent dignity, Geoffrey mounted his horse and led his men out the gate, ignoring the speculative glances they exchanged behind his back. Let them wonder where he had been. There was no force on God's green earth that would compel him to divulge that he had lost track of the hour and kept them waiting in order to dally with Lord de Meules's daughter.

They had traveled for some hours, and as usual to Geoffrey's eyes the grass became greener and the flowers brighter with every mile that brought them closer to Belvoir. Henry had been riding directly behind Geoffrey, so he slowed his horse to allow the boy to trot alongside him. Though Geoffrey told himself that what he did and with whom was none of Henry's business, still he was concerned that Henry might feel his cousin's honor may have been compromised, if he knew that Solange had been alone with Geoffrey. Some discreet investigative conversation might not be remiss.

"I know you are kin to the de Meules family," he told his squire, "so I thought you should know that they will shortly be visiting at Belvoir, when Solange's brother, that is, Lord de Meules's son, returns from London."

Neither word nor look betrayed any feeling Henry may have had regarding his lord's unintended mention of Solange's name. He merely smiled noncommittally and said, "I shall look forward to such a visit, except perhaps for cousin Gilbert. He can be a bit overbearing on occasion."

"I consider myself warned," Geoffrey replied, then he noticed that the front of Henry's tunic had begun to squirm and bulge most alarmingly, and as he watched with amazement, a tiny white furry head emerged from the neck opening, followed by little feline paws with needle-sharp claws which grasped for purchase in the squire's chest as the kitten wriggled from its confinement. Geoffrey had given Henry the charge to care for Tamsin's gift until they arrived in Lydford, but he hadn't expected the boy to take the task so personally.

"Ouch!" Henry yelled, plucking the small animal away from his skin and holding it up by the scruff of the neck. "Behave, Snowflake, or you go back in the sack." As if in reply, a tiny pink tongue emerged from the cat's mouth and complacently licked Henry's chin.

"Snowflake?" Geoffrey echoed with amusement. "You have named the thing?" It was one thing to give a name to one's horse, but to a cat?

"It seemed an appropriate name," Henry replied with dignity, not meeting Geoffrey's eyes as he arranged the little beast in the saddle in front of him. "She did not like being in that sack for so long."

Geoffrey chuckled, diverted by Henry's serious expression. "Did not like it, did she? I would keep a watchful eye on little Snowflake if you intend to perch her there for very long." He shot an amused glance at the kitten seated directly in front of Henry's groin. "She may become nervous riding like that, and you may wish to father children someday." He rode on ahead, secure in the realization that Henry was more concerned with safely transporting a gift for a little girl than in the adult concerns of men and women.

29

At first, Alyssa was affronted, then she became worried.

As soon as Geoffrey arrived home, he insisted upon a thorough cleaning and freshening of the entire castle in preparation for his guests' arrival. New sweet rushes must be put down on the floor of the great hall, and it did no good to remind him that they had been changed only a few months ago. All of the tallow candles must be replaced with beeswax, despite the greater expense, because beeswax candles smelled better and smoked less, and were there enough fur coverlets in the bed-chambers in case the nights were cool? Even the stables were to be completely mucked out, and could Maud possibly do something about the state of Tamsin's clothing?

Alyssa's first reaction to all of this was to think that her stepson found fault with her housekeeping, when neither he nor his father had ever complained before. It was completely unlike Geoffrey to take such a concern about domestic details. Usually he cared only that he was comfortable and his belly did not rumble. For the rest he had, until now at least, placed complete trust in his stepmother; and Alyssa was start-ing to feel insulted that he had somehow found her maintenance of his household to be lacking.

Her insult soon turned to concern. As the days passed and Geoffrey continued to insist upon perfection, she worried that he had become demented in some way, to be so changed. When he insisted that all of the dogs who resided in the great hall be evicted to the bailey while the

350

de Meules family was visiting, she was certain that Geoffrey had gone completely insane.

But all her fears were laid to rest the morning she entered the great hall to observe Henry and Ulric the stableboy dragging the dogs out in compliance with Geoffrey's wishes. The screen in front of the doorway that deterred drafts concealed her presence, and she overheard Henry remark to Ulric, "I certainly hope my spoiled cousin Solange is worth all of this effort. She is only a girl." Ulric grunted in reply as he pulled on the collar of the dog who was strenuously resisting being evicted from his usual place near the master's chair.

In that moment, the answer to all was realized by Alyssa, and she smiled as she turned and went into the buttery, Henry and Ulric never noticing that she had overheard them. Geoffrey was not criticizing her housekeeping, nor had he gone insane. He merely wanted everything to be perfect to impress Solange. Alyssa doubted preparations would be taken to such an extreme were it merely Lord and Lady de Meules who were expected to visit. It was all for Solange, the girl Geoffrey had called out for when he had been delirious. Alyssa became very curious to meet this young lady, who was obviously very important to Geoffrey, whether he admitted it or not. She went along with all of Geoffrey's suggestions and prepared the castle as if the king himself was coming to visit, wondering if the unknown Solange, who had practically been under Geoffrey's nose all along, would be the one who would finally supplant the grief for Milesenda in Geoffrey's heart.

On the day that a messenger sent ahead had told Geoffrey to expect the arrival of his guests, he spent the entire morning on the wall walk behind the parapets, watching the valley for their approach. When finally, he spotted their horses, he hurried to the stairway and practically jumped down the stairs to meet them in the courtyard, though if he had been thinking rationally would have realized it would be another hour before the slow-moving group would actually enter Belvoir's gates. To his annoyance, his leg wound chose today of all days to plague him and he limped visibly as he paced and waited, brushing imaginary dust from his clothes and checking to confirm that his leather gloves were in place.

Alyssa and Henry joined him shortly before the de Meules party arrived, exchanging amused glances behind Geoffrey's back at his obvious display of nervous anticipation. To Alyssa, observing her stepson allowing his feelings to show outwardly was a joy to be thankful for. Every smile, every frown, every caring thing he did brought him one step further from the brooding, mournful creature he had disintegrated into after Milesenda's death.

When at long last the travelers passed through the gatehouse and into the bailey, Geoffrey had eyes only for Solange at the rear of the group, perched on her plump pony. She smiled at him, but a poke in his back from Alyssa reminded him of his duties as host. With a look of regret, he turned to Lord and Lady de Meules, leaving Henry to assist his cousin in dismounting.

"Welcome to Belvoir," he said to Lord de Meules, who swung down from his horse and shook Geoffrey's hand. Geoffrey turned to help Lady de Meules from her horse with a polite, "I trust you had a pleasant journey, my lady."

They replied with polite greetings as Geoffrey drew Alyssa forward to be introduced. "May I present my stepmother, Lady Alyssa."

Lord de Meules bowed, his wife curtsied as she was introduced; then Baldwin indicated the fourth member of his family, a stocky man like his father, black-haired like his mother and sister, who had dismounted unnoticed by Geoffrey. "My son, Gilbert," de Meules said. Geoffrey extended his hand to Gilbert but the other man did not notice. He moved forward as if transfixed to approach Lady Alyssa, with the briefest "Your servant, my lord" tossed by rote to his host.

The younger de Meules gazed at Alyssa like a lovesick calf, and as his parents looked on with amusement and Geoffrey stared in amazement, took her hand and pressed a fervent kiss to her fingers. "My lady," he intoned in a reverent voice. "Had I but known that such a beautiful flower as yourself resided here in the countryside, I would have visited much sooner."

Alyssa smiled but firmly extricated her hand from Gilbert's grasp with a noncommittal, "Welcome to Belvoir, my lord." Geoffrey for his part was enraged. How dare this insufferable brute make eyes at his stepmother! His stepmother, for the love of Christ! Did the man not realize that her husband had been dead barely three years? It would have been rude in the extreme for Geoffrey to knock Gilbert down and beat his face in when he had not even had the opportunity to wash away the dust of travel, but oh how Geoffrey was tempted!

A tug at his sleeve diverted Geoffrey and he turned to greet Solange, his anger at her brother forgotten as he looked at her lovely face. With both their families observing, he could only give her the briefest kiss on the back of her hand as a polite greeting, when what he really wanted to do was to sweep her up in his arms, kiss her passionately and tell her how much he had missed her. He had to content himself with saying it with his eyes.

Alyssa invited the travelers to come inside and refresh themselves as several of the grooms came forward to take the horses to the stables, and as they entered the keep Solange asked, "Where is your little girl, my lord?"

All conversation ceased as Geoffrey replied, "She is in the nursery. Would you like to come up and meet her?" He ignored the shocked looks of her parents and brother as he led Solange to the stairway which would take them to the upper floor. Let them be shocked at the knowledge that he had an illegitimate child. He would not hide her away or pretend she did not exist for anyone. He took Solange into the nursery, and as always, Tamsin greeted him with hugs and kisses.

After returning her ebullient greeting he set her on her feet and crouched down to put his face at her level. "Tamsin dear," he said, "I have someone here for you to meet. This is Lady Solange. Solange, this is Tamsin, my daughter."

Tamsin looked up at the visitor, her blue eyes wide with curiosity. As Solange looked down at the two of them, her heart filled with love for the two blond heads, the two sets of big blue eyes looking up at her, two people very different but so very much alike. "Hello, Tamsin," she said to the girl. "I have been looking forward to meeting you."

Geoffrey was a bit uncertain as to how Tamsin would regard Solange. She had seemed to view Henry as a rival for her father's affection when the boy had first come to Belvoir, though she had soon adopted him as a member of the family and now adored him like a big brother. With Solange, however, the affinity was immediate. "I have a kitten," she told Solange. "My Da brought it for me, and Ree helped him. Do you want to see it?"

Solange looked at Geoffrey with amusement. "Who is Ree?" she asked.

"That is what she calls Henry," Geoffrey replied as he straightened up. "She calls her godfather Mun when his name is Edmund, and she calls her aunt by the name of Bell. Speaking of whom, here she is." He turned to Isabel's cot and picked up his sister who had been napping. The girl mumbled sleepily, then laid her head on her brother's shoulder and continued her nap. Geoffrey returned the child to her cot with an affectionate ruffling of her tousled brown curls. "She is not very sociable at this moment," he apologized to Solange. "And her name is actually Isabel. You will have to make her acquaintance later."

Tamsin, disliking having her father and his friend's attention diverted, pulled at the fabric of Solange's skirt. "Come see my kitten now!" she demanded and took Solange's hand to lead her to the corner where the important feline reposed.

Geoffrey watched them with a smile as his daughter showed her pet to Solange, who dutifully exclaimed at the cat's beauty and at Tamsin's good fortune in having a Da who provided such lovely gifts. He was relieved and gladdened that the two girls had taken to each other so easily. However, he was also concerned about Solange's brother down in the great hall no doubt making eyes at Alyssa and anticipating further advances. With numerous and fervent promises to Tamsin for Solange's return to play with her and the kitten, he took Solange's arm and returned with her downstairs. Geoffrey was undeniably happy that the two girls had taken such a quick liking to each other, and he found himself wishing that Solange's visit might never end.

*****

The next day Geoffrey invited Solange to see Lydford and its environs. He was half afraid that a girl would not be interested in fields and villages, but then of course Solange was no ordinary girl. She responded to the suggestion with enthusiasm.

He mounted her on a mare from Belvoir's stables to allow her pony to continue its recuperation from their long journey, and they proceeded out into the warm sunshine of Devon's summer. First they rode out into the fields and Geoffrey stopped to speak with some of the farmers as he showed Solange how the crops were planted in several long rows rather than in many short ones, to minimize the number of times required to turn the plow oxen, animals who enjoyed being uncooperative. He explained to her about the rotation of crops and how each field was allowed to lay fallow every third year. Solange was impressed. In fact, she responded to all she saw with an enthusiasm and appreciation which reminded Geoffrey of his own reaction when he had first arrived here as a child. Solange exhibited the same feelings of wondrous attachment that he had felt. He was proud of Belvoir, and it made his heart soar to see Solange's eyes shine as he showed her what was important to him.

As for Solange, she was glad to see Geoffrey's demesne not only because she enjoyed it, but also because Geoffrey so obviously loved the place. She was prepared to love Belvoir not only on its own merits, but also because of the lord of Belvoir as well.

They ended their tour at the village, walking their horses down the dirt road which bisected Lydford. Geoffrey pointed out the church (though not mentioning that he had attempted to marry Tamsin's mother there), the mill and blacksmith shop situated near the river's edge, and nodded greetings to the villagers they passed.

"You seem very friendly with these people," Solange remarked.

"They are not merely people," Geoffrey replied. "They are my people. Their welfare is my concern and their protection is my duty. They are my friends, almost my family. Can you understand that, Solange?"

"Yes, my lord, I understand that very well. It must be wonderful to have such a sense of belonging, of purpose. I have never felt that back in Exeter. My parents want to keep me immured in the keep all of the time as if fresh air was dangerous, but here at Belvoir, with you, I feel free and happy."

Geoffrey looked down at Solange from atop Storm's back, a warmth melting his formerly icy heart at the realization that Solange felt almost exactly the same about Belvoir and its inhabitants as he did. And Lord, she was so beautiful! Though she had no features in common with Milesenda, whom he had previously idolized as the epitome of feminine charm, still she fired his senses in a way he had never known before. Her fine, almost delicate features and that glossy midnight hair enchanted him, and her fiery, vivacious disposition combined with a youthful innocence delighted him. She had again gone out without a veil in her hoydenish way, and a few tendrils of silky black hair escaped from her braids to float in front of her face in the breeze. He wondered how the people going about their daily lives around them would react if he were to lean down from Storm's back and kiss her. He almost took the chance, but instead stiffened and frowned at what he saw behind her. Solange, seeing only the frown and the dark emotion in his eyes, but not its cause, drew back as Geoffrey suddenly swung down from his horse and approached the girl he had seen pass behind Solange's horse.

It was Kerensa, carrying a full pail of water in each hand, having apparently just come from the well in the center of the village. She was hugely pregnant, and Geoffrey's heart constricted with fear at the sight of her. His paralyzing terror at the sight of a pregnant woman, any pregnant woman, was something he was afraid would never leave him.

He took the pails from her hands as she gaped at him in surprise. "You should not be carrying these heavy things," he scolded.

"But, my lord," Kerensa protested at the unseemliness of a Norman baron carrying water pails for a peasant. Geoffrey, however, brooked no argument as he carried the buckets across the road to the cottage where Kerensa now lived with her husband Dewi. She could only follow and open the door for him, with Solange glaring holes in his back as she sat forgotten on her horse in the middle of the dirt road.

Inside Kerensa and Dewi's cottage, Geoffrey set the pails down with a gruffly ordered, "Sit down" to Kerensa. She obeyed, saying, "Thank you for bringing those in for me my lord, but there was no need."

"Where is Dewi?" Geoffrey inquired, pacing about the small cottage and trying not to look at Kerensa's protruding stomach.

"It is his day of obligation, my lord." As Geoffrey's tenant, Dewi was required to work in Belvoir's fields for three days of each week.

Kerensa smiled slightly to herself as she saw past Lord de Graville's gruff manner and realized that it was a disguise for his concern. Though she had been too young at the time of Milesenda's death to understand then what had happened, the story of the young lord's love for her and the effect of her tragic death had become something of a legend in Lydford. Though she was not quite yet a mother, her maternal instincts were nonetheless aroused by Geoffrey's concern.

"He should not have left you alone now, when you are..." Geoffrey waved a hand in the general direction of Kerensa's bulging belly. "I will send someone out to the fields to fetch him back, and then he is to stay with you until the child is born and you have recovered from your travail. I do not want you left alone again, nor are you to carry or lift anything heavy."

"But my lord, it is Dewi's-"

"I know, his day of obligation. His obligation is suspended until the child arrives. There will be no need for him to make up the time."

"Thank you, my lord. You are most generous."

"Consider it a gift to my godchild," Geoffrey said with outward nonchalance, but inside wondering with quiet terror if Kerensa realized the danger she was facing. He looked around the cottage, nodding with approval at the stack of firewood next to the hearth and the sturdy furniture made by Dewi's own hands. He was taking his responsibilities as a husband and soon to be father seriously.

"Kerensa, how are-" he shuddered briefly. "How are you feeling?"

Kerensa smiled and brushed one hand over the mound of her belly. "I feel fine, my lord. Tired much of the time, but otherwise I feel well. Emma says the baby should arrive any day now."

Her last comment was the wrong thing to say, for Geoffrey went pale with fear and he looked as if he were about to bolt. "Not ... not now?" It was a combination of a question and an exclamation of panic.

"No, not now," Kerensa replied. "But soon, I hope. The naughty baby has been kicking me most unmercifully." Her hand moved as the baby chose that moment to give truth to its mother's words, and Geoffrey stared in horrified fascination.

Kerensa could not help but be amused at this sight of this very large man, a baron, a man she knew had gone into battle and faced death with fearlessness, reduced to trembling helplessness at the sight of one pregnant girl sitting on a stool. At that moment he looked very young and boyish and completely uncertain of what to do with his hands. Inspiration guided her next words.

"Would you like to feel your godchild's kick?" she asked, encouraging him with a look to place his hand on her rounded frontage.

Geoffrey shook his head and backed up a pace, but it was a small cottage, one room as were most of the villager's homes, and he could not go far.

"Do not fear, it will be all right," Kerensa insisted, and Geoffrey was drawn against his will to step forward and allow Kerensa to take his right hand, his left being clenched firmly in the folds of his tunic. She placed his hand on her belly, and even through her gown and his glove he could feel the healthy kick of a baby clamoring for its life to begin. He felt life, not death beneath his hand.

But, he remembered, so had Milesenda appeared the last time he had touched her so, and a few hours later, she was dead. He snatched his hand away as if it had been thrust into a fire, and backed towards the door.

"I must go," he insisted. "But I will send someone to stay with you until Dewi gets home."

"Yes, my lord. I thank you," Kerensa said, realizing that perhaps she had been too forward and pushed Lord de Graville a bit too far. "Your lady must be wondering what has become of you."

His lady! In his concern for Kerensa, he had completely forgotten about Solange, abandoned in the roadway. He ducked out the door, wondering if she had returned to the castle without him, but she remained where he had left her, holding his horse's reins in her hand and staring at him with an expression that, had he been more perceptive at that moment, he would have recognized as a storm about to break over his head. But he failed to read the warning, as he noticed young Ulric, who worked in his stables, a few yards away. He called the boy over.

"Ulric, I have an important task I wish you to accomplish for me."

"Yes, my lord?"

"Go out to the fields and find Dewi. He is most likely working on the wheat harvest in the north hide. If not, seek out Edmund and he will know where to find Dewi. Tell him he is needed at home, and that I said for him to come right away. Go now, hurry." He sent the boy off with a tousle of Ulric's rough hair, and the boy sped away to accomplish his mission. One more thing Geoffrey needed to do to set his mind at ease that Kerensa would be cared for.

He turned to Solange and said, "I will be right back," not noticing that she did not reply as he strode quickly down the path to the home of the village midwife. Emma responded to his knock with questioning eyes.

"Go and stay with Kerensa if you would please, Emma," he requested. "I have sent Ulric out to fetch Dewi home."

"Kerensa! Is it her time?" Emma hurried out the door and turned toward Kerensa's cottage.

"No, she is not in labor now. But I still do not believe she should be alone when she is so near."

"I will go and see her immediately, my lord," Emma replied, not questioning what might seem to some people to be an excess of concern on the part of the young Baron de Graville. She of all people understood his somewhat irrational reactions to breeding women, having also been present when Milesenda had died.

Satisfied now that he had done what he could, he returned to where Solange still waited and took Storm's reins, leaping onto the horse's back, and they both walked their horses towards the castle. Solange's silence as they returned to Belvoir's stable was uncharacteristic. All day she had chattered ebulliently about how beautiful Belvoir was, how adorable Tamsin was, how she enjoyed the fresh sweet air of the countryside. But since he had stopped to help Kerensa with her buckets, Solange had said not a word. Perhaps she had run out of things to say.

When they entered the warm quiet stable and he helped her down from her horse, she pulled away from him for the first time. He glanced quickly to make sure he hadn't forgotten his gloves, but they were firmly in place. Dismissing her mood as his imagination, he started to remove the saddle from the horse Solange had been riding. Geoffrey, as usual, had ridden bareback.

Geoffrey had still failed to read the storm warnings, when Solange asked in a tight voice, "Is it yours?"

Confused, Geoffrey looked at her, the saddle still clutched in his hand. Was what his? This stable, the horses? Of course they were his and she knew it. "Is what mine?" he asked innocently, and then the storm broke over his head with fury.

"Oh, do not play stupid with me, my randy lord!" Her eyes flashed daggers. "You know perfectly well what I mean! I did not come all the way here to be humiliated in such a manner! To be left sitting in the road like some sort of fool while you visit with your, your mistress! When that child is born will you bring it here to live with you as well? Maybe I should return to Exeter today!"

He was so surprised by her outburst and her outrageous assumptions that he could only stare at her, the saddle still clutched forgotten in his hands. Her anger was so vivid, so intense, that when she stepped toward him he actually backed away from her, ending up with his back against the wall.

After staring at her in dumb confusion for a moment, understanding dawned. She believed that he was the father of Kerensa's unborn child! But nothing could be further from the truth. "But, Solange," he began.

She tapped her foot. "Yes, my lord. Cozen your way out of this if you can! That girl is Tamsin's mother, is she not?"

Now Geoffrey was angry as well. What did she think he was, some sort of satyr who would ravish anything remotely female? "That girl has a name," he informed her. "It is Kerensa, and she is neither my mistress nor is she Tamsin's mother. I told you Tamsin's mother died in childbed. Did you think I had lied? Do you think so little of me that I would lie to you about something like that?"

When Solange didn't answer, he demanded, "Answer me! Do you accuse me of lying to you?"

He was so angry at her for her assumption he felt like shaking her, but he had such a tight grip on the saddle that he probably would be incapable of letting go of it.

When Geoffrey was angry, most people backed away, trembled, stuttered, couldn't meet his eyes. Solange did none of these. She stood up to him, as much as her diminutive stature allowed.

"What do you expect me to think?" she demanded with smoldering eyes. "You practically fell off your horse to go to that girl, with not so much as a word to me. You left me out there while you visited with her, and I could see that she is very pregnant. I shall believe you when you say that girl is not Tamsin's mother. But what about the child she is carrying now? Can you truthfully say that is not your child?"

"Yes, I can truthfully say that. Kerensa is a married woman, and her husband Dewi is her child's father. I should know. I arranged their wedding. I will be their child's godfather, but if you think she is, or ever has been my mistress, you are mistaken."

Solange still looked doubtful. She also looked so beautiful in her anger that Geoffrey felt an urge to drop the saddle on the floor and pull her into his arms. But he wasn't entirely certain she wouldn't try to take his dagger from him and plant it between his ribs, despite being half his size, so he kept the saddle in his hands in case he needed it with which to defend himself.

"Will you swear to me that you have never touched that girl," she demanded, then added quickly when he glared at her, "Kerensa."

"I kissed her cheek on her wedding day," he replied with a sneer. "Will you have me hanged for it?"

"You know what I mean!"

"I swear to you I have never touched Kerensa in the manner which you imply, that I am not the father of her child, and she has never been my mistress nor will she ever be. Does that satisfy you? For the love of Christ, Solange, she is carrying a child, and no matter who the father, a breeding woman should not be carrying anything so heavy as pails of water, nor should she be left alone when she is so near her time." Just the thought of what Kerensa would soon be facing made Geoffrey feel sick.

Solange pouted for a moment, considering while Geoffrey waited like a condemned man about to hear his sentence. Then she smiled, reprieving him. "Very well, I believe you when you say you are not the father of her child. But why should you be so extraordinarily concerned about another man's wife bearing a child? From what I am told, it is a common occurrence."

The answer to Solange's question was something so close to Geoffrey's heart, so tangled in his emotions, that revealing it posed the risk of exposing his vulnerability, of giving that part of himself he had kept locked in ice for over six years. But since knowing Solange he had felt that ice slowly begin to melt away, drip by warming drip, liberated by her smile. He realized that he cared very much for her opinion of him, that he craved her good regard, and winning, or keeping it, entailed that risk on his part.

He set the saddle he had still been clutching on the floor and sat on it, elbows on his knees as he shoved his hands through his hair, and prepared to bare his soul. Staring at the hem of Solange's gown in front of his feet, he took a deep breath.

"As I told you, Tamsin's mother died in childbirth. She died just a few minutes after Tamsin was born. Not only did she die, but I was with her. I was there and I was helpless to prevent it. I do not think it is vain to say I am a strong man, but all of my strength could not save her. She died in my arms, because she had born my child, and I felt as if I had done her to death with my own hands. You cannot possibly imagine how that made me feel. I loved her, and my love killed her.

"Ever since then the sight of a pregnant woman has terrified me. I nearly went insane the night my stepmother gave birth to Isabel. I was certain she would die also. Any time I see a woman about to give birth, I feel sick, helpless. I know the danger she will face, and I would do anything to assure her safety, but I can do nothing. It does not matter that I am a knight, a baron, a warrior. I would rather face a dozen armed enemies with no weapons save my bare hands, than to face the terror of seeing another woman die in childbed. It matters not if she is a woman in my family, someone I know, or a stranger. It matters not who the father is or if she has given birth before without adversity. I still experience that helpless panic. That is why I escorted Kerensa to her home, why I rudely left you without explanation. I know it is eccentric, perhaps even a bit demented for me to be so obsessed about something I cannot control, but I cannot prevent the feeling. I can only hope that you will understand, and forgive me."

Vocalizing these secret parts of his soul was a catharsis for Geoffrey, a cleansing. At the risk of appearing weak, he had never specifically told anyone of his fears, but telling Solange now was a relief and a release. Sharing the fear, he realized, made it diminish and relinquish the hold it had had on his soul. Unsure of Solange's reaction to his revelations, he continued to stare helplessly at her feet until he felt the touch of her hand on his head. Looking up he saw that her eyes were brimming, and as he watched a single tear rolled down her cheek. "Of course I forgive you, my lord, and I apologize for being angry with you. I did not realize how you felt about such a situation. I saw only that you paid attention to another woman."

"My lady Solange," he said with the tiniest of smiles, "I do believe you are jealous."

"Yes," she admitted. "I was jealous."

Geoffrey had returned what Solange had once said to him about being jealous as a joke, but suddenly he was no longer amused. He was, however, astounded that Solange should feel jealous toward a woman she had believed him to be fond of. Jealousy was a lover's emotion.

Don't fall in love with me, he thought, looking at her face but unable to say the words aloud. Don't fall in love with me because I cannot return it as you deserve.

"There is no need for you to be jealous," he said to her, hoping to dispel any foolish romantic notions she might have.

Then Solange did the most amazing thing. She turned and sat on Geoffrey's lap, putting her hands on his shoulders.

"Truly?" she said with shining eyes, and Geoffrey realized too late that she had misinterpreted his words. She obviously believed that she had a premier place in his heart above all others, and while it was true he had feelings for her, he would not, could not, allow himself to call it love.

However when he looked into her deep dark eyes, neither could he disillusion her. So she remained sitting on his lap, her dainty little hands possessing his broad shoulders with a touch, smiling at him, her earlier anger dissipated in that quicksilver manner that both amazed and enchanted him. Leaning back against the wall behind him, he allowed her to settle herself more comfortably on his lap. He had demolished a great emotional barrier by confessing to her his fear of childbirth, and now felt free to speak of less serious matters. But he still kept his hands at his sides.

"You sat like this, on my lap, the first day I met you," he reminded her. She smiled at the memory. "I enjoyed it at the time, but it occurred to me later that it was not a wise thing for you to do, to be so trusting of a man you did not know."

"But I knew I could trust you," Solange insisted. "Even though I did not know you at the time, there was something about you, a kindness in your eyes, that told me you were a compassionate and honorable man.

It made me feel so much better to be able to tell someone that I was upset."

Geoffrey could agree with her about her last statement, but he was not so certain about the compassionate and honorable part. If she only knew about the lustful feelings she inspired in him, especially with her sitting in his lap, she wouldn't think him honorable at all. He was treading on thin ice and he knew it. Not only treading on it, but stomping on it with both boots and all his weight. Solange was simply too tempting.

She looked up at him with those big wide eyes, a trace of her tears of sympathy still shimmering through her smile. He had an urge, sudden and intense, to undo those glossy braids and free her hair from its proper confines. His lecherous mind suddenly imagined that silky black hair spread out in a shining fan over his pillow; conjured up images of her yielding her sweet innocence to him which were in direct contradiction to the honorableness she had attributed to him. She was right there, sitting on his lap, touching his shoulders, but he dared not touch her in return. His reluctance was due not only to his deformed hand, but to the knowledge that once he did touch her, he feared he would be unable to stop himself.

"May I tell you a secret, my lord?" she asked, whispering though they were quite alone. He nodded, wondering what confidence she was going to entrust to him now. "When you were at Rougemont last, and when we," she stammered a little and glanced down for a moment, "when we kissed, I enjoyed it very much."

Geoffrey found himself stammering a bit himself as he replied, "Are you saying that you wish to do it again?"

Solange's nod of assent was both artless and seductive, and Geoffrey was after all, only a man, with no claims to saintliness. When she raised her mouth to his, he obliged her.

It was a soft kiss at first, a forgiveness for their earlier argument. He allowed himself to put his arms around her and draw her closer as her arms encircled his neck and their kiss deepened. She fit so perfectly here on his lap, the softness of her petite form fitting in perfect concert with the hard planes of his chest, as though God had fashioned their bodies expressly for this closeness. His tongue stroked everything reachable in her mouth, and she proved that she had learned well the lesson in kissing he had begun to teach her in the garden at Rougemont. The pleasure he felt was terrifying, and his common sense began to desert him with Solange in his arms.

The sound of the stable door slamming made them jump apart and look up to see Gilbert standing over them with murder written on his face. Geoffrey jumped to his feet and dragged Solange up with him. She took one look at the boiling rage in her brother's eyes and promptly buried her face against Geoffrey's arm, clinging to him for protection. Geoffrey, jerked too suddenly from sensuality to confrontation, was speechless. His face flushed a dusky red as Gilbert said, "I demand an explanation, my lord de Graville!", and Geoffrey counted himself fortunate that Solange's brother was not carrying his sword.

"You have eyes in your head, de Meules," he retorted, when he had found his voice.

"Yes, and those eyes show me my host defiling my sister's virtue in a stable!"

"Her virtue is intact," Geoffrey stated sullenly, hotly embarrassed at having been caught in *flagrante delicto*, as it were, but retaining enough of a sense of humor to wonder for a moment if Gilbert's indignation was more for what Geoffrey and Solange were doing, or for the fact that they were doing it in the stable.

"And only due to my timely arrival, by the looks of things," was Gilbert's terse reply. He reached for his sister's arm. "I shall trust, Solange, that you were not aware of the consequences of your actions and were led astray by this degenerate lecher. Come along now. I shall take you inside to your mother."

Solange shrank away from her brother's hand. "No," she said mutinously, shaking her head. She reminded Geoffrey of Tamsin in one of her obstinate moods.

"Do not defy me in this, Solange," Gilbert ordered. "Come with me now and I will refrain from mentioning this incident to our parents."

"Perhaps you should go with your brother," Geoffrey suggested, not wanting to get her into any more trouble.

That she felt he had betrayed her was evident in the look of hurt on the face she showed him, and he felt like a dog for sending her away. Leaning down to her ear he whispered, "Believe me that I do not wish to send you away. I only wish to spare you punishment, and I promise to make it up to you later, my sweet."

She acquiesced then, smoothing her skirt with one hand but allowing the other to trail deliciously down his arm in an innocently provocative gesture before stepping away from him to accompany her brother. Gilbert reached to take his sister's arm but she would have none of it, wrenching away from him defiantly without words, only a brief but scathing, sharp glance of resistance. Sadly, Geoffrey watched the two walk away from him, but after only a few steps Solange turned, looked up at Geoffrey, and blew him a kiss. Gilbert went red with anger at his sister's action, Geoffrey smiled broadly, and Solange flitted away from both men before her brother could lay hands on her again. Gilbert muttered in Geoffrey's direction, "I shall be watching you, my lord de Graville!" as he escorted his sister out of the stable.

He had been stupid, Geoffrey thought as Solange and Gilbert disappeared out the door and, presumably, returned to the keep. Stupid to allow himself to practically maul his guest's daughter in a lowly stable where detection was virtually guaranteed, to run the risk of destroying her reputation when she was too young and innocent to understand the potential consequences. But his lips tingled with the memory of her kisses, and his chest felt tight at the remembrance of her embrace. Young and innocent and naive she might be, but nonetheless, she was bewitching him much more profusely than any experienced siren ever could. Perhaps it was best that Gilbert had caught them when he had. With the effect she seemed to have on him, he doubted if he had the strength or resolve to prevent himself from destroying her virtue, or, even worse, to prevent her from getting under his skin, through his protective ice barrier, and into his heart. Damn, that anxiety still did not prevent him from hoping for an opportunity to be with her again, and the realization of his weakness for her was formidable and terrifying, and yet somehow exhilarating as well.

30

He was giving Tamsin a ride on his horse the next afternoon, as always finding supreme joy in spending this time with his daughter seated in front of him, even if it was only trotting in circles around the paddock, when he saw Gilbert approaching the fence. With a bit of trepidation, he guided Storm to that side to meet his guest, wondering if another confrontation was about to ensue. Thankfully Solange was inside, safely in the company of her mother and Lady Alyssa, and with Henry sitting on the fence in a position to be a witness, Gilbert appeared today to be more affable towards his young host than he had been the day before. He actually smiled as Geoffrey dismounted with Tamsin in his arms.

Henry jumped down from his seat on the top of the fence and bowed as his cousin approached, and Geoffrey took advantage of his trust in his squire, and Tamsin's affection for Henry, to hand his daughter into the boy's arms and request, "Please take Tamsin inside to Maud." He stepped over the fence, kissed his daughter and promised her, "I will come and get you in a little while."

As Gilbert watched with amusement, Henry said, "Yes, my lord," but set Tamsin on her feet and took her hand rather than carrying her. "She prefers to walk on her own," he explained as the two of them walked toward the keep.

Gilbert cocked one dark eyebrow at the sight of his cousin escorting a small child. "When you brought him here," he said to Geoffrey, "I thought it was to be your squire, not a child's nursemaid."

"He is an excellent squire." Geoffrey defended. "He handles his sword well, is an excellent horseman, and is brave and loyal enough to be trusted with matters of importance, including my daughter."

"A pretty child," Gilbert observed. "She has a look of you."

Geoffrey was surprised. "She does not look like me," he said quickly. "She looks like her mother."

"Well then, produce the mother and we shall compare."

"Her mother is dead."

"My condolences," Gilbert said but with little sincerity. "Do you have many more bastards about?"

Geoffrey tensed in offense. "Tamsin is my only child," he said stiffly, refusing to use the word bastard.

Gilbert nodded, apparently satisfied. "I was speaking to your step-mother this morning. She is a very courageous woman, raising her child with no husband to protect them."

"I have protected them since my father's death," Geoffrey said, wondering what Gilbert was getting at. "I shall continue to protect them, with my life if necessary."

"Yes, I understand it almost came to that after Pevensey. Lady Alyssa is an extraordinarily beautiful and charming woman, and intelligent as well. It must be very lonely for her, a widow with no man to warm her bed at night."

For a moment Geoffrey stopped breathing, then took a step towards Gilbert. Excessive height was not a characteristic enjoyed by the members of the de Meules family, but Gilbert suddenly found himself eye to eye with the much taller and very angry Baron de Graville as the younger man jerked him off his feet by the front of his tunic. The fabric strained and threatened to rip away as Geoffrey shook Gilbert furiously.

"You touch my stepmother," he gritted between clenched teeth, "You so much as look at her cross-ways, and I swear I'll cut out your heart with a dull knife."

"A dull knife?" Gilbert enquired. "Am I not even offered the courtesy of your finest, sharpest blade?"

"No," Geoffrey countered. "An old, dull blade will cause more pain, and give me the added satisfaction of your slow, lingering anguish."

Gilbert replied with dignity, "I assure you I have proffered no offense to the lady."

Geoffrey's glare was disbelieving; Gilbert's, challenging.

"And what if a man wished to offer her honorable marriage?"

Geoffrey's mouth very nearly fell open at the incredulousness of what Gilbert was suggesting, and he involuntarily loosened his grip on Gilbert's tunic so the other man dropped back to his feet.

"She is barren," he lied, quickly, anything to dissuade Gilbert's interest.

Gilbert arched one dark eyebrow. Now it was his turn to look disbelieving. "That pretty baby at her skirts seems to state otherwise."

"That pretty baby is my sister and I will thank you to keep your covetous hands away from her as well," Geoffrey glowered. He was appalled at the possibility of his stepmother remarrying, leaving Belvoir and taking Isabel away with her, though he knew it to be selfish. If it was what his stepmother truly wanted, he should not stand in her way, but on the other hand, he had seen the lascivious looks Gilbert de Meules had cast upon many of the maids at Belvoir. He could not credit the other man with sincerity.

"Perhaps," Gilbert suggested, "I should speak to the lady personally. I am a widower, you know, with no children of my own, or at least none that I care to acknowledge."

"No!" Geoffrey shouted the word as he stepped towards the other man, threateningly. Prudently, Gilbert stepped back. He was older than Geoffrey, but Geoffrey was larger, and angrier.

"Your words seem to carry the stain of hypocrisy," Gilbert said from the safety of several feet away from Geoffrey, "after what I observed between you and my sister yesterday."

"That was different," Geoffrey replied. After all, Solange was Solange, a desirable woman if a young one, and Alyssa was... well, she was a woman also, but she was Geoffrey's mother. "Your suit is denied," he stated.

"But I..." Gilbert began.

"I said, denied," Geoffrey repeated. "Lady Alyssa may be my step-mother, but I am the lord of Belvoir and the guardian of her child. She cannot marry without my permission. If I say your suit is denied, it is denied, and that is the end of it. Do not tempt me to violence, de Meules." How glad Geoffrey was of the convenient law that gave him authority over all marriages at Belvoir.

Thoroughly frustrated, Gilbert shook his head, but a small smile did reach his lips as he turned away.

"I believe," he said, "that when you marry my sister, I shall pray that she gives you only sons."

"And why is that?" Geoffrey couldn't help asking.

"Because if you are that over-protective of your stepmother, I shudder to contemplate the fate of any man who might ever court a daughter of yours."

As Gilbert walked away, Geoffrey stared after him until his horse stretched his head over the fence and nudged Geoffrey's shoulder, demanding attention. Geoffrey stroked Storm's nose, then led the horse to the gate and then to the stable for Ulric to water and brush. It was not until he was halfway up the stairs at the keep to return to Tamsin that Geoffrey realized exactly what Gilbert had said. He had used that word which Geoffrey had been avoiding for years, marry, and Geoffrey had forgotten to protest the idea. What was worse, when he realized it, it didn't scare him nearly as much as it used to, as it ought to.

31

It was the fire that made Geoffrey realize that he couldn't live without Solange in his life.

Over the next few days, Geoffrey and Solange intrigued with little success to sneak away from the supervision of her brother Gilbert and their mother. Lady Alyssa, perceptive as always, could not help but notice that Gilbert especially kept an eagle eye on his sister's whereabouts and insisted on accompanying her if she so much as spoke to Geoffrey. Alyssa found Gilbert's protection of his sister to be endearing, knowing that Geoffrey would be even more protective when Tamsin and Isabel became old enough to be attractive to men, but she also knew that nothing would ever come to fruition between Geoffrey and Solange with Gilbert hovering over them like a mother hen.

Lady de Meules required a period of rest in the afternoon and it was during one of these interludes that Lady Alyssa insisted that none other than Gilbert should assist her with some task in the garden that, looked at objectively, could actually have been accomplished by any number of people. But Gilbert, smitten, saw only the lady's smile, heard only her request for his company. Practical considerations and his mission to chaperone his sister, suddenly became irrelevant. He trailed after Alyssa like an obedient puppy.

Baron de Meules had accompanied Henry to the exercise yard and they did not seem to require Geoffrey's company. He took advantage of his unexpected exclusion to search out Solange, being told by Maud that the girl was visiting with Tamsin.

He followed Maud up the stairs and into the nursery, where he observed Solange seated in a chair with Tamsin on her lap. At first, they did not see Geoffrey, and as he watched, Tamsin flung her arms around Solange's neck and gave her a loud, childish kiss on the cheek.

Geoffrey was unprepared for the intense and completely irrational jealousy which coursed through him at the sight. Those were his hugs and kisses which Solange was appropriating! Although Tamsin was an affectionate child and he was accustomed to seeing her embrace Alyssa, Edmund and even Henry, they were family, and still, he was dumbfounded to see his daughter's attachment to Solange, someone she had only known for a short while.

He must have made some sound, for the two girls turned and saw him. He was happy that Tamsin had the loyalty to slide down from Solange's lap and run to him, exclaiming happily, "Da!" as he scooped her up and received the remainder of her kisses. At least she had not given all of her affection to someone else!

Solange approached him as well, smiling. "Tamsin and I were having a most interesting conversation. She was telling me how wonderful her Da is."

As Geoffrey blushed, Tamsin tugged on his hair. "Da!" she demanded. "Can S'lange stay here? I want her to stay here. I don't want her to go away. Please, Da!"

Both Geoffrey and Solange looked away from each other for a moment, embarrassed by the little girl's outspokenness. Geoffrey patted his daughter's hair.

"We shall discuss it later," he said noncommittally. He looked at Solange. "Would you like to go for a ride?" he invited.

"Gilbert?" she inquired.

"Gilbert is occupied elsewhere."

"A ride would be lovely," Solange replied with a smile.

"Me too!" Tamsin demanded, and although usually Geoffrey would want to take his daughter along, still this was a rare opportunity to spend some unchaperoned time with Solange.

"Not this time, sweetheart," he said. "I promise we will take you with us the next time," he added as the child began to pout.

"Do not frown, Tamsin," Solange urged. "Such a pretty little girl like you should only smile. I will come back and see you later on if you like." She smiled at the little girl, who acquiesced to the older girl's affection, wriggled down from her father's arms, and went over to the corner to play with her kitten.

"You manage her most effectively," Geoffrey observed as they left the castle and went to the stable to prepare for their solitary ride.

"She is a darling," Solange replied. "Where are we going to ride to?"

"I will take you to see the river gorge, if you would like," he offered as, with his gloves firmly covering his hands despite the warmth of the afternoon which made them sweat beneath the leather, he boosted her upon Storm's back and bounded up in front of her. Solange put her arms around his waist as they left the stable, but rather than resenting it as he had the first time she had held him so, he now quite enjoyed it, and appreciated the trust she placed in him.

The river gorge he was taking her to see was a mile past the village but away from the path used by travelers between Lydford and Exeter. It was a site where the usually placid river funneled into a rocky crevasse in such a way that the water frothed and foamed wildly before plunging down a short waterfall. It was a beautiful and scenic place and Geoffrey had an inexplicable urge to show Solange all the attractive features in Belvoir's vicinity.

However, they never arrived at the river gorge. As soon as they cleared the castle gates, Geoffrey's gut instinct told him that something was dangerously wrong, and the premonition was immediately confirmed by the sight of ominous gray smoke rising from the village.

With a flap of the reins, Geoffrey urged Storm down the hill toward the source of the smoke, Solange clinging to him desperately as they raced towards the village.

It was the blacksmith shop which was ablaze, foul smoke pouring from the thatched roof above whooshing flames which appeared to be sucking all of the surrounding air into hell. Geoffrey slid down from his horse's back, having forgotten Solange's presence for a moment. She slid off behind him and fell to her knees, but quickly scrambled to her feet. A group of horrified villagers stood staring at the burning building, and as Geoffrey approached a flying ember spun out from the conflagration and landed in the thatch of the blacksmith's house which was immediately next to the shop. The dry thatch ignited instantly, and at the sight, a young woman whom Geoffrey recognized as Hawise, wife of Brand the blacksmith, broke from the group of spectators and ran shrieking towards her home.

Instinctively Geoffrey caught the hysterical young woman in his arms before she could enter the burning building. She struggled in panic-stricken desperation to pull away from him.

"Brand!" she shrieked. "My baby! Let me go!"

Geoffrey had to shout to make himself heard over the roaring of the flames behind him. "You cannot go in! The house and shop are both burning now." With every passing second, flames spread across the thatched roof of Brand and Hawise's cottage; the blacksmith shop was fully engulfed.

"But Brand is in there!" Hawise cried, as if that fact would convince Geoffrey to allow her into the burning building. "He sent me out when he smelled the smoke and said he would bring the baby. But they are still inside! Brand! Brand!" She continued to scream and try to extricate herself from Geoffrey's grasp on her arms.

Geoffrey shook her to get her attention and to stop her hysterical screaming. He disliked handling a woman in such a rough manner, but desperate situations required desperate measures.

"Hawise!" he ordered sternly. Hawise collapsed in sobs against his chest. "I will go in and look for Brand and your baby. You stay here. Tell me where they are. Are they in the shop or the house?"

"In the house," Hawise replied, her voice choked with the tears which streamed down her face. That at least was the lesser of two hells;

if Brand or their baby were in the shop there would be little hope for their survival.

"Stay here," Geoffrey ordered with another small shake to ensure that Hawise was paying attention to him. Over his shoulder, he caught a glimpse of Edmund, sensibly organizing the villagers into a line starting at the river's edge, passing buckets of water hand to hand to throw onto the flames. Geoffrey turned towards the burning building only to be stopped by another pair of frantic hands. Solange had remained at his side during his confrontation with Hawise.

"Let me go with you!" Solange demanded, clutching at his gloved hand.

"No," he shouted back with insistent finality. Of all people, he would not allow Solange to risk her life in that inferno. "It is much too dangerous. I will not allow you to go in there. Stay outside!" He knew how much Solange disliked being commanded, but he did not have time to convince her with niceties.

"But I want to help you! I want to be with you! You will be in danger." Amazingly, tears were streaming from her eyes as much as from Hawise's. Could it be she was afraid for him?

"If you wish to help me," he shouted, setting her away from him and as far from the fire as his arms would reach, "help them!" He swept a hand towards the line of people attempting to douse the flames, but not really expecting her to assist them. Solange was a lady, and would most likely not wish to sully her tender hands on the rough handles of the peasant's buckets. But as long as she stayed away from the fire, he would not complain. "I do not want you to be injured," he added fervently.

Solange reached for him; for a moment he wondered if she meant to attach herself to him so that he was forced to allow her to accompany him. Instead she stood on tip-toe and reached for his hair, grabbing a handful in each hand and pulling hard, pulling his face down toward her. Then she kissed him hard on the mouth, a brief kiss but nonetheless intense and desperate.

With a small sob, she pulled back and said, "Go with God, my lord." He stared at her for a moment, his mind in turmoil. Then he recalled the burning buildings, Brand and his child trapped inside, and spun away from Solange. He dashed toward the house, pausing only to grab one of the water buckets and pour it over his head, drenching his hair and shoulders before he pushed open the door of Brand's cottage and plunged into hell on earth.

In the few moments that he had been dealing with Hawise and Solange, the flames had spread across the entire roof of the cottage and down the wall which separated the house from the blacksmith shop. The entire cottage was filled with smoke, and above him the burning roof crackled ominously. It was a small cottage, only one room, but filled as it was with blinding smoke, it appeared endlessly huge and terrifyingly menacing. It had been hot outside, but that was as nothing compared to the heat in the cottage, and the water Geoffrey had poured over himself for protection from the flames evaporated in moments. Breathing was difficult, and sight impossible.

"Brand!" he called out, coughing as the acrid smoke burned in eyes and throat. "Brand! Can you hear me? Where are you?"

He pitched blindly forward, arms outstretched, straining to hear any human sound over the hellish roaring of flames above and around him. His sense of balance was compromised by the smoke, and when he came up against something hard, a table perhaps, he tripped and fell to the floor, banging his head painfully against a wood surface. His head hit the object hard enough that it moved, and immediately after the jolt he heard the distinctive bleat of a small baby nearby.

Pulling himself to his knees, he felt in the direction of the tiny sound. His hands burned painfully in the leather gloves, but he would not take the time to remove them as he groped about, feeling and listening.

It was a cradle that he had hit with his head when he fell. He groped inside and, thank God, felt the body of the baby inside. Carefully feeling for the head, he lifted the baby out. The child had made no sound other than the one brief cough that had led Geoffrey to the cradle, and he feared the baby was now dead or close to it.

He held the tiny form up and pressed his ear against its chest. No sound, no movement. He could barely breathe in this fiery hell; how could a tiny baby accomplish it?

Inspiration hit him in the midst of his panic. He recalled a game he had played with Tamsin when she was an infant. He would blow into her face, and she would gasp at what seemed to an infant to be a large blast of wind, then she would giggle at the game.

Hot embers and burning bits of thatch were falling from the roof, and Geoffrey hunched his shoulders to protect the infant from the falling embers, feeling them searing his back as they burnt holes in the fabric of his tunic. He held the baby's face in front of his own and blew sharply. No response.

Please, breathe! he prayed, unable to bear the thought of having to present Hawise with a dead baby after his promise to save it. His mouth almost touching the face of the infant, he blew again, trying to puff his own living breath into the body of the child.

Twice, thrice he tried the maneuver that had been a game with Tamsin but which now was deadly serious.

The baby coughed. A beautiful sound! He blew in its face again and the child began to cry.

Wasting no time in prayers of gratitude, Geoffrey scrambled to his feet, clutching the baby against his chest. At eye level, the smoke was thicker than it had been at the floor, and all around him was the crackling of flames and the ominous creaking of the building about to fall down about his ears.

"Brand!" He yelled again, though his throat burned painfully with the effort. "For the love of Christ, Brand, can you hear me?"

He heard two sounds at once, from his right a sound that could have been a faint moan, and from his left the screechy sound of something solid falling apart. From within the dense smoke a pillar of fire fell toward him like some horrid monster intent on murder, as the cottage's wall collapsed.

Without time to run and not being able to see what was around him, Geoffrey could only turn his back and hunch his shoulders to protect the baby from the falling beam. It hit him across the shoulders and the back of his head, hard enough to drive him to one knee as he desperately fought to keep from dropping the baby. The beam was solid enough to inflict pain as it slid to the floor. He quickly shifted the now-screaming infant into his left arm, hoping he wasn't hurting it with his roughness, and felt his head and shoulders with his free hand to make certain he wasn't on fire. He felt no flames, though his head felt as if a horse had kicked it and his hair was sticky with what he presumed was blood.

Flames were around him, above him, and he knew he could not stay in the cottage much longer. He had heard a sound just before the beam had fallen; a sound that might mean Brand was still alive. He waved his free hand in front of him, trying to disburse the burning, choking smoke, trying to see in the direction from whence the small human sound had come.

There - to his right. The smoke shifted for just an instant to reveal a large lumpy shape on the floor just a few feet away.

"Brand!" Dropping clumsily to his knees, clutching the child to his shoulder, Geoffrey crawled the few feet to where Brand lay groping about on the floor and faintly gasping, overcome by the smoke.

"Thank God I've found you!" Geoffrey grasped Brand by the arm, trying to pull him up. "We must get out of here now." He tugged on the other man's arm, pulling him into a sitting position.

"Baby," Brand gasped, flailing weakly. "Find baby..."

"I have the baby," Geoffrey told the near-unconscious man, but Brand was apparently too muzzy-headed from the smoke to understand. He pulled away from Geoffrey and continued to grope about on the floor for the baby Geoffrey was holding.

"Brand!" Geoffrey shouted, shaking the blacksmith. "I have your baby, and we must all get out of here before the roof falls in. Here, hold him so I can help you up." He pressed the baby's body into its father's arms, and when Brand felt his child and heard its cry, came to realize that the child was found and, for the moment at least, alive.

With the baby being held by Brand, Geoffrey's arms were free to get Brand to his feet and out of the cottage. Of course, it would have to be Brand, the only man in Lydford with size on Geoffrey. A smaller person he could have simply picked up and carried out, but Brand topped Geoffrey by several inches and outweighed him by at least two stone. It didn't help any that Brand was also half unconscious.

Geoffrey could feel his own consciousness fading in the choking heat and smoke. He knew that he and Brand and the baby had only moments to spare before they were overcome or burned to death. He grasped Brand under the arms and by sheer force dragged the man to his knees, attempting at the same time not to be too forceful that Brand might drop the baby.

Brand's head lolled, and Geoffrey was getting desperate. "Brand!" He screamed the man's name again with what little voice was left to him. "For the love of Christ, man, move!"

Brand coughed heavily and with Geoffrey using all of his strength to pull him up, struggled to stand. All around them flames crackled and walls groaned ominously, with the smell of burning wood and thatch searing Geoffrey's eyes, nose and throat. The almost non-existent air he was attempting to gasp in was so hot he felt as if his guts were on fire as well. Both Geoffrey and Brand swayed and stumbled as the blacksmith finally gained his feet, clutching the baby to his chest.

For the first time, Brand seemed to notice who it was that was attempting to save him. He peered blearily into Geoffrey's face and gasped, "My lord!"

"Don't my lord me now," Geoffrey croaked tersely. "Just get your arse outside before the place comes down on our heads!"

Geoffrey's orientation, his sense of where they were in relation to the doorway of the cottage, was obliterated by the smoke, fire and terrifying roars and groans. They weren't in a house, they were in hell, with no way out and the inferno all about them. Through stinging eyes, Geoffrey cast about desperately for the doorway. To one side the smoke seemed slightly less dense and he could only pray that safety lay in that direction.

He grasped Brand's free arm and pulled it over his shoulders so that his own shoulder pressed into Brand's armpit. The larger man's weight, increased no doubt by his weakness, almost drove Geoffrey back to his knees. He stiffened his back, and his resolve, and put his arm around Brand's waist. "Do not drop the baby!" he admonished through parched lips, and dragged Brand towards what he prayed was the way out.

Two steps, then three, painfully gained, and the smoke became slightly less dense in front of them. A brief glance reassured Geoffrey that the baby was still in its father's arms. They had almost gained what did indeed prove to be the cottage's doorway when a burning section of the roof fell in almost on top of them. Geoffrey warded off the falling, flaming matter with his free arm but a still-solid piece of wood flew from the burning thatch and hit his head, then fell to the floor at his feet.

Thoroughly terrified and near-blinded with pain and fear, Geoffrey stomped and kicked at the flames in front of him, then with a be-moaned, "Mother of God! Help me!" he pulled with all the strength left to him and plunged through the last barrier of smoke and flames, into at long last the sweet clean air outside the cottage.

He was literally blinded by the sunlight after his time in the smoke-filled cottage, his stinging eyes unable to function in the sudden change. It seemed as if he had been in that burning building for hours, though it had actually only been a few minutes. Before he could think or move or thank God for his deliverance, a shower of water poured over Geoffrey and Brand, running down their faces and nearly drowning Geoffrey, but he was nonetheless exceedingly grateful for the coolness it provided.

He took a few more steps, Brand and the baby in tow, to be certain they were away from the cottage. The two men coughed and gulped sweet fresh air into their tortured lungs, and Geoffrey could hear shouts in front of him and flames still crackling behind him. He rubbed his eyes to try to clear them, praying the smoke and heat hadn't perma-nently blinded him.

Red. The first thing he saw was red - Edmund's red hair. His friend held the bucket whose contents he had just poured over Geoffrey's head, and Edmund's eyes were huge with fear and as green as emeralds.

"Your hair was on fire!" Edmund gasped, explaining the deluge he had poured over Geoffrey.

"The baby!" Geoffrey attempted to croak, turning to Brand to see if the baby was safe. The child gulped convulsively, then began to scream lustily. Geoffrey had never heard such a beautiful sound in his entire life.

Edmund pried the crying infant from Brand's grasp, and relieved of their precious charge, the two men fell to their knees in identical states of exhaustion and trauma. Brand crumpled to the ground, but Geoffrey's consciousness snapped alert with a sudden bolt of terror-stricken panic multitudes more intense than any he had suffered in the burning cottage.

Solange! The last moment he had been aware of her she had been insisting on accompanying him. He had thrust her away but had no idea if she had obeyed him or not. What if she had after all followed him into the blacksmith's house? She could even now be burning or crushed to death in the building behind him. Now that he could see-a little-he struggled to his feet, looked around and screamed her name.

Except that no sound emerged from his tortured throat. The effects of the smoke and heat and sheer terror rendered him mute and straining, and impervious to Edmund who was trying to check him for injuries, while at the same time juggling the crying baby in his arms.

Geoffrey was maddened by fear for Solange, half inclined to return to the burning cottage in search of her, despite the fact that it was now entirely engulfed in flames which whooshed hellishly as taunting lines of fire spit out and up like devil's tongues. He called for her again, his abused throat feeling like it was being torn to shreds, and this time the sound emerged, more a sob than a bellow, but enough to carry across the short expanse of trampled grass between the blacksmith's house, which was at the edge of the village, and the river bank where Lydford's residents were scooping water into buckets to pass up to the burning building.

He sensed more than saw that Solange had heard him. With some unknown force, his mind realized that she was aware of his desperate fear, and with unerring perception his gaze swung to those villagers at the river's edge.

Solange's head snapped up as she heard Geoffrey call to her. Anyone not knowing her would have never believed her to be a nobleman's pampered daughter, so untidy and downright grubby did she now appear. Her veil was gone with no trace. One of her braids had come loose, the wavy black hair a disordered tangle. Her face was dirty and the front of her gown was wet from neck to knees.

Most amazing of all, she held a bucket of water in her hands, which she dropped at the moment she heard Geoffrey call her name. She quickly clutched the shoulder of the woman next to her - Hawise, Brand's wife - and with cries of gladness and tears of relief, the two women raced toward Geoffrey and Brand.

Though smaller, Solange won the race, pulling her skirts up indecently to her knees to facilitate running. Geoffrey did not notice that she had somewhere lost her shoes as well as her veil, nor did he notice Hawise running to be reunited with her rescued husband and baby. His eyes were only for Solange, though when he tried to step toward her, his legs lost their last vestige of strength and he floundered as if his legs had turned to water beneath him. He fell back to his knees at the moment Solange reached him to throw herself into his arms, falling to her knees along with him.

Though his legs were weak, his arms found the strength to encircle her and hold her tight, thanking God in gulping gasps that she was safe, clutching at her hair and pressing his face into her neck, ignorant of the stares of Edmund and the other villagers, unheeding of Hawise as, with her child now safely in her arms she tried to thank him for saving her family, or of Brand sitting at his wife's feet catching his breath. He wanted only to hold Solange, his precious little Solange, who, thank God, had not followed him into the burning building, but who was safe and whole and sweet in his arms and he vowed with ardor never to allow her far from his protection again.

When he was assured that she was unharmed he finally drew back enough to look at her face, smoothing back the disordered black tresses with shaking hands which felt as if they had been permanently fused to his leather gloves, to gaze into her eyes, huge with fear relieved and shiny with wetness. The tears streaming down her cheeks left clean streaks on her otherwise filthy face. She looked the grubbiest of ragamuffins but at that moment Geoffrey didn't care if she had been rolling in the hog byre, as long as she was unhurt. He wanted to tell her how afraid he had been for both himself and for her, how grateful he was that she had not gone into the burning house, but his throat hurt too much and his tortured brain could not determine what to say first. So he settled for adoring her with his eyes and allowing her to cry and exclaim over him.

"My lord, my lord! I was so afraid you were never going to get out of that place!" she gasped in a sobbing voice. "You are injured!" she exclaimed, reaching up to wipe at his forehead. Her hand came away sticky with his blood which ran across his forehead, into his eye and down his cheek from a gash on his temple. Her searching hands came across a painful lump at the back of his head, and that and his shoulder felt as if he'd not only been kicked by a horse, but pelted with bricks as well. But he didn't care about his injuries just now. He would survive.

"What," he gasped with rasping voice, "where were you? I was worried you might be in there." In there, they both knew, meant the burning house whose flames were now being dampened somewhat by the villager's efforts.

"I was helping," she replied, "helping with the water buckets as you requested. I am afraid I was clumsy at first and spilled the first few, but I wanted to do my part to assist in fighting the fire."

Geoffrey stared at her in astonishment as bloody sooty drips fell unheeded from the singed edges of his hair. Though he had never considered Solange to be a typical indolent Norman noblewoman, still the fact that she had dirtied her lily-white hands, as well as her face and hair and clothing, to assist his peasants with their disaster amazed and affected him.

"Why?" was all he could ask.

Solange blinked as fresh tears threatened to spill from her brimming eyes. "Because you care for these people and are concerned for their welfare. Because you risked your life to save another. I could do no less than my small part to aid them as well. My lord, I was so afraid! Please promise me never to do something like that again!"

The last thing Geoffrey ever wanted to do again was to repeat what he had just experienced, but he could make no such promises to Solange and maintain his honor at the same time. If the need ever arose again he could do no less than what he had just done, though he would pray that such a situation would never again befall him.

Neither, however, would he lie to Solange, so he simply did not answer her plea. He only wanted to hold her and he did so until the trembling started; the quivering shudders that follow an experience of extreme terror. Though he had risked death before, he had never before been so completely and utterly terrified not only for himself, but for another as well.

His convulsions reminded Solange, who was holding him just as tightly, that he was hurt and she leaned away from him, exclaiming anew at his injuries.

"You are coming home to have your hurts attended to," she stated with the commanding authority females tended to assume over an injured man. She employed the same no-nonsense demeanor his step-mother would at such an occasion, and Geoffrey knew better than to disobey. His only hesitation was engendered by the situation in the village and the fear that the fire might spread.

His struggle to his feet was akin to that of a newly born colt, and just as ungraceful. Solange clung to his arm and though she was small and slight, still her physical touch gave him a modicum of strength. He felt a hand on his other arm; it was Edmund, who said, "Lord, Geoffrey, I have seen you in some states but this is the worst. You should go to the keep and have that gash seen to before you bleed to death. I can finish here. I believe the fire is under control and we need not fear it spreading."

If Solange was surprised at the familiar tone Edmund took with Baron de Graville, she did not show it, merely nodding in agreement at his words. Geoffrey glanced at the blacksmith's house and shop. Because flying sparks from the forge made it more vulnerable to fire, the buildings had purposely been built apart from the rest of the village, and now that most of the fuel had been consumed, the water being poured on the flames was helping to diminish them. That realization compelled Geoffrey to comply with Edmund's suggestions and Solange's insistence. With her help, he turned to start the painful, clumsy walk up the hill to Belvoir, his horse having wisely decamped for the safety of the stable as soon as Geoffrey and Solange had dismounted.

He stopped only to check on the condition of Brand, who had been moved to sit in the shade of a tree away from the fire. He sat with his baby in his arms and his wife wiping his face with a wet cloth, a few bruises being his only injuries. Geoffrey waved away their ebullient thanks and allowed Solange to take him home.

Halfway up the hill they were met by Gilbert and Henry on horseback, flying down the hill to investigate the smoke. Both men reined in their horses and flung themselves from their saddles upon seeing Geoffrey and Solange, and Gilbert jerked his horse's reins as he approached Geoffrey with anger evident in his face.

"What have you done to her!" he demanded with a horrified look at his sister, whose face, neck and hands were smeared with blood, adding to the grime she had accumulated herself while filling and passing water buckets.

Geoffrey wiped away blood from the still oozing gash on his forehead as Henry rushed to his side to offer his assistance.

"Lord, this is all I need," Geoffrey muttered, not bothering to couch his words in the Norman French he had been using out of courtesy since his guests had arrived. Before he could explain that he had done nothing to Solange, the girl stepped between Geoffrey and her brother with her hands on her hips and her own flash of anger. Geoffrey, having seen those sparks before, stepped back and said nothing, grateful that Solange's ire was not directed at himself. Gilbert, he could handle; Solange, he was not so sure about.

"You idiot, Gilbert!" she shouted at her brother. "Can you not see that my lord de Graville has been injured! He was almost killed rescuing a man and a child from a fire, and if you had any compassion at all you would show some concern for him, you oaf! I am merely dirty; he is hurt!"

Gilbert spared barely a glance for Geoffrey's injuries despite the fact that the younger man's face and hair were covered with soot and blood and there were holes burned through his tunic. He looked at his sister and said, "You are bleeding, and if he is the cause of it I shall kill him myself."

Solange was becoming more exasperated by the moment. "I am not bleeding," she stated as if explaining facts to a very small child.

In reply Gilbert stepped forward, wiped a finger across his sister's cheek, and held it before her eyes. "That, dear sister, is blood. Do not try to protect this brute. He shall pay dearly for any hurt he has done to you."

"Mine," Geoffrey said, first in English, then remembering to revert to Norman French for Gilbert's understanding. "It is my blood you see on her skin, and I apologize for bleeding on her." He turned to Solange, dreadfully sorry for not having realized that when he had held her he had been smearing his blood all over her. He would have tried to wipe the stains from her face but there was no part of his person or clothing which would do anything but make it worse. "I am sorry, my sweet," he said to her.

"There is nothing for you to be sorry for," she stated, then turned her flashing anger back to her brother, slapping at the finger he still held in the air. "Go away, Gilbert!" she shouted. "You should have no grievance against Lord de Graville. He has done nothing to hurt me; he has risked his life, and he is injured! He stands here bleeding while you blather. Go away, you crude insensitive boor, and I hope you fall on your sword."

Despite his hurts, Geoffrey had to smile to himself at Solange's vitriolic defense. "Yes, Gilbert, go away," he said, a little mockingly, then turned to give instructions to Henry.

"My lord, what has happened to you?" the squire asked anxiously.

Geoffrey made light of his injuries. "A few scrapes," he said, though Henry looked disbelieving. "I have a task for you. The blacksmith shop and Brand's house have burned. Go down to the village and make certain that the fire is completely extinguished, and see that Brand and his family have a place to stay until the buildings can be rebuilt. Edmund will know if any cottages are vacant. Report back to me when you have verified that the fire is dampened down to the last ember."

"Yes, my lord!" Henry said. "Here, take my horse. I can walk down to Lydford."

Geoffrey did not want to admit that at this moment he doubted he would have the strength to pull himself onto a horse's back. "No, you take your horse. It is not much further to walk. Go on, I want a full report that the fire is out."

With a nod of assent, Henry obeyed, mounting his horse and racing down the hill towards the village as Geoffrey and Solange ignored Gilbert and resumed their progress towards the castle. In addition to his other injuries, his old leg wound was killing him and he could not avoid a noticeable limp.

Gilbert almost obeyed his sister's order to go away, but after staring for a moment at Henry's dust, grabbed his horse's reins and followed his sister and Geoffrey on foot. With obvious reluctance, he offered Geoffrey a shoulder to lean on to assist his painful journey up the hill.

"If you fall over," he stated with disgust, "you might knock my sister down and injure her."

As the three of them passed under the portcullis Gilbert muttered, "I find it incredible that you, a Norman baron, would risk your life and put my sister in danger for the sake of a dirty peasant and his hovel. They are only English serfs after all, and can easily be replaced. It is foolish to ..." His sentence went unfinished as Geoffrey pulled away from him in anger.

"Those peasants are my people, my responsibility," he said, the anger he felt towards Gilbert's callous attitude bringing more pain to his tortured throat as he spoke. "And yes, I would risk my life for any of them just as I would for my family or even for you though I doubt you deserve such consideration. What you should wonder is, would any of them risk themselves for you if you were in such danger. Consider that!"

"Yes, Gilbert, consider that!" Solange echoed as she and Geoffrey approached the steps to the keep, leaving a perplexed Gilbert standing in the bailey staring after them.

In the great hall, Lady Alyssa waited anxiously. She had seen the smoke as well from the castle's vantage and had dispatched Gilbert and Henry to investigate, somehow knowing that if there was trouble in Lydford, her stepson would be in the thick of it.

"My Lord de Graville has been injured," Solange stated unnecessarily as Geoffrey limped to the nearest chair and fell into it.

"And you, my dear," Alyssa inquired, looking at Solange's bedraggled state, "are you hurt?"

Solange shook her head. "Then perhaps," Alyssa suggested gently, "you might wish to retire to wash and fix your clothing."

"Not until my lord's injuries have been cared for," Solange stated with immovable firmness as she brushed Geoffrey's hair away from the gash on his forehead.

In that moment Alyssa's opinion of Solange increased considerably. She had liked the girl at first sight, but admired her even more now.

Good, Alyssa thought. Not afraid of a little blood and dirt, which anyone spending much time in Geoffrey's company would be sure to encounter, and apparently more concerned about seeing Geoffrey's hurts attended to than about the reaction of her parents should they catch her in this bedraggled state of dishabille. A girl of strong will and convictions. Just what Geoffrey needed.

Foresight had prompted Alyssa to have her basket of medicines and bandages at hand as soon as she had realized there was a problem in the village. She plucked out a clean piece of cloth and handed it to Solange. "Press this against the wound until the bleeding stops," she instructed and under Alyssa's guidance Solange held the cloth against Geoffrey's lacerated forehead.

"Tell me what happened," Alyssa requested as she began to cut away what was left of Geoffrey's tunic to put salve on his burns. He hesitated to allow his stepmother to bare his chest with Solange present, but Alyssa spared him no modesty and ruthlessly sliced away the filthy shreds of fabric. Before Geoffrey could open his mouth to tell his stepmother about the fire and Brand and the baby, Solange launched into a passionate account of the incident, stressing Geoffrey's bravery and risk to the point of embarrassing him.

When his forehead had stopped bleeding and his burns had been washed and salved, Alyssa touched his wrist and glanced at him with a question in her eyes. Would he remove his gloves? With a tiny shift of his eyes towards Solange, who was wiping the soot and blood from his face, he shook his head with a small but firm motion. It didn't matter if his hands were burnt or bleeding; he was not yet ready to take off his gloves in Solange's view. Solange did not notice the silent exchange between Geoffrey and his stepmother. She merely instructed him to sit still when he twitched.

When the two women had tended his wounds as best they could and given him a cup of wine to soothe his parched throat, he took himself to the garderobe to bathe away the filth he had accumulated. Only then did Solange consent to go upstairs to fix her hair and clean up as well. Geoffrey was grateful that Solange did not consider him so badly hurt that he might need assistance with his bath. That he could not allow. The temptation would be too great.

He also refused his stepmother's suggestion that he go to bed after finishing his bath. Maternally, she wanted to tuck him safely into his bed like a child at the first sign of any injury or illness, but though his body felt like hell, his mind was reeling with realizations, decisions and desires. Sleep was something he absolutely could not accomplish, nor did he wish to.

After washing, putting on clean clothing and going to the nursery to check on Tamsin, he did go to his bedchamber, but not to sleep. He paced and agonized and prayed and thought and paced some more, realizing finally that there was only one course of action he could take. With trepidation, he left the safety of his room and descended the stairs in search of Baron de Meules.

*****

The hall was devoid of females when Geoffrey returned. He passed Moll on the stairs on his way down, and she informed him that Lady de Meules was still napping and Lady Alyssa and Solange had gone to the stillroom where Alyssa intended to teach Solange how to make the salves and medicines she used in caring for Belvoir's sick and injured.

He sent Moll off with a smile and a dismissive pat on the backside, appreciating the fact that she had remained discreetly in the background since Solange's arrival at Belvoir, though it had been some time since she had been with Geoffrey in a carnal way. He doubted she lacked for companionship. There was, after all, a garrison of soldiers in residence at Belvoir.

Baron de Meules sat at a table in the hall conversing with some of those knights, who withdrew respectfully as Geoffrey approached.

"I heard there was a ruckus in the village," de Meules said. "A fire of some sort, and that you had been injured." He glanced at the scabbed-over gash on Geoffrey's forehead. "How do you feel?"

In truth, he had seen men who felt better than him being carried off the battlefield on their shields. But he was too proud to say so. He made light of his injuries though he knew he looked like death warmed over. Though the bruises and burns on his head, shoulders and back would heal, he suspected the gash on his temple would leave another scar, and the singed ends of his hair were ragged and uneven.

"A word with you in private if you please, my lord," Geoffrey requested as he poured himself a cup of wine from the jug on the table, then led Baron de Meules to the small office and closed the door behind them.

The older man sat in a chair and watched with curiosity as Geoffrey paced and stared at the floor before speaking. For his part Geoffrey was terrified, sick and disgusted with himself, and yet at the same time elated. He was about to break a vow, but doing so would bring him a treasure.

He finally grasped the wine cup he had set on the table and quaffed the liquid in a gulp, but there was no courage to be found in the bottom of the cup. His face was sweating with his nervousness. He wiped it with a sleeve, then pushed back his ragged hair, wincing as he accidentally touched a painful bruise.

"My lord, I wish to speak to you about Solange," he finally said. His throat still felt as if it had been scraped with the rough side of a piece of leather, and he couldn't be certain if it was from the effects of the heat and smoke he had suffered, or from his own jitters.

"Solange?" de Meules said with interest. "Where is Solange? The little minx has snuck off and hidden herself again, and it is becoming a tiresome habit."

"I believe she is with my stepmother at the moment," Geoffrey said, and de Meules was satisfied then that his daughter was in safe hands. Geoffrey did not mention where Solange had been earlier in the day. If her father was unaware of the danger she had been in while in Geoffrey's company, his continued ignorance would not harm him now that she was safe.

Geoffrey's shaggy hair had fallen back over his forehead and again he pushed it back. This was so difficult! He swallowed and cleared his throat, stalling as Baron de Meules looked at him expectantly. He wanted another cup of wine, in fact, he wanted a lot of wine, but he knew that even that would not make what he had to do any easier.

"My lord, I wish, that is, I want, or rather I need ..." his boyish stammering embarrassed him, and from the heat in his face, he knew he must be blushing horribly. *Just spit the words out*, he told himself crossly.

"My Lord de Meules, I request the hand of your daughter Solange in marriage."

The fatal words were spoken, impossible to retract. Just saying them made Geoffrey feel drained and tired. Hearing them, a wide grin spread over Baron de Meules' face.

"I was hoping it would come to that," he said. "When Judith died, I suggested Solange to your father, but she was too young then. I am glad to see you have waited for her."

"I was not waiting for her," Geoffrey said uncomfortably, though what he really wanted to say was, *no, I did not mean it, I cannot marry her*; but of course he could not insult Baron de Meules in such a manner. "I was not ready to be betrothed then," (*I am not ready now*, his inner self screamed), "and my father recognized the fact, but now I need a wife, and I want Solange. Do you still feel she is too young for marriage?"

"No, no, not at all. She is seventeen, time and past she was wed. I will warn you though, so that later you do not accuse me of deception, that she can be a stubborn and disobedient little thing when the mood strikes her, and her mother says her needlework leaves much to be desired."

"I am aware of those flaws," Geoffrey said, feeling like a man being led to the gallows.

"Good, good," de Meules said with a complacent smile. "About the dowry - there is a parcel of land, not large mind you, only about five hides, but still-"

"Father Mathieu can make the dower arrangements later," Geoffrey inserted with an indifferent wave of the hand. Baron de Meules' eyes widened at the unconcern of his future son-in-law towards this important part of the marital negotiations.

"Very well," he said, "then it is decided." He stood and shook Geoffrey's hand, sealing the contract, and the younger man responded with a smile that involved only his mouth, not his eyes.

Baron de Meules turned toward the door. "I shall summon Solange and her mother and inform them of the arrangement. When would you like to come to Rougemont to celebrate the nuptials?"

"No," Geoffrey said, stepping between de Meules and the door. "Do not summon her just yet. I wish to ask her myself, in private if you do not object."

"Ask her?" de Meules said disbelievingly. "There is no need to ask. We shall tell her what has been decided. I know I allowed her to refuse the last time, but it is time for her to stop being a spoiled child and to realize what is best for her."

"No," Geoffrey said again. "I shall ask her, and the betrothal will be finalized only if she accepts. There will be no summoning or insisting. I will not have her if she is unwilling. This I insist upon. There are considerations." Unconsciously he slid his left hand into the folds of his tunic.

"Considerations such as the child?" de Meules inquired with raised eyebrows. "I know the little blond-haired girl is your bastard. There is no doubt she is your get. What do you intend to do with her?"

It still angered Geoffrey to hear someone refer to Tamsin as a bastard, but he had learned to control it. He looked de Meules straight in the eye. "The child has a name. It is Tamsin, and I have no intention of doing anything with her. Yes, she is illegitimate but she is no less my daughter, my flesh and blood. Her mother died giving her life, and I have raised her until now. I shall continue to raise her. She likes Solange, and Solange is fond of her. I would not marry Solange if it were otherwise."

Clearly, Baron de Meules was taken aback at Geoffrey's insistence upon keeping his bastard daughter even after his marriage. But, the baron reasoned, the child at least was a girl and if Solange did her duty and quickly gave Geoffrey a son, it would be that future son who would inherit Belvoir. And with the mother dead in childbed, there would be no pesky leman about making claims on Geoffrey. If the younger baron had other mistresses, they were apparently discreetly hidden and should not trouble Solange. The advantages of a titled, wealthy, landed son-in-law such as Geoffrey de Graville outweighed the disadvantages.

Lord de Meules's lips twitched a bit. It was a matter of pride, he realized. Young Baron de Graville did not want to think his bride was being forced to marry him. However, de Meules was certain Solange would agree to Geoffrey's proposal. He had seen how his daughter looked at the man – in exactly the same manner a starving person might look upon a freshly-cooked haunch of venison.

"Very well," de Meules acquiesced. "I shall not protest having the decision be Solange's, though I still think it unnecessary. When do you intend to ask her?"

"Now," Geoffrey said. *Before I lose my courage*, he thought. "I thank you for your approval, and I shall inform you of Solange's reply." He bowed to his future father-in-law and started to leave the room to search out Solange.

"My Lord de Graville," de Meules called after him. "There is one more thing." Geoffrey turned politely back to his prospective father-in-law. "I do not suppose that I can persuade you to cut your hair before you marry my daughter? Something more suitable to a Norman baron?"

"Not even for a moment," Geoffrey replied without hesitation. Even if it were not his own preference to wear his hair in the longer English fashion, there was still Solange. She had touched his hair once and called him her golden knight. That in itself was reason enough to leave it long.

"I thought not," de Meules replied as Geoffrey took his leave. The older man shook his head in amusement behind Geoffrey's disappearing back. This was quite unconventional. Though Geoffrey was a worthy prospect for a son-in-law, who had ever heard of the prospective bride being given the decision when her father had already decided? De Meules could only hope that his daughter had the good sense to accept Baron de Graville's proposal. He feared that if Solange were coerced in any way, Geoffrey would discern it and refuse to put his mark to the contract. The boy had his fine qualities, chief among them land and a title, but was more than a little eccentric.

*****

Geoffrey found Solange in the stillroom with his stepmother, watching intently as Alyssa concocted one of the herbal remedies she used to treat wounds. From the smell of it, Geoffrey could tell that it was the same stuff she applied to his cuts and bruises, and he hoped he had no need of it again soon. Both women turned to him with smiles when he entered the room.

"How does your head feel, Geoffrey?" Alyssa asked, putting down her mortar to push back her stepson's hair and check the gash on his forehead.

He stepped away from her ministrations. She would have to treat him like a child in front of Solange!

Alyssa, a bit miffed at Geoffrey's avoidance, relaxed when she saw the worried glance Geoffrey directed at Solange. "I am sure you are fine, my lord," she muttered, and desisted any further maternal maneuvers.

"My lady Solange, I would like a word with you," Geoffrey said with stilted formality, and both women raised their eyebrows at his wooden tone. Solange stepped towards him, thinking he meant to speak to her at the other side of the room, but he opened the door and motioned for her to precede him out.

With a glance of farewell to Lady Alyssa, Solange passed out the door and accompanied Geoffrey as he wordlessly escorted her out of the keep and across the bailey. Just as they approached the steps on the inner side of the curtain wall, Henry approached them.

"I have just returned from the village to give you my report, my lord. The fire is out, though still smoldering a bit, and there have been no injuries other than those suffered by Brand and yourself. Edmund has taken Brand and Hawise and the baby into his home until the blacksmith shop is rebuilt, and–"

"Thank you, Henry," Geoffrey said dismissively. "We shall discuss it later."

"But–" Henry protested, aghast at Geoffrey's apparent lack of interest in the situation in Lydford.

"Later," Geoffrey repeated as he took Solange's elbow to escort her to the steps.

Henry's mouth gaped open in surprise, but snapped shut when Geoffrey turned briefly back to him. "Henry," he instructed, "find Lord de Meules, that is Lord Gilbert, and keep him occupied for a time."

"Yes, my lord," Henry replied obediently, but he doubted Geoffrey heard him as he was already mounting the stairs with Solange in tow.

To Henry, Geoffrey's mood might appear uncharacteristic, but the squire was unaware of the nervousness which curdled in Geoffrey's stomach with the thought of the course upon which he had set himself.

He knew every step of the stairway he climbed with a puzzled Solange at his side, knew each rough spot which might trip up an unwary foot, every worn spot where water pooled after a rain. He walked on the outside, keeping Solange closer to the wall as they went up. At the top, they encountered the guard walking the parapet, and Geoffrey dismissed the man with a nod.

The guard bowed and descended the same steps that Geoffrey and Solange had used, to stand guard at the bottom step, defending if not the security of Belvoir, then the privacy of his lord and the lord's pretty lady.

Geoffrey was a bit astonished to see that it was still daylight. After all that had transpired today, he was surprised that night had not yet fallen. They were on the east wall with the castle behind them casting a long shadow reaching down the hill towards the village which still lay in the afternoon sunlight, but which would soon be embraced by the castle's shadow. Geoffrey leaned against the edge of the crenel, his elbow very close to the faint dark spot his childhood near-disaster had left on the stone.

"What did you wish to speak to me about?" Solange asked.

Oh, Lord. Geoffrey suppressed a sudden, rabbit-like urge to bolt and run. He stared at Solange as terror mounted in him. Weeping Jesus, but this was difficult! He had been brave before, but this required a special courage which he was not sure he possessed.

Solange was looking at him expectantly. He had the absurd notion that he should kneel when he proposed, but she would probably think him a complete lunatic if he did so, and she would never consent to marry him then.

In that case, perhaps he should fall to his knees, but some vestige of pride kept him on his feet.

Get a grip upon yourself, Geoffrey. You are a grown man with a child, not a green boy encountering a woman for the first time.

"Solange," he began.

"Yes, my lord?"

"Solange, I have spoken to your father."

"I should hope so, my lord," was her calm reply.

The response confused Geoffrey, but she added, "as the host, it would be most rude if you did not speak to your guests."

He was unable to smile at her little jest as he tried to think of all the reasons why he shouldn't marry her. He was too old for her for one thing, a worn and world-weary twenty-two to her fresh and innocent seventeen. He was scarred; his leg, his face, and his left hand was an ugly thing that would surely revolt her. He didn't love her.

I want a son, I need an heir, I want someone to talk to in the dark of night when I can't sleep.

"Yes, well I have spoken, that is, asked him, that is to ask you," he found himself stammering like the green boy he had just told himself he was not, then with a will gave birth to the words all in a rush, quickly before he could call them back.

"Solange, I would like you to be my wife. Will you consent to marry me?

A pregnant pause ensued, but only for a moment as Solange's face bloomed with a smile so beautiful it was almost painful to see. *Say no,* he wanted to shriek. *You deserve someone better; you deserve someone who will love you.*

"Yes, I will marry you. But my father-"

"Your father has agreed, but I told him the decision would be yours to make." Geoffrey's gloomy apprehension was beginning to dissipate in the warmth of Solange's happiness. But there was more, things Solange did not know, which she should be made aware of before making an irrevocable decision. Tamsin, she knew about, and Moll he need not mention. That was over. But there was a much more serious concern, and it was hanging at his left side.

"My decision, my lord? My decision is yes."

"There is something you should know first, circumstances you should take into consideration before you make a final determination," Geoffrey demurred, knowing that his manner was a bit stilted but unable to prevent it. "Before you agree to be my wife, you must understand everything about me ... you must know ... Solange, can you marry a man who is not whole?"

"Not whole?" Her eyes showed her confusion. She inspected him up and down but saw no flaws, only a beautiful, handsome man whom she adored. "My lord, I don't understand," she stammered.

It was now or never. There could be no more prevarication. He had to do this. He had to let her see the worst of him, even if she ran screaming away from him. A deformity as hideous as his left hand should not be revealed on a wedding night. He put his hands behind his back as Solange looked at him quizzically, pulled off his gloves and let them drop to the floor behind him.

"Before you decide, Solange, there is this." Quickly, before he lost his courage, he pulled his left hand out from behind his back and held the hideous thing naked before her eyes.

She didn't scream, she didn't run away, in fact she did not even have the good sense to look revolted. She just stood there looking at him calmly. Was she blind?

"Is that it?" she finally asked. "Is that the horrible secret you have? Your hand?"

He nodded and put down his hand, confused by her reaction, or rather her lack of reaction.

"But I have seen it before," she said

Seen it before! He knew he had been careless with his gloves lately, but he didn't think he had been that careless. When could she possibly have seen it? His confusion must have been evident, because she added, "That day I came across you sleeping in the grass on the hilltop outside Exeter. You had no gloves on and your hands were resting on your chest."

"Did you not find it - sickening?" Geoffrey asked, with disbelief at her unconcern.

"No, although I have always been curious to know how it happened. But you have taken such pains to hide it, so I thought it was something you did not wish to discuss. When you told my father you wished to marry me, did he consider it to be an impediment?"

"No, he never even mentioned it." Could he have been wrong, Geoffrey wondered, to hide his wound like some sort of perversion for which he would be shunned? Could it be that people, Solange included, considered it to be merely another scar, which most knights possessed? No one around him seemed to care much about his deformed hand. Tamsin certainly did not, his stepmother was constantly telling him it was of no consequence, Edmund and Henry were unconcerned, and Moll hadn't cared about it either. And most of all, here was Solange, whose regard he cared for desperately, telling him she had seen it and had not been disgusted in the least! He leaned back against the parapet, a bit stunned.

"Will you tell me now how this injury happened, my lord? If we are to be married, I believe I have a right to know."

In his amazement at her easy acceptance of his injury, Geoffrey had almost forgotten that he had asked Solange to marry him, and that she had accepted. *We are betrothed now*, he realized with a start, but still, he hesitated to tell her about his first battle.

"Please tell me," she entreated with big eyes, and he knew in that moment that it would be his lifelong weakness to be unable to refuse that entreating, enchanting gaze of hers.

"It was at Mantes, in Normandy, shortly after I first met you in your father's stable. I was with the king's army with my father, fighting to retake Mantes from the French. My horse was killed out from under me, and my sword knocked from my hand. I was reaching to retrieve it when a French foot soldier armed with an axe..." He made a chopping motion with his right hand which told the rest. He glanced out through the crenel and over the green fields of Belvoir. "My father was killed in the same battle."

When he looked back at Solange, she had tears in her eyes. As had happened when he had told her about Tamsin's birth and Milesenda's death, he felt cleansed and renewed and free somehow after the telling. Keeping the pain inside all the time had made it grow and fester, he now realized, and sharing the painful experience went far in exorcising the demons.

"Do not cry," he said at the sight of her tears. "I cannot bear to see you cry."

Obediently she wiped her tears away on her sleeve. "It makes me so sad to know these things have befallen you. I wish I knew witchcraft and could devise some way to take away your pain, or had some magical power to reverse time and prevent your tragedy."

"Such talk is blasphemy," he warned.

Why, he wondered, did he now feel so complete and happy? He, who had vowed never to marry, never to allow anyone but Tamsin to get close to him, had confessed his deepest darkest secrets to a woman, and had betrothed himself to marry her. It wasn't just because his experience in the fire had scared him, it wasn't merely his intense lust for her, it was Solange, herself, who affected him.

As he mused, Solange did something which amazed and shocked him, and she did it so quickly that he did not think to prevent her. She reached for his maimed left hand and held it in hers, just as if it were a normal, whole appendage. After a moment of panic, he relaxed and allowed the touch.

"I do not claim to be an expert on the subject," she said, "but I believe it is customary to seal a betrothal with a kiss."

He needed no urging to comply with that hint. It was a gentle kiss, tender and sweet like Solange herself, and Geoffrey gathered her close, clasping her with ungloved hands for the first time. The joy that she was his, that she had accepted him scars and all, made him dizzy with happiness.

He could have gone on kissing her forever, did they not need to breathe, and when that requirement forced them at last to separate, he took her hand and drew her to the parapet wall, standing with his arm across her shoulders as together they looked out over the fields, woods and village, peaceful in the deepening shadows of late afternoon.

"This is my demesne, Solange," he said. "Will you be happy sharing it with me?"

She put her arm around his waist and leaned against him. "Oh, yes, I will be very happy here, if I am with you." Then she looked up at him earnestly. "What about Tamsin, my lord? Will she object to my being here?"

"After what she said earlier today, I rather believe she would object if you were not here," Geoffrey replied. "Tamsin loves you, and I am certain she will adore having you as her stepmother. I doubt she will plague you with the cruel tricks I employed on my stepmother when my father first married her." Then he became serious. "However, I want to tell her the truth about her real mother when she is old enough to understand."

Solange nodded. "I will try to be a good stepmother to her."

Feeling more content and purposeful than he had in years, Geoffrey drew Solange close to him and together they looked out over their demesne. "I have always wanted to live in the countryside," Solange admitted. "I remember when I was little and I heard my parents speak of betrothing Judith to you. I did not know who you were then of course, and I did not know what marriage was, but I recall being terribly jealous of Judith at the thought that she might be going to live outside the walls of a town, in a place where the air was sweet with no fishy smells from the docks, where there were flowers and fields rather than stones and walls. Of course I was very sad when she died, and I did not wish it on her. I still think of her at times and miss her. Should I feel guilty now that I have taken her place?"

"You have not taken her place," Geoffrey said firmly. "I did not ask you to marry me because our fathers once thought to betroth your sister and I. I want you, yourself, regardless of who your sister was or who your father is. I would not have married Judith even if she had lived. At the time my father told me of this possible betrothal, my-" he checked his tongue just before saying "my first wife"- "Tamsin's mother was pregnant with her and I would not have consented to wed anyone else."

"Did you love her?" Solange asked, and Geoffrey knew without being told that she was referring to Milesenda.

"Yes," he answered simply, and wisely Solange did not pursue the subject. She tightened her arm around Geoffrey's waist and turned to him, pressing her face to the folds of his tunic near his heart. "I love you," she said, her voice muffled by the fabric. "I love you and I love Tamsin, and Lady Alyssa and all of Belvoir. I know you must think of Tamsin's mother often and I would not try to prevent you. But still, even if she knows I am not her real mother, do you think Tamsin might consent to call me Mother after we are married?"

"I am certain she will want to call you Mother," Geoffrey replied, returning her hug but refusing to echo her words. He kissed her brow, then pointed out through the crenel opening. "Look, there is your brother and Henry," he said. They looked down to see the pair approaching the keep, whatever excursion Henry had created to keep Gilbert away from Geoffrey and Solange for a time having apparently been completed. As their horses disappeared under the portcullis, Geoffrey warned, "Your father no doubt will be wanting to announce our betrothal to our families, and we should talk to Tamsin first so that it does not come as a surprise to her. We should go down to the keep now. It will be dark soon anyway." He allowed himself one last, brief but intense kiss on the mouth, then stepped away to offer her his arm to go down the stairs.

"Yes, my lord," she said with mock obedience and a girlish smile as she took his offered arm and turned with him towards the steps.

It was at the tip of his tongue to tell Solange that now that they were betrothed to be married, that it was no longer necessary for her to address him as My Lord, and she could simply call him Geoffrey. But he held his tongue. He had said that to Milesenda, and henceforth she had called him My Geoffrey. He didn't think that even now, even though he had in a manner reconciled himself to his loss of Milesenda and felt he would be happy being married to Solange, he could not yet bear to hear that endearment from another woman's lips. He hoped that Solange had not noticed that when she had said she loved him, he had not returned the sentiment, though he had been tempted to.

32

Within days all was arranged, contracts drawn up and the dowry decided upon, and the de Meules family departed for Exeter to prepare for the wedding which would take place in one month. Everyone seemed satisfied with the betrothal; Lord and Lady de Meules, assured their daughter was well provided for; Lady Alyssa, happy that her stepson would no longer be lonely and brooding; Tamsin ecstatic when told that Solange was soon to be her mama; and as for Henry, whatever made his adopted family of the de Gravilles happy, made him happy. Even Gilbert seemed pleased when things were made official, relieved no doubt that he need no longer be his sister's watchdog.

A betrothal ceremony was held in Belvoir's great hall, presided over by Father Mathieu, and at Geoffrey's insistence, all of the citizens of Lydford including to the poorest peasant were invited to attend and to partake of a feast afterwards which was set up on tables in the bailey. Lord de Meules and Gilbert seemed inclined to protest at their future son-in-law's penchant for associating with his serfs, but Geoffrey insisted and when Solange stated that it was her desire as well that everyone be included regardless of rank, her father and brother ceased their protest. Knowing that none of his people outside of his family, Edmund and Henry would be able to travel to Exeter to celebrate his actual wedding had prompted Geoffrey to insist upon his rather unconventional invitation.

The day upon which Solange and her family departed dawned sunny and warm, a good day to travel. It had rained during the night after the fire, a good soaking rain that had fortunately soaked the embers of the burnt-out buildings beyond any possibility of re-igniting. Already workmen were clearing away the rubble and preparing to rebuild the structures.

Geoffrey rode out a little way with the de Meules family, just past the village where the path led to the hills across the valley. He was reluctant to see Solange go; now that they were betrothed she was his responsibility to protect, and though he knew she was still under the guardianship of her father and brother, still he was well aware of her penchant for escaping their authority.

When they reached the far edge of the village Geoffrey put up his hand and said, "I would like a word with Solange before you depart."

He took her horse's reins and led her off the path to where a small copse of beech trees offered them a modicum of privacy. Solange rode a pretty mare which Geoffrey had given her as a betrothal gift. Although a gift of value was expected from a betrothed groom to his bride-to-be, most men gave their intended bride rings or other jewelry. Geoffrey had broken tradition with his gift of an exquisite horse, and Alyssa had smiled with memory as she told him that his father had done the same when she and Raymond had been betrothed. Solange's new horse was all black with the exception of a white diamond on her forehead. The fat sleepy pony had been left behind in Belvoir's stable as a gift for Tamsin.

Behind the trees, Solange's parents exchanged amused glances at the thought of their smitten son-in-law preparing to say his good-byes.

When they were out of earshot of the rest of the family, Geoffrey looked down on Solange. He sometimes wished she wouldn't smile at him like that, like a lover. Still holding her horse's reins, he said, "I do not want you venturing out into the streets or countryside alone anymore. It is dangerous, and until I am there to protect you, you are to stay at Rougemont. And no loitering in the stables!"

It was the wrong thing to say and he realized his mistake immediately. Her black eyes flashed and she kicked out at him with one foot, though he easily caught her ankle in his hand before the blow connected.

"How dare you command me in that manner!" She struggled unsuccessfully to extricate her foot from his grasp. "You are neither my father nor yet my husband, to order me about in such a loutish way!"

"Not yet your husband!" he responded with equal anger at her willfulness. "In case you have forgotten, my dear, that betrothal ceremony we celebrated last evening was as binding as a marriage ceremony, and no one would deny me my husbandly authority over you. Did I wish to take you back to Belvoir now, remove you to my bedchamber and consummate the union today, right now, not even your father would stop me!"

He saw real fear leap into her eyes at his harsh words, and immediately he regretted them. When she argued with him, he tended to forget how young she was, and how she disliked being dictated to, and now he felt like a hound for frightening her. Letting go of her ankle, he said, "I am sorry, Solange. I did not mean what I said. I would never do anything to hurt you, believe me."

"Then why do you suddenly dictate to me as if you were the king?" she asked, rubbing at her ankle in pretended injury.

"Because I worry," he replied. "Because I am concerned when we are apart and I cannot protect you from any adversity. Because I would be devastated if any harm came to you. It causes me to act in an uncharacteristic manner."

Under his contrite words, her anger softened and disappeared. "Very well, I forgive you," she said regally.

He smiled and said, "Would it be better if I were to ask, not to command but to request, that you have a care for your safety until we are together again, and that you take an armed escort if you leave Rougemont? May I beseech that you take such precautions so that your betrothed does not arrive at our wedding with gray hairs over his worry concerning your safety?"

Putting it in the form of a request rather than a command procured the desired results, and he tucked that lesson away for future reference.

"Of course my lord, if it will put your mind at ease," she assented with a most mature demeanor.

"It will," he replied, which was completely true. Already the insomnia that had plagued him in the last few years had been alleviated.

"What about you, my lord?" Solange asked. "If I am to have a care for my safety, it is only fair that you make me that same promise. Will you promise not to risk your life in another fire? Will you promise to avoid the fistfights that you men seem to enjoy so much?"

Geoffrey was a bit taken aback at Solange's request that he be as careful with his wellbeing as he expected her to be. His desire to make her happy compelled him to agree to her request.

"Yes, Solange I will have every care for my safety in order to arrive at our wedding with nary a wound nor burnt hair. As for fisticuffs, now that your brother and I will no longer be required to endure each other's company, the chances for that are very slight."

Solange showed him a satisfied smile, showing that she was well aware she could bend her betrothed to her will so easily.

Geoffrey glanced behind him to where he knew her family waited on the other side of the trees. "I should not delay your departure any longer. I am certain your parents are eager to return to Exeter to make the wedding arrangements."

"It is all my mother can think of now. She talks constantly about gowns and the work required to make them." Solange's brow wrinkled in consternation. "I hope she does not expect me to help in the sewing."

"Heaven help her if she insists," Geoffrey commented with a smile. He leaned forward and kissed her brow, intending to escort her back to her waiting family, but she surprised him by leaning from her horse and clinging to his neck in a childlike manner, seeming most reluctant to leave him.

"Tell me you will be in Exeter soon, my lord. I will be so unhappy to be away from you."

He pried her hands from his neck and held them between his own. The leather of his gloves was dark against her fair skin. "It will be only a few weeks, Solange, and after we are married I shall bring you home to Belvoir." He kissed her again, but only a light, almost fraternal touch, because he knew if he allowed himself anything more, her father and brother would be obliged to drag them apart. "Come now," he urged. "Your family is waiting for you and I do not wish to cause any friction with them."

She complied, but with reluctance, and accompanied him through the trees to rejoin her waiting family.

"Please tell Tamsin that I am eager to see her again, and I hope she enjoys the pony," Solange entreated, and Geoffrey agreed to do so. He didn't have the heart to tell Solange that Tamsin had taken one look at the fat sleepy pony, turned up her nose and demanded a ride on her father's stallion. He was afraid that his daughter was becoming a bit of a hoyden. If he wasn't careful, the next thing he knew, she would be wanting to wear breeches and carry a sword, and no man would wish to marry a woman who did that. But then, the thought of Tamsin someday growing up, marrying and leaving Belvoir devastated Geoffrey. Perhaps he should encourage the breeches and sword.

They emerged from the trees and joined her family at the roadway. "Farewell, my lady," he said with a salute, formal in the presence of her family. "A safe journey to you all," he added to the group in general, and with a small nod to Gilbert, who had looked disapproving when Geoffrey had led his sister into the trees, he turned his horse's head back towards Belvoir, suddenly not wanting to see Solange riding away from him. It was, he realized with chagrin, going to be a very long month.

*****

Once the de Meules family had left Belvoir and Geoffrey was alone again, everything seemed different. From the moment he returned within the familiar confines of the keep's walls, he was nagged by a plaguing feeling he could neither identify nor dislodge. It made him irritable and snappish, and most of all, desirous of privacy. He left Storm in the care of Henry, who looked hurt when Geoffrey walked out of the stable without a word to his squire, merely tossing the reins in the boy's direction and turning on his heel. Geoffrey would apologize later for his rudeness, but for now he needed to think.

He returned to the spot at the top of the wall where he had proposed to Solange, but thinking of much more than only his upcoming marriage. He leaned across the rough stone of the crenel and stared out at the view which was as familiar to him as his own hand, but which still gave him joy, peace and wonder to see. From his vantage, a legion of shades of green greeted him, each a greener here than any to be found elsewhere in England, the tops of the trees, the shrubs and hillocks touched with the last kiss of the sun as dusk approached. Geoffrey was proud of his estate, and the knowledge that Solange was willing, even desirous, of living here with him brought back that same sense of wonder and belonging that he had experienced as a child. Although he hadn't gone looking for it to be so, Solange was even of noble blood. His father would have approved.

But as his wandering gaze moved from the fields dotted with fluffy sheep to the village, the winsome feelings froze in his chest. Was it chance or fate that led his eyes with morbid determination to a certain small cottage at the edge of Lydford? He had never been inside Milesenda's cottage since that one time shortly after her death, and other tenants lived there now, but he had never forgotten the simple place where he had loved and lost, where he had experienced life in its most exhilarating form and death in its most tragic. He always averted his gaze when he was forced to pass the cottage, but now he stared at it from afar with a morbid, painful regard, remembering with a pang things he had said and done there, and vows he had made.

What had he done? *What had he done?* How could he have forgotten - or ignored - the oath he had sworn to Milesenda? Just because she had died, just because five years had passed, did not mean he was released from his vows. A knight's oaths did not expire. *"I swear to you, on my honor, that I will marry no one but you, and I will always care for you, and for our child."* His own voice came back to mock him, insidious, a snake hissing in the grass. He had fulfilled the last part of his oath, that was true, caring for Tamsin not only out of obligation but out of overwhelming love. But he had callously abandoned his vow of lifelong love, his vow to marry no one but Milesenda, because a pretty, bewitching little girl had turned his head. What sort of dishonorable churl had he become? Just because he was lonely for companionship and craved Solange's affection, just because he lusted for her mightily, just because his estate needed the security of an heir, he had conveniently set his knightly principles to the back of his mind, covered them up and ignored them. And now he was damned. His soul was destined to hell, or worse, to eternal purgatory, thanks to his sins. No amount of confession or absolution could restore the honor that had been forsaken.

And Solange, what had he done to her? She was innocent, a guiltless victim of Geoffrey's perfidy. Not only had he made her fall in love with him, but had also made her an unknowing accomplice to his dishonor. He had put his mark to the betrothal contract; to break it now was not only impossible, but would only add more sins to his already huge burden of them. What damned him even more was that he did not want to break the contract. He wanted Solange to be his wife, wanted her at his board and in his bed, wanted her to be Tamsin's stepmother. He felt like a rat, trapped between two very large and hungry cats, with no hope of escape.

Had he been a more devout man, he would have sought Father Mathieu's counsel. But a priest's advice had never given him comfort, and he had felt a disaffection towards his father's cousin ever since the day Mathieu had refused to marry Geoffrey and Milesenda. Of course Mathieu had only been doing his duty and was not personally responsible for any of Geoffrey's problems, still the antipathy had grown of its own volition. So he stayed at his lonely post on the parapet, oblivious to the guardsman when he passed on his rounds, hating himself more with each minute as darkness finally fell and obscured his views of field and village.

He stayed up there even after it was full dark, turning his back to the outer wall and sliding down to sit on the cold stone walkway with his head in his hands, trying to justify what he was doing. Solange was a treasure, and any man would be fortunate to have her, temper and all.

But were the rewards of her companionship and the promises of her bed worth the forsaking of his honor? It was a question without an answer, and it would not have mattered if there was an answer. He could change nothing now, short of dying, and he was going to have to learn to live with it.

When he finally descended the steps and returned to the keep, it was to discover that he had completely missed the evening meal. No matter, he was not hungry. However, he had not only missed the evening meal, but the entire evening as well. He went to the nursery to sit with Tamsin, but she was asleep. His stepmother and Henry had also retired to their respective beds. He hadn't realized how long he had been up on the wall until he came looking for company and found none. Edmund was not even there for him to talk to, being at home and no doubt comfortably bedded with his wife. Geoffrey doubted Edmund would care much to be interrupted from Carys's charms to keep company with a friend suffering torments in his soul. That left only a flagon of wine, another of usquebaugh and his horse for companionship, and for the first time since he had been sixteen, he got blind drunk and passed out in the corner of his horse's stall.

Alyssa took him to task the next morning after Ulric had stumbled over him sleeping off the effects of his lonely binge. The frightened stable boy, believing his lord to be ill, injured or dead, had run in a panic for Lady Alyssa after finding Geoffrey. Along with Henry, they arrived back at the stable just in time to see Baron de Graville stumbling out, clutching his head and grimacing at the spinning, pounding pain. If there hadn't been witnesses present Alyssa would have dragged her stepson inside by the ear, but she was forced to settle for icy formality.

"A word with you in private if you please, my lord," she requested, and from the frosty tone of her voice, Geoffrey knew he was in for it now. He followed her obediently inside the keep and to the solar, each step feeling like the kick of a horse's hoof to his head.

He sank into the window seat and listened to his stepmother scolding him roundly for his immature behavior - getting drunk and sleeping in the stable! - his rudeness - not appearing in the hall for the evening meal and making everyone worry until a guard reported his whereabouts on the parapet - his cruelty - frightening poor simple Ulric who had thought Geoffrey was dead when he had literally stepped on the lord's recumbent form in the stall he had come to clean - and his shamefulness - setting such a bad example for Henry who worshipped the very ground upon which Geoffrey walked. Geoffrey bore it all in silence, praying that she would stop yelling so loudly, not because he feared being overheard, but because it made his head hurt even more, and wondering how she would react if he were to vomit at her feet.

Fortunately, he was not forced to test the limits of his stepmother's patience by being sick, but when she finally finished her tongue-lashing and demanded, "What do you have to say for yourself, Geoffrey?" he was afraid his head would burst. He knew he deserved her ire, but still it surprised him. She rarely showed a temper. He was more accustomed to her calm reasonableness, and he appealed to it now.

"Mother, do you not realize what I have done? I have betrothed myself to be married."

"That is no excuse for your recent behavior."

"In allowing myself to marry, I have forsaken everything my knight's honor stands for. I am abandoning my oath, the vow I swore to Milesenda that I would never marry another, that I would love no one but her. I feel like the lowest slug on the ground, without honor."

"And exactly when did you realize that you had lost your honor?" He looked at her for clarification, not quite following.

"You seemed happy enough until Solange and her family left. Is it only her absence that causes these realizations of dishonor?"

"Yes," he admitted. "I did not fully discern at first what I had done. Solange's presence distracted me." He looked out the window with a pensive gaze.

"You men!" Alyssa exclaimed. "You allow your pride and honor to run and ruin your lives. Will pride and honor provide you a life's companionship? Will pride and honor warm your bed at night?" Geoffrey gaped at his stepmother, aghast at her utterance of what was for her a very crude expression. "Will your pride and honor give you a son, or a mother for Tamsin? Will they provide security for your estate and your family? Will they bring you love?"

Upon hearing the word love, Geoffrey's head snapped around. He fixed his stepmother with his best lord-of-the-manor scowl, but Alyssa was unimpressed.

"Love is undeserved if honor is abandoned, if sworn oaths are forsaken. I swore an oath to Milesenda..."

Alyssa took two swift steps which placed her directly in front of her stepson's seated form and grasped his face tightly. Under her hands he was as cold and stiff as human flesh could be and still live. She stared intently at his face and he was forced to look her in the eyes.

"Milesenda is dead," she said firmly, interrupting him. Geoffrey was a rock, his eyes ice.

"I want you to say it, Geoffrey. Milesenda is dead. Say it."

He was frozen, his voice uncooperative, but under his stepmother's unrelenting gaze, he repeated obediently, "Milesenda is dead." The phrase rang through his head like a shout in an empty church, echoing through his brain and bouncing from the edges of his soul. Though he had said the words before in one form or another, never before had they had such an effect on him as now under Alyssa's command. "Milesenda is dead," he said again, and the words were a knife, severing the rope which had bound rocks to his heart. The weight fell away, leaving his heart unencumbered, and he realized with a soaring feeling of flight, that his stepmother had been right all along. Milesenda was dead, and nothing he would ever do with his life would change that, but if she could have predicted her demise, she would have wanted him to be happy. She would never have required him to endure a lonely life for her sake. But he still worried about his broken oath.

"You are not forsaking nor abandoning any oath or your knightly honor by marrying Solange," Alyssa told him, removing her hands from his face, and though Geoffrey wished her words could be true, he knew it could not be so simply because she believed it. She sat down next to him and took his hand in hers - his right hand, and he was grateful she was not inclined to pursue that issue right now. "I realize that your relationship with Milesenda was never blessed by the Church, but if you had been legally married, you would have taken marriage vows."

"The vows we spoke to each other were as binding as any administered by a priest," Geoffrey said.

"I do not doubt that. But Geoffrey, if you and Milesenda had been married in the Church, you would have sworn the same vows your father and I swore - that we were husband and wife until parted by death. Until parted by death, as you and Milesenda have been parted. You do not lose your honor by marrying this long while after her death, Geoffrey dear. Loving Solange and making her your wife does not forsake your honor nor your oath. Rather, I believe it honors Milesenda's memory by making your life meaningful and by raising your child in a complete family."

Geoffrey dropped his eyes and stared at the floor without really seeing it. After a minute of silence he looked up again at his stepmother. "Until parted by death," he repeated musingly. "Is it really that simple, Mother?"

"Yes, Geoffrey, it is that simple. Do not, please, fret about lost honor when none has been lost."

He had no reason to doubt that Alyssa was correct. He took her hand and offered it a brief, honorable kiss. "Mother, you are the wisest person I have ever been privileged to associate with." She smiled and patted his head, as she might do to a very small boy, but he did not object.

His stepmother was right, he realized, in fact, she had been right all along but he had been too stubborn to accept it. He could be happy; he was allowed to be; he had a right to be happy. He remembered how he had felt after the fire, that he might as well have died in that flaming building if he could not have Solange by his side, in his bed, a part of his life. When Dewi and Kerensa had been married, Geoffrey had realized then that he was waiting for Solange to grow up, and now that she had, he was glad that they were to be married. It had made him feel guilty to be happy about it because he felt that allowing himself to be happy would show a lack of respect for Milesenda. But as Alyssa had pointed out on more than one occasion, if Milesenda had truly loved him, she would only wish for his happiness. He would marry Solange, and he would be glad he had overcome his reluctance to allow someone to get close to him, and perhaps, just perhaps, he would grow to love his wife.

Alyssa watched the emotions and realizations move across her stepson's face like scudding clouds in the wind, revealing a peaceful, happy countenance in their wake. It had finally happened, she thought with exultation. Her stepson had finally thrown off the burden of guilt and loneliness which had encumbered him for the past six years, and she was certain that Solange would be an excellent wife for him, and a loving stepmother to Tamsin.

Geoffrey stood up as if to leave, but a thought occurred to him and he turned back to his stepmother. "Mother, much of what you have said to me could apply to you as well. My father has been dead for several years now, and yet you have not remarried. Father loved you very much. I know he did not love my mother. You were, you are, the love of his life, and I know he would wish for you to be happy as well."

Alyssa smiled. "I am happy, Geoffrey."

"But are you not lonely for … companionship?" Geoffrey couldn't help but think of Gilbert and how smitten his future brother-in-law had been with Alyssa.

"I am not lonely with my family around me," Alyssa said, and Geoffrey was relieved that Gilbert's name was not mentioned. "But if I am ever so fortunate as to meet someone as special as your father was, I shall follow my own advice."

"You would have my blessing, Mother," Geoffrey affirmed.

In a light voice, his stepmother quipped, "Well, certainly not before we get you married. And the first thing you need to do is take a bath, immediately. You smell like the vintner's dregs, and steeped in horse as well. I hope we are not going to have to endure any more of these unpleasant episodes of drunkenness from you."

"You have my word, Mother," Geoffrey promised. He hoped he never again had to suffer a head as huge as what he had felt when he had awakened this morning, although he realized with surprise that his headache had disappeared sometime while he and Alyssa had been talking. It was with a light step, and a much happier disposition than he had possessed the evening before, that he bowed himself from his stepmother's presence to go and bathe away the stench of his foolishness, change into clean clothing, and prepare himself for his upcoming marriage.

33

One of the first things Geoffrey did in preparation for bringing his bride to Belvoir was to arrange to marry off his former mistress. With a little luck, he betrothed her to a farmer from Launceston whose first wife had died and left him with several rambunctious children to care for. Though it had been a long time since he had bedded Moll - long enough to be certain that if she bore any children they would not be his - still she made suggestive eyes at him on occasion, and he did not want her at Belvoir when Solange arrived.

He knew that Moll had been with other men during their liaison, and he strongly suspected that one of them was his squire, Henry. Geoffrey had by purest chance observed Moll coming out of the stable one day with a look of supreme satisfaction on her face, and a few minutes later had seen Henry come out the same door, looking dazed. Geoffrey had chuckled to himself, vastly amused at the thought of Henry receiving his initiation into the pleasures of the flesh at the hands of an experienced woman like Moll. He only hoped that Moll had been as gentle and understanding with Henry as Milesenda had been with Geoffrey. He had never expected Moll to be faithful to him. It was not that sort of relationship. They had shared their bodies, Geoffrey and Moll, but never their minds or their souls. It had been superficial, a meeting only of flesh, but at the time it had been exactly what he had needed.

If the farmer to whom Moll was quickly betrothed wondered at why Baron de Graville personally arranged the marriage of a servant and provided her with a dowry, he wisely did not comment or ask questions, but took Moll away to his home outside Launceston. Watching them leave, on horses from Belvoir's stable, Geoffrey breathed a sigh of relief at having tied up that loose end and went inside to prepare for leaving for his own wedding.

*****

Once, he returned to the clearing in the forest which had been a special place for him and Milesenda. He had not been there since before her death, but little had changed. Wildflowers still carpeted the shores of the small lake, their scent full in the still heat of summer. On an impulse Geoffrey threw off his clothes and waded into the cool water, swimming about and then floating on his back as he remembered playing in this same water with Milesenda. The memories were like the water on his skin, cool and pleasant. The lake seemed somewhat smaller than he recalled. As he waded out of the water and sat down in the sunshine to dry off before putting his clothes on, he could even recall his old, frightening nightmares without concern. Those nightmares had centered in this very place, but they had stopped when he had been reunited with his daughter, and he no longer had cause to fear bad dreams. Now that he was going to be married, he could sleep at night, although once he had Solange in his bed he did not anticipate sleeping that much. He could look forward to nighttime activities much more pleasant than what he had experienced in the dark days after Milesenda's death, when at some times his sleep had been filled with trembling, sweating anxiety, or he had not slept at all and the wakefulness was as bad as the nightmares. All that was in the past now, though as the water evaporated from his skin and he began to pull his clothing back on, he looked down at the flowers around him and allowed himself to remember himself and Milesenda frolicking there, naked as fauns and laughing like children. He thought for a while about the woman who had taught him about love and lovemaking, though the memory of her image was blurred, like looking through ripples of water.

From the thick hedge of bushes surrounding the clearing he heard sounds of rustling and giggling, telling him he was not as alone here as he had thought he was. Pulling on his boots, he gathered up Storm's reins and left in the opposite direction. Let other lovers tryst in this place. He would not come here again. It was not a place for him and Solange. They would have to make their own memories and find their own special place.

The dogs were happy to be allowed back into the hall after Belvoir's guests had left, especially the large brown hound whose seniority allowed him pride of place next to the master's chair. When Geoffrey let one arm hang down over the side of his chair, the hound insinuated its head under that hand hoping to be scratched, the dogs also being unconcerned about how many fingers Geoffrey possessed, as long as he used what he had to pet them. While he obliged the animal his eyes were half closed and to look at him one might think him about to fall asleep. But he was very much awake and alert, as he watched his stepmother putting the finishing touches on a new tunic she was sewing for him.

It was not at all out of the ordinary for Alyssa to be sewing clothes for her stepson. She had been doing so almost since the day she had married his father. But this tunic was different from the others she had made for him. This was for him to wear on his wedding day.

He had told her there was no need for her to go to all that trouble, but Alyssa had over-ruled him.

"This will be my only opportunity to see a son of mine married, with Stephen destined for the priesthood," she said, and so he let her have her way and watched silently as she lovingly created a handsome garment of the finest blue samite, dark blue to match his eyes, she had insisted and she fussed maternally with gold embroidery at the neck and hem. Most likely she had chosen the gold thread to match his hair, he thought with an inward groan. He should just be glad he wasn't being married in the winter. Alyssa would have insisted on velvet.

She tied off what he hoped was the last stitch of the elegant gold trim, then stood up with the finished tunic in her hands. "Stand up, Geoffrey," she requested. "I want to see if this fits you." She held up the tunic as if to place it against his shoulders.

"Mother!" he protested, shrinking back in his seat and glancing furtively about the hall in fear that any of his men might have noticed his stepmother fitting his clothes on him as if he were a baby in napkins. His face flamed and the dog under his hand made a whining sound of protest at the cessation of his scratching.

"Oh, Geoffrey!" Alyssa sighed with exasperation at his stubborn male pride. "Very well, accompany me to the solar to try this on if you please. I have an important matter to discuss with you in private anyway."

He followed her into the solar where in privacy she stood him next to the window and held the tunic up to him, then instructed him to hold out his arm while she checked the length of the sleeve. The sunlight flowing in through the window glinted from the gold thread. Even Geoffrey had to admit it was a fine garment.

Satisfied that the tunic would fit, Alyssa folded it carefully and placed it on top of a chest. Then she sat down with a serious set to her mouth and Geoffrey took the seat next to her, wondering what her important matter was. Perhaps she wished to purchase another tapestry to hang in the hall, or was having a problem with the servants. He wondered if she knew about Moll and why Geoffrey had sent her away. Geoffrey would be willing to wager that his stepmother knew all about that. He doubted there was anything at Belvoir that she was not aware of, and was grateful that she did not embarrass him by mentioning the incident. Perhaps-

"Geoffrey, I should go."

"Where do you wish to go?" he asked. "You know I will take you anywhere you wish to visit. But if it is to be somewhere away from Lydford, can it wait until after we return from Exeter, after my wedding? We are leaving in only a few days. But when we get back, if you like I will take you to visit your family at Arden. It has been a long time since you have seen them-"

"No, Geoffrey, I do not mean that I wish to go visiting. After you are married, I intend to leave Belvoir, permanently, perhaps move to a convent."

"What!" Her words hit him like a rock thrown at his head, spinning his senses. Did his stepmother actually plan to leave Belvoir? "Mother, what are you saying?"

"Very simply, I am saying that when you bring Solange here as your bride, I will give her my keys and then leave here, to live somewhere else away from Belvoir."

"But, why? Are you angry with me? Have I treated you unkindly? How could you possibly wish to leave here? Belvoir is your home." Geoffrey was confused and astounded at this sudden pronouncement from his stepmother. He stared at her, searching for an answer.

"Geoffrey, I am not angry with you. Surely you understand that I cannot stay when you bring Solange here as your wife."

"Then I will not marry her."

Now it was Alyssa who stared at Geoffrey with disbelief. "You cannot be serious!" she gasped.

"Oh, yes, Mother, I am serious." He hated what his stepmother was forcing him to do, but he would not, could not, allow her to leave Belvoir. "If you cannot live under the same roof with Solange, then there will be no marriage." He raked a desperate hand through his hair. "Lord, all this time you have suggested, cajoled, insisted that I marry, and now that I am about to, you will not accept her? I thought you liked Solange." He was completely confused, and desolate. Just when he had thought everything was settled, arranged, and everyone was happy; his stepmother's unbelievable decision was changing everything.

"But I do like Solange. I like her very much, and that is why I will leave." Alyssa's words made no sense to Geoffrey, and his expression showed it. He jumped to his feet and paced for a moment, then glared at his stepmother. "I am sorry, Mother, but I do not understand what you are talking about."

"If you will sit down again, I will explain it to you," Alyssa offered, and Geoffrey complied, this time folding himself onto a low stool at his stepmother's feet rather than taking the chair he had been sitting on.

Perhaps if he appeared smaller, more childlike, his mother would take pity and not leave him.

"Geoffrey, I have managed the household here at Belvoir since your father and I were married," she began.

Geoffrey interrupted, "And you have done an excellent job of it, Mother. No estate could ever enjoy a chatelaine as superb as you."

Alyssa smiled. "Thank you for the compliment, Geoffrey, but I was not fishing for praise. The point I am trying to make is that when you marry Solange, she will be Lady de Graville, your wife and the mistress of Belvoir. There can be only one chatelaine. Two adult women managing the same household can only cause dissent and problems which you do not deserve, nor will you appreciate. It will not be fair to Solange to have her mother-in-law hanging about watching while she goes about her duties, and it will not be fair to you to encourage the sort of resentment that such a situation can create. So in the best interests of all of you, I intend to go and live somewhere else as I said, perhaps at a convent."

"What about your best interests, Mother," Geoffrey challenged. "Is this what you really want, to spend the rest of your life in a convent? I did not realize you had a vocation for a religious life."

"I do not have such a vocation," Alyssa admitted. "Although once I threatened to flee to a convent."

"When did you do that?"

Alyssa smiled slightly, remembering. "When your father first asked for my hand in marriage. My father was reluctant to marry me to a Norman, but when I heard that he might not allow it, I begged and pleaded and then stated I would go to a convent and be miserable for the rest of my life if my parents refused Raymond's suit. When they realized I was serious, they allowed the marriage."

"That sounds as if you were in love with him, rather than accepting an arranged marriage."

"I was. I loved your father from the moment I saw him, before I ever heard him speak or even knew his name. From the first moment I saw him in my father's hall at Arden, I knew I would spend my life with no one else. I didn't care if he was Norman or English or even if he had been a Celt. I saw him standing there, so handsome and serious, with an adorable little boy tugging at his tunic hem, and I ... but we are speaking about your marriage, not mine. When I came to Belvoir as a bride I had no mother-in-law to contend with. It is only fair that Solange does not have to deal with one either."

"So," Geoffrey said with that stubborn set to his mouth which to Alyssa's observance was very much like Raymond had been, "you will retire to a convent though you have no religious vocation, merely because you think it will make life easier for your future daughter-in-law if you are not here." Alyssa nodded. "And what about your own children, especially Isabel?"

"Isabel will come with me, of course."

"You will deprive me of my sister, my only sister, to satisfy this whim of yours? I will not allow it, Mother. Isabel is my responsibility as well, and I deem it to be in her best interests to stay in her home. I am her guardian, after all. What kind of life can that be for a child, immured in a convent for the rest of her life through no choice of her own?"

Now Alyssa looked concerned. "But, Geoffrey, I cannot leave my child."

"Then do not leave your children. I realize Stephen is settled at the priory, but your other children need you, and we need you here. I cannot imagine any dissension between you and Solange after we are married. She respects and admires you. She is young I will admit, but I believe she is mature enough to get along well with you. I shall command it," though he realized it even as the words left his mouth that his commands rarely influenced Solange. "Besides," he cajoled, utilizing his most charming smile, "who will mend my clothes if you leave? Solange is a poor hand with a needle."

"If you did not outgrow or destroy your clothing at such a rapid rate, there would not be nearly as much need for mending," Alyssa pointed out. "There are any number of servants who can assist Solange with that task if she needs it."

"It is not only a matter of mending clothes," Geoffrey said, becoming serious. "The estate needs you, Isabel needs you, I need you. I cannot allow you to leave us all because you fear possible disagreements between you and Solange." Although Geoffrey was not terribly fond of his future mother-in-law, finding her to be somewhat vacuous and not very intelligent, he could learn to live under the same roof with her if he had to.

"It is not that I fear disagreements, Geoffrey. I hope you do not think that either I nor Solange is that petty. It is because I believe Solange should be allowed to manage her own household without my presence."

"But, Mother, Solange is very young and she cannot manage this household by herself. Surely you realize that you are needed here."

"She can learn. She is only a little younger than I was when I first came here."

Geoffrey's patience and good humor were at an end. "No. I will not allow it. I will not allow you to move away from Belvoir, and I will not allow you to take my sister away nor to deprive Tamsin of her grandmother. If you insist upon forcing the issue, I shall send a message to Baron de Meules canceling the wedding."

"Geoffrey, I cannot believe you would repudiate that sweet young girl who adores you, and with whom you have sworn a betrothal contract. That is something which certainly would be dishonorable and unchivalrous, as well as unspeakably cruel to Solange."

"It would give me no pleasure," Geoffrey said. In fact, he thought, it would be like cutting out his heart. "But you leave me no choice."

"Is my staying here that important to you?"

"Yes, of course it is. How can I let you leave, when you have saved my life. When you have been the source of sanity which makes me realize the truths that I am too dense to see by myself." Though he smiled as he spoke, he was very serious. A normal life without his stepmother's presence was unimaginable, although he realized with a jolt that a life without Solange was just as unimaginable. Was it too much to ask for a man to have both a wife and a mother?

Alyssa sighed, acceding to her stepson. "Very well, Geoffrey, I will stay. Perhaps Isabel will be happier living at Belvoir, and I will train Solange to be chatelaine of Belvoir. But once she has learned to manage the household on her own, if there seems to be even the slightest hint of resentment, I will retire as I planned."

Geoffrey stood, put his hands on Alyssa's shoulders, and gave her a brief kiss on the cheek. "Thank you, Mother. I am confident there will be no problems at all when Solange comes here. How could any intelligent person fail to enjoy the pleasure of your presence?"

Alyssa smiled affectionately at her stepson. "You should save that sweet charm for Solange, Geoffrey dear."

"I will," he agreed, then turned to the door. "If you are finished poking me with your pins, I have some matters to attend to at the stable. Henry and I must decide which horses to use for the trip to Exeter."

"Yes, I am finished poking you," Alyssa said. "But you have reminded me of one other thing I wished to say to you. I hope you realize that I do not make a habit of attempting to control your behavior, however there is one thing I insist upon."

Geoffrey couldn't look his stepmother in the eye, wondering if she was going to say something about his former liaison with Moll. He almost blurted out, *but it has been over for a long time*, but before he opened his mouth, Alyssa continued, "On the day of your wedding, I absolutely forbid you to go anywhere near a stable. I will not have you going to your wedding night smelling of horse, nor risk dirtying your new clothes. Is that understood, Geoffrey?"

"Of course, Mother," Geoffrey quickly agreed. Good, she was not going to bring up the subject of Moll. In light of that, he did not consider her request to be at all unreasonable. He left the solar with a smile, but as he crossed the bailey to the stable his expression became serious as he considered what his stepmother had said about the possibility of leaving Belvoir to allow Solange free rein as mistress of the household. Alyssa's motives were, of course, unselfish and in what she considered to be the best interests of her family, but no matter how matters went between his wife and his mother, he would never willingly see Alyssa leave Belvoir on a permanent basis. If she should wish to marry again, of course he would have to agree, though with reluctance. He could not imagine Belvoir without the presence of his mother.

*****

The days and nights had seemed to drag until the de Gravilles could depart for Exeter, but finally they arrived at Rougemont the day before the wedding. It was a large group traveling from Lydford to Exeter to witness Geoffrey's marriage. Not only were Henry and Alyssa going, but also Tamsin and Edmund, as well as the accompanying servants, men-at-arms and baggage carts. Only Isabel had been deemed too young for the journey, and had been left at Belvoir with Tamsin's former wetnurse, Olwyn, returning to the castle to care for her, since Maud's services were required to care for Tamsin on the journey and in Exeter. Father Mathieu was ill and remained in Lydford.

Tamsin was dreadfully excited at the prospect of her first trip away from home, a trip which would culminate in her obtaining what she had always lacked, a mother, though she had to be persuaded to leave her pet kitten at home. Geoffrey had insisted upon Edmund's presence at his wedding. He knew that his future in-laws would be disapproving of his inviting a peasant to witness his marriage to their daughter, but Geoffrey intended to over-ride any objections they might present. He was going to need the stalwart presence of his best friend at his side, the support of someone who knew what he was feeling.

While on the road halfway to Exeter, Edmund informed Geoffrey that Carys was breeding again. With that announcement, Geoffrey was struck by pangs of guilt at having taken Edmund from his wife's side while in a delicate condition, but it was too late to turn back now, and he suspected that Edmund had waited until then to tell him, for just that reason.

Edmund for his part laughed when Geoffrey referred to Carys's pregnancy as a delicate condition, reminding the baron that Carys had worked in the fields until mere hours before giving birth to Cerdic, and he had no reason to think this second pregnancy would be any different. Geoffrey had no choice but to cover up his fears with a smile and congratulations, and to cuff his friend on the shoulder and growl, "For the love of Christ, Edmund, do you give the poor girl no rest?"

Edmund grinned and shrugged. "Carys does not require much rest, Geoffrey. She is a big strong girl." It was a joke around Lydford that Edmund, who was short of stature, had to look up to gaze his wife in the eye, and he obviously preferred it that way.

At Rougemont there was also a large contingent of guests invited to witness the marriage of the daughter of the Lord Sheriff of Exeter to the somewhat reclusive Baron de Graville of Belvoir. So many guests filled the castle to overflowing, that Henry and Edmund were obliged to bed down on the floor in the hall, as Geoffrey had when he had been there before departing for Normandy. That had been the first time he had met Solange, and now he was here to become her husband. The thought seemed to release a flock of butterflies in the pit of his stomach.

He had not yet seen Solange, though he had been at Rougemont for several hours. It appeared to be customary to seclude the bride from her bridegroom until the actual marriage ceremony. Rougemont was abuzz with preparations for the enormous banquet which would celebrate the wedding tomorrow. It was anticipated that the feasting, dancing and drinking would last for several days, long after the bride and groom took their leave. In the castle's kitchens, sumptuous dishes of wild game and fowl were being prepared, enough it seemed to feed an entire army. But then, there were enough guests present to comprise an entire army, or so it seemed as Geoffrey responded to seemingly dozens or hundreds of congratulatory slaps on the shoulder from guests who appeared to have already begun to celebrate. However, despite the bustle of activity and arrangements in progress, there was little Geoffrey needed to do other than to present himself at the church tomorrow. His preparations had been made.

After seeing Alyssa and Tamsin settled in one of the guest chambers, Geoffrey was descending the stairs to the hall in search of a cup of wine when a young page approached him.

Bowing respectfully, the boy said in a secretive voice, "My lord, the lady Solange requests your presence in the solar, if you please."

With an amused smile, Geoffrey followed the boy across the great hall to the solar. Trust Solange to find a manner in which to circumvent the conventions while her parent's backs were turned! He was glad of the opportunity to see her, wanting to tell her that Kerensa and Dewi's baby had been born two days after the de Meules family had left Lydford. Geoffrey was now the godfather of a healthy boy child, and had provided the traditional natal gifts of salt, eggs, and a silver coin.

The page left him at the doorway to the solar, and when Geoffrey went in, he thought at first that someone had played a trick on him, for Solange was nowhere to be seen. But after a moment of casting about he saw her, huddled in the deep window alcove.

The window embrasure was wide enough to support two benches, one facing the other. Both were padded and velvet-covered, a comfortable place to sit and especially popular for ladies plying their needlework, due to the proximity of the large window supplying ample sunlight. With this thought in mind, Geoffrey doubted Solange had spent much time there before today. Like Geoffrey, she preferred being outside in the sunlight, rather than inside watching it come through a window.

She was huddled on one of the benches, her feet drawn up on the seat and her arms clasped about her legs. Her forehead was pressed to her knees and she either did not see Geoffrey or was ignoring him.

Wondering what new game she was playing with him now, he stepped in front of her and patiently waited for her to acknowledge his presence. When she did look up to him, his heart nearly stopped.

Her face, naturally fair of complexion, was deathly pale and streaked with tears; and those beautiful dark eyes which usually enchanted Geoffrey were now red and rimmed. She looked as if she had not slept in days.

Geoffrey's first inclination was to fear she was deathly ill, and he fell to his knees before her, grasping at her hands in a panic.

"Solange! What is it? You must tell me!" He kissed her fingertips, praying fervently that whatever had upset her so was within his power to rectify.

She looked at him briefly, then turned her gaze towards the window and extracted her shaking hands from his grasp. He thought for a moment that she did not want him touching her with his maimed hand, but recalled that she had declared it to be of no consequence to her. He was, however, wearing his gloves today, due to the number of people present at Rougemont whom he did not know. Completely nonplused, Geoffrey rose from his knees and sat on the seat across from his betrothed. "Solange," he begged, "please tell me what is bothering you."

She still wouldn't look at him, but she did finally speak. "My lord," she said in a wooden voice, "I cannot marry you."

Geoffrey's breath stopped, and he felt a stabbing pain in his heart, a cutting sense of loss. At first he was incapable of speech, amazed and devastated by Solange's repudiation of their betrothal. He wanted to throw himself at her feet, bury his face in her lap and beg her to marry him despite her refusal, but icy pride quickly settled in, freezing his soul to protect him from the hurt as it had before.

He would not beg, he would not even debase himself by asking her why, because he knew. It was his hand after all. Though she had told him at Belvoir that it did not bother her, she had come home and had obviously had time to reflect and realize she didn't love him after all. It had merely been the trauma of the near-fatal fire that had made them both act uncharacteristically. How foolish he had been to think that an aristocratic Norman woman would truly want to marry him, a deformed man with an illegitimate child who preferred the company of English peasants to that of Norman nobility.

Very well, so be it. Solange's father, he knew, could very well force his reluctant daughter to marry him anyway, but Geoffrey would rather be lonely the rest of his life than to marry a woman coerced into it by beatings and confinement. He would take his child and return home, and not make this mistake again. Let Solange marry someone else, someone who was perfect.

He found voice enough to choke out, "As you wish, my lady," and rose to leave before she had a chance to notice what she had done to him. As he walked out of the room and swept aside the leather curtain at the doorway, he tried to keep his back stiff and his shoulders straight, but it was like trying to carry his horse.

Two more steps out of the room and that much closer to being on his way back home to the safety of Belvoir's walls, when Solange's sobs broke out with the force of a dam being swept away by a raging flood. He had only heard weeping that intense once before in his life, from himself after Milesenda had died. The sound of it stopped him in his tracks, and melted his heart. Damn, why was she doing this to him, plunging a knife into his heart and soul by breaking their betrothal the day before their wedding, and then twisting that knife by weeping as if her heart was broken?

Perhaps there was more to this than he realized. Reluctantly, wondering if he wasn't asking for more pain, he turned and pushed back the curtain at the doorway to look back at Solange, whose face was buried in her hands as she wept. If she didn't want to marry him, why was she crying like this? His concern and regard and, dare he allow himself to feel it, love for her conquered his pride just as surely as the Norman army had conquered the English at Hastings.

He went back to her and again knelt in front of the window seat, gently prying her hands from her tear-streaked face. "Tell me," was all he said.

Solange immediately flung her arms around his neck and clung to him, nearly knocking him over with the intensity of her embrace. If ever a person needed to be comforted, it was here and now, so he held her until her weeping finally abated into childlike little gulps and hiccups. He lifted her back onto the padded bench and sat next to her. When she crawled into his lap like the smallest child, still clinging to his neck, he was surprised and even more confused. A minute ago she had said she would not marry him, and now here she was acting as if she could not bear to have him an inch away from her. He doubted he would ever in his life truly understand a woman, especially this one. Finally he had to put his hand under her chin and tilt her reddened face up to his. "You must tell me, Solange. I think I have a right to know. Why do you no longer wish to marry me?"

Of course she had to argue with him. She was his Solange. "I did not say I did not wish to marry you. I said I cannot."

"And why is it that you cannot?" Breaking a wild stallion to the saddle was easier than fathoming this conundrum.

She whispered to him as if afraid of being overheard. "Because I am afraid, my lord."

Afraid? This he could not believe. He did not believe that courageous little Solange was afraid of anything. What was there for her to fear, she who had dared to don boy's clothes and sneak from her father's keep to be with him; who had wanted to risk her life in the fire to be with him; who had stood up to her intimidating brother on more than one occasion to champion him. Geoffrey didn't think Solange would be afraid of anything. "What is there to be afraid of?" he asked.

She hesitated before explaining further, as if gathering up her courage, then finally said, still in a low secretive voice, "I am afraid of what you must do to me when we are ... in the ... on the wedding night." She said the words wedding night in the same tone she might use to speak of the deepest pits of hell. Geoffrey almost laughed in his relief. That was what all these dramatics were about, the maidenly fears of a virgin bride. And here he had been convinced there was some serious problem.

"Solange, sweetheart," he comforted her. "There is no need to be afraid. What we do on our wedding night we will do together, with each other. I will not merely be doing it to you." He was surprised at her ignorance of conjugal relations. He knew she was a virgin, but still, he thought she had some idea of what transpired between a man and a woman in bed, especially this soon before their marriage. Was this not something her mother should have explained to her? "Has your mother not spoken to you about our wedding night?" he asked.

Solange nodded. "Yes, she told me this morning, and now I am so afraid, so scared that I do not believe I can go through with this. You must hate me now, my lord." She turned her head away from him again.

"No, Solange, I do not hate you," Geoffrey stated firmly. Lord, what had Solange's mother told her? "Tell me what your mother said to you," he requested.

"Do you really wish to know?"

"I really wish to know."

"She said … that when you are my husband I must submit to you in all your, your b-baser desires, no matter how disgusting or painful I find it to be. She advised me to say my rosary beads when you do these horrible things to me and to pray that you finish quickly, and also to pray that I conceive quickly and bear you a son as soon as I can." She hid her face against his shoulder, as if embarrassed to look at him, so that her words were muffled and Geoffrey had to strain to hear. "I had no idea marriage would be so f-frightening."

Solange's words stunned Geoffrey, who had never heard anything so incredulous in his life. Rosary beads? No woman he had ever been with had brought a rosary to bed. Obviously Lady de Meules did not enjoy the physical aspect of her marriage, and he found it amazing that Solange's father had managed to beget five children on a woman like that. His voice was a bit choked as he managed to ask, "Is that all she told you?' Solange nodded again, sniffling a little against his tunic.

In his mind Geoffrey cursed his soon-to-be mother-in-law for imparting her narrow, bitter feelings to her daughter. Geoffrey had always felt, from the way Solange had enjoyed kissing him, that despite her inexperience she would be a lusty and enthusiastic bed partner; but it appeared that her mother was doing her best to suppress those emotions. He was going to have to convince her otherwise if he did not want her running in fear from the priest tomorrow, if she even got as far as the church door.

This was not how Geoffrey had anticipated spending the day before his wedding. He was aware that even now, Henry, Edmund and even Gilbert were gathering up jugs of wine and Rougemont's household knights for a truly sodden pre-wedding celebration, to the point where one might wonder how many of the male guests would be capable of standing tomorrow. Geoffrey had been hoping that his friends and the other guests would not be offended if the bridegroom abstained from allowing himself to become too terribly drunk on this occasion, because he wanted to be able to remember his wedding, both the day and the night, without having to cope with a huge, painful head.

Perhaps Henry and Gilbert and the others could celebrate without him, because if there was going to be a wedding at all, he had to convince Solange that conjugal relations were not horrifying, that they actually could be very pleasant. Though Geoffrey was not a boastful man, he could honestly say he had never bedded a woman who had left his bed less than satisfied. He was, however, astute enough to realize that he could not state that to Solange in exactly those terms. Patience and tact were what was required here.

He drew Solange's head against his chest and petted her hair, just as he had done the first day he had met her in the stable when she had cried in his lap before. She did not pull away or cringe in fear of him, and he took that as a good sign. In fact, she snuggled quite comfortably against him, not at all appearing to find his touch painful nor his embrace disgusting.

"Solange, do you trust me?" he asked.

"Y-yes," she said, her voice soft against his shoulder.

"Do you know anything of ..." he hesitated himself, shy now at discussing this subject in graphic terms. He was more accustomed to doing it rather than talking about it, "of marital relations, other than what your mother said to you?" Solange shook her head, still not looking at him. "Solange, sweetheart, normally I would not encourage you to disbelieve what your mother tells you, but I believe she is -" he should not say, an idiot, "incorrect in her description of these things."

"Then why would she say them?"

"Perhaps she feels that way, and if she does I pity her, but it is not like that for everyone. Many people enjoy, um ..."

Solange supplied the word, "Fornicating?"

Geoffrey nearly choked. "Is that what your mother called it?"

"Yes. She said you must be experienced at fornicating, since you have fathered a child."

Geoffrey's opinion of his mother-in-law was lowered even further by that revelation. He frowned slightly. "I do not like to call it fornicating, Solange. I prefer to call it lovemaking."

"Lovemaking? That does not sound nearly as awful as," Solange swallowed the word at Geoffrey's frown, "the other." She looked up at him, entreating. "Tell me about it, my lord. If I know what to expect, I will not be so afraid."

He had been afraid it was going to come to this. How could he discuss such an intimate subject with a woman? But this was not just any woman, this was Solange, soon to be his wife, he hoped. "If I describe to you what to expect on the wedding night, will you promise to still marry me?" he asked.

The tear-stained face nodded slightly. "Yes, my lord. I will trust and believe in you."

Her trust and belief was a large responsibility, and Geoffrey hoped he could earn and keep them. He had never considered himself a teacher, although Henry was learning very well the knightly skills and principles that Geoffrey was teaching him. What he had to teach Solange was infinitely more delicate and difficult. He cleared his throat and uttered a silent but fervent little prayer for guidance. Where to begin? *Perhaps at the beginning*, a sarcastic inner voice suggested.

"Solange, when I have kissed you, when we have kissed each other, did you find that to be disgusting?"

"Oh, no," she answered without hesitation. "I have enjoyed that immensely. It makes me feel like a part of you, like we are part of each other. I never before felt such a feeling of excitement, of exhilaration and fear at the same time, with a tingly, dizzy feeling all over, and..." she stopped and blushed. "I must sound very silly."

He hugged her briefly. "No, you are not at all silly. I feel exactly the same when we kiss. It is called desire or lust, and it is a normal feeling when a man and woman are beginning to make love."

Solange looked very surprised. "My lord, do you mean to say that kissing is a part of for-, lovemaking?"

"Yes, Solange, it is a part of the entire act. Did you not know that?" Solange shook her head.

"No, I thought it was something very pleasant by itself. My mother never said anything to me about kissing."

Another discredit to Lady de Meules' account. Geoffrey sighed. "Kissing is not only a preliminary to lovemaking, but it is also an imitation of it, and the feelings of excitement you described go much beyond the contact of our mouths. The act of lovemaking is very similar to kissing, but with different parts of the body."

She looked up at him with eyes slightly narrowed. "My lord, have you also felt this ... excitement when we have kissed?"

"Oh, yes Solange, I have felt it most intensely."

"So if you enjoy kissing with me, and you feel this sensation of excitement, then does that mean that you wish to fornicate with me?" At his censorious look she amended, "I mean, lovemaking."

She had no idea how much he wanted that very thing. "Yes, Solange, I very much wish to make love with you."

At Geoffrey's words Solange jumped away from him, and he put down his hands. Let her flee if she must. He would not frighten her further by trying to detain her. However, she fled no further than the other side of the window embrasure, and looked at him carefully from the other bench. "Solange, I do not intend to take you here and now," he said, a bit more gruffly than he had intended. She reminded him of a wild forest creature, with her eyes huge in her face and her expression wary, like a cat poised to bolt should the dog give chase. "Sweetheart," he entreated, holding out his hand to her but not touching her, "I would not, will not hurt you, I swear."

"Promise?" she asked in a childish voice.

"I promise, on my honor, I will never do anything to hurt or frighten you. I will not force you to do anything until and unless you are ready. More than anything, I do not want you to be afraid of me." She relaxed her wary stance then, and dared to approach him, standing at his knee. Her chin came up, her pride returned.

"I apologize, my lord, for behaving childishly. I will not be afraid if you say there is nothing to fear."

He smiled, touched and honored anew by her trust. It was a wonder to Geoffrey to be able to smile so freely. Not so very long ago, he had felt that if he allowed himself to smile, his face might crack in half and leave his soul exposed. Knowing Solange had changed that for him. Young and naive though she was, her innocence tinged with an unconscious sensuality, she had liberated his smile, liberated his soul. He would never do anything to erode the trust she had in him. He took her hand, and she allowed it. "Will you sit?" he asked, indicating his knee.

Nodding, she climbed back into her place in his lap, and for a minute they sat without speaking, accustoming themselves to each other again, allowing their heartbeats to synchronize.

"Is it all right now?" Geoffrey asked. "You are not afraid of me?"

Solange looked up at him and shook her head. "No, my lord, I am not afraid of you. But I am curious. Are you ever afraid?"

"Many times," he answered. "Just recently I was very afraid that my betrothed might refuse to marry me." He had meant the words to be teasing, but much more feeling filled his voice than he had intended. Upon discerning the emotion he had unwittingly uttered, Solange stared at him, realizing for herself that it was within her power to hurt Geoffrey as well, not necessarily physically, but in his heart. She leaned up and kissed his cheek, just below the scar. "I will never hurt you either," she said softly, and with her words, the last bit of ice on Geoffrey's heart slid away and melted forever. He put his arm around her and rested his chin on top of her head. It felt good to no longer be cold.

"Will you tell me the rest now, my lord? You had said that the lovemaking done by a man and woman was like kissing, but with different parts of the body. I do not understand what parts of the body you mean."

Geoffrey had almost forgotten, the lesson had not yet been completed. He shifted uneasily. "Surely you have noticed that the bodies of men and women are different," he began. "It is those differences which allow us to do ... to have ... to make love." His stuttering was juvenile, but he could not avoid it with such a difficult subject to describe, and to phrase it in a way which would not frighten Solange. "Women have, that is they are ..." He gave up on that angle. Solange was a woman. She should know how her own body was formed. "Men are ..."

Before he could determine the correct descriptive words, Solange offered, "Big and hard and flat." She put her hand on Geoffrey's chest, which indeed was big and hard and flat, especially compared to Solange, who was small, soft and rounded. Despite her astuteness in analyzing the part of him she was touching, there were the other, more intimate parts, of which she was yet ignorant. Though he felt uncomfortable in the extreme, and wished fervently that there was some way for Solange to simply know what to expect on their wedding night without him having to say it out loud, still he felt an obligation to educate her, to correct the obscene misconceptions her mother had infused her with.

"Solange, have you ever seen a man, uh, naked?"

She nodded, and at Geoffrey's shocked look (for he had been expecting a negative answer) she reminded him, "I have seen you, my lord, that day on the hill." As Geoffrey recalled, he had on that occasion been nude only from the waist up, so Solange was not completely correct. Before he could remind her of that fact, she added, "and once I accidentally entered the garderobe while my brother was in the bath." Her voice lowered. "He has hair all over, like a dog," she added in a tone which made it obvious that she found male body hair to be an unpleasant feature, and Geoffrey was suddenly glad of his own lack of hairiness.

"So, you saw then how a man is formed below the waist?"

Solange shook her head. "No. There was a girl with him and she blocked that part from my view. Then Gilbert shouted at me to go away, and I left." At least once she had obeyed a direct command, Geoffrey thought with gratitude. He loosened the arm he had about her waist, in case she wanted to flee as she found out more about marital relations.

"Solange, you must know that a man is formed differently than a woman." Solange nodded and looked up at him earnestly, a student waiting to be taught. "A man has an ... an appendage, which a woman does not have."

"An appendage? Where?"

They were, after all, about to be married and she was going to know him in the most literal sense very soon. His face flamed with the most fiery blushing he had ever experienced, but he took her hand in his. "Here," he said, placing her little hand on his groin.

Unbidden, his loins sprang to life under her innocent touch, and upon feeling his arousal, she jerked her hand away as if it had bitten her. "What is that?" she gasped.

He kept back the ordinary term he would have used. It was a soldier's word, not suitable for the ears of a young lady. He summoned up his soldier's courage to continue the description. "That is the appendage I told you of. Remember I told you kissing is an imitation of lovemaking, but instead of my tongue-"

She interrupted him. "You will put that in my mouth?" Her look of horror almost made him laugh, but he stifled it. "No, not in your mouth," he assured her, though privately he had to admit the idea had attractions. "It goes ... um ... elsewhere."

"Where?" she demanded.

Unable to utter the words out loud, Geoffrey looked pointedly at Solange's lap. Following his gaze, comprehension dawned in her, and she clasped a hand to her mouth in a horrified speechless gasp.

Geoffrey was devastated. He had frightened her again. But the worst was over. Of course, there were details, nuances not yet explored, but the basics were at least revealed. The finer points would have to wait until the wedding night. It might be easier to teach her and make it a pleasant, rather than terrifying experience with practical demonstration rather than mere description. He reached again for her hands. She had in the course of the last few moments slid from his lap to sit next to him, apparently no longer trusting what might be going on in his lap.

"Solange, sweetheart, I know it sounds frightening when I attempt to describe this to you. You will have to trust me that it is not nearly as bad as it sounds. I must confess to you that pretty words are not my skill. I am a knight and a farmer, not a storyteller who can couch words in their proper manner. But I promise you this, as I promised you before, I will never hurt you or frighten you, or force you to do anything you do not wish to do or are not ready for. I promise and swear to you that I will do all in my power to please you, to pleasure you and to make our marriage a pleasant experience for us both. Nay, more than pleasant, it can be-" he slipped to his knees before her, grasping her hands in his in the manner of the taking of a vow, "it will be delightful and exhilarating, if we are together. This I swear to you by all I hold holy."

It was unusual for Solange to be in a position to look down upon Geoffrey; usually it was the reverse, with him towering over her. But he remained kneeling at her feet, holding her hands, begging her with eyes and heart to believe in him.

After a breathless moment, she leaned toward him and kissed his forehead, a gesture that was almost maternal. Her smile was beautiful and peaceful. "My lord, I have known since I met you that you were a most special person." She freed one of her hands from his, and smoothed back his hair which had fallen over his forehead. "I will trust you, I do trust you, and I will not be afraid if you are there to guide me. This I promise to you as well, my lord, because you know I love you."

"Geoffrey." As he said his name to her, her little face tilted slightly, eyes wide. "You must know that my Christian name is Geoffrey. I would like you to call me by my name. This my lord nonsense is unnecessary. Will you do that for me, Solange?" He felt comfortable now encouraging her to address him informally, no longer fearing comparisons to Milesenda.

The sound of his name had never sounded so sweet as when it came from Solange's lips. But then she frowned slightly and said, "My mother said it was not proper for a woman to address any man by his Christian name, especially her husband."

"Does she never call your father by name?"

"Never in my hearing," Solange insisted. "I have never heard either of them address each other as anything other than my lord or my lady, when they speak at all."

Geoffrey hoped fervently that his marriage never deteriorated to that level of indifference. However he had to admit that his father and stepmother had been formal in public as well, and he knew they had loved each other.

"If you feel more comfortable with my lord in the presence of others, I will not argue its use. But you will make me a happy man if you will remember at other times that I prefer simply Geoffrey."

Solange smiled mischievously. "Of course, Simply Geoffrey."

He grinned and stood up, intending to kiss her, but the sound of footsteps in the corridor outside prevented it. A moment later, Lady de Meules entered the solar and when she looked to the window embrasure, it was to see the intended bride and groom sitting demurely on opposite benches, not touching in any way, the bride with her head bent over a bit of convenient embroidery, the bridegroom gazing pensively out the window, and fervently hoping without daring to look, that the embroidery was not upside down.

"My lord," Solange's mother said icily. A muscle twitched in Geoffrey's cheek, but he suppressed the chuckle that had threatened to burst forth, rose and bowed to his mother-in-law. Solange refused to look at either of them. Lady de Meules' voice was as cold as a stone wall in midwinter. "It is not proper for the betrothed couple to consort together until the wedding is celebrated, and that is not until tomorrow. I will have to ask you to remove yourself from my daughter's presence until that time."

Though outwardly Geoffrey was the epitome of decorum, inwardly he was wondering if Solange's mother had ever hugged or kissed her daughter, and he rejoiced that Solange had become a loving, affectionate person despite her mother. Their home would be infinitely happier, he vowed to himself, but outwardly he deferred to the older lady.

"I apologize, my lady," he said in his best courtly voice. "I will remove myself immediately." He turned and bowed toward Solange, who nodded just as formally and silently, also following the proper procedure for her mother's benefit. "Until tomorrow, Lady Solange," he murmured and left the room, letting the leather curtain over the doorway fall behind him as he left the room and strode down the stairs, hoping fervently that Solange would not suffer too much of a tongue-lashing from her staid parent.

34

The day that Geoffrey had once sworn would never happen bloomed with promise. His wedding day. The past few days had been hot, with a sweltering heaviness to the air that only late summer can induce. This day, while warm, was much more temperate than had been experienced lately, and Geoffrey was glad of that fact. With the air a little cooler, there was less chance of him sweating through his elegant new tunic, as he remembered his stepmother's stern instructions not to dirty himself before the wedding. Though he doubted Alyssa would chastise him publicly if he disobeyed that directive, still he did not wish to distress her. To that end, he had suppressed his desire to spend some time that day with his horse in Rougemont's stable, and hoped the beast would forgive him his neglect.

So now instead he stood in the monk's garden behind the great cathedral of Exeter, where shortly his wedding would take place at the church door between imposing twin towers. He had attended other weddings and knew what the procedure would be. The civil business of reading the marriage contract, listing the contents of the dowry and the exchanging of vows completed at the front door, the more spiritual aspect would take place inside the cathedral, with the newly married couple, their families and guests entering to hear Mass among the forest of ribbed columns, after which they would return to Rougemont for a celebratory feast which no doubt would last for two or three days, long after the bride and groom left the company to consummate their marriage elsewhere. Geoffrey smiled to himself as he thought of the first part of the proceedings. Because part of Solange's dowry was comprised of land, she would be required to prostrate herself at his feet at that point, and he wondered how that would sit with her pride.

Of more concern to him than the wedding, the Mass or the feasting was the consummation of his marriage, the act which would make it all binding and irrevocable, and which would make him and Solange forever one. Geoffrey had had the foresight to insist upon the use of a bedchamber with a door which could be bolted from the inside, to ensure their privacy. He had no intention of consummating his marriage with a gaggle of drunken guests listening on the other side of a curtain and hoping for a glimpse. That at least he could do for his new wife, to spare her any embarrassment.

He loved her. The realization had come to him at the moment she had said she could not marry him, though he had not recognized it immediately. He had told himself over and over that he did not love her, even as recently as the day he had asked her to marry him, but he had been deceiving himself. Now he understood with mature clarity that he was in love with his betrothed, and had been in some manner since the day of their first meeting when she had sat on his lap and cried, and believed him to be an English servant in the bargain.

It was amazing, he reflected, how he had been conquered, not by knights or armies, but by children.

When Milesenda had died, their child, a tiny girl child, had conquered his dark despair which would have driven him to join his lover in death had not the existence of their daughter brought him back from the edge of the chasm. Tamsin had taught him to live again, and Solange had taught him to love again, both of them children, both of them innocent, but innocence was, he realized, a most potent weapon.

And Solange, who had still been a child when he had first met her, and had appeared even younger than she was due to her diminutive stature, had by simply admiring him, trusting him and loving him despite his cold heart, conquered that icy barrier he had erected around his feelings, freeing him to laugh, to love, to truly be alive. Though he knew he would never again be quite the playful, carefree boy he had been before Milesenda, all boys grew up and exchanged a child's pursuits for a man's responsibilities. He was no different, and it had taken the love of a child-woman to make him realize it.

He also realized, with something of a jolt, that it was possible for a man to love two women. He admitted his love for Solange to himself, but that did not change the fact that he still loved Milesenda and he always would. He thought that by things Solange had said to him about Tamsin's mother that Solange was astute enough to realize this, that though death did not end love, neither did it prevent love. Geoffrey had been too stubborn to admit that fact, but the young Solange had somehow known it instinctively, and had made Geoffrey believe it despite his pigheadedness.

So now he was whole and happy, and ready to be married. One thing did make him nervous though, and that was the wedding night. Despite his assurances to Solange the day before, or perhaps because of them, Geoffrey now felt uneasy, insecure, almost frightened himself at the thought of tonight's bedding. It was a huge responsibility for a man, to guide his bride through the surrender of her virginity, and as he looked down at his big hands, ungloved at Solange's request, his concerns were legion.

Geoffrey's considerable size had always been an advantage before. In warfare and in dealing with rambunctious horses, size and strength served him well. Men who were his friends envied his longer reach, while those who had been his enemies had died because of it. Even when he did not intend it to be so, he could intimidate people simply by looming over them. And therein lay the problem.

Not only was Solange smaller than him, but she was also smaller than other women her age. Though emotionally and spiritually Geoffrey knew her to be strong and competent, still in body she was a fragile thing, easily broken by an ox such as he. For the first time, Geoffrey wished he had been built more like Edmund. At least then he need not fear doing his bride bodily harm by laying with her. But he was a big man, and she was a small woman. He might kill her, right there on their marriage bed, amongst the dried forget-me-not flowers which would be sprinkled on the bed to encourage the conception of a son.

The fear that he might hurt her despite all his care did make him sweat, and when Edmund poked his head around the garden door in search of Geoffrey, it was to find his friend standing white-faced among the monk's vegetable patch.

Edmund took one look at Geoffrey's stricken face, and clasped his friend's shoulder with concern. "What is it?" he asked. "Are you ill?"

Geoffrey shook his head wordlessly. He looked at his friend and flopped his hands in a gesture of helplessness. "I am not ill, Edmund. I am nervous."

Edmund nodded, thinking he understood what his friend was feeling, being married himself. "Do not be nervous, Geoffrey," he advised with a little chuckle. "The whole thing will be over soon, and you can move on to the more ... pleasant activities. Just don't look at her father during the ceremony. Oh, by the way, the bridal procession has left the castle. I hurried here so that I could tell you to be ready to meet them at the cathedral door, but I imagine it will be a while yet before they arrive. Everyone in Exeter is lined up along the streets to see the bride; it will be slow going for her to get here. Lord, Geoffrey, but she is a pretty little thing. That hair of hers must reach to her knees when it is unbound, and she is wearing a bright red silk gown and a garland of flowers on her head. Your Solange is very beautiful, Geoffrey. You are a lucky man."

Geoffrey was paying little attention to his friend's dissertation, other than a small secret smile at the mention of Solange's red silk gown. Bright red for love and joy. So Solange had dared to have a gown made from the fabric he had given to her. But he did not need Edmund to remind him of the beauty of his betrothed, nor was he nervous about the marriage ceremony itself. He fixed his gaze firmly on a late-season legume across the garden before he spoke to his friend.

"It is not the wedding ceremony which concerns me. It is the wedding night."

Edmund's red eyebrows quirked up. "The wedding night? I wouldn't think that should concern you. I think you should know what you are doing. I believe it is the virginal bride who is supposed to be jittery." Geoffrey blanched at Edmund's uttering of the words virginal bride, and the redhead misinterpreted the look. "Don't tell me that you two have already, um, already...?"

"Of course not," Geoffrey said sharply.

"That is a relief," Edmund replied. "That brother of hers looks to be a nasty sort. I would not want to be on his bad side."

Geoffrey snorted. "I can handle her brother."

Edmund was becoming impatient. "Then what is it, pray tell?"

Still refusing to look his friend in the eye, Geoffrey said with anguish, "Edmund, I've never been with a virgin. What if I hurt her?"

Edmund stared at him for a moment, then threw back his head and shouted with laughter, while Geoffrey glared at him angrily.

"Weeping Jesus," the redhead gasped, shamelessly stealing his friend's favorite oath. "I do not believe it. The great and powerful Baron Geoffrey de Graville, veteran of war, defender, slayer of men, is afraid of a tiny little girl!"

"I am not afraid of her, I am afraid of myself." Though he was horribly embarrassed with this discussion, he had to talk about it to somebody before he bolted headlong in the direction of Lydford. Edmund could be trusted to be discreet where Geoffrey's foibles were concerned. "Look at me," he directed with anguish. "I am a big gawk of a thing, and she is a fragile little flower. I am afraid that when I lay with her, I will hurt her with my desire for her, crush her or ... oh, I do not know, Edmund! I think this was all a mistake."

Edmund hooted with derision, which did not sit well with the Baron de Graville. "Fragile little flower!" the redhead repeated. "Is that really how you perceive her? Let me tell you something about women, Geoffrey. They are far stronger than you may believe. Why do you suppose it is women who bear children rather than men? Because a man simply could not do it, we are not strong enough. If you are too rough and hurt her, she will let you know for certain and you will both learn from it.

Lord, Geoffrey, she is the one who is supposed to be nervous about the wedding night, not you!"

"Oh, she is," Geoffrey replied. "She almost refused to go through with the wedding because she was afraid."

"There, you see," Edmund said, although Geoffrey was not certain yet that he did see. "You are the experienced husband and father here. Just be gentle and guide her through with patience, and you will both survive and perhaps even enjoy it. But what made you think she was afraid of this?"

"She told me so, yesterday."

"You saw her before the wedding?" Edmund was amazed. "Carys and I were forbidden to lay eyes upon each other, once it was found out she was, I mean, once we decided to marry."

"You do not have to mince words with me," Geoffrey said, finally able to smile now that his friend was embarrassed too. "I know how soon after your marriage little Cerdic was born, and I can count."

Now it was Edmund's turn to blush. "We would have married in any case. I do love her, Geoffrey, so much it hurts sometimes."

"I know the feeling," was the quiet reply.

"Well then if you love her, do not be afraid to lay with her. You may be big, but I doubt you will hurt her, otherwise all large men would have to become priests."

"Perish the thought," Geoffrey said fervently.

"As for her nervousness, just tell her the pain and blood are only the first time, and then it will be wonderful."

"Pain! Blood!" Geoffrey was aghast. All of his carefully constructed assurances to Solange began to unravel at Edmund's words. "I did not know there would be pain and blood involved." His eyes were wide with apprehension.

"You really have never been with a virgin."

"Of course, that is what I have been trying to tell you," Geoffrey paced about a little, raking his hands through his hair, before standing to confront his friend. "Can this pain and blood be avoided?" he asked.

Edmund shook his head. "No, but if you are patient and you love her, it will not distress her. I think it will upset you more than your bride."

Geoffrey drew himself up to his full height. He was not going to fall prey to cowardice at this point. "I will do this," he said, more to himself than to Edmund. "We will consummate this marriage, and I will use the patience of a saint if needs be if she is uncomfortable or nervous. I do love her, and I will not let the fears of either of us inhibit our lives."

Relieved, Edmund clapped Geoffrey's shoulder. "I knew you could be made to see reason, Geoffrey. Now I think you should proceed to meet your bride. The procession should be here soon, and you would not wish to start off your married life by keeping her waiting at the cathedral door."

Resolute, Geoffrey reached into the small leather pouch he had hung on his belt and extracted a gold coin, which he handed to Edmund. "Can you break this in half for me?" With his missing fingers, he could not grasp the coin tightly enough with his left hand to apply the strength required to split it, but with a little grunting Edmund was able to do the job. "I shall give this to the priest," the redhead said, and Geoffrey nodded. At the wedding the priest would give one of each half to the bridal pair, to symbolize their becoming halves of a whole.

"You will be there, won't you, Edmund?" Geoffrey asked anxiously. "I need you to stand beside me, at my right side, during the wedding ceremony."

Edmund chuckled as he nodded. "Of course I will be there, Geoffrey. There is no force in this world which could induce me to miss this, your marriage day. And look, Carys made me a new tunic." He spread his arms wide to show the new garment to his friend, a fine green frieze. "She threatened me with death if I dirtied it," came the chuckled confession.

Geoffrey smiled as well. "My stepmother made the same threat to me."

"And you do look splendid," Edmund teased. He walked around Geoffrey in a tour of inspection. "You may outshine the bride, nay, you may outshine the sun itself." Edmund quickly danced away from Geoffrey's fist, taunting, "You may be bigger, but I am faster."

"It is my advanced old age," Geoffrey conceded. "It makes me decrepit." He was, after all, older than Edmund by approximately one month.

Edmund laughed at him, hands on hips. "Decrepit!" he echoed. "If you think you feel decrepit now, wait until tomorrow morning. If either you or your bride can walk, you won't have done your duty."

Geoffrey blanched a bit at that, but recovered and joked, "That is something that you will never know. Neither of us will so much as put our noses out the bedchamber door for at least a week."

Edmund's eyebrows shot up in derision. "What about food, water, the chamberpot?"

"We shall have water and the chamberpot provided beforehand. Food will be unnecessary."

The redhead was still skeptical. "A newlywed bride and groom, and no food for a week? With all of that activity and no sustenance, you will both be withered corpses by the time anyone dares to batter down the door."

"Ah, but what a manner in which to perish!"

The two men shared a last bachelor laugh, but all too soon Edmund was urging. "We had better remove ourselves to the church door, Geoffrey. The bridal procession will surely be here soon, and you do not want to begin your married life angering your lovely bride by keeping her waiting to become a wife." Geoffrey opened his mouth but before he could speak Edmund was reassuring him, "Yes, yes, I shall be there, at your right hand, prepared to wrestle you to the ground should you appear about to make a run for it. And if you look as if you are about to faint, I shall burn a feather and wave it under your nose to revive you."

"Thank you," Geoffrey said somberly. "Go ahead, I will be there shortly. I need just a minute to myself. No need for guardianship; I have no intention of an escape attempt. I promise!" He urged his friend toward the garden gate and thus persuaded, Edmund departed with a look that clearly informed Geoffrey that if he dawdled too long before presenting himself to be married, Edmund would call reinforcements to drag him to it.

Though he did truly need a few more moments alone before becoming a husband, Geoffrey would require no coercion to do it. Solange's need of his understanding, her requirement of his patience, would give him the strength and courage he needed for himself to consummate their marriage successfully, to make it the beginning of a happy and passionate life together. Though knowing Solange, their lives would not be without some conflict; that would be the spice which would add flavor to their marriage.

After Edmund had left him alone, he patted the small leather pouch hanging from his belt, from which he had extracted the gold coin he had given to Edmund to convey to the priest. Still residing in the pouch were the two gold rings he would place on Solange's hand as they became man and wife. They appeared small enough to fit on the hand of a child, but he knew they were the proper size to fit comfortably on Solange. Alyssa had had the forethought to measure the circumference of Solange's finger with a string before her family had left Belvoir last month, so that Geoffrey could have rings made to fit. Geoffrey himself would never have thought of such a thing. He had never given Milesenda a marriage ring, just himself, and the brooches with which she had been buried. The two fine gold rings Geoffrey now carried would be placed briefly on his bride's thumb, then moved to the first and then second fingers, invoking the Holy Trinity, before being set permanently on the third finger of her left hand, where the gold bands would circle the vein which led directly to her heart. Geoffrey wondered briefly why it was not customary for the husband to also receive marriage rings from his wife. Just as well, he reflected. He had only the merest stump of a third finger on his left hand, not enough to hold even one ring.

Along with the rings was another piece of gold, a fine glittering neck chain that he had chosen to give to Solange as a morning gift after their wedding night. He would not present her with brooches as he had for Milesenda. Not only would it open wounds only recently healed, but it would also not be fair, to either Solange or to Milesenda's memory, to repeat the same gifting which had begun his first marriage, the marriage which had really been no marriage at all. The giving of twin brooches was an English custom, rooted in Saxon tradition. Though Solange, like Geoffrey, spoke English as her first language, she was still a Norman woman, and he hoped she was Norman enough not to notice his substitution.

Milesenda. He could not avoid thinking about her now, as he was about to be married to another woman. His first love, the mother of his firstborn child, she would always hold a place in his heart. It was still a bit of a surprise to him to be able to think about her, remember her, without his heart breaking. At one time, he would never have believed such a thing to be possible. He was grateful beyond measure that Solange exhibited no jealousy toward Milesenda, that she did not attempt to deny Geoffrey his memories. Young as she was, she possessed an innate wisdom which had previously escaped Geoffrey. His little black-haired child-woman had made him see truths he had not known existed, and he thanked God for her.

But there was, he realized, one thing he had to do in his heart before he could give himself to Solange and truly allow himself to love her. If he had had the acumen to do it earlier, he could have saved himself years of anguish.

Milesenda had died so swiftly, so unexpectedly, that before his mind had been able to perceive what was happening, she was gone, torn from his life in the blink of an eye. No time, no opportunity, no realization to be able to prepare himself, to accept, to conceive of farewells. It had been like being taught to swim by being suddenly and unexpectedly being thrown into deep, cold water, only much, much crueler. If he hadn't had his daughter, his stepmother, and most of all, his Solange, to teach him to swim in the lake of life, he might never have surfaced from beneath the black water of despair.

He would, in a way, always love Milesenda, and would always mourn the life they had been unable to share. For years, he had railed and raged against Fate and God the and unfairness of his life, but his tears and grief and pain had not brought Milesenda back. He had been a fool to believe they might. Geoffrey was certain that his stepmother, in her own quiet way, had privately mourned over his father in the same way. He wondered if she would ever be inclined to marry again.

He stood up, straight and tall, though even with his height he still could not see over the wall of the garden in which he stood. But still, he turned and faced toward the west, toward Lydford. In a few days he would bring his new bride there, but for now he saw, with his heart and mind, if not his eyes, the sweet and gentle woman with the honey-brown hair. He imagined her at their little lake, shrouded in the mist of early morning, her image indistinct as memories frequently were. When he closed his eyes and lifted his face to the sun he could still see Milesenda, smiling, strands of her hair floating in a silent breeze, one hand raised in farewell. She seemed to move away from him, though she did not walk, the misty fog enveloping her like a curtain made of angel's hair. It was almost like the dreams he had had shortly after her death, but it was no longer a nightmare. He understood now.

Her mouth moved and spoke to his soul. Unconsciously he raised his own hand, as the mists around Milesenda thickened and concealed her from his view. But this time he did not panic nor scream nor despair. A peace filled him, a closure of a wound left too long exposed. Milesenda was gone, not completely, because she lived on in her daughter, and certainly not forgotten, but still irrevocably ended. Geoffrey sighed, but only once.

"Good-bye, my love," he said, then opened his eyes and went in to his marriage.

35

ENGLAND, DEVON,
YEAR OF OUR LORD 1097

Henry de Lessay was in mortal peril, in fear for his life.

To look at him, one might not believe such a thing. He sat in a charming meadow carpeted with wildflowers, in a clearing in the woods near his home, next to a pretty lake, just big enough to swim in. Sitting next to him was a pretty girl, nay, a beautiful girl, looking at him with adoring eyes. To the casual onlooker he might be considered to be a fortunate man indeed.

But what threatened his life was the fact that his pretty companion was only fifteen years old, and if her father caught her with him, Henry would be a dead man. It wouldn't matter that he hadn't lain with her, that her virtue was intact, that he hadn't even kissed her. He'd never even touched her, other than within the bounds of propriety. He knew her father, knew him better than he knew his own father, and there was no doubt whatsoever in Henry's mind that were they to be discovered here, alone, despite the chaste nature of their companionship, he would still be a very dead man within moments.

So why was he risking life and limb in her company? It wasn't even so much that he loved her. He'd always loved her, as far back as he could remember. It was because she followed him everywhere, even when he tried to evade her. He thought he'd been clever and eluded her, thought this secluded area would be a place where she wouldn't find him, but no sooner had he dismounted from his horse, sat down and taken off his boots to rest, than she was there, swinging down from her own horse, her skirts pushed up indecently high so that she could ride astride.

"Henry! Why did you not wait for me?" she demanded, as she sat down next to him.

"How did you find me?" he demanded in return.

"You cannot hide from me, my darling. I can smell you!"

He sniffed at himself. "Do I stink?"

"No, you do not stink, you silly boy. But I can still detect your scent wherever you go."

"Jesus." He didn't bother anymore to apologize for cursing in her presence. She caused him to do it so often, he'd given up the apologies after the hundredth time. "Why do you insist upon following me?" he asked.

"If you would refrain from running away, I would not have to follow you."

"I run away from you to protect us both from your father's wrath."

"You didn't answer me earlier. It was rude of you to leave without helping me. Is not a knight required to assist his lady?" Henry had to restrain himself from rolling his eyes. She was a beauty, but rarely acted like a lady.

"I was hoping to avoid answering you, to save you hurt by refusing."

"But Henry, I want to! You know I am ready."

"You are too young."

"If you won't teach me, I shall ask someone else. Do you really want one of the garrison soldiers to teach me?"

"That will never happen. They are even more terrified of your father than I am."

"How can you be terrified of my father? He loves you."

Her father would certainly no longer love Henry if he was aware that they were alone together here. But the naughty girl just would not understand that.

"You should teach me what I ask, Henry! We are betrothed. It is your duty to teach me the things I need to learn."

"We are not betrothed."

"Of course, we are betrothed. If we are to marry, we must be betrothed first."

"We are not going to be married either."

"But Henry, do you not love me?"

Henry sighed. They had been over this ground before.

"Yes dearest, I love you. But we are not betrothed and we are not going to be married. And I am most certainly not going to teach you to do *that*. And I am certain nobody else will be willing to risk their lives to do so either."

She stood up and stamped her foot, committing murder upon the flowers beneath her. Henry had seen her temper before but it still both scared him, and aroused him, a feeling he tried very hard to disguise. He was a knight, had fought in battle, had a scar or two to prove it, and yet he was more terrified at this moment than he'd ever been before in his life.

"Yes yes yes!" she shouted. "I am ready for this. I am old enough, and strong enough, no matter what my father says!"

He leaped to his feet as well and glared down at her. Though she was a tall girl, he was an even taller man. He put his hands on his hips and attempted to look formidable.

"Tamsin de Graville, I am not going to teach you to jump your horse over the fence!"

****

ENGLAND, DEVON,
YEAR OF OUR LORD 1098

Henry de Lessay was a liar.

For the past year, he had been telling Tamsin he would not under any circumstances teach her to jump her horse. He kept a close watch on her to make sure she didn't convince anyone else to do it either. Nobody could resist those big blue eyes of hers.

It wasn't that Henry doubted her abilities on horseback. She was, after all, Geoffrey de Graville's daughter and rode as if she and her horse were one. She could even handle a stallion, though her father had, thankfully, convinced her to ride a mare most of the time. But the thought of any danger coming to her had steeled Henry's resolve to resist her pleas about trying for fences.

But finally, he knew he could resist the notion no longer. Tamsin's patience was wearing thin and he knew if he didn't help her, she'd try it by herself. So now, today, he'd become a liar. He'd said so many times he would not allow this, would not teach her to do it, and yet, he was going to do so anyway, against his better judgment.

He had at least persuaded her to wait until her father and stepmother left Belvoir to visit Lady Solange's family in Exeter. Lord de Graville's stepmother did not go to Exeter with them. Things had been awkward between Lady Alyssa and the de Meules family since the day that Henry's cousin Gilbert, brother to Tamsin's stepmother, had formally requested Lady Alyssa's hand in marriage, and she had gently declined him. Gilbert had seemed to be crushed by her refusal, but had quickly married another woman, one who seemed to bear a bit of a resemblance to Lady Alyssa.

The next obstacle to the jumping lesson had been Tamsin's clothing. As soon as Henry said he would agree to this lesson, Tamsin threw her arms around his neck and kissed his cheek in thanks. If she'd been beautiful and tempting at fifteen, at sixteen she was even more so, and he'd quickly detached her from himself and set her away from him, before he forgot who she was, and who he was. She hadn't noticed the abruptness of his action, merely sat down at his feet, grasped the hem of her gown, and started to rip it up the front.

"My god, Tamsin, whatever are you doing!" Henry bellowed.

She looked up at him with those irresistible big blue eyes. "I cannot ride properly in these skirts. I need my legs to be free. You always get angry with me when I pull them up."

Of course, he got angry with her. She felt no shame at pulling up her skirts to ride and exposing her long, pale, beautiful legs. How she'd never managed to let her father see such scandalous behavior was beyond Henry's comprehension.

"Wait," he entreated. "There must be some other method."

"I know!" Tamsin, thankfully, stopped trying to rip her skirt and stood up. "Braies!"

"Braies?" Henry repeated stupidly. No, she could not be considering it? But yes, she apparently was.

"Yes, silly, braies. Those things you wear on your legs."

"I know what braies are," he replied with dignity.

"Are you certain?" she asked with teasing eyes. "You look as if you had forgotten. If I am going to jump, I will wear braies."

"You cannot do that, Tamsin," Henry entreated, though realizing at the same time that telling Tamsin she could not do something was usually a waste of breath. "Anyway, where would you get a pair of braies, and a tunic?"

She was thoughtful. "Well, my brothers' clothing is too small. William is getting taller but he's still not big enough. Oh, that reminds me! Mama is going to have another baby."

Henry's eyes goggled. "Another! And your father allowed her to travel in her condition?"

Tamsin giggled. "Da doesn't know yet. Mama said she won't tell him until they return. You know how he gets."

Henry was well aware of how his lord got. Geoffrey de Graville was the strongest, bravest man Henry had ever known. But show strong, brave Geoffrey de Graville a woman's pregnant belly, and he was reduced to a trembling puddle of fear, which everyone in Lydford was aware of, despite how hard Geoffrey worked to disguise it. How he'd managed to survive his wife bearing five children – including a set of twins – was unimaginable. And now a fifth pregnancy, a sixth child? Henry's mind boggled. He was aware of why his lord had this unusual trait. Lady Alyssa had told him of the circumstances of Tamsin's birth.

But he wasn't sure if Tamsin knew the complete details of that dark time in her father's life.

So, Tamsin was not the only person deceiving Lord de Graville. However, Henry was certain that once his lord discovered his wife's deception, he might be angry, but not nearly as angry as he would be if he discovered Tamsin's deceptions. Lady Solange would survive her husband's anger, but Henry was not at all certain about his own survival.

"I think," she said. "I shall have to wear yours."

He had a sudden unbidden, and unacceptably erotic, vision of Tamsin stripping off his clothes to wear herself. He backed away from her. "No!"

Her smile was brilliant and mischievous. "Not the ones you are wearing right now, silly! I shall sneak up to your room and steal some others. But you are so tall, I shall have to cut them off to fit me."

If she did so, Henry reflected, it would not be the first time he'd had his clothes stolen. Once, shortly after he'd entered Lord de Graville's service as his squire, a set of his clothing had disappeared from his bag while they'd been in Exeter. He had never discovered what had happened to them, and his lord had merely provided him with replacements without comment.

So now Henry was not only making himself a liar, but he was also throwing away his honor, his discretion, and his better principles. The lesser of all evils in this situation was going to be to give Tamsin a set of his clothes to alter, and to teach her to jump her horse while she wore them, and to pray with every fiber of his soul that they weren't caught in the process.

*****

It worked. The whole crazy, unacceptable scheme had worked. She had successfully jumped her horse over the fence, wearing Henry's spare, hacked apart clothing, and not only had they survived, but they had managed it without detection. Henry had almost died on the spot when she'd approached the fence, but the horse and girl had sailed over smoothly, landed firmly on the other side, and then, she'd turned the horse around and did it again. She dismounted and strode towards him with triumph in her eyes and her thick blond braids swinging.

"That was wonderful! You should have allowed me to do it sooner! How could you say it was difficult?"

"Allowed you? I haven't allowed you to do it yet!" he croaked. "Come, let us get this horse back in the stable quickly, before anyone sees you like that." He indicated her new, boyish wardrobe, but tried not to notice the feminine breasts under his spare tunic as she breathed heavily with exertion. For once, she obeyed him and obediently led her horse into the stable and helped him arrange for the beast's food and water.

"Can we do this again tomorrow? Da and Mama aren't back yet."

"No, Tamsin dear, it is still too dangerous. If Lady Alyssa catches you, catches us, she will tell your father when he returns, I am certain."

"I don't think she will find out. Grandmama isn't feeling well, she has been in her room all day."

"She is ill?" Henry exclaimed in a panic. The only woman on earth that he loved almost as much as his lord's daughter, was his lord's step-mother, though not in the same way he loved Tamsin. His love for Lady Alyssa was completely maternal, while his love for Tamsin was completely lustful, degenerate lecher that he was. Though he could hardly be blamed for his love for Tamsin. How could he not love her? Her beauty, spirit and bravery had owned his heart since the day he'd first arrived at Belvoir.

"I'm sure it is nothing," Tamsin assured him. "Isabel is with her." Then she looked at him with her direct blue gaze. "Thank you for today, Henry. It was wonderful!"

Henry shook his head as he placed his horse's saddle in its place. "Tamsin de Graville, you are going to give me gray hair. In fact, I think you already have."

"I do not believe that. Let me see if you have any gray hair."

She was so childishly entreating that he bent his head towards her and she put her fingers into his thick, disordered brown curls to search for the imaginary gray strands. But after only a moment he realized she was not looking for signs of age. She was running her hands through his hair, smoothing the curls between her fingers, and before he could react, she threw her arms around his neck and kissed him on the mouth.

Despite his better judgment, he couldn't help but put his arms around her waist in response. But he was shocked beyond belief when her mouth opened against his, and she thrust her tongue between his lips and started stroking his teeth. Though his body immediately flushed with heat, and his manhood sprang to life like a dragon, he still had the presence of mind to jerk back and push her away.

"Sweet mother of God, Tamsin, where did you learn that!" He felt destroyed inside that some other man had possibly been kissing her.

"I saw Da kissing Mama like that. They didn't know I saw them." Henry was relieved, that Tamsin had learned to kiss only from observation and not from actual practice.

"Your father and stepmother are married. They are allowed to kiss each other," he said stiffly, hating how the words made him sound like a boring old man.

"When we are married, I will kiss you like that every day."

Henry sighed. She was still after that notion. How long had he been telling her? It seemed like his entire life. "Tamsin, darling, my sweetheart. We are not going to be married. We are not betrothed."

Her eyes started to moisten. "But Henry, I love you! You love me too, don't you? You wish to marry me, don't you?"

Henry had to turn away from her, because the sight of her love shining from her eyes cut his heart into shreds. Of course, he loved her. Of course, he wanted nothing more than to be her husband, her lover, her life. But it was impossible. There was no way in the world a man such as him could ever be considered a worthy candidate for her hand, even if Tamsin was illegitimate. She was still Lord de Graville's beloved, cherished, and only daughter, and Henry had nothing to offer her other than himself and his love.

But those were not enough. He owned nothing other than what Tamsin's father, Baron de Graville, had given him. Though Henry's father possessed a fine estate in Normandy, Henry would not inherit it.

He had two older brothers and several healthy nephews before him. Henry's horse had been a gift from Tamsin's father, as had been his suit of mail, his weapons and armor, the very clothes he stood in as well as the ones Tamsin had appropriated. The de Gravilles had fed and housed him and treated him as a member of the family since the day he'd arrived at Belvoir at the age of fifteen, as Lord Geoffrey's squire. Baron de Graville had even knighted Henry himself, and had generously provided a fine celebration for the event. It had been the proudest moment of Henry's life, the day he'd placed his hands in those of Tamsin's father and sworn him his fealty.

He'd adored Tamsin from the moment he'd met her as a little girl, but somehow over the years, the adoration had evolved from fraternal, to lustful. Why could she not have remained a little girl, so that he could resist her? Tamsin the woman was too beautiful and loveable for her own good.

He felt her hand touch his back but he used all his strength to keep it turned away. "Henry," she entreated. "Ree!" It was even worse when she used her childhood nickname for him. "Don't you like kissing me?"

"Too much," he muttered.

"I want to ask you something."

Finally, he turned back to look at her. As long as she didn't touch him, and he could restrain himself from touching her, he might be able to answer her question. He just prayed it was not going to be a request for a higher fence.

"Henry," she looked down for a moment, biting her lip, then asked, "Are you a virgin?"

He almost collapsed on the spot. "Weeping Jesus, Tamsin, you cannot ask me that!"

"Why not? I am a virgin."

You had better be, he thought. He sat down in the straw and put his head in his hands while the memories flowed over him.

The woman, Moll, had been a servant here at Belvoir, and it was no secret that several of the garrison knights had enjoyed her favors. She had even been in the bed of Baron de Graville, before he married

Henry's cousin Solange. And one day, while a sixteen-year-old Henry had been working in this very stable, Moll had come in, closed the stable door, and practically dragged Henry into an empty stall and made him a man. There had been other women since then, but none that he had ever loved. None like Tamsin.

She was still looking at him for an answer. How could she ask him something so personal, something that should be none of her concern? Because she was Tamsin de Graville, that was why. "Ree? Tell me! Have you lain with a woman?"

"Yes," he finally admitted. Maybe the knowledge would dissuade her from him. But he was wrong. She just smiled at him.

"Good. When we are married, it would be helpful if one of us already knows how to do it. I am waiting for you."

Did the girl have any idea whatsoever what her words did to him, how close they came to destroying his self-control? He forced himself to be gruff with her, so that she wouldn't try to kiss him again. "You should go change back into your own clothes, before someone sees you." He turned on his heel and walked away, knowing without looking that she would be hurt by his abruptness. But it was for her own good, he reasoned.

*****

ENGLAND, DEVON,
YEAR OF OUR LORD 1099

Henry de Lessay was doomed. His soul was doomed, his body was doomed, his honor was doomed.

For the past year, he had been telling Tamsin over and over that they were not betrothed, that they were not going to be married, and that he was certainly not going to give her the details she requested from him about his sexual experience. He did, however, supervise her again as she jumped fences on her horse, knowing he could not stop her, short of tying her up. He was only amazed at the miracle that kept her from her father's detection. If Henry had had a daughter like Tamsin, he would have clapped her in a convent as soon as she started to develop her womanly curves.

Those curves continued to tempt him, now that she was seventeen. He avoided her like the plague and yet she still managed to catch him alone on occasion and try to kiss him.

He even dreamed about her. Baron de Graville had generously allowed Henry the choice of any bedchamber in the castle for his own use, and he had chosen one at the top of a tower. The window there gave him a fine view over the fields and village, and it was also as far as he could get from where Tamsin slept. But even that distance did not prevent him from his dreams. He dreamed that he kissed her without reservation, dreamed about touching her, dreamed that she whispered his name. He woke up in a sweat, but even awake he could still hear her whispering his name.

He couldn't believe it, but his bedchamber door was opening, and her whispering became louder. "Henry? Are you asleep?"

Perhaps if she thought he was asleep, she would go away. Why had he not thought to bar the door? He'd never imagined that even hoydenish Tamsin would be so bold as to come here, to his bedchamber, in the middle of the night. He lay still and squeezed his eyes shut. But still, he heard a rustle of fabric as she walked right in the room and a moment later, felt something soft brush his arm. He opened one eye a crack, hoping she couldn't tell in the dark.

It was her hair that had brushed his arm. Her hair was unbound and flowing around her shoulders and over her breasts like a river of molten gold. He could see it even in the dark, with only the moonlight giving a glow through the open window. Her hands moved, and he had to give up all pretense of sleeping as he realized she was holding a sheet around her body. He gasped as she dropped the sheet to the floor, pulled back the cover over him, and climbed into his bed.

Henry de Lessay was a man. Only a human man. He was not a stone statue; he was not a saint. He was only a sentient, sinful man, and the woman he loved beyond all reason was in his bed with him, naked, warm, her soft curves pressing against him as she kissed his neck and ran her hands through the hair on his chest. "Henry, I want you," she murmured. "I love you."

His sinful arms had to hold her. There was no other choice. He clasped her tight, groaning at the feel of her full breasts pressed against him. "Oh, God, Tamsin," the words were almost a sob. "I want you," he echoed. "I love you. But -"

At that, her finger pressed against his mouth, shushing him. "I love you," she repeated. "Don't think of anything else. Just love me."

Despite the destruction of his soul and honor, Henry could do nothing else. He kissed her hungrily, touched her, loved her. She was, as she had continually told him, a virgin. At the moment she became no longer a virgin, she did cry out, and he hated the small pain he obviously caused her, kissing it away until the pain subsided and the passion could triumph.

Afterwards she cuddled up beside him as if this was the most natural, allowable thing in the world, laying her head on his shoulder and playing with his chest hair. "My God, Tamsin, what have we done?" he moaned, both deliriously happy and terrifyingly distraught at the same time.

"Don't you know what we have done?' she asked brightly. "I thought you were the one with experience."

She simply did not comprehend the gravity, the danger of what they had just done, and he knew perfectly well what it was.

"I'm so sorry, sweetheart. I should not have allowed, I should have had more control, Jesus, I am a dog!"

"I am not sorry, Henry. I am ecstatic," she declared. "And you are not a dog." She sat up suddenly, kneeling next to him, and he tried not to salivate at the sight of her breasts swaying in front of his face. Yes, he was a dog. "Do you think I have gotten with child tonight?" She actually smiled as she pronounced the fatal words.

He felt like weeping. He wanted to say, "Please, God, I hope not," but he couldn't make himself utter the words. It might erase the smile from her face.

"We should not have done this, darling."

"Yes, we should have. When we are married we can do this whenever we want."

He opened his mouth to repeat the words he had told her so many times already, but she would not hear them anymore. "Don't say it, Ree! We will be betrothed, and we will be married, and I will love you. You cannot stop it."

She was right. He could not refrain from loving her. It would be easier to pull the moon out of the sky. All he could do was hold her and put his face against her hair, and tremble with how much he loved her.

Surprisingly, they slept, but fortunately Henry awoke in time. It wasn't dawn yet, but the sky was a little less dark. He shook her shoulder gently. "Tamsin, wake up," he whispered.

She opened her eyes slowly, and smiled at him sleepily. "Good morning, my love."

"Tamsin, you have to leave. Go back to your own bedchamber before anyone finds you here." They didn't have the luxury this time of Lord de Graville being away from home. He was just down the stairs in the lord's bedchamber with his wife. If he discovered Tamsin here, in Henry's bed, if he even suspected it, Henry's death would be slow and painful. Geoffrey would disembowel him, pull out his entrails, and use them to suspend his carcass from the castle walls, leaving it there unshriven until the birds picked his bones clean, as a warning to other men who might consider touching Tamsin.

"Please," he entreated. "It is not safe for you to be here."

With a pout, she agreed, pushing off the covers and reaching for the sheet she had worn when she'd arrived, wrapping it around her bosom and pulling her hair out from under it. Henry sat at the edge of the bed watching. "Don't come back," he warned. "It is too dangerous."

"Oh, Henry," she scolded. "Why are you so timid?"

"Because I enjoy being alive."

She just smiled, leaned forward and put a hand on his chest, spreading her fingers among the brown hairs. "I like this," she said. "And this," she then put her hand on his head and played with his curls. "And this," she kissed him again, but quickly, though he was still tempted to sin again when she did so. Then, with a swing of her head that caused her hair to brush his arm again, she went to the door and slipped out, calling over her shoulder, "Until next time!"

He went to the door after she'd left, looked out and watched as her sheet-clad form disappeared around the corner, and prayed as he'd never prayed before that she arrived at her own bedchamber without detection. Then he returned to his bed and flopped down on it in utter exhaustion.

"You are doomed, you idiotic, lecherous fool," he said to himself. "Utterly doomed."

*****

For the next few days, he avoided both Tamsin and her father as much as possible. He busied himself in the stable, and in the bailey practicing with his sword with the garrison knights. He went to the chapel and prayed, anything to keep from meeting either Tamsin's or Geoffrey's eyes. Until the day of his utter doom, when Baron de Graville came up behind him, clasped his shoulder and requested, "A word with you, please, Henry."

It sounded like a request, but of course, it was a command, and like a puppy who had relieved itself where it shouldn't, Henry followed his lord into the small office just off the great hall where estate business was conducted. Baron de Graville sat in his chair behind the table, while Henry stood before him in agony, staring at his feet. After a moment of suspenseful silence, Geoffrey asked, "Well, Henry, do you have something to tell me?"

Henry was astonished at the lack of rage in his lord's voice, but he still knew himself to be doomed. His life would end today, at the age of twenty-seven. He was tempted for a moment to try and justify himself. *But, my lord, she came to my room in the dark, naked, with her hair unbound, and she seduced me.* No, he respected and loved his lord too much to tell him such a thing. It would be best if he merely knelt, exposed his throat, and begged Geoffrey to do it quickly. But he was frozen, paralyzed, and unable to either move or meet Baron de Graville's eyes. He heard the older man sigh.

"Henry, I know you have never been a chatterbox. But I've never known you to be quite this reticent. But I suppose I cannot be surprised. I once found myself struggling for words, in this situation."

Henry could not quite imagine Baron de Graville ever being in a situation like this. He could only continue to study the toe of his boot.

"Tamsin spoke to me this morning," Geoffrey continued. "She told me everything."

Everything! He finally looked up at that, staring at his lord's face. If Tamsin had told him *everything*, why was Geoffrey smiling, and not reaching for his dagger?

"She asked me for permission to marry you. I know it is customary for the bridegroom to ask permission from the father rather than the bride, but you know Tamsin. She will do things her own way." Henry could only stare, transfixed, unable to form words. He felt his mouth opening in astonishment. "What say you, Henry? Will you have my daughter's hand in marriage?"

"My lord!" was all the words Henry could utter. "My lord, but,"

"I know, Henry, you have no land, no inheritance. That does not concern me. Do you love Tamsin? She assures me that she loves you beyond all reason."

Henry could only nod.

"Good. I had hoped so. You know that my prime concern is for Tamsin's happiness, and I am overjoyed that you are what makes her happy. I remember when you first came here, as my squire, how you held her hand and protected her, and how she always trusted you. I thought, that young man will make my child happy. I'm glad you waited for her to grow up." Geoffrey leaned forward and said, in a lower voice, "We need not tell her about Moll."

Henry was so astonished, so relieved, so utterly unbelieving that his lord not only was not murdering him in his boots, but rather was giving

Tamsin to him like a gift from God, that his knees felt weak. He did, however, finally find his voice.

"My lord, I wish nothing more than to be Tamsin's husband. I love her beyond all reason as well, and I cannot tell you how happy it makes me that you approve of me as your son-in-law. But,"

"Yes," Geoffrey interrupted. "About the land. When I married your cousin, her dowry included a small parcel of land. It is not far from here, only a day's ride. Solange and I have always intended for it to be Tamsin's dowry, so it will pass to you when you two are married. It's not a large estate, but a very pretty little place, and it will solve the problem of your inheritance. And, I hope, dissuade you from taking Tamsin away to Normandy to live with your family?"

"My lord, I would never consider such a thing! My family is here, in Devon. At Belvoir."

"I am relieved and gladdened to hear it. Now, go find Tamsin. I'm sure she will want to know that you have agreed to be her husband. I can only imagine the tantrums I would have to endure if it was otherwise. We can make the announcement tonight in the hall, if you both agree."

"Thank you, my lord, thank you!" was all Henry could think to say. He was tempted to kneel and kiss his lord's hand, but that would look silly. Geoffrey stood up, walked around the table, and offered his hand. When Henry took it, his soon to be father-in-law actually gave him a brief hug.

"Welcome to the family, Henry," he said, then nudged him to the door, a hint that Henry was only too happy to take as he strode out in search of his betrothed.

She must have been lingering just outside the door, for it was only a moment until she was in his arms. "See!" she laughed triumphantly. "I told you we would be betrothed. I told you we would be married!"

"I should have believed you," he agreed, kissing her now without fear of detection. "But did you really tell your father *everything*?"

"Well, not quite everything," she admitted. "That will be our secret. But it had best be a short betrothal. Just in case."

"Tamsin, it has only been a few days. You cannot know if you, um, conceived that night."

"I know. But I hope so."

"You are incorrigible. And adorable. And I love you."

"Let's go celebrate!" She took his hand and started to drag him towards the staircase.

"Tamsin, no! We are not married yet, and besides, it is daylight!"

"I know. I want to see you better this time. You want to see me too, don't you?"

He would give his soul to see her naked again, and to see her better, but he was still cautious. "Not here. Your family is all around." In fact, two of her brothers were only feet away at that moment, her father was only feet away in his office, her stepmother, Geoffrey's stepmother, Isabel. The castle was full of people going about their everyday lives and they would all be scandalized to see Henry and Tamsin scampering up the stairs to his bedchamber, even if they were betrothed now.

He took her hands, and leaned down to whisper in her ear. "Go to the stable, get your horse. I will follow in a short while."

"Where should I go?"

He kissed her briefly, chastely, but with promise. "The clearing by the lake."

THE END